THE ALMANACK

Recent Titles by Martine Bailey

AN APPETITE FOR VIOLETS
THE PENNY HEART
THE ALMANACK *

* *available from Severn House*

THE ALMANACK

Martine Bailey

severn
House

This first world edition published 2019
in Great Britain and the USA by
SEVERN HOUSE PUBLISHERS LTD of
Eardley House, 4 Uxbridge Street, London W8 7SY.
Trade paperback edition first published
in Great Britain and the USA 2019 by
SEVERN HOUSE PUBLISHERS LTD.

British Library Cataloguing in Publication Data
A CIP catalogue record for this title is available from the British Library.

ISBN-13: 978-0-7278-8863-1 (cased)
ISBN-13: 978-1-84751-983-2 (trade paper)
ISBN-13: 978-1-4483-0195-9 (e-book)

All Severn House titles are printed on acid-free paper.

Severn House Publishers support the Forest Stewardship Council™ [FSC™],
the leading international forest certification organisation.
All our titles that are printed on FSC certified paper carry the FSC logo.

Typeset by Palimpsest Book Production Ltd.,
Falkirk, Stirlingshire, Scotland.
Printed and bound in Great Britain by
TJ International, Padstow, Cornwall.

To my grandparents, Alf and Emily Hilton,
who made the fields and hedgerows
come alive with country lore.

Who Am I?

I with a vizard-mask am born,
To show my face the world I scorn;
And though the curious searchers strive
Me of my vizard to deprive;
Although they bite their nails and frown,
Long as I can I'll keep unknown,
Nor am I without cause this shy,
For when bold mortals me descry,
I at that very moment die.*

---

* Solutions to all riddles can be found at page 323.

ONE

A Riddle

Insensible as clay, deaf, dumb and blind,
I yet possess each passion of the mind,
Rage, tenderness, guilt, joy and fear
Dwell in my breast and in my words appear.
Some at my sight you'll see with horror start –
While others fondly press me to their heart.
But though the object of a strong desire,
Ungrateful folk oft doom me to the fire.

The 30th to 31st day of July 1752

Luminary: Sun sets 35 minutes after 7.
Observation: Venus is in the Ascendant and shows
many perturbations.
Prognostication: An unlucky day for travel.

'An unlucky day for travel.' The phrase tolled like a doom bell in Tabitha's skull as she woke. Wincing against the over-bright morning, she groped a hand to the other side of the bed, but found no warm flesh there, only cold rumpled linen. Raising herself stiffly, she pushed skeins of hair from her face. No doubt her gentleman had gone to the privy or, even better, to settle her bill. Busy voices and clatter from the downstairs of the inn told her she'd slept exceedingly late.

Her first stab of misgiving was heralded by the disappearance of the gold sovereign from the table. And where was her box, her trunk, her bag? In a twinkling she was up on bare feet, scrabbling beneath the table, beneath the bed. 'The black-hearted dog!' she cursed, then a tremor shook her voice. 'No, no. My mother's money . . .'

Casting around the room in despair, she found even her flowered silk gown had vanished. After pulling hard on the maid's bell, she laced the few garments the rogue had spared her over the top of her stale shift. Here was her quilted petticoat and satin stays; but not a thread remained of stockings, cloak or hat. Ill-matched with this scanty apparel, the villain had left her fancy ribboned shoes neatly at the bedside.

A scrawny serving girl appeared.

'The gentleman in black and green. Where is he?'

'Why, he got the early morning flyer, madam.'

'But he said . . .' Oh, what did it matter what he had said? 'I have been robbed by the rascal! Fetch the landlord.'

The Malmsey-bloated landlord appeared at the doorway, his face pinched with suspicion.

'Look, sir! I have been robbed – by one of your patrons, no less.

And he's taken a deal of money I owe my mother.' Her eyes pricked at its mere mention.

'Now hold your horses, missy,' grumbled the landlord. 'Even if he were a gentleman, I never set eyes on the fellow before you led him to your chamber. I charged his drinks to your bill, just as he asked.'

She wanted to spit in the rogue's eye. Lifting empty palms, she cried, 'The villain has taken every farthing I own, and my box and clothes besides. What am I to do, sir?'

Pushing the door closed, the landlord took a few steps towards her. 'So? Is it the magistrate you be wanting?' He lifted his bushy brows, knowing the answer well enough.

She shook her head, unable to disguise her wretchedness. 'But my bill of charges . . .'

'That scoundrel's made a proper fool of you, young miss. Mend your ways, is my advice. If you don't want any trouble, clear off smartish and I'll wipe the slate.'

Chastened by his kindness, she mumbled, 'I shall repay you when I can.'

'Repay me by keeping clear of this inn, you hear?'

The little maid hung back after her master had left, jittering excitedly. 'Some of these villains carry the timetables to all the rattlers – sneaking from inn to inn, forever acting the stranger. Travelling folk be easy pickings to them.'

Wearily, Tabitha remembered her own sorry plans to strip the fellow of his purse and abandon him at first light. If only she had woken first. What a fool she felt herself – the biter bit, indeed.

Tabitha had intended to hire a carriage to take her baggage to Netherlea, but now she was forced to walk. Though she was morti-fied to appear outdoors in such undress, it was at least a fine summer's day, the sun shining bright upon the hard-baked road. Down Chester's Bridge Street she strode as fast as she might, past high-gabled brown and white half-timbered mansions, avoiding the eyes of strangers. Passing the bridge tower, she crossed the River Dee in a throng of hawkers and market folk, weaving to avoid horses' hooves and the pole-ends of sedans. On the far side, she turned aside for the water meadows and near-forgotten path to Netherlea. Passing a familiar sandstone tomb, she idly traced the gritty image of a spear-bearing woman, just as she had on a hundred childhood errands. It had been the local custom to make a wish there, to some pagan witch or other. What was her wish now? Everything she truly wanted was impossible: to have her money back and more besides, to have Robert at her side again, to be a thousand miles away, inhabiting another, carefree life.

The events of the previous night blazed in her mind as she marched steadily on beside the river. Two days had already passed since the date she had told her mother to expect her. Robert had kept her back in London, promising a fine farewell, so she had bought herself the flowered gown and ribboned shoes. Their encounter had ended with violent words in the street; he complaining that his wife was ill, at which Tabitha replied she hoped the malady would prove fatal. Then the coach had run tiresomely late, trundling along rutted byways and through naked and uncivilized land for mile after mile. Chester's church bells had been ringing eleven chimes, the moon a sickly crescent, when the coach rolled into the walled city.

When she had strode into the smoky fug of the White Lion, all eyes had risen and fixed upon her. She wore her hem raised high to show scarlet heels and pretty ankles. Sending the landlord's boy upstairs with her box and bags, she sauntered to a table by the fire. Taking her seat, she laid her head back against the panelled oak, content to breathe in pipe tobacco and hops, and find herself blessedly motionless.

'The gentleman's compliments,' the tapster had announced, setting a bottle of garnet-red claret and two glasses down before her. From the chimney corner, the said gentleman tipped his hat in her direction – a lean-faced cove, in a coat of black with green frogging. She had not turned a trick since meeting Robert, but now that he had scorned her, what price a loyal heart? Rapidly, she calculated. After she had given her mother five pounds, and paid her fare home again to London, she would have less than twenty pounds to keep herself afloat. Sitting upright, she banished weariness and turned to her admirer, posing a coquettish question with her eyes. Slowly he approached, and though his deep-pocked visage was not quite as handsome as the shadows had promised, she thought him no less agreeable than many another.

Setting his tricorne on the table, he poured her a glass of claret. 'Have you travelled far?' His voice was hoarse and low, with a faint Irish lilt.

'From the capital. I miss it sorely, already.'

'You are seeking business tonight, lady?'

Well, straight to business he goes, she thought sourly, at the same time affecting laughter. 'I should rather say I am in pursuit of pleasure, sir.' No, that wouldn't do; she was not about to give the goods away for free. 'Most especially, with a kind and generous gentleman,' she added airily.

He leaned towards her and narrowed his grey, gleaming eyes. 'Why, just today my banker gave me a fresh-minted sovereign of the prettiest gold. Is that . . . agreeable?'

After a pause, Tabitha nodded, raising her glass. 'Now business is done – let us raise a toast to pleasure.'

He took a long draught of claret, then delved in his pocket and pulled out a globe-shaped silver article. Turning it upside down, he flipped open the top.

'That's a curious trifle.' She leaned forward to gain a better view. It was formed in the shape of a human skull, but about the size of a bantam egg. He had swung its jaws open on a hinge, revealing a silver watch dial marked with Roman numbers and circled with gold. The time was accurate: it wanted only thirteen more minutes to midnight.

She reached out to touch it, but he snatched it to his chest.

'Hold. His teeth are sharp. Death has his bite, see?'

With great care he closed the mouth and displayed the miniature skull on his palm. It was gruesomely beautiful, decorated with tiny figures, mottoes, hollow eyes and bared teeth. Across its domed brow was a familiar scene from Robert's collection of curiosities.

'Death bearing his scythe and hourglass,' she murmured. 'Standing between a castle and cottage with equal favour. A *memento mori*; a reminder we all will die.' Then, meeting the Irishman's eye, she uttered a favourite remark of Robert's: 'So passes the glory of the world.'

'Now who would have thought a girl of the night would fancy herself a scholar?' he said coolly. 'It's almost midnight. Time lost cannot be won again; that is my creed.' Pocketing his macabre toy, he extended a hairy hand towards her. With barely an instant's hesitation, she let him lead her up the staircase.

Her chamber had not been the cheapest the inn could offer, but she was glad of the wide, damask-draped bed and feather-plump mattress. He pulled her towards him the moment the door was closed, and she put up a lively performance, running her fingers up and down his body and coaxing him ever closer to the softness of her flesh. Aha, there was the pretty *vanitas*, a solid lump inside the silk of his coat. Distracting him with burrowing kisses, she helped him from his coat, and at the same time slipped the silver skull into the secret pouch inside her petticoat. After that, the gentleman had applied himself manfully, but she had been glad he made no great effort to prolong their congress. Before she fell asleep, she had mused that the gruesome watch alone would turn the night's venture to profit.

The silver skull. Pausing on the grassy path, she rooted inside her petticoat and pulled out the watch, swinging it like a pendulum on its silver chain, gratified to feel it hang as heavy as a bag of silver. She placed it to her ear: it had stopped ticking. Then her predicament struck her. Skin the dog alive, she couldn't even pawn it. If the thief was riding the coaches, the watch must have been stolen from some traveller, and might be searched for in Chester. She needed to keep it secret until she could find a trusty fence, down in the capital. Until then, not a soul must see the grinning skull.

Moving on, she made an inventory of all her other losses: her favourite gown and ruffles; a coral bracelet given to her long ago by Robert; laced linen that conjured happier days abed; a shell mirror; a token in the shape of Venus allowing admittance to Vauxhall Pleasure Gardens. It was mortifying to turn up at Netherlea as ill-dressed as she had left it. The shame of it burned like a branding iron.

Again she heard an echo of the past. All the previous day, a farmer's wife on the Chester coach had prated from her almanack. 'Today is a day of misfortune on the roads – an unlucky day for travel.' Beneath the shade of her saucily tipped bonnet, Tabitha had rolled her eyes, wondering at what a credulous age she lived in. But was not her own mother a devotee of the same *Vox Stellarum* almanack, making a ritual of marking the days, and reading the prognostications without fail?

A little whimper escaped her lips – she had lost her mother's letter with her stolen box. Yet there was no need to reread the tremulous lines, she had them by heart . . .

It would be best, Tabitha dear, if instead of posting the money for the infant you delivered it here by your own hand, for I must have words with you, of a grave and private sort. There is something afoot that may only be an old woman's foolishness, yet I can confide it to no one else in the world. Come quickly, dear, before July is ended, as I fear time may be short. I should dearly love to see your bonny face once more, and pray your sharp wits prove a fretful old matron wrong.

Your affectionate and ever-loving,

Mother

How her heart had sunk when she first opened the letter, recalling her shameful departure from Netherlea more than a year past. It was a reminder, too, of a blood oath, unthinkingly sworn one desperate winter's night. Her fingers felt sticky; she fancied, too, that they smelled faintly of iron and salt. Devil take it, why must she venture back? Netherlea was a village of countrified clods, gossips and whisperers. Yet it also held her mother's home, where Tabitha had been born and reared, and whence she had, with much relief, escaped. In London she had kept her past tucked away like dirty clouts, hidden behind the baubles and glitter of her new life. Now, with a sense of dread, she took the soiled memories out once more. She must keep her visit short, and her secret secure.

The riverside path was deserted that morning; from the golden motes in the air, she guessed most folk must be hay-making. Crossing a well-remembered meadow, she drank at an icy brook and breakfasted on bilberries fresh from the earth; the taste of them, tartly sweet, was fresher than any food she had eaten in years. Thereafter her way grew easy and she passed the succeeding miles serenely. She had forgotten the lushness of the Cheshire sward in midsummer; the murmur of insects on the wing, the wildflowers that bedizened her path. Idly she picked meadowsweet, wild rose and ragged robin, twining them into a chain and then winding it in a circlet through her hair. Why, in London she often paid twopence for half-dead twists of heather. And truth be told, her diminished costume was suited to the glorious heat, leaving her arms bare of all but her thin shift.

Ahead of her loomed the high peak of Beeston Castle, casting a fairy-book silhouette against the blue sky. Pulling off her pinching shoes, she walked barefoot on the silky grass, enjoying the coolness between her toes, inhaling bruised mint. How many times had she walked this path? Here was the cave where a band of village children had conspired to sleep one night, until a flurry of lights sent them shrieking home again. Joshua, their leader, had said they were the torches of dead Roman soldiers, hunting children to work in their mines.

There had been peculiar objects buried in the dirt, she remembered now. Turned to stone by witches, they had seemed, the blackened knives, spearheads and bracelets; all of them magical, especially the thumb-sized figurines like petrified fairies. Sometimes their finds were snatched and used as charms by the village women. Mostly, she recalled taking relics up to Bold Hall, where the De Vallorys' steward paid a penny for every trifle they found. She paused at the hollow oak where the children had often played and now found warm embers and charred animal bones. Tinkers, she thought, or tramps halting on the road.

She left the wood, and soon Eglantine Hall and its park came into view. The ancient Tudor tower stood intact and impressive, but the house had been shot to a soulless shell in the Civil War. The sun flashed on only a few mullioned windows rising above the ruins.

A stone fish pond glittered through the undergrowth; a boon to a sore-footed traveller. Slipping through the shrubbery, she crept to the water's edge. Above her, she caught sight of a wisp of smoke, rising from the tower's barley-sugar twisted chimneys. So Eglantine Hall was tenanted, for the first time in years. She must be silent and secret – but no one was going to stop her bathing her raw toes.

TWO

A Riddle

It bears me many miles away,
Yet in my room it's there.
It has no wings to soar and play,
Yet lifts me through the air.

It is the craft of fastest motion,
Yet has no need for sail nor oar,
With speed of thought I cross an ocean –
One instant and I'm on the shore.

The 31st day of July 1752

Lammas Eve

Luminary: Moon rises 24 minutes
after 4 of the afternoon.
Observation: Mercury the Messenger
is with the Moon.
Prognostication: Unsettling change is at hand.

N athaniel Starling lifted his spyglass to his eye and surveyed the view from his lofty perch on the roof of Eglantine Hall. Over in Netherlea, groups of villagers moved like ants, dragging branches across the green to the unlit bonfire. It surprised him that such customs had survived the wars, but tonight was Lammas Eve, accounted by antiquaries a most uncanny night. If the old rites were followed, tomorrow the loaf-mass would be baked from the first corn and carried to church to be blessed. Tonight, however, would be rather less holy. Did these rustic maidens and their swains still chase each other in the greenwood? That plump-cheeked dairymaid was forever playing the coquette when he called at the farm. He resolved to stroll over when the first fire was lit.

Nathaniel pulled aside a lock of unwashed hair and, through his eyeglass, surveyed the road to Chester. He saw none of the usual passers-by: the vagabonds heading for Tinkers Wood, or Mr Dilks the parson bowling along to Bishops Court, or Sir John's brother, Doctor De Vallory, returning from a consultation in a coach that bore the family crest.

Neither was there anything astir behind the diamond panes of Bold Hall. It was a fine old manor from the days of the Tudors, three storeys of blackened antique timbers laid in stripes and chevrons over white plaster. In what luxury that man lived. Sir John De Vallory had not a care in the world, save for pocketing his rents and choosing how to spend his money.

The task Nathaniel was set upon – to introduce himself to the man and gain his trust – made him sick with apprehension. Yet he had to do it. Death and bones, even the contemplation of it made Nathaniel weary. He yawned. All night he had been puzzling his imagination hot with slow stranglings, the anatomization of cracking bones and steaming guts, and today his spirit felt as filthy as his stained hands. Later he would strip himself of his night-stinking clothes and dive into the pond to sluice himself of these horrors. His every atom felt unclean.

Taking a draught of ale from the leather jug, he turned his eye to the woods: massy green foliage intersected by twinkles of silver dancing on the river. Sir John's fields were a chessboard of ashen oats, silk-green barley and yellow, ripening corn. He yawned. The zephyrs cooling his cheek were perfumed with flowers, and wood pigeons cooed from their roosts in the stone walls below him.

Suddenly the sound of splashing water reached his ears. Perhaps that fat drake had returned and he might have roast duck for dinner? But leaning over the battlement he saw instead a woman seated on the banks of his private bathing pond. He made a silent inspection of the intruder. Not the usual coarse village girl, but a fine-looking woman, tantalizingly half-dressed in expensive underclothes. Nat held his breath as she dabbled her toes and leaned back lazily on her palms, her strong face uplifted in the sun's beams, eyes closed and unpinned hair tumbling groundwards. A garland of Ophelian wildflowers crowned her head.

Jerkily, he directed his lens across her form, wondering who in Heaven's name she might be. And why was this nymph so scantily dressed? To bathe, perhaps? Or had she a lover nearby, for whom she had pulled off her gown? No: his spyglass showed him no companion; she was as self-contained as a nut in a shell, lost in languorous oblivion. He leaned forwards, wondering where he might have seen her before. Was she an actress perhaps, a beauty he had once admired on the London stage? Her lips parted, and a moment later her song drifted upwards, fainter than the murmuring brook and the fluting of the pigeons.

'And then my love built me a bower, bedeck'd with many a fragrant flower;
A braver bower you ne'er did see, than my true love did build for me.'

The savagery of the night was banished at once. The air was magically still.

'Oh, fragrant flower,' he whispered. 'Oh, glorious nymph.'

He was resurrected from his long sojourn in the stews. Why did he sink to such vileness when he so longed for beauty? Perhaps he could compose poetry again, poetry worthy of this Euterpean muse. He turned the brass dial to frame the woman's languid, dreamy face, and her image filled his eyes, so close he might reach out and caress her cheek. Oh, sweet God; it was happening again, as it did almost every sap-high summer. Would he never learn? Imbecile that he was, he was falling in love.

THREE

A Riddle

Though I'm nothing that breathes, I'm dreaded by all,
And strange to declare, owe my rise to a fall.
I am always around, but I've never been seen,
You take pains to avoid me, but can't escape me,
I may choose to visit when you're old and grey,
Or if fortune foretells it, I'll grasp you today.
Manners dictate I give you strong embrace,
As I settle a final cold kiss on your face.
Whether I meet you in prayer, dread, or hate,
I will find you, I promise –
I am everyone's fate.

The 31st day of July 1752

Lammas Eve

Luminary: Sun rises 24 minutes
after 4 of the morning.
Observation: The Sun enters Leo at
which time Saturn is retrograded.
Prognostication: A complication that is worse
and better, good and bad.

Hearing voices raised in merriment, Tabitha slowed her pace
as she neared Netherlea. Through a gap in the foliage, she
saw the familiar great oak, spreading its branches over
Church Common, and behind it Netherlea's ancient church and
splendid modern parsonage. A bonfire was being built, by a crowd
she knew only too well. There was Zusanna the dairymaid, whip-
tongued queen of the village gossips, laughing shrilly with the young
bucks, one hand at her waist and the other holding a tankard. Cam,
her black-bearded giant of a husband, reclined on the grass with a
jug at his side – perhaps dozing, perhaps watching his wife. Huddled
at the church wall were Zusanna's mother Nell Dainty and her two
cronies, passing judgement on their neighbours like three grey-haired
harpies. Tabitha felt a powerful reluctance to show herself there so
ill-dressed. Instead, she took the shady lane that followed the brook,
wondering how in the Devil's name she might find herself a fashionable costume in such a backwater.

Soon the brook broadened where the tide ran down from the mill
race. At the ford, she lifted her hem and strode nimbly across the
stepping stones. She had sung ten verses of her ballad before the
thatch of her mother's dwelling peeped above the treeline; she
quickened her pace, anticipating an affectionate greeting. Rounding
the final turn, a squat wattle-and-daub cottage came into view, golden
brown thatch sagging over the windows like a bonnet pulled low
over two wide-set eyes. Behind the wicker fence, pink, yellow and
purple blossoms ranged around canes of green beans. It was hard

to credit that she had lived upon that tiny square of earth for nineteen years, reluctantly drilled in every homely art by her mother, from baking to brewing to mending and cleaning. This time, prodigal though she was, she would try to be a worthy daughter. She must fortify herself to talk with her mother and ask forgiveness for calling her a hypocrite, and worse.

From the perfumed garden, she entered the gloom beyond the open door. Not a jot had changed. The blackened fireplace cast a thin red glow across the rag rug to her mother's empty wooden chair. There were few possessions: a shelf of ancient platters, oddments of brass, a few pieces of time-polished furniture, while above her head hams and herbs hung from the ceiling beams.

'Is the kettle boiling?' she called, an ancient jest of theirs, for her mother's kettle boiled perpetually on the fire hook.

A figure stepped out from the back room – a slender young woman who pulled up, stock-still, like a frightened coney. Tabitha started too – dressed in a white cap and apron, the girl had the uncanny appearance of being the phantom figure of her own younger self.

'Who are you?' The girl had a sweet voice, high-pitched with surprise.

'I am Tabitha Hart, Widow Hart's daughter. I might ask you the same.'

Making a curtsy, the girl said, more warmly, 'It is me, Miss Tabitha. Jennet Saxton. You gave me such a startle, I couldn't think who you were.'

Tabitha could barely remember Joshua's stepdaughter, save as a slinking, silent child. Had she grown so quickly in the last year?

'Mother!' she called towards the bedroom. 'I'm home.' She had pulled up a wooden chair to the fire before she noticed Jennet's woebegone expression. 'What ails you, girl?'

Receiving no reply, she sprang up and lifted the curtain between the parlour and the bedroom. What she saw there threw her heart hard against her ribs. On the narrow bed stretched a figure that was her mother and yet not her mother at all, a small figure lying as if asleep in a nightgown and cap. Behind her, Jennet mumbled, 'It were only yesterday . . .'

Her mother's face was swollen, and mottled with patches of bluish red. Like the round eyes of a hideous doll, two copper pennies lay upon her eyelids. Tabitha sank to her knees at her mother's bedside, taking a cold, resistant hand and pressing it against her cheek.

'I've come too late,' she whispered. If only time might turn around. If only she could have been spared a few moments more before her mother's spirit had left this earthly realm.

She was still kneeling by her mother's bed when the bass notes of men's voices in the parlour roused her. Jennet pulled back the curtain and whispered, 'Miss Tabitha, the parson and the doctor have come a-calling.'

Tabitha hauled herself up, woefully aware of the sun-pinked flesh displayed above her stays. Damn that plaguey thief! Her mother would have been mortified by her appearance. Rifling through the few garments in the room, she found a modest grey linsey gown and bodice. She was a good hand's-breadth taller than her mother, but beggars, as she was coming to comprehend, could not choose their dress. She swallowed back a little sob. The fabric felt like arms enfolding her, very soft from long wear, and smelling of lavender and her mother's body.

'Parson, Doctor.' Tabitha cast her eyes to the floor – whatever rumours Netherlea might whisper of her, she was determined to behave with propriety.

The doctor rose, a puzzled look on his grave face.

'You are Widow Hart's daughter, newly returned from London? Tabitha by name? A sad homecoming for a daughter.' With kindly condescension, he touched her hand; she rubbed her nose, and tried to smile, despite her wet eyes. The doctor wore the black fur-trimmed robe of his profession – though, as Sir John's own brother, it was said he practised medicine only from a noble vocation to help his fellow man. As he sat, Tabitha drew up a wooden stool for herself.

'Sirs, pray tell me what has happened? Mother wrote to me to come home. I cannot comprehend—'

Parson Dilks broke in. He was as different from the doctor as a sow's ear was from silk; a bloated toad, squashed into her mother's narrow chair.

'God moves with hidden intent,' he rasped. 'You must console yourself that your mother is safe with Christ now. Your neighbour, the constable, Mr Saxton, found her drowned in the river. He tried his best to rouse her, but . . . too late, on this occasion.'

'Drowned? But no one knew the river better than Mother.'

The doctor nodded in sympathy. 'I am afraid your mother's mind was disordered somewhat since the springtime. We all observed how she forgot her duties, arrived and departed at unexpected times, went wandering in the night. I am afraid the softening of the brain is a common plight of those who age before their time.'

'But she was no more than forty-five years of age.' Tabitha's voice rose in indignation.

'It is a hard life for a widow, I fear, though it was agreed that young Jennet here should call each day and help her.' The doctor nodded at the girl waiting in the corner. 'Yester eve, alas, she must have had one of her fancies, and gone out wandering in the woods.'

Tabitha closed her eyes tight, trying to hold back tears. 'Come quickly, dear,' the letter had begged, 'before July comes to an end.'

When she recalled herself again, the parson was speaking in his grating voice, familiar to her from a thousand sermons. 'Tomorrow will do, after the Lammas service. And, you'll need to borrow the pauper's coffin.' He cleared his throat. 'That is, unless you mean to purchase a coffin yourself?'

Tabitha shifted uneasily. 'Sirs, upon any other day I should have provided my mother with only the finest oak, and an engraved head-stone too. But I was robbed this morning of all my money by a rogue who rides the coaches. I had no choice but to walk from Chester with only the garments on my back. I am entirely penniless.' She lifted the corner of her mother's apron and wiped her eyes.

Parson Dilks could barely hide his satisfaction. She would never forget his tirade when she had left Netherlea. 'Strumpetting baggage!' he had shouted down the lane after her. 'Abandoning your brat to the care of your mother!'

As if at his cue, he asked, 'I trust you will soon return whence you came?'

'Certainly. But you must understand that my lack of funds constrains me at present.'

'Dilks, you are not for setting this unfortunate out on the road tomorrow, are you? What of charity, man?' demanded the doctor.

Through his clenched, yellow teeth, the parson replied: 'My dear doctor, it is the parish that pays for this cottage, and Widow Hart's stipend. I must consider who is worthy to be lodged here.'

The doctor tapped his cane impatiently on the floor. 'May I make a suggestion to you and to your parish board? Appoint this young woman as her mother's successor as village searcher. Else she is left without a roof for her own head – or her child's.'

Tabitha shook her head. 'I cannot do that, sir.'

'Where else will you go without funds?' the doctor asked.

The parson turned his unwholesome features to Tabitha. 'Are you even aware of the searcher's duties?'

Bewildered, Tabitha gave a little nod. 'Yes, sirs. I often accompanied my mother in her duties. To lay out the dead when the doom bell rings. And to write down the cause of each death in the Book of Mortalities.'

The parson shook his head. 'What of Nell Dainty? She has herblore and has waited long for this cottage. You employ her yourself in your garden, Doctor. She is deserving of charity.'

'Alas, I regret I cannot recommend her as searcher. She is competent at lesser tasks, preparing herbs and simple distillations, but her penmanship is poor. Tabitha, I recollect that you can read and write to a good standard?' The doctor was watching her closely, coaxing her to comply.

'I can, sir. I can read any book fluently, thanks to my mother's teaching, and I write a good gentlewoman's hand.'

'There were certain allegations made,' the parson retorted. 'This . . . female . . . is not respectable.'

The doctor turned to him, still courteous, but very cold. 'Should you like me to refer the matter to my brother? He always had a certain fondness for Widow Hart and her daughter, as I recall.'

As Tabitha listened she had time to gather her wits. 'I confess, a few weeks here to tidy my mother's affairs would be a great kindness, Doctor. Then I will be on my way.'

'Then it is agreed. I will recommend the appointment to my brother.' She felt the doctor's smile fall upon her like a benison.

From a second curtained chamber came a sudden raucous sound of wailing, growing ever more insistent. As both men made ready to leave, the doctor pointed his cane towards the curtain.

'And here is another reason to lodge Tabitha here, Parson. Now the child need not be paid for by the parish, either.'

The parson's expression brightened. 'That's very true, sir. You are ahead of me in your arithmetic.'

As Jennet carried the struggling, bawling infant into the parlour, both men turned and made a hasty escape.

Two hours later, the child at last lay red-cheeked and exhausted in her linen-cushioned basket. Tabitha watched her warily, as if she might at any moment rouse herself again. Little Bess was no longer the drowsy babe-in-arms she had last seen; she was a stocky creature, as tall as Tabitha's knee, and every inch of her bold and wilful. From the moment Jennet carried her into the parlour, the little maid had stared at her with undisguised dismay, her tiny lip trembling as she clung to Jennet's gown. Dressed in a stained bonnet and smock, she toddled round the room, her grubby fingers poking everywhere they shouldn't. After a long and tedious period of assessment, Bess had bravely made an approach to Tabitha, gaping upwards at this tall woman who was entirely a stranger.

'Ma-ma,' she babbled, and Tabitha stepped dutifully forward, forcing a rigid smile. But from the expression of terror in the child's face, she might have been an ogress. Bursting again into tears, the child scurried at surprising speed back to Jennet and buried her face in the girl's skirts.

'See how my mother has spoiled her,' Tabitha complained; the child would not even take a spoon of bread mush from her hand. But then, she had not given Bess a thought this last year or more, save only to earn the five pounds she paid yearly for the child's keep. The notion of being this peevish brat's new guardian appalled her. She could think only of one solution, and that was to rid herself of her quickly, before she hurried back down the highway to London.

FOUR

A Riddle

On man's vitals I constantly prey night and day,
And with fretting and vexing, I wear them away.
I force him to search with a diligent eye,
To find out the thing he's least willing to spy;
For when he has found it, it makes him look sad,
Nay, a hundred to one, but it makes him turn mad.
Though my colour by most is allowed to be green,
And I soon grow apace, I more often demean.

The 31st day of July to the 1st of August 1752

Lammas Eve to Lammas Day

Luminary: Moon is in decline 54 minutes
after 1 of the morning.
Observation: Saturn sets 34 minutes after 11 at night.
Prognostication: Trouble is stirring for one
of High Rank.

D usk was gathering fast as Nat sank down below the great
oak tree, trying to draw no attention in his direction. Around
him, a gathering of young fellows were sprawled; a few
he recognized as labourers from the estate, broad-shouldered as
bullocks, with mud-caked boots and bovine wits. Fifty yards away,
on the Church Common, the newly lit bonfire was already six feet
high, sending flames of scarlet and gold leaping into the air. He
gazed upwards, easing his neck after a day bent over his quill. Soon
the night would be black, for the young moon was still hidden below
the horizon. Above their heads shone the leaden pinpoint of Saturn,
his ring invisible without a spyglass.

The talk all around him was of the new calendar and the disappearance of eleven days.

'Can you credit it? Parliament is saying, after the third of
September, the very next day is to be the fourteenth of September!'

'Codswallop, in't it? Eleven days sliced off our lives? What about
us wages?'

Nat wished he had a memorandum book to collect his observations. He must write a humorous piece: *The Observations of Old
Hodge upon the Gregorian Calendar*.

A better-dressed fellow broke in, with an air of authority. 'The
length of your life won't change, Ben. 'Tis only the date that's
changed.'

'Aye, but 'as them Parliament fellows told the geese to fatten
eleven days early for Michaelmas? And bid the Glastonbury Thorn
to blossom well afore Christmas?'

There was laughter at this. Another voice piped up: 'The farmer says them calendars has got out of kilter with the sun and stars. So all the pay days and birthdays and feast days has got to be changed.'

'Lammas is Lammas. Mother Nature knows that. Come Lammastide the seed grows as fast by the moon as by sun,' persisted Ben.

Nat wondered if any of them knew the astronomical reason for that. Over the coming weeks the vast sphere of the harvest moon would swing close to the earth, looming heavy and bright almost from sunset to sunrise, a vast celestial lamp by which to gather the crops home.

Through the gloom he spied the approaching dairymaid. 'Any more of this excellent cider?' he called, raising his tankard.

'Just for your good self, sir? Or is you standing a round for the lads?' Her eyes gleamed amber in the firelight, and her lips were wet.

'I'll stand a round, Zusanna.' As he handed her a sixpence, her fingers, warm and sticky, were slow to withdraw.

The other drinkers grunted approval as cider splashed into their cups. Turning to acknowledge them, he noticed two newcomers had joined the throng; the first, from his silk coat, could only be Francis De Vallory. It was the first time he had seen the boy at close quarters. His face was unattractively long, the goatish impression accentuated by a jutting chin, and he held his tankard awkwardly, as if his knobbly wrists might snap. Nat could see little resemblance to the boy's father. His mother must be a bloodless sort of woman, to have produced such an heir.

His companion was a marked foil to him – handsome to a classical degree, and possessed of eyes as large as a prize heifer's, which laughed in the firelight but contained no warmth. Again and again he flipped a coin up into the air and caught it on the back of his hand, with the practised knack of a racketeer. Nat puzzled over where he had seen the lad before; those mocking eyes and oily curls. Yes – he was known as Darius, one of the hawkers, peddlers and ne'er-do-wells that camped down by the river. So the milksop lordling had a liking for such low company? The Devil only knew what his father made of that.

The word 'dead', uttered in a low voice, drew him abruptly back into the general conversation. 'Drowned, she were. By the stepping stones. Buried tomorrow.'

'How'd she drown there? T'int no more than waist-high.'

Nat tilted his head quickly to catch the reply.

'I heard she gone crack-headed, old dame Hart. She'd gone a-wandering in the moonlight, all alone. Din't know night from day no more.'

Nat stared. That was preposterous. Widow Hart had been upright and shrewd; he remembered her bright eyes lighting up her girlish features. Whenever he called at her cottage, their conversations had been lively and spiced with pleasurable intrigue. Yet she had been naïve, he could see that now; unaware of her own significance as the searcher, the recorder of the village's mortalities.

'Her daughter is back.' That was the better-spoken voice again, succeeded by silence. It belonged to a burly fellow in a sober brown coat, with a young female at his side – perhaps his daughter?

'Who's back? That Tabitha? Back from London?' demanded Zusanna from Nat's elbow, where she had slunk in close to press her leg against his. 'So why don't she show her face then?'

The man half-turned to the fire. He was a broad-faced fellow, with lightish hair tied in a ribbon.

'She's keeping watch by her mother tonight.'

The dairymaid snorted. 'Is that what she told you? Hell-cat!'

Nat, deducing that this newly arrived daughter might well be the nymph he had seen at the pond, found himself speaking aloud. 'This Tabitha is Widow Hart's daughter?'

At once, he wished he could unsay his words. The burly man, whom he now recognized as the local constable, took a few steps toward him, peering down into his face. 'Who are you, fellow, that wants to know?'

Before he could answer, Zusanna said silkily, 'It's only Mr Starling, Joshua.'

'Only Mr Starling.' The man's voice was hard and flat. 'And what is your business here, Mr Starling?'

The labourers turned to watch. The young girl at the constable's side pulled on his arm, eager to leave.

'Whatever my business is, it is certainly none of yours.'

Damn it! Nat couldn't stop the drink from putting provocations in his mouth. In the hush the only sound was the crackle and spit of the fire. The De Vallory cub was watching too, plague take him.

'Joshua,' Zusanna wheedled. 'Don't be ill-tempered.'

It was no use – the constable's face loomed over Nat.

'I've been watching you, Mr Nat Starling. I've seen those papers you're forever sending down London way. Now what might they be about, I asks myself? I have powers to intercept the post in the King's name. Mark my words, I will find you out.'

'Father, please.' His daughter tugged at his sleeve.

Nat flinched to think of his latest commission being publicly exposed, a crude re-telling of *The Ladies' Secret School for Pleasure*. Or even worse, any hint of his and Widow Hart's inquiries into the parish records.

'Be my guest,' he said, sweeping off his hat in a gesture of mock gallantry. 'Though if a gentleman cannot correspond privately with his friends, this is not the free and fair England I once believed it was.'

Gratefully, he heard a rumble of 'Ayes' and 'Hearken to that,' from the men around him. The constable, it seemed, was not a popular man.

'We shall see,' Joshua barked. Then, drawing his daughter away with him, he turned and left the gathering.

Nat wiped his mouth, wondering what manner of inconvenience he had just brought down upon his own head. One thing was certain – he must not allow that damned constable to pry too deeply into his affairs. Boyish laughter broke into his thoughts. The De Vallory heir and his swarthy friend Darius were watching him, dark and light heads conferring close together. Pox the pair of them! He wished he had not drawn the whippersnapper's attention.

'Shall I tell you what goes on at Lammas Eve?' Zusanna whispered, drawing her arm through his. ''Tis a night to go wandering, deep in the woods. You've heard the song: "*It was upon a Lammas night, When corn rigs are bonnie . . .*" She sang tunelessly, tickling his neck with her hot breath.

Nat pulled away to look down at her. 'So it's a night for lovers to take to the forest? To break old bonds, forget tedious old husbands and abandon oneself to the corn spirit?'

'Aye, it be that.' Zusanna held his eyes.

'I shall bear that in mind, then, my dear. Good night, all.' He heard a little squeal of dismay from the dairymaid as he leaned hard on her shoulder to stand up, before setting off alone across the green. He hoped that no one had noticed the direction he walked was quite opposite to his lodgings at Eglantine Hall.

FIVE

A Riddle

A tall and slender shape I bear
No lady's skin more white and fair:
My life is short, and doth decay
So soon it seldom lasts a day.
Yet to mankind I'm useful ever,
And many hidden things discover;
Which makes all those who round me tend,
To with a sigh lament my end.

31st day of July to 1st day of August 1752

Lammas Eve to Lammas Day

Sun rises: 43 minutes after 4 in the morning.
Observation: Seven Stars rise 52 minutes
after 9 at night.
Prognostication: Hidden truths will always out.

T abitha watched a flock of birds wheeling in a pink sky limned
with gold. Just beyond the garden stood the skeleton of a
tree, where a blackbird perched, his lonely song fluting in
the still air. The garden was as still as a waxworks; the distant sound
of the river a melodic surge and fall. It was her first spell of peace
since she had woken that morning; she would have liked to write
to Robert, but their parting had made that impossible. Jennet had
gone, at Tabitha's insistence, to join her friends at the Lammas
bonfire. Thankfully, Bess was again deep in slumber, making tiny
curling movements with her fingers. It was time for the night watch.

By the light of a new wax candle she began her mother's laying
out, washing her mottled flesh and placing sweet rosemary and
lavender in its hidden folds to keep her body fresh. Next, she dressed
her, thankful that the death-rigor was leaving her limbs. Muttering
apologies, she garbed her in her best Sunday gown of blue stripes.
Then every ribbon, knot and braid had to be loosed to allow her
soul to escape her body. Easing the cap from her head, she unwound
the wiry grey plaits and fetched her comb. A bloody wound was
revealed on her mother's scalp. She lifted the candle flame closer
to inspect it, lying ugly and gaping and darkening to black.

She had seen drowned folk before, and knew that when the tides
sent bodies drifting down the Dee, a body could be bumped and
scraped along the riverbed. But this was no such wound for her
mother bore no other marks or scratches. She tried to imagine her
mother falling directly on to a sharp stone, but she could make no
sense of it. Neither was there any of the foam that usually besmirched
the mouths of those who drowned.

The candle had burned a good few inches when she allowed herself to rest in the chair at her mother's side. Muttering a few half-remembered prayers from her childhood, she felt her eyes droop. She was near drunk with tiredness, ill-equipped for the coming days of mourning.

Sleep claimed and held her fast, until in the depths of the night a movement at her side woke her. There stood the child Bess, prattling to herself in the darkness. In the candle's guttering glow, she saw tiny fingers lift and stretch upwards to grasp her mother's dead hand.

Suddenly all Tabitha's stoppered rage ignited: at Robert and his conniving wife, at the Irish thief who had duped her, at the spiteful parson – and mostly at this hindrance, this child who dared to live when her own mother was lost to her forever. Before she could stop herself she pushed Bess aside, and the child slipped to the floor. A moment later, her scream split the night.

At once shame, hot and queasy, overcame Tabitha. Her anger left her and she felt instead ferocious pity. Bess had only wanted to greet her old playmate – God only knew what fond hours the two of them had shared together. She pulled the child on to her lap, clasping her squealing, wriggling body. For a long spell, she did her awkward best to hush her, until her sobs ceased and her little body slackened into sleep. Then, wary of waking her, she gently set her down.

Tabitha felt wide awake once more. Through the window, a scrap of moonlight shone, and she could sense the garden exhaling its night scent. Beyond that, the thicket began, and the path to the river. A sudden sound, two stones clinking together, alerted her to something moving. Possibly a darker shape – or perhaps not. She stood very still, straining her eyes to catch a glimpse but discerning nothing. There were plenty of creatures living in the wood, she told herself: foxes, owls, even a badger or two. A long spell of silence passed. The only sound was the rattling tremor of leaves lifted on the breeze. The creature must have turned back and gone.

Wondering what time the day would break, she looked about her for her mother's almanack. Not finding it on its usual shelf by the Bible, she began a thorough search: under the bed, in the linen box, even feeling beneath the mattress. Next she searched the parlour, still without success.

Somewhere in the cottage was a small wooden box, where her

mother's few precious objects were collected. She sank to her knees and groped for it in the alcove beside the fire. A tinkling sound led her fingers to a small piece of ironwork. She held it up to the candle: it was nothing but a stubby square-headed nail head, rather rusty and dirty. Abandoning it on the mantel, she paced back and forth. If the almanack was missing, had someone taken it? No, it was more likely that her mother had hidden it away. She returned to the bedroom, and explored the thatched ceiling.

Every year her mother spent a precious shilling on the Chester almanack, entitled De Angelo's *Vox Stellarum*, and every day she consulted the little book, her calendar, diary, horoscope and entertainment. Her mother had been no poet, but she had once called it the loom on which she spun her life; a frame that carried the warp and weft of her days. It was a guide to the sunlit hours, a reminder of when the moon was dark or bright, and a reckoner to plan each season's tasks. Though she struggled to comprehend their exotic symbols, she puzzled over the charts of astronomy, watching the sky in eager hopes of eclipses, meteors and comets. De Angelo's prophecies, on the fates of countries and kings, were deliberated on as profoundly as any events at hand in Netherlea. Yet her mother's supreme pleasures were the cunning Enigmas and Riddles, which entertained her busy mind for the whole twelvemonth.

Groping with her hands along the roof beams of the far corner, Tabitha found an unfamiliar small object tacked to the wall, and, lifting the candle, discovered a tiny wooden cross. She knew it to be made of rowan twigs, a protection against evil. Her mother had always disdained such country claptrap – but latterly, it seemed, she had been fearful enough to make such a charm. Growing more alarmed still, Tabitha felt beneath the eaves until she found a recessed space, barely a foot wide. There sat the box, locked but with no sign of the key. Shaking it, she found it rattled.

There had been a time when Tabitha had lived entirely upon her wits and her fine form, sharing rooms off the Strand with her friend, Poll Shepherd. It was Poll who had shown her how to lift a few extra coins, or even better, a pocket watch, and leave the gentleman none the wiser. 'Bleed a few drops and they don't even feel it,' had been Poll's advice, and thus, the curious art of the picklock had formed part of Tabitha's education. Now, taking a long pin from her mother's shelf, she unfastened the box's crude lock within minutes. Lifting the lid, she found a fold of paper containing a lock of her own father's grey hair, a pair of ancient buckles, and a faded pink ribbon her mother had worn on her wedding day. Then a sheet of fresh paper fell out, newly inked in a large and fine hand. She read it rapidly, puzzling over its dedication:

A Riddle for Mistress Hart

I see you as you watch and spy,
Consumed with curiosity;
A maggot feeding on the dead,
And feasting on calamity.
Don't think you'll end my sovereign power –
'Tis you whom worms will soon devour.

D

Tabitha read it twice again. Who would have sent her mother so vile a threat? But as she glanced upwards, the rowan cross confirmed the truth: her mother had been terrified, had pleaded with her to return – and she had done so too late. She closed her eyes tight, and rocked herself in the chair. For a long spell she hated her own self, her vanity and self-regard.

The loathsome verse still lay on her lap. Who might this 'D' be? Her mind raced through a dozen possibilities. Then, reaching into the bottom of the box, she found the current edition of De Angelo's almanack.

Tabitha opened it with a new wariness. There were the usual familiar pages: the twelve signs of the zodiac, the high water tables, the list of kings and queens and the astrological judgements upon the year. And there, as she had always done, her mother had neatly penned her observations, in the margins and spaces of every single day.

The year of 1752 had begun dully enough, save for a remark, at Ash Wednesday, that she had awaited Tabitha's letter for a whole month. Otherwise, it was much as any other year: *'I visited Old Seth, he is gaining strength,'* and *'I wrote in the Book of Mortalities how Mistress Cox did die in childbed.'* She almost slipped over the first indication of her mother's unease:

1 May Day. Beside this, her mother had written: *Woke tonight in great fear. I know who killed Towler, and why.*

Towler? Who was he? She knew no one of that name in the village. Was he a newcomer, or a passing traveller? She read on rapidly until, a month later, her mother's cramped handwriting spoke again of her fears. Tabitha lifted the candle and read the words twice, to be certain of their import:

8 June Whitsunday. *I believe the culprit has marked me. He looked at me, hard and knowing. He followed me here this night and I stood silent behind the door, very afeared.*

Tabitha hurried on, rifling through pages. Here was another:

24 June St John the Baptist. *D followed me silently in the woods but I retraced my way to Nanny Seagoes and stayed with her.*

With sinking spirits, Tabitha saw her own name again.

15 July St Swithin. *I wrote this day to Tabitha and told her to hurry. I long to have her here.*

A few days later, she asked again: *When will Tabitha come? D is so well regarded here that I can make no accusation.*

Then, only three days ago: *I am more easy. D paid me no heed today upon the High Street; perhaps it is all a lonely woman's fancy.*

And there it was, yesterday, the final entry, on the day on which she had drowned.

30 July Day Before Lammas Eve. *D watched me today with a secret eye when no one else was looking. I must stay indoors till Tabitha comes.*

Tabitha clapped her hand over her mouth and swayed, her gorge rising. When she laid hands upon this D, she would rend him limb from limb. Wait – had he not killed the hapless Towler? She ploughed back again through the pages. Though Towler was not a name she knew, surely his death must be in the Book of Mortalities. She must alert the constable tomorrow, and this D must be arrested for his murder.

Then she found the very first entry, and almost laughed aloud at the oddness of it.

23 April St George's Day. *Towler, Sir John's favourite hound, died today very sudden from a violent fit. The gamekeeper rebuked me for enquiring the cause, making an ill jest that I need not enter a dog in the list of mortalities.*

What in the Devil's name was a dog's death to her mother? The doctor's words returned to her: 'Your mother's mind was disordered since the springtime.' Tabitha leaned back in the chair, her thoughts chasing each other. Lonely women grew fond of cats and dogs, of tame blackbirds and squirrels; yet such soft-heartedness had never been her mother's way. She had been the quick-witted daughter of a radical preacher, a clever woman with a sharp eye for her neighbours' follies. She would no more grieve over the death of a hunting hound than the neck-twisting of a cockerel.

Suddenly the candle fizzed and died; a grey dawn seeped into the room, casting shadows across the bed. Her mother's corpse seemed to have shrunk in the night, her cheeks sunken to the skull, the skin a waxy death mask.

Tabitha stood broad awake in the grainy light. Her mother had been the only soul on earth who had cared for her, fed her, consoled her. She looked outside at the brightening sky, hearing the chirrups of waking songbirds. Someone hereabouts had harried and frightened her mother, or perhaps worse. But he had not taken Tabitha's return into account. Her first step must be to identify D, discreetly, privately, without arousing a jot of suspicion. And if D could be proved to have raised a finger to harm her mother – by inflicting a fatal head-wound, for instance – she would not leave Netherlea till she had avenged her, and brought the cowardly monster to justice.

SIX

A Riddle

A house I am, but not of size
To take in more than one;
I'm often viewed with wary eyes,
Though I'm a foe to none.
Four sides I have, but of what made
Depends not on his voice
Who is to sleep within my shade –
It's left to others choice.
Though freehold is my small estate,
No vote it e'er can give;
Yet thousands, fattening in state,
Upon my inmate live.

The 1st day of August 1752

Lammas Day

Luminary: Day is 14 hours and 42 minutes long.
Observation: Mars is returned to the
Quadrant of Saturn.
Prognostication: The month will see much
use of Fraud and Deceit.

Contrary to the almanack's prediction, it rained on Lammas Day; low clouds hung smoke-grey, spitting out spots of rain. Tabitha pulled her shawl tight around her shoulders, waiting at the cottage gate for the parish men to take her mother to the churchyard. Dully, she noticed the door latch was broken, the wooden rod had been snapped in half. She ached for a bumper of brandy, or a quick tot of Madam Geneva. Lord, the gaiety of the hot London streets seemed as distant as the moon.

The handcart trundled into view, bearing the ugly parish coffin. She followed it at a sombre pace through the rain, her back and skirts growing damp. After a jolting passage across the river, they reached the village, where a sprinkling of mourners appeared with heads bowed at their doors. By the time they reached the graveyard, a rain-spattered huddle had formed behind her, mostly crones and old fellows leaning on canes. She nodded at those she recognized, mortified that she could afford neither a bite to eat nor a sip of ale for them. Nanny Seagoes waited at the lychgate, muttering to her how sorely she would miss the widow; and her mother's aunt, an upper housemaid at the hall, stepped forward and pressed Tabitha's hand through fine white gloves. That was the worst of it – having no mourning clothes. Her London friend Poll had owned an elegant black silk, very low-cut with ebony ruffles, that made a great show for a funeral or a hanging. If she could have worn such a gown, Tabitha felt she could have borne anything, even this dreary gathering.

Keeping her eyes low and her hands clasped, she took her place by the graveside. Was her father anywhere close by? she wondered. Her mother used to leave flowers and a little heap of smooth river stones at his grave. Then the bishop's man had visited and ordered all such churchyard trash to be removed. In later years she had forgotten to ask her mother exactly where Father lay. Now it pained her to think of man and wife cast apart, even in death.

Remote and dull, she heard the parson begin the service, only rousing herself when he raised his white finger in reproof. Widow Hart, he said, though she had striven to serve the Lord, had been guilty of turning a blind eye to lewdness. He is throwing scorn on me, Tabitha thought, twisting her mother's pink wedding ribbon tighter and tighter around her fingers. Dilks, she repeated fiercely in her head. D, D, D. Had the parson struck her mother a blow to the head and then thrown her into the river? Thrills of fury prickled all over her skin. Yet now was not the time to set a match to that powder. Instead, she stood grimly beside the burial pit.

Her mother's bundled body was lifted from the public coffin and lowered down upon a sheet into the wet clay. At a sign, she cast a nosegay of rosemary into the grave, mumbling a farewell. Cold damp earth fell in spadefuls on to the wretched bundle, but could not conceal a thin foot, with yellow toenails, that poked forth from a rip in the shroud. Tabitha pressed her fist to her mouth, making a supreme effort not to shame her mother with tears. She wanted to spit in the eye of the whole poxy world.

Gruffly, the parson informed her that it was now her responsibility as searcher to complete the Book of Mortalities. Devil take it, her duty to note the reason for every death in the parish had slipped entirely from her mind. While he concluded his business with the gravedigger, she made her way to the vestry. The leather-bound book was laid out ready on the table. She glanced at the sad records, touching the pages like a talisman – her mother's writing was as neat as any clerk's, filling page after page of the book. So this was the world her mother had inhabited: a dreary room, filled with dusty ledgers and ancient quills, old wax and candle stumps.

A moment later the parson appeared and stood at her shoulder. 'I need to oversee the first entry. A drowning is something of a rarity.'

She hesitated, glancing quickly at his pouchy, wrinkled features. 'There was a wound to her head. Might not that have been the means of her death?'

'You heard the doctor's reasoning. Drowning.' His mouth set spitefully. 'I'll have no disputatious women here.'

She wanted to argue, but only sighed and bent over the book.

'A new page?' he asked sharply. She lifted the sheet, showing him the previous page – filled to the last line with cramped records. Very slowly, he told her what she must write: *Thirtieth day of July 1752 – Elizabeth Sophie Hart – Widow of Ambrose Hart – Aged forty-five.*

He watched her dip the quill, then tap away the surplus ink to get a neat line. 'Don't make a blot,' he rasped. 'Now, at the end, you must give the cause of death. Write *Drowned.*' He was standing so close she could smell his mouldy breath.

He watched every stroke, from the great curl of the initial 'D' to the final flourish. As she lifted the quill, the bell rang out the time: it was three o'clock and the walls seemed to shake around them. Parson Dilks' mud-spattered boot tapped impatiently. 'Come along now.'

'The ink must dry. You said there must be no blots.' She smiled guilelessly into his ugly face, but he responded not one whit to her charms.

'As soon as it's dry, place the book back in the chest.'

When his footsteps had fallen silent, she slumped down upon the bench, feeling a dull pain pulse in her skull. Only when all was still did she lift the scribed page and delicately prise it apart from its predecessor. The tiny dabs of wax she had slipped between the pages had performed their deception well; it was a trick she had seen a dozen times, performed by false-letter men, or by swindlers inserting fake deeds for signature. With extreme care, she tore out the newly inscribed page, and screwed it up tightly into her pocket. Then she began writing again, exactly the same record – but now in its proper place, on the right-hand page below the last entry – *Thirtieth day of July 1752 – Elizabeth Sophie Hart – Widow of Ambrose Hart – Aged forty-five.*

Her quill hesitated above the page. This book would be her mother's only memorial; there would be no headstone carved for her. Tabitha would not end her mother's life with a lie. She set the quill aside, leaving a blank white space where the cause of death should be written, and hoped no one would consult the book for a good long time. Briefly, she prayed under her breath that she could soon return and scribe a true and honest cause of death.

Placing the Book of Mortalities back in the box, she noticed the Book of Baptisms lying there, too. Idly, she lifted it out, and leafed through pages completed in neat copperplate by the parson. She found it quickly enough, a second Elizabeth Sophie Hart – though this one, now known as Bess, had been baptised on 10 January 1751. In the space for the name of the child's mother was written *Tabitha Hart*, with *Absconded* inscribed in small letters beside it. She felt a stab of mortification to see it written plain like that, like a rebuke to a fugitive. Where the child's father's name was generally stated, that space also remained an obstinate blank: taunting, provoking, empty.

SEVEN

A Riddle

Before the birth of either Time or Place,
I reigned a despot over boundless Space:
But though I did my ancient throne resign,
Still half of this vast globe is mine;
To me the stars their brilliant lustre owe,
While drowsy mortals take repose below.
Me poets love, and crafty villains prize,
When they would hide an intrigue from your eyes;
I blind the sight and can confuse the brain,
Pray reader tell me, what's my name?

The 3rd day of August 1752

Lammastide

Luminary: Night increases to 9 hours
and 53 minutes.
Observation: Saturn sets 34 minutes after 11 at night.
Prognostication: Females in general may
face shame and other calamities.

N at was drawn to Tabitha's cottage in the manner of a moon captivated by a planet. Finding a grassy bluff within sight of the hovel, he threw himself down on his back. Above him spread the whole celestial panoply pulling him into infinity. He trained the lens of his telescope along the curvaceous windings of the constellation of the Serpent. Then he fixed his eye upon glittering Andromeda, and next on Saturn's yellow sphere.

He rolled on to his stomach. Soon his spyglass was fixed upon the cottage. The lovely Tabitha was still awake, judging by the golden light at the window. He could see only shadows, flickerings, a quiescent presence. Yet it was a pleasure to be so close to her. He had considered calling on her, explaining that her mother had welcomed him, and offering his assistance. No, he could not do it. The truth was, he enjoyed this secret state of attraction; a circling attendant in no danger of collision.

He had few enough pleasures these days. Something was wrong with him, he was sure of it. Since his own mother had urged him to come to Netherlea he suffered violent, angry passions towards his neighbours. And now Widow Hart, his only friend, had died. He thought of the day he had first come across her in the church vestry and asked her advice in consulting the records. Her kindness made him regret not telling her the entire truth, claiming he wanted to see the Dove family's history to make a fair copy for his mother's Bible. What harm had it done? The lonely old dame had enjoyed showing him books of burial, marriages and births, and directed him to his mother's birthplace at Red End. Arriving at the latter he had been shaken: the hamlet was a tumbledown ruin. Standing ankle deep in mud and dung he had asked himself: Who then am I?

Widow Hart soon guessed what he was up to. 'Courage,' she had said once. 'You will find your place in the world. You are like my daughter. A dullard's life would suit neither of you.'

'I scarce know what I want,' he replied. 'Only that I must be my own man.'

She laid her thin fingers upon his arm. 'Time is our greatest healer.'

'Time is also our greatest teacher,' he replied dryly, 'yet he does have a habit of killing all his pupils.'

Winged shadows flitted across the stars; a pair of tawny owls making tremulous cries. On the path below he could hear another creature moving as quietly as a leaf blown along the ground. He stiffened: there was no breeze tonight. Nat twisted around and listened hard, hoping the interloper would not see him. Suddenly the dark shape of a man loomed directly over him.

'Who are you?' Nat asked, feeling wholly to the disadvantage.

'I wondered what you was, lurking in the grass. Starling, is it? Want a drink?'

The shape squatted down beside him and Nat sat up on the grass.

'I know you. Your name is Darius, is it not?' In the faint starglow he recognized the tar-black eyes of Francis De Vallory's drinking companion.

The youth took a long tug from a bottle and handed the cheap liquor over. For once, Nat took only a moderate sip, watching Darius all the while. 'Your friend is not with you?'

Darius grunted dismissively. 'No. He don't need to catch his own dinner. Be that a spyglass?'

Reluctantly, Nat let him take a turn, directing him to a few notable objects in the sky.

Darius lowered it from his eye. 'That's a mighty handy instrument. And you know what all them stars foretell?'

'If you mean drawing up horoscopes, then no, I don't. I study astronomy. There's nothing magical up there. Observation and mathematics are my tools.'

Darius snorted. 'My family all has the second sight. And I's known clever men who can read the future in the sky. What happens above must happen below.'

Nat shook his head, irritated. 'Tell me then, if the heavens are so easy to read, why these prophets always fail to accurately predict deaths and wars and disasters?'

Darius leaned back on his elbows. 'So you don't believe the ancient paths? You would not care if I set a curse upon you?'

'Be my guest.' Though Nat spoke coolly, the youth was needling him and he gave in to a foolish desire to goad him in return. 'I'll wager you a shilling. I will predict an event that will occur with absolute certainty. And you must do the same. Then we'll compare the validity of your hokum against my observations.'

Darius nodded; Nat could see the gleam of his teeth and eyes.

They both rose and Nat handed him the telescope, pointing with his finger to the dark gap between the constellations of Perseus and Cassiopeia. 'If I were a mountebank astrologer, I should say, "Hearken at this fireball which proves that a great calamity will soon befall us." But as a rational man, I simply ask you to observe Nature's glory and marvel.'

He helped Darius find the spot and waited. It took only a minute until even with his naked eye, Nat also saw the firework flash and trailing tail of a shooting star, moving faster than lightning across the firmament.

'How'd you know that would happen?' Darius asked, handing back the telescope.

'Mathematics.' He chose not to explain that at this date meteors flew in a deluge in that part of the heavens.

'You vouch you saw what I predicted?'

'Aye.'

'And your prediction?'

'You don't believe in curses. So you'll not be minding if I curse our pert new neighbour.' Darius jerked Nat's telescope in the direction of the lighted window of Tabitha's cottage. 'It may take a while longer'n your trick, but I predict she'll meet misfortune before the year is out.'

Nat felt his face glow hot. 'Damn you for a sharper! What has she ever done to you?'

'What's she done to you, more like? Jumping like a rabbit to her defence, eh? Francis told me all about his night with her, when she was but a fresh pullet on the market.'

The tinker raised a pale outstretched hand towards the lighted cottage and began to speak an incantation in a gibberish tongue.

Whatever he was chanting, it sounded cruel and ugly and potent.

Nat stood up, struggling to master the desire to strike Darius in his smirking face.

'Hold your tongue, you devil!' Then turning on his heels Nat made for home, furious that he had let the rogue draw him in.

'So you do believe in the old ways!' Darius crowed after him. 'Or why you be so rattled? Come on, hand over that shilling and be done with it.'

Old ways indeed! Nat brooded miserably as he hurried along. Of course he did not believe in such claptrap. And yet, to hear Tabitha being profaned was intolerable. Nonetheless, the philosophical part of his nature asked: why should he fear a tinker's curse?

Perhaps there were old ways of wickedness, he concluded. Ancient tricks that worked by persuasion and domination to browbeat the innocent. These were the dark dealings of alchemy and spell-casting that modern, educated men must resist. And why resist them? Because there was some lingering power in such malice, after all.

And he had recognized Darius's sinister aspect since first clapping eyes on him. When was it he had seen him first? It had been well before the Lammas bonfire, when walking home from Widow Hart's. Damnation, it had been the night she died. He had reckoned him to be a poacher and let him pass without regard. But the memory jolted him sufficiently to unloose a further image of Widow Hart that same night. All evening she had been distracted, her thoughts elsewhere, her actions clumsy. Then she had pleaded with him to stay longer. As he took his leave she had peered over his shoulder and asked, 'There is no one out there?'

The garden and beyond had appeared empty and so he had reassured her. Then, no more than a quarter of a mile along his path home, he had glimpsed the poacher he now recognized as Darius.

Pox that blockhead of a constable; there was no one here in Netherlea he felt able to confide in. All the dark way back to Eglantine Hall he was agitated by the pain that he had failed to help a fellow human and, by doing so, unwittingly contributed to Widow Hart's death.

EIGHT

A Riddle

I am no sooner known to be,
Than all the great take leave of me;
To have me, all their cares employ,
But when possessed I quickly cloy:
I serve the ladies when alone,
To show their handy skill upon,
And when assembled, give them pleasure,
Upon their backs their chiefest treasure.

The 3rd day of August 1752

Lammastide

Luminary: Sun rises 43 minutes after 4 in the morning.
Observation: Mars and Venus are so near
the Sun they will scarcely be seen.
Prognostication: Many transcendent actions
upon the stage of the world.

'Father says it's best if you come out today.' Jennet was bouncing Bess on her knee, an hour after daybreak on Monday morning. 'Let's go up to the hall and lend a hand for the harvest.'

Tabitha pulled the bedsheet up over her shoulders. In civilized society, no lady rose before ten, or breakfasted before eleven.

'You go.' She yawned. 'I'll not give those jabberers any more to gossip about. And take the child with you.'

Jennet put Bess down and stood up. 'No, I will not be your nursemaid today. I shall go to the hall on my own, then, and earn my shilling a week.'

Tabitha's heavy eyes opened in surprise. The girl did have some pluck, after all. And a shilling a week – that was better than being stranded here all day with the child.

Once they set out, it was good to feel the summer sun like balm on her face and shoulders. Above their heads, a great armada of clouds sailed through a china-blue sky. Even Bess was content on her leading strings, delighted with every tiny pebble and feeding butterfly.

The previous night the parlour had been serene for once; Bess sat on a rug, cheerfully casting wooden pegs about, while she and Jennet ate vegetable pottage. Seeing Joshua hesitate on the threshold, a foolish fit of sentiment had coursed through her, and she had jumped up from the table and run to embrace him. His broad face, though weathered, had not lost its agreeable boyishness. He had once again been the fond companion of her childhood: a partner in rapscallion games, and the bestower of her first sweet kiss.

When she tried to grasp his hands in hers, he backed away uneasily. 'So at last you are home again,' he mumbled.

She pulled a stool to the table for him and offered him a plate of pottage; to her surprise, Bess waddled over with a coloured peg as a gift and clambered contentedly on to his lap.

Tabitha asked him how he fared these days. 'Good, good, though I'm right sorry my business in Chester kept me from your mother's burial. As constable, I am right-hand man now to Sir John, who campaigns to be a Member of Parliament. And we've a new house. You remember the Grange? Too big for me and Jennet; we rattle round it like two dried peas. 'Tis a pity Mary scarce had time to furnish it – she'd have had it as fine as fivepence by now.'

She was glad he could speak of his dead wife so calmly. His disappointment when Tabitha had left him behind in Netherlea had been terrible. She could not stay in such a nowhere place, she had protested. London was her Promised Land. So Joshua had married Mary, a widow with a good dowry and a quiet-mannered daughter, Jennet. Learning by letter that Mary had died, Tabitha had been pricked with pity, even in the midst of her gadabout London life she had felt sorrow for her oldest friend.

When Jennet disappeared to the back room, Tabitha whispered to him, 'I must talk to you privately, regarding Mother. As the constable. Alone.'

He frowned but nodded. 'Call on me tomorrow suppertime. Come take a look about the Grange. Jennet can sit with Bess.'

Now, walking through the sunlit morning woods, Tabitha considered what facts she might lay before Joshua over supper. Catching up with Jennet, she asked, 'Did you see my mother the night she died?'

'Not me, but Father did. I was round earlier that morning to take Bess away to the Grange – your mother had some business or other. Then, when Father came home that evening, he set off to carry the little maid back. It was about nine o'clock by then, but he said the cottage was all dark and deserted. Father said she must have got it in her head to call on Nanny. He wasn't best pleased.'

'Jennet, when was the door broken?'

'I don't recollect. A few days ago perhaps?'

'Well, Mother would have said something. Did she?'

The girl crinkled her face in thought.

'So perhaps it was broken the night she died?'

Jennet halted, startled. 'Goodness. Father said the door was open. But there was no one there.'

'And my mother always bolted the door at night.' Tabitha scooped Bess up in her arms to stop her straying towards the nettles. 'I want it repaired at once. I don't feel safe.'

'I can run and fetch Darius. He fixes all such things in the village.' Jennet's face shone with sudden joyous mischief.

'What are you so cheerful about?'

'Oh, me and my friends think Darius is the handsomest lad in all these parts.'

Tabitha smothered her own smile, thinking that Joshua would find his stepdaughter a handful sooner than he reckoned.

'So, my mother knew this Darius?'

'Aye, he used to help her – cheapest carpenter for miles.'

Another D. He might have repaired articles, but did he break them too? Recollecting the date of Towler's death, she asked how long Darius had been in the neighbourhood.

'Must be a year, I reckon. Aye, he were here last harvest.'

So the lad had been in the village when the dog died.

Arriving at the stepping stones, she and Jennet each took one of Bess's tiny hands, and swung her across the river, shrieking with glee.

'He lives on Tinker's Meadow. I can go fetch him for you, if you like.' Jennet was as eager as a hound in the traps.

'Perhaps not,' Tabitha said gently. She was sure Joshua would not want Jennet trailing after some bonny-faced tinker boy.

On Church Common, the remnants of the bonfire lay in a patch of scorched earth. Beyond that stood the mottled grey church, and the circular wall of the graveyard. It was a blow to remember her mother lay there, beneath that rippling blanket of turf. And there was Dilks' parsonage above it, three storeys of red brick with twin white chimneys like the ears of a hare. A low flight of steps led up to the pedimented white door. Every year the villagers grumbled as they handed over their hard-earned tithes to Dilks – money or chickens, corn or rabbits. Had her mother in some way threatened the parson's grand style of living?

The church bell was ringing seven in the morning as they hurried along the dusty track of the High Street, past the few shops and untidily thatched cottages. It was busy with early trade, though to

Tabitha it looked a small and shabby sight. Barrels banged and
thundered across the cobbles, and the blacksmith's anvil rang out
as a line of horses waited in his yard. The De Vallory Estate Office
gleamed, with new glass windows and a brightly painted crest
swinging on its sign. Next door stood the pillory, a warning to any
who breached the law. Tabitha herself had barely escaped Parson
Dilks' threat that she should be punished there. If she had not fled
to London, she might have been forced to stand with neck and arms
locked tight while the villagers pelted her with rotten food or worse.
While the infamous mobs of London changed their direction like
the wind, she knew country folk had mighty long memories.

As the thought crossed her mind, she saw a trio of elderly women
by the wayside gaze at her with no attempt at friendliness, and
wondered just how far the rumours about her private trade had spread.
The three harpies cast black looks at Bess, too. Lord, she hoped her
mother had not suffered similar scorn. She needed to confide her
suspicions to Joshua, and then escape this viper pit for good.

At the magnificent gates of Bold Hall, Tabitha let her fingers trail across
gilded ironwork. They were locked; they had to take the long way
round, up the servants' path. Nevertheless, she could not help but be
impressed by her first sight of the hall. It had been refurbished as shiny
as a jackdaw, drawing the eye to its black timberwork in chevrons
across clean white plaster. The sun caught in a thousand tiny panes of
window glass. The smell of money reached her: the breeze-borne scent
of perfumed gardens and clean laundry, utterly different to the village's
stink of poverty. It stirred some hidden part of her and she greeted it
with relief, like a genteel friend well met on a night in the stews.

A score of women were at work in a cruck-roofed barn at the rear
of the hall, preparing food and filling leather flagons for the
harvesters. A flurry of surprised stares and nudges ran around the
room at her appearance, but Jennet and she were ushered to a trestle
board, and matters began well enough. Their task was to cut large
pieces of cheese and wrap them in leaves, then pack them tightly
in basket panniers. Bess was collected by a cheery girl who oversaw
the other children in a private yard.

A pleasant serving woman bustled over, announcing that once
the midday fare was delivered to the fields they should all get a
share of the broken food, as well as the promised twopence a day.

Keeping her head down, Tabitha listened as the hubbub rose around her. A mouthy old dame bragged of the money her soldier grandson sent her. 'One whole pound a year, and not a finger to lift for it!' Tabitha had once earned double that sum in a single hour in the metropolis. She rolled her eyes as it went on; country women, jostling for supremacy like ewes around the trough. They cared not a jot for fashion or gentility or taste – instead, they were rivals in breeding dutiful children, wielding the petty power of kinship. Now there was endless jawing about the corn maiden: who should make it, where to hang it and what of that sorry one made back in '47? She yawned. Menial work was such a waste of life. Absentmindedly, she tore morsels of bread and cheese from the heap and slipped them into her mouth. Jennet looked up in alarm and shook her head.

A familiar voice cut through the clamour. 'Why, look what the cat dragged home from London town . . . If it in't that brazen-faced Tabitha Hart!'

She looked up to see Zusanna approaching, her wide hips rolling in a snowy white gown, her yellow-lashed eyes bright with triumph. The gaze of all present fell upon them both.

'Zusanna?' she called back. 'Still here, up to your neck in cow muck, are you? There is a world beyond Netherlea, or have you not heard?'

Zusanna made a scoffing sound like a vixen's bark. 'Oh, aye. Be that the same world where trollops do parade with no gown upon their backs? I heard how you dressed so fine to make your grand return. Or do you trouble no more with clothes, since you strip yours off that often?'

The room fell as silent as the grave.

'Well, 'tis better sport than lying with my own kin. Is Cam your nephew or your stepbrother? I never can recall.'

Zusanna banged down the plate she was carrying, and Tabitha pushed herself up, standing tall. She had a devilish urge to slap Zusanna's lardy face.

'I know what you are up to!' Zusanna cried. 'Your beguiling of Mr Starling is no secret to me.'

Before she could floor Zusanna, a heavy hand clapped down on Tabitha's shoulder and held her firm. 'Come with me.' Her great-aunt Sarah spoke with cold authority, even as Tabitha turned and glared into her lean, tight face. 'Or I'll throw you out before them all,' she added in a frigid whisper. She turned next to Zusanna.

'For shame. Tabitha has lost her mother, and here you are, goading her like a fish-wife. And for the rest of you, get back to work; or be off now, but you'll not get a farthing.'

Obediently, Tabitha followed her great-aunt out of the barn and down a bare passage.

'I am ashamed of you. You don't help yourself, do you?' Stopping suddenly, she grasped one of Tabitha's hands and inspected it. 'I remember your bobbin-work. You used to have neat fingers, not like those caw-paws back there. I can give you work in the stillroom here – but it's only for your mother's sake, mind.'

Mindful of her need of money, Tabitha bobbed and smiled. Even better, she knew such favour would outrage Zusanna.

They passed the kitchens, walking through heat like an invisible wall. Through the doors, she glimpsed scarlet-faced servants sweating in shirtsleeves, cloths wound like turbans around their heads. In the stillroom, though, it was cool and high, newly rigged out with a chequered tiled floor and walls lined with bottles and earthenware pots, neatly labelled. Two women sat up to attention as her great-aunt came in.

'Jane, you know Tabitha, my niece the Widow Hart's girl? And you, Nell. Make use of her.'

Jane, a bran-faced girl, no more than sixteen, lifted her face from the table where she was grinding something pungent in her mortar. Nell, older, nodded warily. Damn her eyes, she was Zusanna's mother – the same Mistress Dainty who had been the parson's choice for the searcher's position. She was an avid churchgoer and knew much – some said too much – of sickness. But she could barely read nor write, and was a poisonous gossip besides.

Well, there was nothing for it but to be biddable, Tabitha told herself, and indeed, her first day's tasks were easy: rinsing and picking over dried fruits, grinding spices and pushing mixes through a vast hair sieve. For a long time they worked in companionable quietness, until Jane could no longer keep from questioning her.

'Is it true you have been to London town?'

For the rest of the morning Tabitha gave a florid account of the capital. Yes, she had seen the King drive down the Strand in his golden coach – but in truth, he was a miserly soul who dined no better than a shopkeeper. And yes, the latest fashions were for skirts stretched over cane hoops more than six feet wide. And true, she had seen all the Quality parading at Vauxhall Gardens, a place like a paradise of coloured lanterns and lamp-lit scenes where fairy music played all along the Classical walks.

'What food is there to eat?' Jane asked.

She laughed. 'The food at Vauxhall is robbery – five shillings for a piece of ham through which the plate can be seen as clear as glass. It is a place to be seen, not to eat.'

Nell Dainty scowled, her black brows puckered and her mouth pinched tight with condemnation.

But Nell and Jane could not resist gossiping as they worked, and naturally, the De Vallory family was the subject of their greatest interest. Tabitha slowed in her tasks to listen: how his Lordship would be wanting a new London house once he was elected to Parliament, and how the doctor would move into the hall and take charge in his absence.

'I'll be right glad to have the doctor as the new master,' said Nell, whose wariness of Tabitha was in conflict with the natural looseness of her tongue. 'He at least has brains, unlike some I could mention. He has seen the world too, and uses his physic in God's service. But, of course, he's not the firstborn – and then there's what that astrologer fellow told his father.'

'I've forgotten that old tale,' said Tabitha.

'Something about Sir John being born in the house of the Sun,' Jane supplied. 'He was the golden boy, predicted to be a great, shining man. And the doctor was born under some lesser influence – wise but solitary. Or so the fellow told his father.'

'If you was to ask me,' said Nell, 'it is a shame Sir John be the elder brother. The doctor wouldn't charge these scandalous rents just to buy himself votes. And the Good Lord only knows what will happen when Master Francis takes his place.'

'When I was a girl here, Master Francis was known for his singularity,' Tabitha mused with feigned innocence. 'They said every single one of his tutors was dismissed. Has he grown any wiser, now he is a man?'

She remembered Francis as a pallid boy, too delicate to play with the village children – Joshua had once walloped him in a bout of boyish mischief. The lad had screamed and fallen to the ground in a shaking fit, and Joshua had run away, only to receive a whipping from his own father.

Nell could not resist the bait. 'It in't like me to speak ill of the family, but that boy don't have a shred of sense. Parson Dilks was engaged to tutor him in Latin and that, but when he couldn't grasp book-learning, he thrashed him to within an inch of his life. Master Francis wouldn't have nothing more to do with learning after that. There's bad blood between them two, Master Francis and Parson Dilks. Did you hear that last sermon?' Nell scoffed. 'He good as called the lad womanly. I'll eat my own bedstraw if that one ever sires an heir.'

Tabitha struggled to keep from laughing. She'd known plenty of molly boys, many of them married lords with wives in the country. In town, they had their own bathhouses and taverns, where they wore paint and wigs and frills and no one gave a fig.

'That doesn't mean he can't father a child.' Lord, she had heard of some wives forced to go to bed in breeches for the sake of an heir.

Nell pulled a long face. 'I wouldn't know about such matters, thank you very much. An abomination, I call it. And the parson is watching him like a hawk.'

'And what does Sir John say of it?'

Nell shuddered theatrically as she shook her head. 'It's not for me to speak of the quarrels that go on in this house,' she muttered. 'So I'll say nothing at all.'

Tabitha grew used to the work and the company. At dinnertime, they stopped work to eat broken food and shared a cake that had cracked in the oven.

'Look,' Jane called, peering through the window as Tabitha sat with eyes half-closed, savouring fine Bohea tea with a whole lump of sugar stirred into it. 'Outside in the yard. It's that fellow from Eglantine Hall.'

'Who's that?' Tabitha remembered the smoke rising from the twisted chimneys.

'Mr Starling.'

She looked through the window and felt herself stop still in her tracks. A man stood outside, chatting to the stable boy beside a glossy black horse. He might have flown to Netherlea straight from King's Coffee Shop at Covent Garden. He wore his hair long and untidy, and was clad in a coat of shagreen, with a loose neckcloth and riding boots. She knew his rig-out was intended to give a devil-may-care appearance, no doubt mightily studied in advance before a mirror. In short, it was a London rake's notion of how to dress in the country.

She peered closely at his face. Did she perhaps know him? Or was he simply one of the type she and Poll knew too well – a Peep-o'-Day

Boy who frequented the same inns and theatres as they did? She measured him at medium height, lithe and very pale; she could see good bones and a touch of puckish humour to his features. Without turning in her direction, he strode rapidly away and in through a side door. She turned back to face the room, hiding her disappointment.

'Who is he?'

'Mr Starling. Don't you know him? He's from London too.'

'There are thousands of folk in London, Jane. I don't know them all.'

'Well, he come here a few months ago. Sir John give him the old hall for a peppercorn rent. We've seen lights burning through the night up there. They say he's writing his poems. I never heard of such a thing.'

Good God, not a poet! Again, Tabitha wanted to laugh. He would be all verse and no purse.

'Zusanna said his name this morning. Why does she think I have ought to do with him?'

'Well, everyone thought you knowed him – for he asked about you at the bonfire.'

'I don't know this fellow from Adam. You are sure of it? He asked after me?'

'Aye. He wanted to know if you was Widow Hart's daughter.'

'Did he now?' The malicious verse she had found in her mother's box sprang uneasily into her mind.

'And then him and Constable Saxton nearly come to blows.'

'No. Not Joshua? What did he say?'

'The constable warned him off,' Jane replied, with an annoying smile, as a murmur of agreement rose from Nell. 'Some of us has already wagered you and he will marry before the year is out.'

Lord save her from such witterers. 'That's the biggest heap of claptrap I ever heard!'

A curl of mischief lifted Jane's lips. 'So – are you not going later to the constable's, to have him show you round his grand new house?'

Oh, fiddlesticks. If she even hinted at a private matter, it would spread through the village like wildfire.

'Constable Saxton's bought a nice leg o' mutton,' Nell said innocently. 'He asked the farmer's wife to roast it this afternoon.'

'There is nothing between us, I assure you.'

Neither Nell nor Jane replied. Both turned aside, hiding mocking little smiles.

NINE

A Riddle

A riddle of riddles – it dances and skips;
It is read in the eye, though it cheats in the lips;
If it meets with its match, it easily caught;
But if cunning will buy it, 'tis not worth a groat.

The 3rd day of August 1752

Lammastide

Luminary: Sun sets 15 minutes after 7.
Observation: The Moon is in the
Ascendant approaching Mars.
Prognostication: Sullen and froward tempers
will excite men to action.

Tabitha set out for Joshua's house and entered the wood, her
footsteps a rhythmic pattering on the dry earth. She was
vexed that her encounter with Joshua provided entertainment
for the village gossips. Mr Starling, though, was a different matter;
an image to turn over and inspect with pleasure.

Near the heart of the wood, she found the glade where her father
had once burned charcoal; it was hushed save for rustling leaves,
punctuated by the alarmed *pink-pink* of a bird. Her mother was
proud to have married her sweetheart, choosing hard life and happiness over the ease and rank she had been born to. But time had
struck her husband down swiftly with a wasting sickness, taking
him to God before he was even thirty years of age. Tabitha had no
memory of him, save from the words her mother had used to conjure
him: a strong and solitary man, rooted deep in his modest plot of
woodland. His work kept him at long nightly vigils over his fire,
reading the moon for weather lore, sitting so still and quiet that
deer and badgers were his regular visitors. What a waste of a life.
And here was she, lacking even the funds to have her mother and
father buried side-by-side in the churchyard. The poor have no
memorials, she thought bitterly: her father's last charcoal stack was
a mere heap of tarry earth, overrun by dandelions.

'I am sorry, Father,' she muttered. When she returned to London
she would try to send money to erect a pair of graves.

Still standing in reverie, she heard footsteps approaching – heavy
steps, men's steps. Joshua appeared, dressed in a silver-buttoned
coat more fitting for a party than a country stroll. 'I came to walk

with you.' He looked into the distance, where the trees tangled
thickly. 'A man has been seen here, skulking in the woods towards
dark.'

He took her arm and she walked beside him, laughing off his
concerns. Yet, as they walked, a recollection of being watched
haunted her for a moment. Yes, on the night she sat vigil over her
mother, someone had stood as still as shadow, watching from outside,
in the darkness.

The Grange was a monastic house and grain store, owned long
ago by the Canons of Chester. It had once, too, been the source
of the village children's wilder fancies and games of 'dare'. Picking
her way over the cracked flagstones, Tabitha found that it was
only a squat building with a lichen-blotched roof, slits for windows
and a grim, nail-studded entrance. She forced some enthusiasm in
reply to Joshua's pride. The interior was even less impressive: a
disused great hall standing empty, with birds' nests in the beams,
while the smaller rooms housed soot-black fireplaces and farm-
house benches. She tried not to look at Mary's spinning wheel,
gathering dust in a corner. It would be harrowingly cold here,
come winter – but by then she would be indulging herself in the
lamp-lit shops of the Strand, on her way to a warming glass of
something strong.

However, the mutton, served with onion sauce, was excellent –
and she was glad of it, for Joshua's sake. He was striving to impress
her. Damn Netherlea, in any other village, the prettiest girl should
have been overjoyed to live with Joshua and make a home even of
this chilly house. She watched his broad and resolute face. Time
and responsible work had dulled her old friend; she could barely
glimpse the handsome rapscallion boy. And he was a widower, poor
man, so seemed old before his years.

After supper, they took their ale out to a bench in the walled
garden, where Joshua had scraped out a few rows for vegetables.
Outdoors, the evening retained the warmth of the day, darkening to
a bluebell tint. They watched a flock of swallows whip back and
forth, feeding on invisible insects.

'So, Tabitha, what is it you must tell me?'

She told Joshua briefly of her worries: the blow to her mother's
head, the notes in the almanack about a visitor named 'D'.
Could it be the parson? The constable listened, narrowing his

eyes thoughtfully. When she'd finished, he fetched an oil lamp and studied the cramped pages of the almanack.

'Your mother always was prone to odd notions. Look how closely she studied this humbug. The calendar has its uses, but the rest of the almanack is old women's nonsense – all dreams and fortunes and fates.'

'It wasn't a dream that she found herself at the bottom of the river.'

'You weren't here, Tabitha, to see the change in her. There were times I found her fast asleep in the daytime. She had a short temper, too.'

'Maybe that came about from caring for a child? She was no longer young.'

'There is not sufficient matter here to make charges. As for suspecting Mr Dilks – it is a monstrous accusation.'

She sighed, disappointed. 'Would you tell me what happened that night? To put my mind at rest?'

His was the mirror of Jennet's account. It had been agreed that Jennet should take Bess home with her, to afford her mother some peace, but at ten past nine in the evening, according to Joshua's pocket-watch, her mother was not in her cottage.

'The door was open and I called out, but the place was deserted. It was late, I needed to rise early; so, to speak plain, I wasn't over-joyed to carry Bess all the way back here again.' He paused and sighed.

'The door bolt is broken. Did you notice it that night?'

His face clouded. 'I . . . pushed the door. It was ajar. And I left it so, thinking she might be back any moment. But the next morning, I was worried. I wondered if she'd tripped and fallen in the wood, and I went searching. Yes, I believe the door was still ajar at the cottage. I set out to the woods. Then I saw a white cap in the water. When I pulled it out, I knew it was hers, the very worst news. I went to the village and rounded up some men to carry her, and call for the parson and the doctor.'

'Thank you.'

'Be easy. It was quick and merciful.'

'How can you know that?' she flashed back at him. 'Jennet spoke of a fellow named Darius who did small repairs for Mother. He is another "D" who called on her.'

'Darius,' he said. 'That makes better sense. I've a notion that young rogue is running a racket, telling honest folk they need unnecessary repairs. Once inside, he pilfers whatever they won't miss.'

'He's been accused before?'

'I have not yet had the proof to charge him. Was any of your mother's property missing?'

'No. But Jennet is keen I ask Darius to repair the door.'

'No, I will do it. And look into the matter.'

Beneath the darkening dusk, she felt the unease of their situation and scarcely knew what to say next. Maybe it was the carefree habits of her new life that made her make a bad decision; she found Joshua's large, calloused hand and stroked it with the soft ends of her fingertips.

'Please,' she said softly. 'Question Mr Dilks. Put my mind at rest.'

His hand tensed like a bowstring.

'You know I can't deny you, Tabitha. I'll call on him, then. Confront him.'

'Please – no. Go gently. Be a little . . .'

She wanted to say guileful, but she doubted Joshua would approve.

'Could we go together? I'll make a pretext of enquiring about my parents' grave.'

He was moving closer to her now, his leg and shoulder growing warm against hers.

The lamp cast a golden glow, in which Joshua's face appeared suddenly lively.

'Do you want my opinion? I believe the culprit is this Starling fellow.'

'Why? What did he have to do with my mother?' she asked, with a curious sense of annoyance.

'I don't know yet, but Jennet met him in your mother's garden once. Has he bothered you?'

She could answer that, at least, with complete honesty. 'I have never met the man.'

'Well, if he tries to approach you, tell me. I am watching him, and I have intercepted his papers. Disgraceful stuff; tawdry tales of prophecy, and worse. They put even this to shame.' He lifted the almanack.

Tabitha pulled back from him, thinking hard. There was certainly something odd in Mr Starling's interest in prophetic lore. And he had also visited her mother. 'Are you going to arrest him?'

'He's purportedly a gentleman, though he behaves like a ruffian. I have not enough proof yet to go to Sir John. But if I give him enough rope, I have faith he'll deliver himself to the gallows. In the meantime, look to your safety – the man in the woods is dark and tall, too, like Starling. And, now . . .'

He grasped her waist and drew her firmly to him. Here's the reckoning, she told herself, as Joshua's lips met hers. It was not entirely unpleasant; she liked him better than many of the unamiable fellows she had known in London – and to get her way, she would, as Poll used to say, happily entertain the whole kingdom. Yet, in the more virtuous chambers of her heart, she knew that it was wrong to lead him on like this. After a spell of kissing and some fumbling caresses, she pulled away, and asked him to walk home with her to fetch Jennet.

TEN

A Riddle

A word that's composed of three letters alone,
And is backward and forward the same;
Without speaking a word makes its sentiments known,
And to beauty lays principal claim.

The 3rd day of August 1752

Lammastide

Luminary: Twilight ends 2 hours and 8
minutes after sunset.
Observation: Mars with the Sun shows an
excess of heat.
Prognostication: Beware fires, robberies and
voluptuous temptations.

Nat threw his book against the wall, his anger so great he
fancied his whole body was blazing from the core. Again
and again the day's miseries were re-enacted inside his
head. First, there had been a hellish interview with Sir John. After
he had told him his business, the old man had shrunk from him,
recoiling and suspicious. 'Why should I believe *you*? Don't you
dare to breathe a word of this to anyone.' He had made Nat swear
an oath on the Bible. Then he had dismissed him, like a tawdry
beggar.

Later, riding the highway to Chester, that clod Saxton had stopped
him at the turnpike. At first, he fancied it must only be a paltry
local matter. When the constable pulled out the package of papers
from his saddlebag, however, he knew otherwise. To his rage and
dismay, seven days' worth of neatly finished scribing was summarily
torn open and inspected by that straw-headed buffoon.

'You are stealing my private correspondence,' he had said,
sounding like a child.

'Merely confiscating your papers, Mr Starling. The magistrate
may return them if he sees fit.' The dunderhead was evidently
enjoying himself, paying him back for his words at the bonfire.

'The magistrate – would that be Sir John?'

The magistrate in charge was indeed Sir John. The notion of his
reading this Grub Street nonsense was so insupportable that Nat
felt like throwing himself off a cliff.

*   *   *

He had rushed home, but his choleric humour soon drove him outside again; not knowing what he wanted, he had galloped across the common, driving Jupiter on in the heat until the poor animal's coat was slick. On an impulse, he plunged into the ford, surging through the spray like a cannonball. Then, for his horse's sake, he halted on the far bank. For a long time, he sat motionless in the saddle as Jupiter dripped and panted. Nat's own skin was also slick with cold sweat but the eddies of his mind settled back into calmer channels. Perhaps he should turn homewards, after all.

The moon was a crescent fingernail of silver now, casting the sparsest light. Nat could just see the river's streamlets, plaiting and unplaiting like rippling hair. The tides of time. The great genius Newton had said that time flows independent even of the stars, of the universe itself; that rustic fellow at the bonfire had confused calendar time with Newton's unstoppable current. Yet what a strange allegory it was, the river of time. If he was standing here in the now, then to the left, downriver, the past was disappearing away into the night. Time past could never be changed: what was done was done. If only the past did not stay fixed like dead flies in amber. If only he could live his life again.

Upriver, by a quirk of chance, he saw the three triangular stars of the Phoenix constellation low against the trees. Could it portend a chance to rise anew?

Ha, he was as gullible as those fools he scribbled for, those swallowers of penny oracles, horoscopes and dream lore. It was an old and human frailty to seek assurance of the future. If I only knew my fate – was that not mankind's greatest wish?

But what of the now, Aristotle's *nun* – the snatched moment of the present in which we are alive? This *now* was unstoppably transforming his future into his past. If he jumped into the river *now*, his life would be over. His past would be fixed forever, the tale of a strange melancholic youth who committed self-murder. There would be no more history of Nat Starling to write.

Widow Hart must have stood not far from this very spot, he realized; here her life had ended, her spirit been snuffed out. He was suddenly convinced that some mischief had befallen her. His bright-eyed neighbour had not been the sort to be transfixed, as he was, by the black water. The realization woke him from his dangerous mood. Who in this cursed village could have harmed her?

And so he faced a second, eternal question. If he must endure this troublesome life, what the devil must he do next?

'Who's there?'

A man's voice rang out from the trees behind him. Looking over his shoulder, Nat saw the glow of a lantern behind the black branches' silhouettes. He turned Jupiter and approached his interlocutor. Damnation, death and fire, it was that poxy constable and, even worse, the glorious Tabitha – holding hands with him. Not slowing Jupiter's steady walk, he rode directly up to where they stood. Towering above them, he looked down imperiously.

'Constable,' he said flatly, without the slightest nod. Then he turned to his companion, making her a low bow. 'Miss Hart.' What he could see of her face in the lamplight was lovely; her lips parted, all cast in amber. Jupiter snorted and tossed his head. He wanted to empty his soul to her of so many matters: of her mother, his hopes, her danger.

Tabitha dropped the constable's hand like a hot coal. Stepping up to Jupiter she stroked his nose and the great horse grew calm. She laughed as he snuffled at her open palm. Then she looked up at Nat with eyes filled with liquid inquiry. There were a dozen poetical similes for the sensation her gaze caused him – darts, piercings, wounds and arrows – but all sounded ridiculous. Nevertheless, he was convinced that a mute communication had passed between them.

The constable called her name and, without another word, Nat rode away.

It was almost noon the next day when he woke from a shameful, feverish slumber. All the hours of the night he had felt like the mainspring of a watch, winding ever tighter with mounting energy. And he had longed for Tabitha so violently, had in his fancy possessed her again and again, exploring the wetness of her mouth, the intriguing dark mole on the convexity of her breast, had drowned in the oceans of her eyes. He remembered that he had written something, after draining the ale jug, though what it was he could not at first recall. He found it crumpled in his soiled bedclothes, an ink-spattered mass of crossings and hatchings through which he could just make out a verse. He laughed sourly as he read it. Adolescent balderdash, playing upon the eternal struggle between sensual *eros* and wholesome *philia*:

A vessel has she,
As round as a pear,
And sweet and moist in the middle;
'Tis bordered by hair,
And love does flow there
In my dreams – pray you solve me this riddle.

After that he had worked all night with new zeal, until another exquisite dawn rose, as pink as the secret chambers of a shell. He had remembered and rewritten every word that the Saxton imbecile had stolen from him; he would catch the postboy with this second parcel. He would send this paltry riddle too – though it confirmed what he already knew, that his muse had utterly abandoned him. Still, a lewd enigma on one's beloved's eye might, he supposed, be worth another shilling.

ELEVEN

A Riddle

You will find me in madness, disease and despair,
But not in the lovely, the fine or the fair,
From innocent joy I'm eternally banished,
And from pleasure and love my dull presence has vanished.
I am not ever numbered at routs or a revel –
But eternally doomed to wait on the Devil.

The 4th day of August 1752

Lammastide

Luminary: Day 14 hours and 20 minutes long.
Observation: Quadrature of Saturn and Mars,
Jupiter and Mercury.
Prognostication: A siege of other battle in
which the way is blocked.

F ollowing Joshua into the airless heat of Parson Dilks' study,
Tabitha recognized illustrations from Fox's *Book of Martyrs*,
pasted on almost every inch of the walls. She tried not to stare
at the pitiful bodies racked upon machines, screaming in flames,
stretched between trees or devoured by beasts. Even the crucifix in
pride of place on the mantelpiece was a grotesque, the Christ figure
showing His muscles twisted in agony.

'Constable. Miss Hart. You may sit. How may I oblige you?'
Dilks sat behind his desk, a lumbering toad, tapping his fingers
together over piles of paper. Joshua turned to Tabitha, in a mute
plea for assistance.

'Pray forgive me, sir,' Tabitha said, mustering all her sweetness,
'but I worry so about my mother's soul. Were you in the neighbourhood the night she died, Parson? Did you have any opportunity to
bless her poor remains?'

As if she were not even present, Dilks turned to Joshua.

'A minister cannot chase around the parish every time a cottager
expires. As it happens, I was in Chester that same night, at the
invitation of the bishop. I dined at the Bishop's Palace and returned
directly to Netherlea the next morning.' Now he faced Tabitha.

'Your mother was decently buried, with all the necessary rites.
What more do you expect?'

'I am grateful to you, sir.' As before, she found him as resistant to
her charms as if he were made of ancient, shrivelled leather. 'Yet I should
so like Mother to be buried beside my father. When I have the means to
buy a headstone, might you grant such a memorial to be raised?'

The parson seemed to take pleasure in shaking his head. 'Memorials are not for the likes of common old women. They are for freemen and gentry alone.'

He turned abruptly back to Joshua. 'I had hoped you had called about a more godly matter. A widower with a young daughter, and a woman with an unlawful child; you would do the parish good service if you married.'

Joshua had at least the grace to appear astonished at this, though he spoiled the effect by casting a sheepish glance in Tabitha's direction. She attempted a bright little laugh.

'I have been home for only four days, Parson, and I am still in mourning.'

'God created matrimony as a remedy against sin. To avoid fornication,' rasped the clergyman, making poor Joshua shift uncomfortably. What was it Poll had used to say? A cross on the chest, a devil in the breast – the clergymen that Tabitha had encountered in the private rooms of the capital had left her wary of this hypocritical breed.

The silence that followed stretched awkwardly until Dilks broke in, with impatience.

'Well, if you want to make yourself useful, Saxton, you might keep a watch on our vestry. Someone has been tampering with our parish books.'

Tabitha's heart thumped at the memory of her small deception over her mother's entry in the book.

'The sexton has seen a stranger meddling where he should not; by the time I arrived, he had vanished. I intend to keep the records locked away from now onwards – therefore, should you need to perform parish business, young woman, you must apply directly to me for the key. And I expect to see you attend my church henceforth. Your absence has been recorded.'

She nodded meekly, her cheeks fiery with relief. The parson stood, and bid them good day, moving around his desk. Sensing her chance slipping away, Tabitha loitered before a hunting print of a fox caught in the jaws of two fighting hounds, only a little less cruel than the tortured martyrs.

'The hunting season soon returns?' she said.

For the first time, the parson's jaundiced features brightened. 'Yes. Come the autumn, it is a joy to ride with the hounds.'

'It is a pity old Towler passed away.'

Dilks grew still more animated – more so than she had ever seen him. 'The finest pack leader his Lordship ever bred. That kennel master should be flogged for not taking better care of him.'

There was no doubt the parson spoke with sincerity. Unless he was a finer actor than Mr Garrick himself, Dilks was an unlikely dog-killer.

Tabitha strode irritably back to the cottage in Joshua's wake. She was wretchedly tired; her sleep the previous night had been as fragmented as a broken mirror. A dozen times, in half-dreams, she had heard the rattle of harness, the gate's rasp, and steps upon the garden path – but when she finally woke in the darkness, all was silent. Then the strange matter of the latch had surfaced in her mind. How had it been broken, that wooden rod that had held the door safely locked for decades? Had it been violently forced open as her mother cowered in the same bed Tabitha lay in now? The horror of it had led her to picture a hammer blow, falling on a skull as delicate as a hollow shell. She had lain very still, her skin prickling hot. There was no doubt she might be in danger, too. Parson Dilks must have been in Chester the night of her mother's death, said the cold voice of reason. Surely, then, suspicion weighed all the heavier upon this Darius fellow – and also on Nat Starling? At once, the magnetic pull of her attraction to him was commingled with deep and no doubt sensible fear.

She remembered what Poll had called her 'dark transactions'; the contrary desire of a good woman for a bad man. She had known plenty of town girls who surrendered themselves to 'guardians' who later destroyed them. Had not Poll, a lovely, well-schooled, though reckless girl, fugitive from fond parents, surrendered to such a devil? They had always puzzled her, those women who pursued men who rewarded them with pain. What the devil was this dangerous perversity that possessed her, this yearning for Starling to enter and lay claim to her?

In the darkest part of the night she had woken again to a tap at the door – this time a real, resounding rap. Tabitha had got up and moved quietly through the cottage. In the parlour, she picked up the poker and listened hard from behind the front door. She thought she heard a whisper, distinctly young and male.

She suddenly whipped the door wide to find three boys, no more than twelve years old, laughing and showing their heels as they pelted off down the path. One of them turned to taunt her: 'D'ye take a penny for a grope?' With whoops and jeers they disappeared.

She had returned to bed entirely wide awake and miserable. So her old reputation did live on, and would probably follow her to her dying day.

'Are you satisfied now?' Joshua burst out, dragging Tabitha from her reverie as they arrived at the cottage. No doubt his pride was hurt by her renewed refusal of his hand. 'What did you expect – that the parson held some ridiculous grudge against your mother?'

Why was he so agitated? Jennet waited at the door; he was upsetting his daughter too. The girl was eager to leave, fumbling with her bonnet.

'Will you question Darius next?' Tabitha asked, hoping to distract him.

'I sent men down to Tinkers Wood this morning, but damn him, I was too late. He ran off like a hare while I wasted time with the parson. But I have a warrant for his arrest. He'll not get far. As for Starling, I'm hopeful of a warrant to pull him in too.'

As he took his leave, a further reason for Joshua's ill-temper presented itself. Pulling a letter out of his coat, he thrust it at her. To her delight, it bore her own name in Robert's beautiful hand. Only when Joshua and his daughter were far out of sight did she break the red seal.

> *My dearest girl,*
>
> *I am heartily sorry we parted so miserably, my chicken. I write with good news, as business takes me to Chester on the 21st of this month and I shall hold you in my arms again at last. How can I mollify my sulky darling? You must hire for me the finest chamber in the town for that same night, and, once my day's business is done, I shall give you such proofs of my ardour that I swear you shall not sit easy for a week. I write in haste, but much troubled by the wanting of you,*
> *Your most ardent servant,*
> *Robert*

At a stroke, all was as clear as crystal. She would persuade Robert to take her with him back to London and leave this misery over her mother, this hopeless inquiry, behind her. Only seventeen days remained. True, she still needed to find a place to lodge the troublesome infant, but Robert could pay for that, too. Joshua, Dilks – even Nat Starling – all must go hang. She kissed Robert's letter, catching a faint scent of his citrus-sharp cologne. Robert, bless his restless loins, had cast her a line of hope to haul her back to the civilized world.

TWELVE

A Riddle

Almond cakes well iced and fruited,
Sugarplums to children suited,
Toffee pulled with expertise;
Truly are my *first* all these.
Swiftly o'er my *second* stealing,
Comes a startled, happy feeling,
Beating like a cage-bound dove –
When I spy my *whole*, my love!

The 5th to the 13th day of August 1752

Harvest

Luminary: The First Quarter waxing to the
Full Moon.
Observation: The Moon will eclipse Saturn
on the 7th day.
Prognostication: There shall be blood
on the harvest corn.

The harvest gathered speed like a great Wheel of Fortune, its spokes spinning giddily before it came to rest, delivering its judgement on the year. The villagers rose earlier, scythed faster, worked later. The corn had grown to its utmost height, filling the eye in every direction with feathery pinkish-gold; pale motes rained down like hail as weary horses pulled laden carts between field and barn. The labourers' skins turned nut-brown, men stripped to their breeches, shining with pride and sweat. Playing in the corn, children balanced white corn-lilies on their noses, making them stick like beaks until laughter tumbled them away.

Inside Bold Hall, the pace quickened too. A spectacular cake was planned for the noble guests at the harvest feast, and it was a still-room task to make the tiny shapes of wheat-filled cornucopias that would circle its rim. Tabitha was surprised at how hard she found the diminutive arts of confectionery. Like exquisite white cameos, the decorations had to be teased out of wooden moulds, but her clumsiness continually spoiled them – and Jane and Nell's annoyance at having to remake the decorations only made her more clumsy still.

Vexed that she might lose her comfortable position, Tabitha found excuses to go on errands. One afternoon, malingering outside, she came across Nanny Seagoes again, limping across the yard. Tabitha followed her into the cool shadow of the barn and found her seated on a low wall, breathing hard.

'It is I, Tabitha, Widow Hart's daughter. Do you want a hand with the eggs?' At Nanny's nod, she began searching the straw while affronted hens squawked and flapped around her ankles.

'You were a good friend to my mother,' she said, piling still-warm, bluish eggs into the basket. Nanny looked up. Though she was frail-boned and shrunken, her voice was strong and sharp.

'She needed a friend, left on her own with a needy infant. No one should end their days as Elizabeth did.'

A tightness afflicted Tabitha's throat; she swallowed hard.

'I know that now, Nanny. Mother wrote in her almanack that she was glad to stay with you some nights. Was she fretting over something?'

'It's a bit late now to dredge that up.'

Tabitha pulled a final egg from the straw and joined Nanny to sit on the wall.

'I don't believe so. She wrote some odd things down. Accusations. I don't want this repeating, Nanny, but it's got me believing her death might not have been pure accident.'

Nanny peered up at her through rheumy eyes. 'Odd nonsense about a dog, is it?'

'So you believe, too, that Mother's brain had turned soft?' said Tabitha, with some disappointment.

'Your mother? Your mother was as sharp as a pin.'

'But I heard she went wandering in the night. And that she mixed up her days.'

Nanny's drooping lips pursed in contempt. 'Disgusting, what some folk will say. When you come to know old age, you'll find you still know what's what.'

'Nanny, did she ever tell you she didn't want to be alone at the cottage some nights?'

The old dame screwed up her face. 'I don't know about that. But she did stop by and tell me she knew who killed Sir John's hound.'

'That's it. Who was it?'

'She wouldn't say. Said it was dangerous knowledge; that the person she suspected was a person of standing. Then she asked me a peculiar question. How would I make a complaint if I didn't want to go to the Justice of the Peace? Who was above him? I didn't know the answer.'

'The Justice of the Peace – is that Sir John?'

This time, when Nanny lifted her red-rimmed eyes, Tabitha wondered why she had ever thought her slow-witted.

'Justice of the Peace, Squire, Colonel-in-Chief, landlord. And reckoning soon to be Member of Parliament. I told her, only a numkin would want to get on the wrong side of Sir John De Vallory.'

Back in the stillroom, Tabitha pondered her mother's worries, then retreated into daydreams. She pictured Robert's delight at their reunion and began calculating the generosity with which he would prove it. A new gown would be the least of it: one of those sprigged silks with a raised hem to show her ankles and petticoat. For the journey to London, she must also have a flower-trimmed hat to wear at a coquettish tilt, and a fan to flutter. She pilfered a clean sheet of paper from the stillroom cabinet. Then back at the cottage, she wrote a letter to the landlord of the Talbot Inn, engaging their largest chamber and private parlour for the night of the twenty-first in the name of Robert Tate, Esquire.

When the sugar decorations had to be coloured, Tabitha returned to favour. One busy morning, when Jane was packing up a box of cordials, she was allowed to pick up a tiny brush, dipping it into the palette of edible pinks, greens and yellows with a steady hand. She had worn no paint for almost two weeks, but these colours reminded her of the sooty eye-paints and rose-tinted rouges of which she had been robbed in Chester. When Jane complimented her work, she confessed that her talent with brush and paint was only from long practice at a mirror. Her spirits reviving, she began to regale Jane with an account of how women wore their paint in London.

'First the face is made very pale with almond powder; the very height of elegance. Then carmine is doused on a piece of swansdown and coloured just here – on the centre of the cheek. Then take a black patch shaped like a star, or even a coquettish heart, and apply it just beneath the eye. Or even,' she giggled, 'set it high on the curve of the bosom. You can imagine how that draws the gentlemen's eyes.'

The room had fallen suddenly quiet. Tabitha looked up from the flower she was painting to see that Jane was sitting very stiffly, with her head held exceedingly low; the girl cast her a sideways glance of severest warning. She craned her neck and looked around.

Parson Dilks was regarding her with such concentrated loathing that it fair knocked the breath from her lungs. Shrinking back, she also bowed her head low over her work, and fell silent.

'And, behold, there met him a woman with the attire of an harlot, and a subtle heart,' Parson Dilks pronounced, beneath his breath.

Then, picking up his box of cordials, he turned on his heels and left them.

In the evenings, Joshua called at the cottage and repaired the door. He also brought gifts for her and Bess: a loaf of white bread, a length of cotton thread, a crude poppet doll. Yet he continued ill-tempered, no closer to finding Darius.

'I reckon he's disappeared down those secret peddlers' paths to Manchester, or upriver to Liverpool,' he complained. Tabitha wasn't so sure, but she kept her notions to herself, watching Jennet sitting silently by the fireplace. The next day, she was not surprised to see the girl stealthily hiding a bundle under a hawthorn bush. Returning later, she found it packed tight with bread, cheese and bacon. Telling herself to leave well alone, she watched both father and daughter, and pondered the perils of interfering.

As the days passed, she packed up the few of her mother's well-loved goods she wanted to take with her to London. It was then that she came across the macabre pocket watch she had pilfered in Chester. She swung it gently on its silver chain, repelled by its likeness to a laughing skull. Yet there was some very fine etching on the silver, illustrating a dozen reminders of life's brevity. Though she tried to wind it, she could not restart its mechanism. Nevertheless, it had to be worth a considerable sum and she itched to be rid of it.

There was so much that she wanted to be free of. Life as a cottager did not suit her: the tedium of tending the fire, hauling water from the well and boiling all their food in the pot made her want to throw the heavy pail at the wall. She wished to be rid of Joshua's jealousy, too. Surely her departure would be a deliverance for him as well.

'Who was that letter from?' he demanded, on the eve of the harvest feast. 'It bore a very fine seal.'

'I am surprised you did not open it,' she replied wearily. He had followed her into the back chamber, where she was trying to pack up her possessions. Striding towards her, he grasped her wrist so tightly that she cursed him. She tried to pull away but he had twice her bulk and strength.

'Why should I have opened it? Should I suspect you?'

As he stared fiercely into her face, such a fit of exasperation boiled up inside her that she stepped up to him, pushed her elbow up to his and forced his arm out of joint. It was a common street-walkers' trick that Poll had taught her, to shake off unwanted admirers. With a little whimper of pain, Joshua moved back.

'Oh, Joshua. Why do you not just find a village maiden to marry?' When he glared at her in sullen silence, she added, 'Or take a ride to Chester and pay for a tumble?'

'I hate your filthy mouth.' He scowled. 'I wish you were not so . . . worldly.'

'And I wish you were not such a damnable prig.'

'I shall go, then.' Still he stared at her, until a little flame of her old fondness overcame her, and she touched his arm. At once, he trapped her against the wall and kissed her as if he wanted to devour her alive. When he released her, he looked dazed and angry.

It was hopeless. She knew she had to stop this folly, to tell him she was leaving.

He looked at her, unrelieved misery clouding his face; then he left, banging the door so loudly that Bess woke and started to wail.

Alone, Tabitha slumped down on the bed and stared out at the moon, shimmering and mysterious behind a curtain of light rain. She blamed her contrariness on the monthly courses that always troubled her at the month's midward point. Each night, the moon had waxed ever brighter, until now it was a silver doubloon, hanging so low it looked close enough to grasp in her hand. It was a bad omen, she remembered, to gather the last of the harvest in the wet. When she went to bed that night she remained restless, and so was Bess: the child toddled in and hauled herself up beside her on the bed. Mostly the child was a damnable nuisance, though she had to admit there were times when the little chit had her charms. With an insistent squeal, Bess stretched out her arms for Tabitha to hold her close. She guessed her own mother must have embraced her on many such a lonely night.

No, Tabitha told her sternly. She was leaving soon, and it would be a cruelty to indulge her. True, she had not yet found a place for the child, for the moment never seemed apt to begin enquiries. In the meantime, she had decided to leave Bess with Jennet for a few days, and then post her a good sum of Robert's money from London. After all, Jennet preferred the cottage to her own home, and had a natural affection for Bess. And surely it would be best if the child stayed on in Netherlea?

On a whim, Tabitha got up and lit a candle from the embers. She leafed through her mother's almanack from St James' day, to St Lawrence's, to the Harvest Moon. It told her that the morrow was the fourteenth day of August, when for one day of the year human clocks and watches would run true to the minute with the heavens. She frowned over the coming day's motto, '*There shall be blood on the harvest corn.*' Well, there had been plenty of rabbits for the pot that week. Tomorrow, the last panicked creatures would be trapped in the stands of corn before the sharp scythes cut them down. Sowing and reaping, ploughing and gathering, birthing and butchering: it was all Mother Nature's way.

On the morning of the harvest feast, the sky was bright and clear again, and the bustle at Bold Hall reached dizzying speed. The great barn was hung with flowers and corn dollies, and the trestle tables were set out in rows. All the hoard of produce laid by throughout the summer was at last broken out of jars, boxes and baskets. Tabitha's great-aunt called at the stillroom every few hours, to give a report on events upstairs. There was a final panic when a De Vallory sugar crest cracked in half, at which Nell made a silent sign against bad luck.

'And Master Francis has gone off again,' Sarah tutted. She sidled in a little closer. 'What with the wet corn stooks, Sir John was as sharp as a wasp at breakfast.'

'So where'd they think Master Francis has gone?' Nell asked.

'The doctor told him that most likely he is drunk in a ditch. Her ladyship ran off to her chamber, crying as ever.'

Tabitha had noticed the same derisive tone whenever they spoke of Lady Daphne.

Nell began her usual lament. 'To have but the one son, and that one such a—'

'Watch out.' Her great-aunt looked meaningfully down the corridor. In a moment the doctor himself strode in and, after a kindly nod at the women, went to busy himself at the shelves. Tabitha watched him slyly, admiring the plush velvet stretched across his broad back and his fine curled wig. With graceful assurance he inspected the bottles ranged across the top shelves: pennyroyal, peppermint and laurel waters, and cordials of lavender and violet. His brother had overindulged and needed a purge as well as his usual dose of ratafia, he told her great-aunt, asking for some senna and rhubarb as well as nutmegs and Lisbon wine. His clean pink fingers worked deftly, pouring coloured waters into vials and holding the mixtures up to the light.

He smiled at Tabitha. 'Miss Hart. You make yourself busy?'

She rose and bobbed. 'Yes, thank you, Doctor.'

'You look somewhat improved since our last meeting. Grief is no handmaid to beauty.'

He took a few paces over to the table and inspected the board of sugarplums Jane was modelling from red and green preserves. Tabitha had the written recipe in front of her and had been reading the instructions aloud with great care.

'My brother has a tooth for those childish morsels. I confess I am more fastidious. Man produces only two sets of teeth in a lifetime, and I wish to keep mine.'

She smiled up into his clear, intelligent eyes.

'Perhaps when your work here in the stillroom is finished you could help me put order in my papers?'

'Perhaps, sir. But I still hope at some point to return to London.'

He watched her for a few more moments, and she caught sight of Nell tittering at Jane behind the doctor's back. It was no surprise that they scoffed. If he had not been in every way the model of a fond old bachelor, she might have believed the doctor had designs upon her, too.

As the morning passed, Tabitha was kept busy fetching porcelain for their confections and laying them out in precise geometric fashion. There were other errands to be run, too, collecting fresh powdered sugar from the larder, and a special gilt tray from the housekeeper's quarters. At the tail end of one of these forays, Tabitha stole a few minutes to persuade the hall boy to take her letter with the post.

'Here, take a whole sixpence,' she cajoled. 'And no one will know how you earned it.'

The gawky youth had just agreed to put the letter in the post box when a familiar loud male voice made the lad nearly jump out of his braided coat.

'Boy! Go, tell my groom to saddle Acteon.'

The lad scampered away and Tabitha found herself alone in the cubbyhole with Sir John De Vallory himself. He was little changed since their last meeting, nearly two years earlier. His hair was perhaps greyer, and his belly even larger, but the braggadocio he wore like a suit of gold was unchanged. He approached her with a wolfish expression.

'Tabitha. My brother said you were back. Good.' He slipped his arm around her waist. 'We must meet soon, and in private. Christ above, Tabitha, you don't know how glad I am to see you. I have—'

Before he could continue someone bayed out from the hall, 'Sir John! Has anyone seen Sir John? The farmer has ridden here, all in a lather, and will speak to him alone.'

Pressing his tobacco-stained fingers to her lips to signal silence, the master of Bold Hall turned and disappeared through the door.

'Damn, damn,' Tabitha muttered, striking a fist against the wall. What a nincompoop she'd been, to think she could come here to Bold Hall and Sir John would not learn of it. His presence, powerful and musky, still filled the tiny room. Oh, Venus, oh, Cupid; how soon could she make her escape?

No more than an hour later, a different boy in the De Vallory livery pushed his way inside the stillroom.

'A message for Tabitha Hart. You must come at once to Riddings' field.'

Both Jane and Nell turned to give their full attention.

'Who sent you?' Inwardly, she groaned to think that Sir John must already be plotting an encounter.

'Constable Saxton.'

'What does he want now?' She glanced at the boy and noticed for the first time that he was agitated and beaded with sweat.

'You are the searcher, miss? That's who I must fetch.' The boy reached out for the edge of the table to steady himself.

'Whatever's the matter, lad?' demanded Nell.

'There's a dead body been found, hidden in the corn. It's the worst thing I ever seed, ma'am. Some fellow's been hacked to death, right here in our own Riddings' field.'

THIRTEEN

A Riddle

My weapon is exceeding bold,
Of which I think I may well boast
And I'll attack old Colonel Gold
Together with his mighty host.
With my sharp tongue they can't compare
I'll conquer them both great and small,
Though thousands stand before me there
I'll cut but get no harm at all.

The 14th day of August 1752

Harvest

Luminary: The Harvest Moon at Full.
Observation: Mars, Mercury, Saturn and Venus all
direct in motion and very active.
Prognostication: Changes at hand either by
death of displeasure.

Tabitha ran towards Riddings' field, her thoughts turning somersaults. Who had been killed? It could not be Joshua, if he had sent for her – in spite of their last caustic meeting, she felt giddy with relief. Could it be Sir John? The grumbles against high rents, the muted accusations of his overreaching his position – all suggested the villagers' violent opposition. And the Devil take her for a sinner, but she would feel a moment's relief if Sir John conveniently disappeared.

As she pelted along the lane, a cart rattled up in her wake. After gasping out her mission, she was hauled up on to the board and jogged along in a hail of golden chaff. In the distance, the twisted chimneys of Eglantine Hall poked up behind the trees. A little snag of anxiety caught at her mind: she did not want the victim to be Nat Starling, either.

The Riddings' cornfield came into view, and she leapt down, only to slow again as she spotted a tableau of men huddled at the field's edge. After long hours working indoors, she could not help but notice the sky, shining cornflower blue above a row of hayricks as neatly thatched as miniature cottages, while poppies fluttered their venous petals underfoot. Yet there it was, something partly obscured, an object slumped and scarlet against the biscuit-golden corn. She marked the members of the assembled group off as she began to hurry towards them. Joshua was there; even from a distance he looked unsteady, as if drunk on punch-gut beer. The doctor was leaning over what she now saw was a bloody corpse with its face obscured. There was a labourer too, clutching his hat, gaping from a respectful distance, whom she guessed must have discovered the body. And there, kneeling on the stubbled ground, was Sir John himself. Gone was the puffed-up pigeon of a man – he was doubled over, his head bowed, like a broken version of his former self.

The shape was at first unknowable: a punctured sack of torn clothes twisted into an unnatural form. The victim had been kneeling, it seemed, when he died, but had toppled sideways so his face was deep in the standing corn. At least a dozen black-red gashes sliced through the remnants of his shirt, and a terrible wound lay open on his marble-white shoulder. Flies circled above him; Joshua nervously tried to bat them away with his hat. Coming closer, she saw a pair of lifeless eyes like two beads of pale jade. It was Francis De Vallory, heir of Netherlea.

Sir John was crooning over his son. 'You did not deserve this, Francis. How in God's name will I tell your mother?'

Then, turning round and seeing Joshua at his back, he cried harshly, 'Find who did this! I'll see the dog hang high.'

The doctor patted his brother's shoulder, but Sir John lashed out in reply, pushing him so hard he almost stumbled.

'Who the devil could have done this?' he cried, his face pink and his breath wheezing. Looking about herself, Tabitha comprehended a great truth; that the murderer had not only severed the life of one man but diverted the whole community from its ancient course. Quiet, dull, predictable Netherlea had been destroyed forever.

A farmhand now entered through the gate, and Joshua went to meet him. The constable returned a few moments later, and a horrified murmur rose as they identified what he carried. 'The weapon,' Joshua said huskily. He lifted aloft a straight-handled scythe with a cruel, crescent-moon-shaped blade. It was brown-stained, marred with what might have been cotton threads or whitish hair, all congealed along the length of it.

Sir John blanched. 'Who do you suspect, Saxton? Who?'

'I've a warrant out for that tinker they call Darius. I'll pull him in.'

'The tinker?' Sir John's voice trailed away. 'Go and get him. Go on, man.'

Joshua left with the scythe swinging in a sack, as the doctor concluded his gentle examination.

'When did it happen?' Sir John asked his brother.

The doctor pulled out his pocket watch and glanced up at the

sun. Tabitha was just close enough to see the light sparkling on the
tiny hand that moved inexorably around the elaborate dial.

'This morning. No more than two or three hours ago. Men must
be fetched now, to take Francis home.' Then he turned to Tabitha
and announced quietly to all present that she was the searcher now,
as her mother had been. 'She must go with Francis and do what is
right.'

He patted her arm. 'Well done for bearing up. Get back to the
hall now and see to the body.'

Rather than wait to accompany the men, Tabitha slipped away
through a gap in the hedge, to a path she knew led directly to the
hall. As she walked, she listed the items she needed to lay out
Francis: rosemary and other sweet herbs, warm water, clean linen.
The sounds of men and horses gradually subsided until the sensation
of being entirely alone overcame her, bit by bit. The folly of her
wandering solitary along this path, perhaps the one the murderer
had taken, made her pause mid-step. She looked around at the
familiar meadows: all was quiet, save for a couple of magpies
watching her from a post. She glanced down to see footprints in
the mud, heading in the opposite direction, back to Riddings' field.
Three sets of footprints, she noticed. Fearful of meeting three strangers, she walked on even faster.

At the hall she was led up to Francis's rooms by Master Francis's
valet, a sweating, trembling foreigner who mumbled Popish oaths
as he clucked about the room in search of his master's best suit of
clothes. Francis De Vallory lay twisted on a snowy bedsheet, laid
over a bed decorated with embroidered peacocks. It was Tabitha's
job now to transform those hacked remains into a semblance of the
youth he once had been. The valet backed away when she asked
for help in pulling off Francis's boots, so she had to heave at the
stiff limbs alone, all the while struggling to preserve a measure of
the youth's dignity. His boots of fine leather were splattered with
mud, from their tan tops to the fashionable low heels. The vague
recollection of the footprints she had seen on the path chimed in
her mind; one of the footprints had, she was sure, been made by a
heeled boot like this.

She closed her eyes and forced herself to remember. There had
been a set of distinctive hobnail prints, she was convinced of that.
And had there also been a third pair of footprints? Though fear
pricked her like a thousand pins, she decided she must go back to

the path when she had finished laying Francis out. In London there had been much talk that summer of a thief caught by taking the measure of shoe prints left behind in soil.

She began to wash Francis with warm water from a china ewer. Pictures flashed in her inner eye, of the one and only time she had openly conversed with him while he was alive; alone together in the bedchamber of a grand Chester inn, laughing and drinking on his birthday. At just twenty, he had been little younger than herself, and she had liked his cutting humour and sardonic gift of mimicry. At the time she had thought it the most pleasant guinea she had ever earned.

Now she removed his dew-damp clothes with difficulty, for his limbs would not relax from their contorted shape. The sun had baked his wounds, and the fabric of his shirt stuck like fish glue to his flesh. Newly slashed fibres needed careful coaxing to pull them out of hardened scabs. She counted thirteen wounds cut into his snowy flesh, from his shoulders to his buttocks; some so deep that they passed through skin to yellow fat and into white bone. Unwillingly, she thought of his last minutes kneeling in the corn, beseeching his murderer. She could think of no one on this earth who would want to do this. As the water turned rosy red, the sheet became stained too; the bed soon resembled a butcher's block. Behind her, the valet complained of faintness, and finally fled through the door with a whimper.

As she lifted his coat to lay it on his clothes press, a bloodstained corner of paper peeped out of his pocket. With great care, she eased it free and read it. At once she recognized the same hand, and the cruelty, of the missive sent to her mother:

To Francis

A harvest fails when seeds are rotten,
A weak seed fails in fields of tares,
A Noble House needs strength begotten,
In clever, strong and worthy heirs;
The Age of Gold will be reborn
When your blood spills upon the corn.

De Angelo

De Angelo? So 'D' and the almanack writer were one and the same! Had he killed both her mother and Francis? So who the devil *was* De Angelo? Everyone knew him as the author of Chester's *Vox Stellarum* but no one knew the man. It had to be a pen-name concealing D's true identity. And according to her mother's diary entries, D was a local man, a man of high regard. As though handling a pus-soaked rag, she laid the paper out on a nearby table, and hurriedly washed her hands again. Joshua needed to see this at once, and also Sir John. Time was running short – a hue and cry must be sent out to catch this lunatic. Yet first, she had to finish Francis's laying out with the dignity he deserved.

Tenderly, she washed the youth's long face, noting the bloodless echo of his father's features, the cheeks hairless. His skin was pore-less, his mouth as silky and pliable as a maiden's. He was only a youth, she thought, robbed by this monster of an even greater portion of his life than her own mother had been. When she twisted his head sidewards to wash the deepest wound on his shoulder, a dribble of bile-like liquid poured from his mouth, staining the lace pillow with a pool of yellow. It smelled of spirits, and she wondered at his having drunk intoxicating liquor so early in the morning.

With quick movements, she washed his private parts, then, hoisting him on his side, prepared the herbs she must push inside his body to keep him fresh. She had once seen a molly boy slumped in a Covent Garden alley after being violated by a soldier, and had never forgotten the blood-streaked signs of force. Thank the saints, nothing of the kind had been inflicted on Francis.

By the time she had tugged a suit of embroidered silk on to his limbs, the pallid youth bore the look of an effigy. He no longer felt limber; his flesh was stone cold, and the right arm that had been raised, doubtless to protect his head, was impossible to straighten. Filling a second china bowl, she scrubbed ineffectually at the brown lines rimming each of her fingernails. Catching sight of herself in a looking glass, she saw that her apron bore livid pink blotches.

Before she could remove it, a second apparition stood in the mirror beside her: a few feet behind her stood Lady Daphne De Vallory. For a moment their eyes met in mutual astonishment. The passing years had blanched whatever remained of her ladyship's beauty, leaving behind a strange translucence; her hair stood wiry grey beneath her muslin cap, and her complexion was crumpled under white powder.

Lady Daphne's ice-water eyes froze hard. 'What are you doing here, with my son?' She pointed towards the blood-soaked bed.

Aristocratic disdain fought with volcanic fury in her voice. Close at hand, the mistress of Bold Hall's face was corrugated by age, and her hollow eyes showed the skull beneath.

Be bold, Tabitha commanded herself. These people can do you no harm. She spoke gently, as if to a child.

'I was instructed to come here. I am the searcher now. This is my task.'

'What is this?' Francis's mother snatched at the bloodstained paper and stared blindly at the writing upon it. 'He thinks I don't see his continual scribbling?'

Her ladyship's lips tightened, as if restraining a great deal more she would like to say, or in preference spit, at Tabitha. Then, turning, with a creak of her vastly hooped *sacque* gown, Lady Daphne threw the paper into the fire before Tabitha could stop her. In a moment it had been reduced to ash, and a jagged pain exploded at Tabitha's temple as a porcelain shaving dish clattered to the floor.

'You abomination!' the older woman screamed. 'You filth!'

She picked up a brass candlestick, and made ready to throw that, too. Tabitha ran in desperation for the door. By the time she reached the head of the great wooden staircase, she found that her scalp was smeared with bright blood and her eyes felt hot, though she blinked them very fast. Death and damnation! She should never, in a thousand poxy years, have come home.

FOURTEEN

A Riddle

In youth I flew high in the air,
Or bathed upon the water fair,
My person white with slender waist,
On either side with fringes graced,
Till me that tyrant man espied,
And dragged me from my mother's side:
My skin he flayed, my hair he cropped,
At head and foot my body lopped.
And then with heart more hard than stone,
He picked my marrow from the bone,
Such torture did that tyrant wreak,
He slit my tongue to make me speak:
Though mute to ears I speak to eyes.
Disguised I tell a thousand lies,
From me no secret e'er can hide;
I witness malice, lust and pride:
All languages I can command,
Yet not a word I understand.

The 15th day of August 1752

Harvest

Luminary: The Sun rises 6 minutes after 5.
Observation: Jupiter and Mars at the cusp.
Prognostication: The people in a ferment and
unable to settle.

W hen Joshua thumped on the cottage door the next
morning, Tabitha, for once, welcomed his company. She
had been alone with Bess since returning from Bold
Hall, furious with herself for ever leaving London, and growing more
and more frightened. She had come home by way of the Riddings'
but was sorely disappointed: already a herd of cattle had churned up
the footprints on the path. All the long night, the passing bell had
tolled its monotonous dirge, while again and again Francis's body
had sprung unbidden before her eyes. Murder was against nature,
she repeated numbly; to hound and harm and slaughter a fellow
being was unthinkable. Lady Daphne's lashing out at her was unsettling, too. And then there was the discovery that De Angelo – or
someone masquerading as him – had killed Francis and must be her
mother's pursuer, too. Time itself seemed to become like treacle,
trapping Tabitha here while her every instinct urged her to run away.

She had at once got out the almanack and hastily read it, attentive to any connections between prediction and fact. The day her
mother had died carried the prognostication: '*An unlucky day for
travel.*' That same day her mother had written of locking herself
indoors – and the journey she had taken to the river had indeed
been the unluckiest of her life. But the prediction was too ill-defined
and might apply to hundreds of different circumstances, including
her own unlucky journey from London. Much more lucid was the
prediction of Francis's death: '*There shall be blood on the harvest
corn.*' Yet how could anyone, even a skilled astrologer like De
Angelo, predict such butchery – unless he had carried out the
slaughter himself?

Joshua looked harried as he slumped down in a chair. With relief she told him of the riddling verse and her confrontation with Lady Daphne, touching the scabbed lump beneath her hair.

'No doubt her ladyship was crazed with grief. You say there was a paper you found in Francis's pocket signed by De Angelo?'

'Yes. De Angelo, like the almanack writer. Here, I've written out what I can remember.'

She passed him a piece of paper, but he merely glanced at it, and put it in his document bag.

'Well, the original of the paper is destroyed, so this cannot be held valid proof for the coroner. As for De Angelo, it sounds like a hoax, wouldn't you say? I must deal with realities – Sir John is near wild at losing his son; he's locked himself away in his apartments. And the most outlandish rumours are being repeated: that a secret club of gentlemen ordered that Francis be murdered, or that this Darius stabbed him in a quarrel over money.'

He rubbed his weary face.

'I've already questioned the harvest gang. It was one of their scythes that was used; they found it missing, yesterday morning. I'd wager still it's that stranger in the woods who has done this – but for God knows what reason. And now Sir John has ordered me to question that Starling fellow – only he said I must be subtle and not accuse or arrest him, but all of it is to be secret and underhand. What kind of play actor does he think I am?'

He looked at her sideways.

'Then I remembered how you have a sly woman's mind – more fit for the task, maybe.'

Tabitha was unsure if this was a compliment or an insult. 'So what do you want?'

'Come with me now, while it's good and early. Come question Nat Starling, and make him confess to this damnable crime.'

Tabitha had not visited Eglantine Hall since she had played in its ruins as a child. Now the sun burned slowly through luminous fog to reveal the broken skeleton of a once-grand manor – barely a third of its buildings had survived the bombardments of the Civil War. The bulk of the house was no longer habitable: it was a mere skeleton of blackened stone. The only usable quarters were in the ancient gatehouse, from which rose the distinctive twisted chimneys. It was four storeys high, part castle rampart and part monastery tower, studded with oriel windows filled with coloured glass. Crumbling effigies of saints peered down from niches through the mist.

Joshua pushed at the carved door and found it open. Privately, Tabitha hoped Mr Starling had ventured out early that morning, for she was loath to entrap the man for Joshua's sake. They made a rapid, stealthy search of the lower two floors, finding nothing of interest. But at the top of the next dimly lit staircase lay a grand apartment, strewn harum-scarum with a mess of discarded coats and books and hats, overturned tankards and dirty crockery. Tacked over the walls were crude prints of garish stuff: a Wheel of Fortune, mermaids and hanged men, a demon, and a bevy of bare-breasted harlots. Joshua mutely pointed towards them, his brows raised. She looked about in dismay; there was certainly a strange correspondence between these crude prints and the archaic lexicon of the almanack and the threatening verses.

The room had been divided by a cord, upon which hung embroidered coats, ruffled linen and nightshirts, some in grave need of laundering. Beyond stood a musty-looking tester bed, upon which Nat Starling lay half-dressed in shirt and breeches, eyes closed, entirely insensible.

Joshua prodded him with the end of his staff.

'Wake up, you scoundrel, and give an account of yourself!'

The young man did not even stir. Tabitha stepped forward and shook his arm. Lord, he stank of spirits, and the familiar fust of men addled after a long night. She called his name and shook him again, but still he didn't stir.

Joshua motioned to her to stop. 'While he sleeps, we can search this place at our liberty.'

As he began to turn over clothes, stools and boxes, she made a lacklustre show of looking about her; to her relief, he soon disappeared upstairs to search the upper apartments.

Wandering back to Nat's bedside, she studied his sleeping form; it had played often in her fancy since she first glimpsed him in the yard at Bold Hall. Asleep, he was as fine as she remembered, his pallid cheek shadowed with stubble, his lips just parted. His chin bore a black smudge, and his fingers, too, were black from ink. She crossed over to his writing desk. It was made of carved oak, so heavily stained that, if the hue had been crimson instead of black, it could have been taken for some pagan altar. Piles of papers lay scattered, covered in hasty scribbles.

A print lying on a nearby table caught her eye. She laughed noiselessly, for she knew it well – a picture from Signor Aretino's *Remarkable Amours*, titled *The Wheelbarrow*, that depicted a woman propelled upside down, her hands holding a rotating wheel, while a handsome youth impaled her from the rear. Next, she picked up an enamel snuffbox bearing a lascivious Venus, her fingers delighting in the cold slipperiness of worked gold. It was studded with gems and would be worth a good two guineas. But she laid it down again – to be caught pilfering goods in Netherlea would only heap more difficulties upon her.

Her fingertips played over Starling's other goods: a repeating pocket watch, a net of coins, a jewelled pin. Finally, she touched the stiff feathers of his new-cut quills. He had so many, and she needed only one – he surely wouldn't miss it. She pulled out a snowy quill and slid it into her pocket.

A husky voice spoke out behind her. 'Lady, did my eyes mistake me?'

She spun around to find Nat Starling's bleary eyes fixed upon her as he struggled to rise from his bed.

The heat of shame burned Tabitha's skin. 'I beg your pardon. I didn't mean—' She threw the quill back down upon the desk, horribly bent from being pushed inside her pocket.

Nat watched her, blinking, from his mound of bedclothes. 'I'm most obliged to you for calling, and so on – though less so for stealing my quills – but pray, why are you here, at this godless hour?'

She pointed at the ceiling, whence came the sounds of Joshua bumping and scraping.

'I'm here with the constable,' she said as softly she could. 'He needs to ask you some questions.'

He raised his elbows and stretched himself awake. 'Throw me that robe.'

She passed him a green robe of Chinese silk, and he tied it over his sleepworn clothes. Then, padding over to a ewer in his bare feet, he found a jug and lifted it to his mouth to drink. Wiping his mouth on his sleeve, he settled down again on the bed and drew his fingers through dark strings of hair, then smiled up at her. She again noticed his shining tortoiseshell eyes. What was it about this fellow that made him so hard to dislike? She tried to gain the upper hand.

'You do know that illustration is a physical impossibility?' she said, touching it with a casual finger.

He winced, smiling. 'So you come here to correct my knowledge of anatomy, Miss Hart?'

'I am employed as the searcher by the parish.'

'Like your mother?'

She nodded.

'I liked your mother. I was wretched when I heard—' He hearkened for a moment. 'Does that infernal bell mean someone is dead?'

Tabitha nodded, trying to convey a warning with her eyes.

'That is why we're here.'

'Here? Don't tell me Saxton suspects me of some mischief?'

'More than mischief – and he comes at Sir John's request. Take care when he returns.'

She stood very still as furniture moved above them.

'Listen,' he said amiably, pushing disarrayed hair from his eyes. 'You lived in London, did you not?' To her alarm, he added in a conspiratorial whisper, 'I believe I know you.' His smile was mischievous and expectant.

'You know me?' She made an effort to recall him. It was no use; a cavalcade of London gentlemen had paid court to her, but she could remember barely a single face. Was the rogue saying he had known her – in the flesh? No, surely she would remember him, a diamond in the dross. Dismayed, she heard Joshua's footsteps on the stairs.

'And I suspect, Miss Hart, that you are more than what you seem.' He tapped his lips with one long finger as if considering hard. He lowered his head and whispered, 'I heard a man needed five hundred pounds to keep you for himself.'

She did not often blush – but to hear this in Netherlea was not at all welcome.

'Keep that to yourself,' she hissed. And then, recovering herself, 'It is different here. Here, I am without even fifty shillings.' As his roguish grin warned her she had been too forward, she gabbled, 'That is not an offer of my services!'

He tossed his head, laughing. 'So you do not remember me?'

She shook her head.

'Try this one, then – 'tis a puzzle or, technically, a conundrum. The place I saw you is "Where horses' fodder is traded".'

She bit her lip, confounded. His expression was eager, willing her to comprehend. 'I cannot think. Tell me.'

But the rascal only shook his unkempt head. 'Not now. Call again. Alone.'

Joshua came in then and strode over to the bed. 'Roused yourself at last, Mr Starling? Where were you yesterday morning?'

'For goodness' sake, man, I was here. What is your business?'

'You know Francis De Vallory?'

'No,' said Nat defiantly. 'I do not. Why would I be interested in that young cub?'

'Where are the clothes you wore yesterday?'

'What do you suppose those articles are?' asked Nat, indicating the clothes upon the line.

'So where have you hidden the bloodstained garments?'

Nat stood quickly, on the defensive. 'You will find no bloodstained garments here.' Then he added, in a low but clear voice, 'Unless you produce them yourself.'

Joshua's colour was deepening to the colour of plums. 'I have seen you. At night, in the woods. I am a witness to your prowling.'

'I take exercise. It is common land, I believe.'

'Not common to you, Starling. You are under suspicion.' Joshua banged his constable's staff against the floor. 'The woods are out of bounds to you. I'll set a watch.'

'And do you also watch that youth Darius? He lurks about the pathways at night making threats. Is he a suspect too?'

Ignoring this, Joshua turned to Tabitha. 'Your questions?'

Damn him. She had questions, but none suitable to ask before her old friend. She searched her wits. 'Mr Starling, if I might ask – how long have you been here in Netherlea?'

Tight-lipped, he glanced quickly at the constable. 'About six weeks.'

'So you were not here at Easter-tide?'

He shook his head.

'And what did you know of Francis De Vallory?'

'Only that he was Sir John's son and heir – young, conceited, badly-dressed.'

She shook her head at him. 'Whatever your opinion of him, Mr Starling, an innocent youth has been murdered.'

'Forgive me, Miss Hart. I did not mean to be uncivil.'

He sounded suddenly so contrite that she had a startling desire to console him. Mercifully, Joshua interrupted them, bearing a sheet of paper inked with a crude design. 'What do you call this?'

Nat took it. It was an old-fashioned picture of a corn stook, around which young men in doublets and feathered hats were throwing sickles in a species of contest.

'I believe it's called throwing for the neck,' he said casually. 'It's an illustration for a chapbook I'm writing on country customs.'

'Balderdash,' said Joshua coldly. 'You got the notion to kill Francis De Vallory from this trash. I'm taking this to the magistrate. And I'll be back with a warrant, you may be sure of that.'

He turned away to the door, and Tabitha cast an exasperated glance back towards Nat, who shook his head in amused exasperation.

'Take care,' she warned, with silent lips. Then she forced herself to follow Joshua.

FIFTEEN

A Riddle

There is a gate we all know well,
That stands 'twixt Heaven, Earth, and Hell,
Where many for a passage venture,
Yet very few are fond to enter:
Both dukes and Lords abhor its wood,
The prospect of it chills their blood.
Yet commoners with greatest ease
Can find an entrance when they please.
The poorest hither march in state
While drums are beat and parsons prate –
Yet e'en the gravest persons who advance
Cannot pass through before they dance.

The 21st day of August 1752

St Athanasias

Luminary: Today sun and clocks run correct together.
Observation: Conjunction of Venus and Mars.
Prognostication: There will be such fightings and
slaughterings as are not usual.

The crowds at Francis De Vallory's funeral were vast, for the whole county knew that much of the harvest feast had been kept back for the wake. For almost a week, the youth remained above ground, embalmed in a lead coffin in the hall's private chapel; the coroner's inquest pronounced him to have been murdered by persons unknown. Instead of the expected summons from the constable, Nat had instead received a lavish invitation to the funeral, along with a black arm ribbon and hat band. Thus clad, he had waited, as po-faced as he could manage, as an extravagant procession passed out of the gates of Bold Hall, led by nobles in black velvet and culminating in a hearse pulled by six ebony thoroughbreds dressed in waving plumes.

Once he was seated next to a young farmer in the sweltering Great Hall, its walls muffled in a king's ransom of black crepe, he found he had quite lost his appetite for all but wine. He was soon benumbed, both with his neighbour's conversation and the quaffing of spiced claret; his mood brightened only when the sweetmeats were served and he sighted Tabitha Hart sauntering about the room.

'Would you care for a biscuit?' she asked demurely.

He looked up, tipsily flummoxed by her proximity, and took a morsel wrapped in black waxed paper. The motto stamped into the confection read: '*Our Time is At Hand.*'

He showed her the legend and smiled. 'Is it, truly? In which case, may we not talk somewhere in private?'

'Oh, sir, not now,' she said, though she looked disappointed. 'I have to get to Chester by six, and it's a good two-hour walk.'

'I see. Are you not fearful of walking alone after such an outrage?'

'Aye, there is a savage murderer at large,' interrupted the young farmer, a single man. 'I have a gig I might place at your—'

'Ride with me to Chester,' Nat broke in rudely, in his turn. 'Meet me at the stables in a quarter-hour. I'll have you at the market cross well before six.'

For a moment, she looked from him to the farmer, then silent laughter seemed to brighten her eyes.

'Very well. In fifteen minutes.'

He waited fretfully, with Jupiter pacing, until Tabitha arrived with a bundle in her arms. 'Oh, Lord! That is a very high horse you have there.'

As he sat well forward in the saddle, she mounted clumsily from the block, sitting farm-boy fashion behind him, with her legs astride – and, from what he could glimpse, her skirt raised up almost to her knees. Though she couldn't ride for pie, it felt good to feel her sitting warm and ungainly behind him, her arms clasping his waist.

He turned the horse out of the yard. Ahead of them, standing by the gates, a gaggle of women stood watching their approach; Zusanna, the bane of his tavern hours, stood red-cheeked and grim. He had an uncomfortable notion that the dairymaid might cry out some impertinence as they passed.

'I'll take the back roads through the farm,' he decided, leading Jupiter down a bridle path behind the highway instead. The church bell chimed four o'clock as they trotted onwards through the final glory of the afternoon, through stubbled fields and glades that had just begun to wear the yellow tints of summer's passing.

'You didn't come to the harvest feast.' She sounded almost sorry, speaking so close to his ear that her breath tickled him.

'I was avoiding your friend the constable.'

'No mind. All who came said it was the poorest harvest they ever saw, what with there being no merriment on account of Master Francis's death. Sir John was hid away, so there were no healths drunk to the master. But who could blame him, with his only son just murdered? Some said it was an ill omen for Netherlea to have blood spill on the corn. What do you say?'

'Did not the old pagan rites welcome blood at harvest time? It augurs fertility and so on, does it not?'

'Do you believe that?' She angled her head to watch him. He twisted to look at her, with a mocking grin.

'I am sure you think me a dunderhead, but truly? Do not insult me, Tabitha. I do have some sense.'

They came to the orchard, where neat rows of trees bearing perfumed lady apples and cowslip-yellow pippins stood as still and silent as Pomona's grove. He walked the horse up to a heavy-fruited tree, plucked a shining green apple and offered it to Tabitha. With a snort, she discarded it after one bite.

'You are too early, unless you want to fetch a ladder and take one from those nearest to the sun.'

'Ah, the higher the tree, the sweeter the fruit. There is truth to those old sayings. We talked of such matters at Cambridge.'

'Aye? And in which Cambridge tavern was that?'

'At Trinity College, you saucy jade. My professor often talked of it as an allegory. Do you know that there is such a thing as a tree of time?'

He felt her head resting against his back as they trotted on and it pleased him. 'And you are going to tell me all about it.'

'I am. Picture a great tree in your mind. The solid trunk is the past. The past, of course, cannot be changed.'

He felt her nodding, pictured her clear brow, the unruly hair that fell from her cap, and two sparkling eyes that missed nothing.

'The present moment, the 'now', moves like sap up the trunk. The future is represented by branches, the different possibilities ahead of us. Unlike the tree's rigid trunk, our future is malleable and we can choose which branch to take. But the branches we do not choose – the schooling we reject, or the suitor we disdain – those branches no longer exist once time has passed. Indeed, they wither and fall off our tree.'

'So we must make wise choices to pluck the best fruits?' She was quick to grasp the idea.

'Yes.'

'But how do we know which branch to take?'

'Ah, if only we knew. We must be as wise as we can; for as time keeps moving upwards, our branches grow fewer.'

She craned forward to look at him, a perplexed look on her face. 'What is the name of these notions you studied at Cambridge?'

'Philosophy. My professor knew the great Newton himself.'

'Perhaps I was wrong about your being a dunderhead, after all.'

He chuckled but was silenced by her next remark. 'But why do you live as you do, Nat? If you know all these clever things?'

He sighed. 'Well, why do *you* live as you do?'

'That's cheating. I asked you first.'

'But the answer is surely contained in both of our reasons.'

'And that is?'

'I deduce that we are not yet wise.'

'And by God, may we never be!' She repeated the common London toast to folly but added, in a plaintive voice, 'Truly, why do you live as you do at Eglantine Hall?'

'Because I confound myself, Tabitha. Those scribblings and quips I produce are mere shadows of my ambition. I long to be a writer, a poet, but it seems I have only the shabbiest sort of talents. I disgust myself, selling the outpourings of my pen for coppers.'

He told her then of his being reared in Cambridge, in a noble household; his mother was a woman of Netherlea, but she had had the good sense to leave the place and take up a post as Lord Robbins' housekeeper and marry his steward. His Lordship had favoured Nat as a lad, given him access to his great library, and even arranged for his studies at the university. But Nat, like a prize booby, had fallen in with false friends and failed at his studies; a weakness for liquor had undermined his will. Fleeing debt, he had headed for London, still sure of the great literary career awaiting him. Alas, the only work he could sell had been on Grub Street – the riddles and dream books and lewd pamphlets from which he now made a paltry living.

'It is my ambition to write in the new style,' he told her. 'Have you read much of that fellow Defoe, beyond *Robinson Crusoe*? He was an upstart, of course, but truly he overturned the whole business of writing; he wrote in a manner for common people to enjoy, but there is a modern singularity to his work. Do you know, he used to go into Newgate and converse with the felons? Then, in his pamphlets he transports the reader directly into the jail and reports the authentic words of scurrilous villains like Jack Shepherd.'

He could not help but run on, now he had started.

'I believe it is more than just a fashion, this attempt to understand the world we live in – not by creating fantastical conceits about gods and kings but looking unflinchingly at what is here all around us, the poor, the criminal orders, the pimps and whores . . . Oh, forgive me. I suppose you must despise me now,' he concluded, suddenly horrified by his own frankness.

'There is no tree but bears some kind of fruit,' she quipped, sounding not at all insulted. 'Nat Starling, how old are you?'

'Five and twenty.'

He heard her happy, ringing laugh. 'So old? And so educated and well connected. You handsome lump; there are rich branches aplenty dangling above your head. You just cannot see them yet.'

He protested, but was cheered, at least, by that epithet 'handsome', whether he was a lump or not. 'And you, Tabitha? What lies ahead for you?'

'Well, I have no fruitful branches to pick from, as you have. But you are not the only one with regrets. Perhaps I must also leave some deadwood behind me.'

He recalled the curse that Darius had purported to cast in her direction. 'And you are well? Allowing for the sad loss of your mother, naturally.'

'I believe I am improving every moment,' she answered cheerily.

They had arrived by now at the top of Moss Hill, looking down on the valley of the Dee, where a herd of brown-and-white cattle drowsily splashed through the water.

'I shall walk down the hill,' she said, 'if you will help me dismount.'

Together they strolled down the slope, he leading Jupiter by the reins. He glanced at her sideways, trying to guess her thoughts.

'I wanted to talk to you.'

'I guessed it. Did you come to the cottage one night?'

'I did. Well, more than once perhaps.'

'Why? I hope you are not the murderer.'

He grinned at the ridiculous idea.

'No, I wanted to speak to you. I liked your mother very much, she was a friend to me.'

For some time they talked of the widow and he was touched by the regrets they shared; the difficulties of combining a life of liberty with the duty to one's parent.

'The last night of your mother's life she was distracted,' he confided. 'And once I had left her, I saw Darius close by.'

'You called on my mother?'

'If I had only stayed longer she might still be alive. I cannot forgive myself.'

Though they walked on in silence he caught her watching him.

'It is I who need forgiveness,' she said at last. 'I was tardy on the road and too late to save her. Nonetheless, take my advice, Nat. Don't tell Joshua you were with her. He is a solid thinker and needs a scapegoat. Perhaps you will soon return to London?'

With some apprehension, he noted that they had come already to the bend in the river, very close to Chester and its walls.

'I still have business here. I can't leave yet. And . . . if I could make amends? I have written of a great many crimes and indeed it is my pleasure to unpick the puzzle of them. In every inquiry there is the gathering of intelligence, the detecting of past events and following the criminal's trail. I would be most happy to assist you. Whoa, Jupiter. What is this?'

He slowed to stroke the horse's neck. They had arrived at the highway to find a crowd massing towards the city. Purveyors of cakes and hawkers of liquor stood along the road, while sellers of ballads and last confessions shouted their wares. A thrilled murmur rose from the rabble as a band of soldiers overtook them, guarding a rough-hewn cart. Inside it stood a parson chanting from a prayer book and behind him crouched a youth no more than fourteen years of age, his face crumpled and slick with tears. Nat saw, with disgust, that the lad's scrawny limbs were weighted with chains. There above them stood the city gibbet on Gallows Hill, the topmost beam in grim silhouette against the sky. As the cart trundled past them, they could hear the poor lad's sobs.

'Look at that!' he cried. '"The little thieves hang while the great thieves sit on the bench." Where is justice in this land?'

To his surprise, Tabitha slipped her arm through his and squeezed it.

'Poor little runt,' she agreed. 'He has had no life yet. But do you, with all your knowledge of such matters, wish to join him on the end of a rope? Don't make an enemy of Joshua. The gallows is not a pretty end, especially when the corpse is innocent.'

She looked towards the turrets and towers of Chester, rising against the softening golden sky. Across the still air came the tolling of the great cathedral bell.

'Six o'clock. We've been dawdling. Your friend will be waiting.'

But instead of hurrying, Tabitha slowed and stood before him. 'Where are you going tonight?'

He looked down into her eyes that met his with fierce intent. The sun had turned her cheeks a pretty pink. 'Nowhere of consequence. I'll find an alehouse in Chester.'

'Don't,' she said, taking his fingers in her own. Her hand felt very soft and slight inside his. 'Stop throwing your life to the dogs, Nat. Go back to Netherlea tonight.'

'What, while you feast and carouse and the Devil knows what else, I must trot off with my tail between my legs? You have not even told me who this fortunate friend of yours is.'

She again looked towards the city, to the mass of gabled roofs and spires, all of it a tempting labyrinth, then turned back to him. 'I do believe that road leads to a blighted branch,' she said, indicating the city with a movement of her head. 'Do you not think the time has come to pluck our fruits before they spoil? You will think me half-crazed – but would you care to accompany me back home to Netherlea again?'

'I am your servant.' He made a small bow, baffled but bursting with happiness.

'Thank you, Nat. I need to show you something odd that was written by my mother.'

SIXTEEN

A Riddle

My *first* is the term to relate
A circumstance present or past,
And those who love stories to prate,
My *second* will spout away fast.
My *whole* in the days of our youth,
Is what we extremely despised;
And though it says nothing but truth,
Yet it never need hope to be prized.

The 21st to the 22nd day of August 1752

Luminary: Moon at the last quarter.
Observation: The Moon rises at 54 minutes
after noon.
Prognostication: The weak and poor will
suffer oppression.

When Tabitha had said her farewells, she felt Nat's gaze burning upon her back as she continued homewards. Oh Venus, she was developing a bad case of lovelornedness for the fellow, but the delicious contemplation of Mr Starling must wait until they met again the next evening; there was another matter to attend to first. She was damned if Nat was going to be persecuted while ruffians like Darius ran free.

Just beyond the stepping stones, she looked beneath the hawthorn bush. Sure enough, Jennet's basket was carefully hidden from view there, and packed tight with bread and cheese. Placing it back where she had found it, Tabitha continued down the path and home.

Joshua and Jennet were enjoying the last light of the day in the cottage garden while Bess sat at their feet, happily making mud pies. For all the much-trumpeted grandeur of the Grange, it was clear the pair of them preferred the modest cottage, with its bright fire and narrow walls. Joshua rose from her mother's stool with the air of a guilty man.

'Tabitha. We understood you were away until Monday.'

'I had an alteration to my thinking,' she said.

She ruffled Bess's fair curls as the little girl made excited sounds of greeting. With a sigh of contentment, she slumped on to a bench and breathed in the scent of her mother's gillyflowers. Her long game with Robert over, she felt as light and free as thistledown. He would be wondering where she was by now, his evening slowly souring with disappointment. Well, the boot was on the other foot. She stretched with satisfaction.

Joshua pulled his stool closer, appraising her and the bundle she had set down on the grass.

'Jennet,' she called. 'I saw some wild raspberries, back by the dead tree. Would you like to fetch some?'

The girl rose at once, eager to gather the sweet fruit. Once she had left them, Tabitha turned to Joshua.

'If I tell you a secret, would you swear to never tell a soul that I was your informer?'

'I don't care for underhandedness and you know it.' His broad face was uneasy. 'Is it Nat Starling? What have you discovered?'

'No, it is not him. But I might be able to lead you to Darius. Do you promise not to tell – on Jennet's life?'

'On Jennet's life? I'd have to stand by that.'

'Come closer, then. Don't fire off, now. Your Jennet has a hankering for this Darius – it's a common enough folly at her age, for he is handsome, she tells me.' She laid a gentle hand on his own, which was fast tightening into a fist. 'Someone has been hiding food in the hedge, Joshua, and I've no doubt it's your daughter. I've been thinking, you could send a man – not you – to follow her. The youth isn't far away.'

Joshua spat on the ground. 'I'll give that girl such a—'

'Hush,' she whispered, fearful of Jennet's return. 'If you break your oath I'll never speak another word to you. And I shall tell Jennet that you broke your promise, too.'

Joshua breathed hard. 'She needs a mother.' He looked at her, eyes burning with entreaty, and a picture of that dusty spinning wheel sprang up at once in her mind.

'You know I'm mighty fond of Jennet, and that's why I'm telling you this. But more than that, I cannot give you.'

When Jennet came weeping up the path the following afternoon, Tabitha saw at once that her plan had worked.

'I hate my father,' the girl wailed, running into Tabitha's arms. 'He has had Darius put in chains! I never want to see him again.' She raised a forlorn, tear-slicked face, so bereft of hope that the sun might have fallen from the sky.

Disentangling herself from the girl's hot fingers, Tabitha questioned her with all the false astonishment of a Drury Lane board-walker. Between sobs and hiccups, Jennet told her how her father's man had found Darius hidden in the woods.

'But how could they have known?' she demanded.

Tabitha, well-prepared, fielded the question adroitly. 'Who has heard you speak fondly of him? One of your friends, perhaps? If Darius had nothing to do with Francis De Vallory's death, your father is a fair man – he'll soon be released.'

She watched Jennet wipe her pink-rimmed eyes with the corners of her apron.

'Jennet, I have a good notion. It is doling day at the hall; they are distributing all the broken food from the funeral today. Shall we go and fetch some? And deliver a portion to your father's new prisoner?'

At the servery at Bold Hall, they waited in line as the servants doled out portions of sliced meat, bread and a few sweetmeats. Jennet, she noticed, whispered to the servant, and after some altercation was grudgingly handed an extra portion in return. Contenting Bess with a sugar sucket, they strolled back up the High Street, Tabitha watching her young friend shrewdly. She had all the smooth-faced freshness of a girl just blooming into a woman; her reed-like waist was little more than a hand-span beneath her drab linsey-woolsey gown. In a year or two she would be a fair, good-hearted young woman, a credit to Joshua – if she could only be protected from Darius and his type.

'Darius knew Francis De Vallory, didn't he?' she asked.

'Master Francis was a puffed-up coxcomb with more riches than sense,' replied Jennet scornfully. Tabitha was briefly surprised, before she grasped that the girl must merely be repeating Darius's own words.

'But Darius didn't harm him,' she added quickly. 'He wouldn't have. Master Francis lent him money; he was always open-handed.'

'Were they good friends?'

'Aye. Everyone wanted to be friends with Darius. They used to play cards together.'

Naturally, thought Tabitha, and no doubt who won the stake. They were coming up to the jail now, and Jennet hesitated.

'You are the constable's daughter. There can be no objection to your taking the prisoner food in the name of charity.'

Encouraged, the girl ran up to Godfrey, a good-natured fellow who had worked with Joshua for years. A moment later, she beckoned to Tabitha and, leaving Bess with Godfrey, they entered a stone cell, reeking of mildew and nightsoil. Darius lay sprawled on a bed of straw, his ankle chained to a metal ring hammered into the wall. Tabitha saw at once that the ruffian had a mighty high regard for himself, and for his own sulky-mouthed attractions. He raised a pair of smouldering black eyes towards them as they came in, feigning indifference to Jennet's eager inquiries. He devoured every morsel she unpacked from her basket but did not trouble himself to thank her.

Once this was over Tabitha introduced herself, with as open a smile as she could muster. 'Thank you, Darius, for helping my mother around her cottage.'

This was greeted by a blank face.

'I am Widow Hart's daughter. You recollect? There was a broken latch.'

Tabitha held her breath, sensing some deep cogitation behind the carpenter's jetty eyes.

'I'm forever mending stuff for folk,' he growled. He raised his index finger and beckoned Jennet to come up close beside him; as she scurried over like an eager kitten, he spoke softly in her ear, so that Tabitha could not hear a word.

Reverently, she reached for his big-knuckled hand, scarified all over with black symbols like a sailor's. As if granting a boon, he allowed her to caress it, laying his head back against the wall and eyeing Tabitha narrowly.

'You brung my baccy?' he abruptly asked the girl. Dutifully, she set off at once to enquire from Godfrey how some tobacco might be obtained.

Tabitha remained with him, wondering how best to bluff this roister without showing her hand. At last, she pulled herself up to her full height and folded her arms, trying not to look at his mud-caked hobnailed boots. Though the cell was ill-lit she would swear there was a nail missing from the centre of the sole.

'I am the parish searcher now, as my mother was.'

Darius raised his heavy brows.

'Therefore I had to lay out Francis's corpse, and my head is not stuffed with straw, like those of some round here. I found a verse threatening Francis from De Angelo. You know him. What is his true name?'

Darius's head jerked sharply upwards, his eyes so wide that she could see little rims of white around the black discs. There – she was right on the nail.

'Why don't you peach on him and turn King's evidence? It's you or him,' she urged, taking a step toward him. 'So why shouldn't the other fellow swing for it?'

Like the lash of a horsewhip, his hand appeared from nowhere, snaring her wrist. The jolt was so sudden that she stumbled – he pulled her so close towards him that she could feel the heat from his unwashed body. Instantly she put Poll's trick into action, yanking his arm hard in its socket. As quick as lightning, his other fist grasped her hair, pulling it so violently that she yowled.

'You,' he growled. 'You think I don't know about you? Jennet's busybody friend who watches her every move? The poxy London whore?'

He flung her backwards against the wall, and she staggered, winded.

'It's like this,' he said steadily. 'I don't need to peach, or even lift a finger. I know what the future holds for me. I'll not stand trial for this or any other business. It's written in the stars, and it will come to pass. You just wait and see.'

SEVENTEEN

A Riddle

With scarlet cheeks a group of beauties stood,
I cropped their bloom and sucked their blood,
Sweet meat they had, but neither flesh nor bone,
Yet in each tender heart they held a stone
I rhymed and counted but then fell to grief
To learn my fate's to be a common thief.

The 22nd day of August 1752

Luminary: Twilight ends at 44 minutes after 8
of the evening.
Observation: Mercury hastening to the
conjunction with Venus.
Prognostication: Moves afoot to ameliorate the worst
effects in some measure.

As he waited for his rendezvous with Tabitha, Nat felt as
though he had swallowed a nest of squirming vipers. His
pocket watch told ten minutes after six – more than an hour
later than the time they had agreed – when she at last strode through
the ruined stumps of the gateposts and up the drive. He savoured
the moment, watching unseen from the battlements, his heart twice
the speed of his watch's ticking. This had to be the beginning of a
new epoch for him – the conjunction of two radiant planets in the
cold immensity of his life.

He ran downstairs to greet her, then was suddenly too agitated
to take her arm as he led her up to the roof. She had missed the
church bells at five, she said in apology, and got in a muddle about
the hour – he had forgotten there was no clock at the cottage. Today
she looked different from his recollection; not so conventionally
beautiful, but stronger, and more vividly real. He settled on one of
the two chairs he had set in the shade; she paced about the narrow
roof, pausing to lean on the battlements, gazing over the pond to
the church and common, the winding sparkle of the river, and the
distant roofs of Bold Hall itself.

Setting his telescope to her eye, she said, 'This is a good view-
point to watch who comes and goes.'

He took the opportunity to come up behind her, circling her with
his arms to guide the telescope. Gently he pointed it up to the sky
that was slowly deepening to a dark forget-me-not blue.

'Look. There is Venus.' In his mind, he associated the silver-blue
planet with Tabitha, a crystal droplet hanging high beside the Pole
Star. 'When the crisp winter nights arrive there will be many

wondrous spectacles. I'll show you comets and shooting stars, and with luck, the aurora of the Northern Lights.'

'Yes – I should like that.' Her eyes shone. 'You have studied the stars?'

'Yes. I have seen all six of the planets. We live now in an age without equal in learning and science. I pity the Ancients – so much more is revealed to us in this modern age.'

He talked for a spell of studying the heavens with his professor; of comets, auroras and the distant constellations – until he became aware of a sudden change in the air, a bluster that lifted the clinging ivy and rattled the casements. Damn it, he had let her grow cold – she was hugging herself, no doubt willing him to still his tongue.

'You are shivering. Come inside.'

'Yes. Now I must show you my mother's almanack.'

He lit half a dozen candles, revealing that the worst of the mess had been tidied away. Did she cast a curious glance towards the bed in the far corner? Its linen, at least, was fresh and clean. His notions of how this evening might proceed had swung like a pendulum – from a chaste exchange over academic tomes, to a night of lascivious revels. In the absence of London pastry cooks, he had assembled the simplest of meals: a game pie, bread, cheese, apples, and a dish of cherries with scalded cream. Both ate as they talked. She opened her mother's almanack, pointing to the crudely printed pages on which were written Widow Hart's crabbed and cryptic comments. Perplexed, he read of the death of a hound – and, more disconcertingly, of the widow's fears.

'What else do you know?'

She told him of the wound to her mother's head, and of the damage to the door latch for which no one could account; also of Nanny Seagoes' tale, that her mother had discovered the killer of a dog, and lived in fear of him ever since. And now Francis De Vallory's butchered body had been found. Darius was a party to it, she was certain.

'And all have De Angelo in common.' She pointed at a prophecy she had marked in the almanack with a tiny dot of red ink. The motto *'There shall be blood on the harvest corn,'* was printed below the date of Francis's death.

'Both my mother and Francis were sent these but Francis's was destroyed by his mother.' She held out a piece of paper, a verse addressed to Mistress Hart.

'That is monstrous,' he said after reading it, appalled by the venom of the missive. 'You must have been horrified.'

She nodded, a shadow of fear showing in her eyes. 'Nat, what do you make of this riddle?' Tabitha handed him the almanack, open at the page that bore a grotesque mask and verse titled, 'Who Am I?'

'Look, my mother attempted it and wrote "A Murderer?" below it.'

Nat read it with slow concentration. He looked up, fixing her with shining eyes. 'The origin of the word "riddle" is "dark saying" in Old English. It means veiled, like the Greek term "enigma" – "to speak obscurely". So I'm afraid "murderer" is too simple a solution.'

'Why so?'

'A riddle must have two aspects: a deceptive cloak masking an inner truth. "Murderer" lacks the twisting wordplay, the flourishing of the cloak being swept aside. I believe the solution is—'

'A riddle itself,' she interrupted. She took it back and read it out loud: *"For when bold mortals me descry, I at that very moment die."* At the moment we solve it and our curiosity ends, the riddle expires too. It is rather a dreadful jest. And yet so ingenious.'

'Yes. If the almanack writer is "D", he is jesting with those who ponder his identity. De Angelo *is* a riddle.'

'And we must solve it. So who writes these almanacks?' she asked. 'Surely they must be very learned scholars.'

He flicked through the pages, shaking his head. *'Vox Stellarum* – the voice of the stars. Maybe once upon a time great scholars wrote such stuff; but I doubt they do so now. The legendary astrologers, Old Francis Moore, Nostradamus, and the like, are all in their graves.'

He offered her the cherries; she picked one from its stalk, dousing it in cream.

'But my mother purchased this almanack every single year, and its advice was always different.'

'So it may have seemed; yet the compiler need only shuffle the mottos and dates. Ah, look – he's inserted the calendar changes here, the loss of eleven days next month. There is some skill here, but it is not, I suspect, drawn from a genuine horoscope. I should know; I have written plenty of chapbook predictions myself. Dream books, prophecies, prognostications – all pure balderdash.'

'How disappointing.'

'We are all gullible. Who does not want to know their future?'

Spitting out the last of the cherry stones, she counted them with her fingertip. 'Tinker, tailor, soldier, sailor, rich man, poor man, beggar man, thief. Ah – my destiny is to be a thief, it would seem.'

'Aha, Miss Light-fingers! Next you will tell me that cherry stones are a most accurate means of prognostication.'

She threw one of the stones at his face, laughing. 'So, what is your occupation to be, when you finally ripen from boy to man?'

He counted his cherry stones. 'Five. A rich man,' he said, with a smirk.

'Ha! A thief would like to know such a man.'

He made a play of pulling his pockets inside out. 'So plunder me.' He leaned back in his chair, eyes narrowed, challenging her.

'You have not climbed your great tree yet, you wastrel,' she said, unable to suppress a smile. 'Will you help me solve this puzzle?'

Putting the almanack down, he pulled out a large handbill; uncurling it, he fetched his ink and quill.

'Who, then, could be this "D", do you reckon?'

She bit her lip and looked out of the window at the darkening sky. 'Darius. Parson Dilks. All of the De Vallory family, of course: Sir John, Lady Daphne, and the doctor. Then there is Mistress Nell Dainty, who begrudged my mother's position as searcher and her cottage. But I find it hard to picture her wielding a bloody scythe, never mind compiling an almanack.'

She stared hard at the list of names he had inked on to the back of the playbill. 'None of it makes sense. What of D for dairymaid? Or here is another I had not thought of before – the dogman up at the kennels, Willis.'

Nat added Zusanna and Willis to the list. 'Certainly, the dogman must be worth a visit – we must learn how Towler died.'

She nodded. 'Nat, I still cannot comprehend how the coming year is described with such accuracy. Last Thursday there was a rain shower, just as predicted.'

'That is merely a random event. Loose enough arrows, and some will strike home.'

'But all this – this blood and doom and mischance? The prognostication for December is that the year will reach "A violent and bloody end.""

He picked up the almanack and perused a few pages, then looked at her keenly.

'You almost persuade me of your case: that someone has written this with a malevolent purpose . . . that this De Angelo appears to predict the future, but in fact brings these awful events to pass.'

'But who could do so, here in Netherlea? Who could conceive, and then write, such an almanack? Darius is not sufficiently educated. Dilks is unlikely – and he claims he was away from home when my mother was murdered. It is not in the doctor's character, and neither would he kill his own nephew. And as for Sir John, why would he murder his heir? Lady De Vallory I cannot believe capable. True, there is a dark stranger who wanders the woods, but he, of course, may be . . . you. And so, I'm afraid, may the compiler of the almanack.' She turned to his writing desk and picked up a freshly scribed page: 'The Bloody Tragedy of the Monster of Newgate' complete with a stomach-curdling description of the execution.

He snatched it from her hand. 'Don't look at that nonsense.'

Then came the question he was dreading.

'Nat, what business did you have with my mother?'

He reached for his tankard, knowing that she, of all people, would not swallow an easy lie.

'She was an old friend of my own mother's. I told you my mother was born in Netherlea. And I knew she was the searcher.'

'You knew she was the searcher?' A stony cast settled on her features. 'What did you want from her?'

'Information.' His mouth was dry. He took another long draught of ale, his mind in a jumble. The silence that followed forced him to add: 'About my own mother.'

She continued to watch him.

'And about me,' he heard himself muttering. Oh, this was too bad; she was drawing him out like an eel from a basket. And what if she was Saxton's informer? What if he had sent her to seduce him into error with her honeyed tongue? A sensation like liquid ice filled his veins.

'What was your mother's name?'

'Hannah Dove.' He raked his fingers through his hair. 'Tabitha, truly, I would rather not speak of it. Your mother helped me with a matter that was pertinent to me alone.'

'But it may have caused her death,' she protested. 'Are you the man whom the sexton saw reading the parish book in the vestry a while back?'

'Me?' He did have a dim recollection of being disturbed in his perusal by a grimy, bent-spined fellow. 'It may have been. They are public documents?'

'No, they are not.'

'Then I was ignorant of the custom – that is all.'

'I am sorry, Nat. Forgive my ill temper. I am still grieving for my mother.' For an instant, she looked so heartbroken that he seized her hand in sympathy. She squeezed it softly in return. Instead of matters of suspicion, they broke off, and talked a while of London; of the lamplit alleys leading off Covent Garden's piazza, where they had both frequented the same coffee houses and taverns.

'Your conundrum was not so very difficult to solve. "Where fodder is traded"; that is the Haymarket. So when did you see me there?'

'Last season, at the opening of *The Modish Couple*. Seeing you here, without your silks and jewels, I did at first wonder if it were truly you. But there is something remarkable about your face.' He cocked his head to one side and appraised her. 'I might even like you better now, without your paint and feathers.'

'You perverse creature.' Yet she looked pleased. 'That was a remarkable night. My friend Poll had strung pearls in my hair, and I had a new gown of flowered silk; I was quite in love with it.'

'You were standing beneath the great chandelier. Every eye was on you. I swore never to forget you – and now, like a miracle, here you are.'

She pressed his fingers and leaned forward very close, her lips parted – but, like a blockhead, he prattled on. Later, he calculated that was the exact moment he should have kissed her. 'You had that old fellow always with you then – that naval-seeming man.'

'Robert Tate.'

'Was that the old goat's name? He was in no wise good enough for you.'

She shook her head good-naturedly. 'Of course not. And, no doubt, you are?'

'I am.'

With a quick movement she raised his hand to her lips.

'Nat, you are just what I need at present. And I confess: it was

Robert Tate I was to meet in Chester on Friday; yet I came home
with you instead. But before we are distracted – and you are a most
distracting fellow – I need you to apply your clever brain to determine whether any crime was committed against my mother. And,
when you have done so . . . perhaps a reward may be due?'

'I will do all I can to help you,' he said. 'I swear it with my
heart.'

They looked directly into each other's faces; he felt a little breathless He had now a task to perform for her and told himself he
would not fail. As for waiting for her to oblige him, he would wait
until the Last Judgement. She looked on him with her frank brown
eyes; then, without a word, she withdrew her hand and stood to
fetch her cloak, and went to the door, refusing his offer to escort
her back to the cottage.

'I wish you would not go alone. Do take care, Tabitha.'

'I will. I am taking care. You see,' she said, 'the only suspect
capable of all these enigmatical intrigues is you, Nat Starling – or
might my mother more rightly have known you as another "D",
Nathaniel Dove?'

EIGHTEEN

A Riddle

At once to describe my name and my race,
I often attend on the huntsman at chase;
I also can find it is equally pleasant
To wait on the squire, or even a peasant;
But when I conceit myself most highly blessed,
Is when by a lady I'm fondly caressed:
Yet many a child seems to take a delight
To treat me with constant ill-humour and spite.
On me you may always for safety depend,
And consider me both your protector and friend.

The 24th day of August 1752

St Bartholomew

Luminary: Sun rises 22 minutes after 5.
Observation: A trine of the Sun and Saturn.
Prognostication: Men's chief practices will be fraud
and deceit.

'Perhaps Towler left us a trail to follow,' said Tabitha two days
later, as they paused to survey the palatial extent of Sir John's
kennels. These were grander by far than many of his tenants'
homes; a range of brick buildings backing on to a high-walled
exercise yard, with drinking fountains and feeding pens. Reaching
the iron gate, Tabitha cautiously peered through for any sign of Sir
John. Thank the stars, he seemed not to be about.

She had decided it was time to test Nat as an ally. The name of
Dove still worried her – and he was clever, too, which made him
dangerous. 'Would you take the lead in questioning the dogman?'
she asked him. 'Invent some tale or other about the pack.'

'My pleasure.' He gave a confident little bow. He looked quite
the gentleman, too, in russet-brown velvet and glass-polished boots.

Nat rang the bell, and a short, skew-eyed fellow in a leather jerkin
admitted them into a circling mass of barking hounds. He stepped
into the thick of them, with the manner of a gentleman not to be
refused.

'Willis, is it? I come to take a tour, on behalf of Lord Robbins
of Cambridgeshire. You have heard of the Cam Valley Pack? He
has a fancy to make a cross with one of your lord's best hounds.'

Willis commanded the hounds to stay back, and began to show
their points, while Nat complimented every facility, from the great
stove that warmed the interior in winter to the maze of sleeping and
feeding rooms. Tabitha at first stepped warily, but every inch of the
kennels was cleanly swept and swabbed. In any case, her mother's
rough skirts were rags beside Nat's gold-buttoned coat; she had
made a dozen trials of ribbons, kerchiefs and ruffles that morning,

but there was nothing for it but to stiffen her backbone and hold her head high.

In the she-dogs' straw-room, Tabitha watched with distaste as the brood-bitches placidly panted, pups suckling and squirming over their bodies. Nat called the dogman over.

'Lord Robbins has heard report of a celebrated hound. Towler, is it? He is considering a cross with one of his own dams.'

Willis's seamed face looked suddenly cast down. 'You come on a goose chase then, sir, if you be looking for Towler. He were destroyed last Easter.'

Nat shook his head incredulously. 'How so, if he was such a valuable hound?'

'Poisoned he were, sir. Some'll tell you otherwise, but that's the sworn truth. A king of dogs, he were – could follow a scent faster than the wind. Whoever done it is as wicked as any man-murderer.'

'Yet how might such a deed have been accomplished?'

'Someone must have fed him a poisoned titbit, sir – that's my reckoning. Towler was too friendly a fellow, see. And his Lordship kept him half-starved so he always showed fine form, with his ribs on view.'

'But if a stranger came to such a well-guarded kennel,' Nat asked amiably, 'surely the alarm would have been raised?'

The old fellow wiped his brow with a rag. 'That's just it, sir. The day Towler died there was a heap of visitors, on account of the new litter. They was all here, family, neighbours, even blood connoisseurs – all come here to look the litter over and raise a toast to old Towler. Aye, even your mother come along, Miss Hart. The bitch what whelped, Gladsome, was in poor fettle, so we fetched Mistress Dainty to bring a poultice, and Mistress Hart come along with her.'

Tabitha smoothed away all expression. 'My mother?' she repeated. 'I did not know she helped Mistress Dainty tend the dam.'

'Aye, they saved her life,' answered Willis.

Nat picked up a wriggling pup and inspected its muzzle. 'That fellow Darius, who has been arrested over Master Francis's death. Did he ever come here?'

'Him? I shouldn't let a rascal like that near my dogs.'

'You are sure it was not a sudden rupture or distemper?' Nat set the puppy down.

'No, sir; you see, Towler had a queer smell to him when I found him. Poor old fellow, he were perfumed like a Duchess's lapdog.'

Just then, the bell at the gate jangled insistently – with a plummeting inward sensation, Tabitha caught sight of Sir John pulling impatiently at the bell-rope. What poxed luck! As Willis hurried off to admit him, she urgently grasped Nat's sleeve. 'I should rather Sir John did not see me.' She noticed the door to a storeroom standing ajar and, stepping inside, she motioned silence to Nat with a finger to her lips. Ignoring his bafflement, she pulled the door to.

Such was the outbreak of barking and yelping in the yard that she scarcely heard Sir John enter the kennels, but, after Willis had commanded the hounds to be still, Sir John's voice rang out in his usual bombastic tone.

'Nathaniel. What brings you here?'

Nathaniel? She tensed to listen, intrigued by this intimate form of address, as Nat recited his tale of searching for new blood for Lord Robbins' pack. He was playing his part well, she granted him that, sounding remarkably easy as he spun his lies to the master of Bold Hall. Soon the two men's conversation grew less strident, and she could no longer catch every word – no matter, as the conversation dwelt only upon Towler's merits. Then the word 'Francis' reached her, and she crept an inch closer to the door and, moving too quickly, banged against a shovel. Flustered, she reached out and caught the handle mid-fall.

'I suppose you believe Francis's loss advances your own cause,' Sir John said testily.

'No, sir. Not one whit. '

'You left the funeral early. It was not respectful. And I hear bad reports of you.'

'That pains me, sir.'

'Understand this, Nathaniel: my wife is near mad with grief – and my brother has a sickness that even he cannot cure. The timing is crucial, do you hear?'

'I do, sir. I leave for London soon, and can stay away until you send for me.'

Tabitha almost flung wide the door. London? The arrant fellow was deserting her – after all she had done for him by postponing her own escape.

There was a long pause.

'No need for that. Come and go as you will. But don't speak a word to anyone, mind? Remember your oath.'

'I do, sir.'

'Good day, then, Nathaniel.'
'Good day, Sir John.'

After a long silence, Nat tapped at the door and she emerged, dusting off her gown. He attempted a tight smile. 'Well, lady? Your antics continue to astonish me.'

She laughed, but it sounded hollow. 'I assure you the surprise is mutual. Here am I, attempting to avoid your most particular friend, Sir John.'

He raised his brows quizzically.

'He will not leave me alone. He seeks an assignation,' she confessed, with self-mocking humour. 'But it won't do. I will not see him.' She expected him to be amused, but instead he turned upon her a glance of absolute coldness. Grasping her arm and steering her to the gate, he muttered, 'I need a drink.'

Tabitha had vowed never to set foot in the inn's parlour again. She claimed it was too warm within, and they took one of the benches on the High Street instead. They both drank deep, and she puzzled over his change of temper; then, unable to bear the silence, she could not resist baiting him a little.

'I did not know you were so well acquainted with Sir John.'

He answered gruffly: 'I might say the same of you. I am his tenant; we converse when I call on him.'

'Be wary of the old scoundrel,' she said with sincerity. '"Serve a great man and know sorrow", as they say.'

If she had hoped to invite a confidence, this strategy failed: Nat's chin lifted and he looked the other way. 'I find him cordial enough. And, as for what I believe you overheard – I support his bid for Parliament, that is all. It is a matter of my private business.'

She felt chastened, and unfairly too.

After a long, churning silence, he asked, 'So, what do you know of Mistress Dainty?'

She felt dispirited, feeling her trust in him ebb away. 'It could be that my mother witnessed her harming the dog; she may be the mysterious "D", I don't know. She distils remedies too – but why would she poison a hound?'

Once again, they both lapsed into silence until, at last, he broke it.

'I had meant to tell you I must leave for a week or two. But first I must hear Darius's committal at Chester assizes. Are you going?'

She still found it hard to stomach his departure; especially after she had given up Robert, and a new gown and hat, for his sake.

'Yes. Joshua believes I may be questioned as a witness to the condition of Francis's body. When is it?'

'Michaelmas. Only remember, soon we shall lose the eleven days; the second of September is followed by the fourteenth.'

'Is it not all nonsense? To confuse everyone thus.' She looked over to the large notice nailed to the door of the Estate Office, where, as usual, two or three estate workers were slowly spelling out the proclamation. The steward of Bold Hall had given a rule for every particular case affected by the calendar: how wages would be paid and tenancies arranged, and the terms by which apprenticeships should be drawn up.

'The nonsense is that we are eleven days adrift from most of Europe,' said Nat. 'A man might travel abroad and change his time on six occasions in a day. But as for confusion – yes, that is inevitable.'

At the barmaid's approach with a jug, Tabitha waved her away and stood. Villagers were arriving on the High Street as dinnertime approached. God forbid that Joshua should see her in company with Nat Starling.

As they strolled in silence to the river, she picked up a branch and swatted at the foliage. The hedgerow was full of signs of the summer's end: the green nubs of blackberries, tired tansy, a froth of campion. How dare he treat her so casually? They reached the point where she must take the path into the woods while he continued to Eglantine Hall.

He turned to her, asking testily, 'How long can you avoid Sir John?'

'I am doing my best – but he carries great authority hereabouts.'

At that he sighed, as if he carried the weight of the world.

'What troubles you, Nat?'

He looked away irritably. 'May I borrow the almanack?' he asked. 'I should like to make a fair copy.'

'No. I should rather not let it out of my hand. Find another. You might still obtain a copy of last year's edition at the inn.'

'Are you angry with me, Tabitha?'

'Yes, naturally I am angry with you. You are a dunderhead after all,' she told him.

'Am I? Why?'

'A true friendship must be based upon honest dealing.'

He grasped her hands in his and stroked her fingers so gently that her bones melted with pleasure.

'That is a novel plan. I will try it. Only tell me we can still continue as friends.'

She glanced up at his face, for only a moment. It would have been easy to take one step forward and press her lips hard against his. Instead she stepped jauntily away from him.

'You will come and see me, won't you? Will Saturday be agreeable?'

She nodded, inwardly counting the long days, and made a curt farewell, only to castigate herself for a damned fool, once he was out of sight.

NINETEEN

A Herb Garden

What's the regretful herb (1), or the most wise herb (2),
Or the herb where ships may be? (3)
The victor's herb (4), or the King's own coin (5),
Or a bloom for our Blessed Lady? (6)

What's the never-sweet herb (7), or the friar's cowl herb (8),
Or a match made in glittering ore? (9)
The duration herb (10), or the coin-making herb (11),
Or the herb that can ease any sore? (12)

The 24th day of August 1752

St Bartholomew

Luminary: Day shortened by 3 hours and 32 minutes.
Observation: At 3 of the morning Venus
is with the Moon.
Prognostication: A most remarkable discovery
to those of clear sight.

T he sound of a young man's cheery voice reached Tabitha
through the shrubbery. Devil take it, a messenger in the livery
of Bold Hall was standing on the cottage threshold, talking
to Jennet. Tabitha pressed herself between two prickly hawthorns
until the boy had finished his business and strode past her, whistling
a tuneless air.

Once inside the cottage she snatched up the letter and read it
with impatience. It only confirmed what she had expected to
hear:

> *Tabitha,*
> *I must see you without delay. I trust you might spare some*
> *compassion for me.*
> *I await your choice of rendezvous and hour.*
> *Sir John De Vallory.*

When Tabitha thrust the letter deep into the fire, Jennet looked
up from a pile of half-peeled pippins and gasped. 'Are you allowed
to destroy something sent by Sir John?'

'Why not? He does not own me.'

To her astonishment, Jennet burst out weeping and threw down
her knife so hard that it skittered across the floor.

'It is all well for you,' she said, raising a face wet with tears.
'You have Mr Starling running after you as well as Father – and
now Sir John himself. While I—' She broke into sobs again, alarming
little Bess, who began to bleat in sympathy. Fierce with misery,

Jennet cried, 'What will happen to Darius?' She sank her face on to the table, crying, 'If only I might die as well.'

Tabitha sat down and held her tight, stroking her hair. What a capacity for making water this girl's eyes had. There was no helping her, she supposed, for Jennet's first love would soon swing by the neck at Chester gaol; even worse, her own father was to arrange it. Jennet must never know that Tabitha had delivered Darius up to the law – though privately, she had no regrets at all.

'Shh,' she whispered against Jennet's scalding cheek. 'You are too good for a man such as him.'

Jennet jerked away. 'What then? Must I stay here and rot with Father in this . . . pigsty?'

This was said with such a sense of injustice that Tabitha turned aside to hide a rueful smile. Oh, to be a maid of fifteen and in love, she thought. Was there ever a more stupid creature?

'You ran away to London as soon as you could. You weren't a prisoner like me. At least you had a life of fashion and – and freedom!'

When she had quieted a little, Tabitha stroked Jennet's shoulders and looked seriously into her face. 'If you must know, there was many a day I lamented ever leaving Netherlea. I left behind warmth, a place of safety and the only friends I had ever known. Did you know I was robbed by a woman, a procuress, within two days of arriving in the city? She stole my money and, more importantly, my liberty. I had to work for her like a galley slave. You think I had fine dresses and admirers? More like stained shifts and a new customer knocking every hour. That was when I prayed I might die.'

Jennet stared at her with round, red-rimmed eyes. 'I never knew,' she croaked.

Suddenly, the disappointment of the day, the lack of ease between Nat and herself, left Tabitha too weary to continue. With great effort, she succeeded in raising a bright smile. 'Anyway, I ran away – with another girl named Poll. I'll tell you more of it another time.'

Bess had cautiously pottered over, and now grasped Tabitha's skirts. On an impulse, Tabitha hugged both Jennet and Bess, one arm tight around each of them. Were all men rogues? she wondered. And what in Heaven's name would become of the three of them?

'Listen. All may not yet be lost. My mother was in fear of a person she called 'D' before she died; the same person who killed

Sir John's dog, Towler. Your father is convinced that Darius alone is to blame, yet Darius was not at the kennels that day – while Nell Dainty was. Now, you look very pale, Jennet. I wonder if you have a bout of green sickness? Shall we go to Mistress Dainty for a little gossip and a remedy?'

Inside the stillroom at Bold Hall, though, they found only Jane.

'Nell is over at the doctor's while the family are in mourning. She told him what you said, Tabitha; that you have no time to help him with his medicines at present.'

'Oh, did she now?'

Evidently, Nell had chosen to lie, and to pluck this rich plum for herself. Retracing their way to the gilded gates of Bold Hall, they came to where the doctor's house stood in seclusion. A former dower house, it was the oldest building in the village, said to have been built by crusaders from remnants left by the Roman soldiery. Now, seeing it for the first time in years, Tabitha thought it charming: an irregular dwelling of weathered, honey-grey stone. The lawn to the front was a circle of velvety green, and an ancient rose of blushing white rambled around the studded oak door and high-arched windows. They took a narrow path to the back of the house and Tabitha halted for a moment at the garden's edge, breathing in the warm scent of lavender, mint and myriad blossoms, a *pot-pouri* of clean, sweet scents.

In the lower half of the garden, the doctor had created herb beds inside low squares of box hedge; there stood neat bushes of rosemary, pink mallow, tarragon, dill and lemon balm. The further reaches of the garden, hedged all around with laurels, were devoted to lettuce and purslane, and peas and beans clinging to hoops of cane. Banks of irises stood in purple bonnets above the frilled suns of marigolds and spikes of yellow thyme. Only Nell Dainty's bow-backed figure spoiled this Eden as she harvested herbs into a basket, her eyes hidden by a linen sunbonnet. Truly, it would be difficult to imagine more pleasant work on such a day.

Nell caught sight of them and scowled. 'What do you want? I heard about you, out drinking this morning – carousing with that strange fellow that seems to ply no honest trade.'

Tabitha managed to conjure a disarming smile, holding tight on to Bess's leading strings as the child strained to pick the colourful blossoms. 'And a good day to you, Nell. I pray we don't disturb your labours, but Constable Saxton has sent me in search of one of your remedies.'

'What's he after, then?'

'It is for Jennet. Might we beg a sup of water, and you shall hear?'

'If it's for Miss Jennet, I might. Only be sharp about it.'

Tabitha glanced towards the house standing in sleepy stillness, most of the shutters closed and drawn curtains hiding the shadowy interior. This was the one house in the village that Tabitha most wished to peep inside.

But today, disappointingly, Nell led them not into the house but to a separate edifice at the bottom of the garden. At first glance, it looked like a summerhouse, but, on entering, Tabitha recognized it as another stone-flagged stillroom. A glass alembic had pride of place on the stove, distilling a herbal cordial, drop by precious drop. Shelves held rows of bottles, filled with distillations, liquors and essences. With ill grace, Nell pointed to a vat of water, and she and Jennet drank greedily from the ladle.

Tabitha nodded graciously to Nell. 'I wanted also to thank you, Nell – I have just heard from Willis that you helped my mother cure one of Sir John's bitches at Eastertide.'

'You've got that the wrong way about; your mother may have showed her face, but it was my poultice what did the trick.'

Let the crone have it her own way, Tabitha thought, biting her tongue. 'But I could barely believe what Willis told me of old Towler. How on earth might such a wicked deed have been accomplished?'

As Tabitha had hoped, the question appealed to Nell's vanity, and she leaned against the table, her thick arms crossed. 'I'd wager someone lured that hound with a tempting morsel.'

'Willis said he fell into a fit – and stank like perfume. Could it be poison?'

'What else? I'd wager it were another huntsman, grown jealous of the Bold Hall pack.'

'So what did you see of Towler's death?'

Nell's face grew sour with the disappointment of a rumour-monger absent from a public outrage.

'Well, I weren't exactly there on the spot. But by all accounts he was poisoned. Your mother went to look at him before the rest of them came, but I were that busy I never even saw the hound.'

Tabitha believed her. Seeing she was wasting time, she changed direction. 'Is it true that the doctor is sick?'

Nell's head jerked up, with a sharp expression. 'Who told you that?'

'I heard it from Sir John's own lips.'

Nell's thin mouth pursed tight, as if struggling to keep the gossip stoppered up. Then she burst forth.

'The poor doctor. A saint he is, out at all hours tending to any poor soul as needs him. And so considering – he'd rather dose you from his own bottle than give a twinge of pain. And all the while, he is sicker than most of his patients – his heart's blood is failing. That puffed-up brother of his won't hear of it; he says he is the only one who ails, what with Master Francis dead. As for the doctor – it will all be over by Christmas, or so I hear.'

A sudden sound from the garden made the women stand silent and alert; the next moment, the doctor himself appeared, leading Bess by the hand.

'Look who I found, chasing butterflies through my sweet peas.' From near the hem of the doctor's robe, Bess looked up at them with an expression of mischief.

'Pray forgive us, Doctor. The naughty little maid must have slipped away while we consulted Nell.'

Tabitha bobbed to him and grasped hold of Bess's sticky hand. It was true, the doctor did have a haunted look; his skin was fading like old parchment, and his shoulders bowed like a packman's. Could he be another of De Angelo's victims?

'You are in luck. Let me take a look at you, girl.' The doctor motioned for Jennet to sit down in the light of a pretty arched window; he felt the girl's brow and pronounced it clammy.

'Close your eyes. No need to be agitated.' Jennet played her part well, giving every sign of the sleepiness and vagueness of mind common to that curious ailment. When questioned, she described her strange appetites, unnatural yearnings and melancholy.

Nell interrupted with her own diagnosis: 'All she needs is a sturdy village lad to stir up her womb and give her a brood of babies.'

'Is that a rash?' the doctor murmured, gently lifting her hair to feel the pulse at her white throat. Finally, he inspected the blue veins on the inside of her wrists.

'Chlorisis,' he said to himself. 'Morbus virgineus. Do you sleep heavily at night?' he asked his patient.

Jennet nodded, her lips pressed tight together.

'She is growing new bones,' Tabitha said.

'Sleep is good for a mild case of green sickness,' the doctor concluded. 'Nell, go fetch a small vial of Black Drop.'

In search of the remedy, Nell disappeared in the direction of the house.

The doctor watched fondly as Tabitha lifted Bess on to her hip. 'She is very fair,' he said, touching a flaxen curl where it had fallen free from Bess's cap.

'Do not be fooled, sir. She is a naughty little monkey.'

'What of your plans to return to London, Tabitha?'

'They are postponed, sir.'

'And your duties at Bold Hall?'

'I am no longer needed, now the family are in mourning.'

'Ah. Can you read and calculate Roman numerals – for that is how my accounts are arranged?'

'Certainly I can.'

'So might you now assist me? I am not as strong as I was and would like to get my pharmacopoeia in good order by Christmas.'

Nell had just returned and began to bang about the room, dropping heavy implements. Tabitha felt immense pleasure in replying, 'It would be my pleasure to assist you, Doctor.'

'Well, I will need a quiet spell to unpack my boxes. Ah, there are scarcely any days this September – and then I'll be at the Michaelmas Sessions for I don't know how long. So, to be safe, what say you begin at the start of October? You do understand the new calendar?'

'I believe so, sir. That will be just more than a month, then.' Privately, she cast a prayer of thanks to Nat, whose explanations had at last led her to understand the mathematics of the matter.

'Quite so. Very well. For each day I require you, would sixpence suffice?'

Her spirits rose like a lark on the breeze; she agreed at once, overjoyed at the prospect. As Tabitha paid Nell for her medicine, the doctor finally glanced at Jennet.

'Wait until the new moon before you dose yourself, my dear. The end of the Dog Days is an auspicious time for medicines.'

Jennet nodded and curtsied, but it was Tabitha who received a dry but gratifying squeeze of her hand.

TWENTY

A Riddle

One night, a party round the fire I found
Pleased with the cheerful blaze it cast around;
The foremost was a tall and lively lad,
Nimble of thought he seemed, and lightly clad;
A radiant nymph did next the circle grace
Sparkling and brilliant, fairest of her race:
A sober matron then the circle pressed,
Who seemed the guardian of a younger guest;
Apart from all a dreaded warrior sate,
Whose brows overshadowed eyes of vengeful hate:
A father joined the throng in belted pride
And four fair daughters graced his reverent side:
Next I could mark a greedy dull old beau
Who strove, with foppish pride, a ring to show.
Come join me in a heavenly turn,
These famous wanderers' names to learn.

The 29th day of August 1752

Saint Bartholomew

Luminary: The Sun runs faster than
the year by 3 hours and 14 minutes.
Observation: The shooting starts of Saint Laurence
in the east.
Prognostication: Friendship and amity
amongst neighbours.

'I promised I would help you.' With a flourish, Nat waved his hand towards an extraordinary collection of papers tacked across the wall of his chamber at Eglantine Hall. Names, pictures and memoranda were displayed like ragged sunrays around the heart of it: the *Vox Stellarum* almanack. On the cover was a dog cowering beneath a vast Wheel of Fortune, spinning in the sky.

Tabitha's eyes shone, absorbing the whirlwind of information. 'So you did obtain an almanack from the inn. How long did this take you?'

He would have liked to confide the truth; that over the past week it had become a mania that engaged his every waking moment. Instead, he said, 'It is a most intriguing puzzle. I have concluded there are two men working together – Darius who is the minion and De Angelo the master.'

Pulling a red ribbon from her hair, she pinned it between a paper bearing the date of Francis's death and the woodcut of the scything men circling a corn stook. Nat had connected other facts this way, using string, laces and even a tendril of ivy drawn in from the window. He approached to help – their hands touched, and she sprang back as if he had scalded her.

'I have a notion,' he said quickly, 'that the reason for Towler's death was to test a dose of poison. What do you say?'

She pressed her lips together thoughtfully. 'Yes. But poison intended for whom? Neither my mother nor Francis were poisoned. And yet . . .' She removed the paper bearing the name Mistress

Dainty. 'I called upon Nell Dainty and believe we can disregard her. Even better, the doctor has offered me work making accounts of his medicines. Oh, Nat, he is ill. I fear he may be this poisoner's next victim. I intend to keep a close watch upon him, and anyone else who calls.'

He watched her slyly as she studied the papers. Yes, he certainly liked her even better in rustic dress than in paint and pearls.

He moved in closer beside her as she continued speaking. 'But even if the poisoning was to test the dose, why choose Towler?'

'What if the connection is this?' he said. 'Two of Sir John's most beloved possessions have been destroyed – his heir, and his hound.'

Tabitha nodded, slowly. 'So who is it that hates him so violently? A rival for his Parliamentary seat, perhaps?'

'The fellow he is standing against lives down in Northamptonshire. If he sent an assassin to Netherlea, the fellow would have been remarked upon as a stranger.'

'You say Sir John has borne two losses – and, if his brother is being poisoned too, that is a further blow to him. But still, I remember what Nanny Seagoes said – that my mother would not go to Sir John with her fears. I wonder why?'

'Do you trust Sir John?'

'Me? Not at all,' she replied smartly.

'But you like him? He certainly has a regard for you.' His voice whined jealously in his own ears.

'Nat, am I on trial? From what I overheard, you are his great friend, not I.'

That stung him. 'Forgive me.'

Her returning smile might have melted stone. He watched her, unable to take his eyes from her features.

Dear gods, he was indeed a captive of Venus. His attempts at self-discipline had lately collapsed; after visiting the kennels, he had stumbled to the tavern in search of oblivion. Almost at once, Zusanna had slunk down beside him, her creamy flesh pressing hot against his thigh and elbow.

'La, Mr Starling, tell me you are not still moping after that doxy Tabitha Hart,' she cooed. 'We all seen you together – but she's dallying with the constable, you know.'

He did not answer her, but she continued, sinking her mouth to his ear to confide.

'And I'll tell you what no one else will. That by-blow of hers could be anyone's – aye, and I mean anyone's – but she's not Joshua's child. It's common knowledge all round here, he never did have the pleasure. That's why he is always hanging on her petticoat strings, hoping to unlace them.'

The news that the pretty little maid was not the constable's daughter had at first brought Nat relief. Yet, after Zusanna had reluctantly left the inn, a young fellow from Bold Hall had called over to him. 'You's talking about that Tabitha Hart? I am forever calling at that cottage on Sir John's business, but she'll not take his letters. Still, I know Sir John. He won't take no for an answer.'

Since that day, he had known it was only a matter of time before Tabitha became Sir John's. He did have one small compensation. This last week, it had come suddenly to him that this affair of the De Angelo almanack might be his salvation. For was he not a writer, and was this not a story? It was a blood-curdling tale of a great house under attack, of gruesome secrets, puzzles and poisons. True, it might not be quite honourable to wring information from Tabitha, but he could not ignore the extraordinary luck of his being here, at the very heart of it all. He had sent a letter off with the idea of it to Quare of Chandos Lane, and a reply had arrived almost by return. Nat was in luck, the print-seller had said – he was in need of a colourful story. With it came a contract, promising an advance payment of ten whole guineas. In return, Nat must present himself at Quare's office at the soonest opportunity – though first, of course, he must see Darius indicted.

Nat was in a secret ecstasy; he even told himself he might advance his courtship, once he was a celebrated man of letters. But to proceed with the story he had to know everything about the whole affair. The key was Tabitha – the searcher of the dead and, in his opinion, the only intelligent witness.

Through the fine oriel windows the sun sent copper-gold rays spilling across his wall of papers. Nat turned to Tabitha; it was time to fish for facts. 'Tell me, are there any other persons you suspect of being De Angelo?' He recalled she had said the doctor seemed more a potential victim than malefactor.

'I am most uneasy about Dilks,' Tabitha said.

'I made inquiries and he was in Chester that night your mother died.'

'Yes, but as you told me yourself, Darius was near her cottage and is no doubt his instrument, attacking my mother on his instruction.'

'A worthy point,' he conceded.

'Remember, Darius told me he would never stand trial; he said it was written in the stars. He is one of those swindlers who takes money for reading cards and fortunes. He is our strongest link to De Angelo.'

'And if Darius provided the muscular strength to perform these attacks, then anyone, weak, womanly or both, could be driving him to it.'

Tabitha lifted her hand to her head and winced. 'True. What of Lady De Vallory herself? She attacked me; some say she has lost her mind. She is educated, too – the daughter of a Doctor of Divinity. And, I have heard folk say, she is some relation to Dilks.'

He inked his quill and wrote down what she said beside Lady Daphne's name. 'And what of me?' he teased. 'For I believe you said that I must join the list.'

She turned to him, steadfast and grave. 'In that case, why would you help me?'

With a qualm, he remembered his contract with Mr Quare. 'A rake's game,' he quipped. 'To draw you in closer and possess you.'

She smiled and drew away.

'I am ravenous,' she said brightly and, sitting at his table, she did full justice to a pork pie, cheese and apples. Having little appetite himself, he fetched candles to the table; their amber glow seemed to pull the two of them closer, into an island of light. For an instant he fancied he caught her looking over his shoulder towards his bed. But when he looked back again she was smiling modestly at the open pages of the almanack.

'Have you seen the prophecy for September?' she asked.

'Yes. It seems largely to be about the calendar change.'

Tabitha opened her mother's copy, and read out loud from the Prognostications:

'"*I predict that what some do call this Grave-Robbery of Time will bring mighty Confusion and Loss, so mark well the Days in your Almanack. Crafty Wrongdoers will escape Justice, thanks to the blindness of the Fools who stalk them. And may the Fools be condemned while the Crafty triumph.*" Do you understand that as a challenge?' Tabitha asked.

She was as sharp as a razor, he decided. 'That we are the blind fools? His arrogance is remarkable.'

'It is a warning to be careful, Nat,' she said. 'Some in this village need only see those papers on your wall to be convinced that you are De Angelo.'

He glanced over to the wall; in the flickering candlelight, he saw it with the constable's eyes. It did indeed look like the creation of a madman, and a guilty one at that.

At the end of the evening she consented to his accompanying her home; he felt himself walking a good foot taller as they picked their way down the broken-flagged driveway. Wednesday the third of September, he mused, would be an historic night, famed over eons, in which human time would take a great leap forward. True, the universe would not alter; but England's puny inhabitants would at last follow time in line with the sun. Just before the ruined arch that marked the boundary of Eglantine Hall, he stopped, and they looked up at the heavens.

'How far away is the moon, Nat?' she asked.

'A mere two hundred and thirty thousand miles from the earth.'

'Could it be lived upon?'

'Well it certainly has valleys, mountains and other signs of natural geography. But sadly, a journey to the moon is not possible. Think, even at the rate of twenty miles a day, it would take more than thirty years to reach it. And there are no inns upon the way, nor much entertainment on arrival.'

He saw the gleam of her smile in the dark.

'D'you see that tiny red star?' he asked. 'That is Mars, pulsing like a beacon. Now, look to your left. If you watch carefully, we might see the shooting stars of St Lawrence.'

A tingling cold was rising from the ground. Tabitha pulled her shawl tight, and he slipped his own arm tentatively around her waist.

'Look past that bright star,' he murmured. 'Vega is its name.'

If the meteor shower appears now, he told himself, she would be his. He dropped his head close to her, closing his eyes as he smelled her hair and skin and moving his fingers minutely over the taut fabric around her waist.

'Ah,' she cried. He looked up and caught a glimpse of a long tail of silver flying eastwards through the night sky.

'I missed it.'

'It was beautiful,' she said, pressing closer to him as they moved on towards the wood. A lucky sign, he told himself. But maybe it was lucky only if he had seen it himself. Devil take him, was he also being lured by predictions now?

They came into the shelter of the trees. It was velvety dark; they had only each other to hold on to. In time they reached the shining breadth of the river, the banks crowded with swaying black foliage. Nat offered her a hand to lead her across the stepping stones.

'All the farmer's men swear they will not follow the new style,' she said.

'And thus seek to add eleven days to their span of life? As the great Newton says, it matters not which clocks and stars we use to measure it; true time flows equably onwards, just as this river does.'

For a moment they paused, balancing on the flat rocks at the centre of the star-glancing water. Then he helped her up to the firm earth of the bank but did not let go of her hand.

'Yet it's a pretty conceit, is it not, to add eleven days to a life? Eleven days, two hundred and sixty-four hours, or – wait a moment – fifteen thousand eight hundred and forty minutes. If I could add those minutes to my life, what would I do with them? If I knew they were a gift, a supernumerary bonus, unsullied by habit and routine . . .' He pulled her close to him, closing his eyes again.

'A new you?' she asked, with a hint of mockery.

'A new me. Clean of habits and pure of heart.'

'You sound dull already . . .'

He opened his eyes. Both their eyes gleamed in the darkness.

'Tabitha, I could be so much more than I am now. I could write stuff that would set my name in the Book of Fame. If I was worthy, I would rise with the lark, write poetry to rival the nightingale's sweetness. In eleven days, I might find my better self.'

'You can do that anyhow, whatever the date. Begin tomorrow.'

'Ah, I have an excuse. I have another commission at present, and I need to earn my bread. After that, perhaps. And you? If you were given a benefice of eleven days, in which any wonderful, magical event might occur – what would that be?'

A troubled expression moved across her face; for some time, she did not speak. Finally she said, 'Everything I wanted before seems so paltry now. I'll think on it awhile.'

At her gate they both hesitated; then she reached up and brushed his cheek with her rose-soft lips. In a trice, the darkness had taken her, as she disappeared up the path and into the cottage.

TWENTY-ONE

A Riddle

I am an enchanter and soon can create,
A magical spell from invisible air,
I give to the prodigal son an estate,
And to those who are childless a strong lusty heir.

For pining maidens I abate their woe
And make faithless lovers woo their charms,
And on trembling cowards I bestow,
Victory's glory in glittering arms.

To the sick I promise health and ease
And to the grieving I grant a passing spell,
That the dead do walk and talk again
And unspoken wishes finally tell.

To the beggar I a bounty give
And to the lawyer monstrous fees
I grant the criminal hope to live
When on the gallows I bring reprieve.

To conjure up time is my transient power,
Yet my whole duration lasts not half an hour.

The 2nd to the 13th day of September 1752

Annihilated from the Calendar

According to the Act of Parliament the Old Style
of Calendar ceases here, and the New Style takes
place; and consequently the next Day, which in
the Old Account would have been the 3rd, is now
to be called the 14th so that all the intermediate
nominal Days from the 2nd to the 14th are omitted,
or rather annihilated from this Year and this
Month contains no more than 19 Days.

N at is careering along a highway in a carriage of the most
modern style, with well-sprung wheels and a lining of
nail-punched leather. At last he has a great prize at his
fingers' ends. Awaiting him in London is the printing press in which
his scribbled words are at this very moment being transformed;
inked, printed, folded, bundled, cried up by hawkers, and sold for
cash. His story, complete with shocking illustrations, will soon pierce
the minds of thousands of citizens, like a hail of inebriating darts.

As the left-hand wheels of the carriage jerk violently upwards,
he fumbles for the strap; but the vehicle rights itself without slowing
its momentum one whit. In his mind, scenes of absurd satisfaction
unfold. He walks among a fashionable crowd at the Playhouse, and
overhears, 'There – that is him. The man of the day.' He is invited
to private clubs, admitted to esoteric societies; there are countless
toasts raised to his name. And best of all, there is the marvel of the
fresh-inked paper itself – in coffee houses, on breakfast tables and
in servants' halls and low taverns – upon which his own name is
writ in black on white. He knows that he stands on the cusp, and
the intoxication of it is more dizzying than any liquor.

Another great crack sounds from the axle below him, and the
carriage tilts giddily before it rights itself once more. Who the devil
is driving the horses so hard? Raising the window blind, he finds
a grey confusion; fog, or perhaps smoke, covers an arid land. The

road, as far as he can descry it, is rocky, lonely, deserted. He cannot recall ever seeing this highway before. Impatient, and not a little anxious, he bangs his cane on the ceiling. There is no alteration in the speed of the vehicle. He thumps harder; then he pulls down the window glass and thrusts his head outside into the smoky air.

'Driver!' he shouts, eyeing the team of plunging ebony horses. He can just see the fellow's flank and back, muffled in a tattered costume. He is a bulky and peculiarly forbidding figure. 'Driver, stop!'

Is the fellow deaf? Without slacking pace, the carriage crests the hill, and he sees with a throat-clutch of horror that the road plunges steeply at a near vertical drop, down and down. They will all certainly plummet – the carriage, horses, himself and his precious, febrile hopes – to their deaths.

'Stop!'

At the same instant, he knows, in the portentous manner of nightmares, that this is his own entire mistake; that the driver he trusted to steer his way has tricked him. For now he knows that *he* is at the reins; his invisible enemy, the secret prognosticator, his own lurking shadow: De Angelo himself.

The agony of the knowledge forces him awake, choking for air, his heart thumping like the echo of hooves. Alone at Eglantine Hall, he remembers that he has signed the agreement to send Quare the story of the Netherlea Murders. And now, having taken the leap of eleven days in one harrowing night, he has the first inkling that this might have been remarkably unwise.

Meanwhile, Tabitha goes to bed, her mind revolving around Nat's notion of eleven days' addition to her life. She flits rapidly through insubstantial scenes in which she is admired: in a large box at the theatre, taking the floor at a glittering ball, ending the night at a coffee house as dawn pinks across the piazza. Enough of that. She surrenders to the power of those tortoiseshell eyes, Nat's mouth; his strong fingers rake the hair at the nape of her neck. Lips parted, she sinks into sleep.

The bedroom is very still and quiet, the dawn weak and grey. On the wooden chair in the corner sits a woman dressed in faded blue. Tabitha fights off the entanglements of sleep, sits upright and peers at the woman.

'Mother.' She cannot believe her eyes.

It *is* her mother, rising now to sit on the edge of the bed. Tabitha's surprise is a lump in her breast, a blazing heartache, wonder and pain. True, her mother has changed – she is bone-thin, and frail as a feather. Yet her spirit quivers with life, like the light of a candle flaring behind a muslin drape.

'I am so happy you are home,' her mother says.

The pain in Tabitha's breast overflows and blooms into happiness, as if these were the words she has waited all her life to hear. Her mother's eyes are familiar shining blue. Her expression bestows on her child such sweet concern that Tabitha's spirit repeats, 'I am home. All will be well.' Silently, her mother raises a mottled finger to her lips, and Tabitha watches as those lips pucker and age, growing toothless and ruined. There is not much time. Her mother is leaving.

There is no need to ask why she has returned. It is to remind her that she made a promise, here, in this same room, on a night of fury and tears. A blood oath of silence that must never be broken.

TWENTY-TWO

A Riddle

My *first* is laid upon the plate
Of each delighted guest,
My *second* in a thirsty state,
Will suit your parched throat best:
But *both* together form a word
Which, when glad hours are passed,
We grieve to find, howe'er deferred,
Must be pronounced at last.

The 29th day of September 1752

Michaelmas Fair and Assizes (New Calendar)
Luminary: Sun apparently rises and sets at 6
allowing for refraction.
Observation: Opposition of Saturn and Mercury.
Prognostication: Matters go Backwards in
Custom and Law.

Waxen-skinned, blinking in the sunlight, Darius steadied himself, appraising the gathered company with contempt. Turning, he spat over his shoulder at the door of the gaol; then he lifted his chained wrists like a pugilist, taunting his audience in a hoarse, but carrying voice. 'Take a long look, you hypocrites. I am innocent!'

Joshua strode forward, his musket trained upon the prisoner. 'Silence!' He motioned with the barrel towards the prisoner's carriage.

Darius moved with an arrogant, rolling gait, the iron cuffs clanking. Before he climbed inside, he looked at them all in turn, his obsidian eyes raking across each of the spectators. Tabitha, chilled, was convinced his glance lingered longest upon her.

'Darius,' Jennet mouthed hopelessly, and Tabitha held the girl's arm tightly as the prisoner disappeared into the black carriage. Turning swollen eyes upon her, Jennet whimpered, 'How can you let this happen?'

Mr Dilks, who stood beside them, snorted, 'It is the right function of the law, girl, to rid us of such vermin.'

Darius's committal to Chester Castle was thus far proving to be an ordeal for all concerned. Joshua had told Tabitha a dozen times that the transporting of a notorious murderer to the Michaelmas Sessions would be the most worrisome day of his life. 'Only when that evil creature is secure in Chester's dungeon will I be easy again,' he said.

All the arrangements had fallen upon the constable, commencing with his duty to gather Darius and the key witnesses to the case at

Chester Castle by nine of Michaelmas morning. Now, at last, they rattled off towards Chester in a well-ordered cortege. Sir John was carried at the head of the procession in his finest carriage, emblazoned with his coats of arms in shining gold. Around them rode the gentlemen: Doctor De Vallory, the higher servants, a few prominent neighbours, and to Tabitha's surprise and pride, Nat Starling, mounted on Jupiter and wearing his best gold-laced coat and hat. Next in line was the prisoner's conveyance, an ancient black mourning carriage with opaque blinds to hide its inmate from the curious. Then came the third carriage, carrying Tabitha and Jennet, along with Mr Dilks, whose gout prevented him from riding, with the labouring men, who might be called as witnesses to finding Master Francis's body, sitting on the outside.

It was a dull, white-skied day, the air moist and heavy. The carriages rattled along the die-straight Roman road, passing many a fine brick farm and collection of cottages. Thankfully, Mr Dilks soon fell asleep, still weak from having recently been bled. Tabitha tried to assemble a clear statement in case the judge called upon her, but continual worries interrupted her thoughts. Joshua had advised her not to take Bess, so she had asked Nanny Seagoes – but she had fallen sick. When Nell Dainty called and offered to mind the child, Tabitha had been nonplussed. The woman had sauntered around her mother's parlour, scrutinizing the fireplace and tea table, and even the contents of her mother's lace-edged shelf.

'So when is it you be leaving?' Nell Dainty had asked bluntly.

She had an agreement with Dilks to stay until the start of this new-fangled year – no longer Lady Day in March; the new year was now to change to 1753 on the first day of January – but Tabitha was damned if she was going to give Nell Dainty that promise.

'When I'm good and ready,' she had replied.

Nell hadn't faltered; only walked to the window, and examined the view with a discontented sniff.

'Will you mind Bess for me, then?'

Mistress Dainty had nodded sourly. 'I'll bring my knitting. I might even clear some of those dandelions you've let sprout all over the garden.'

Venomous drab! Tabitha had bitten her tongue so hard she nearly drew blood.

'The constable has said I might have to sleep over in Chester if I'm not called the first day.'

Nell lifted the tea caddy's lid and inspected the contents. 'Staying away all the night then, is it now? Well, if that's what the constable wants; he's a widower, I suppose,' she'd said spitefully. 'Get some more tea in, then. And leave plenty of chopped wood for a fire. If I need to do the doctor's work, I'll take the little maid with me.'

It was only now, when Tabitha had leisure to sit and reflect, that she wondered what the devil she had been thinking. How would Bess get on, abandoned to that cratchety busybody?

A rap came at the window, interrupting her thoughts. It was Joshua on horseback, looking tired and ill-shaven.

'The roads are full today; we must stay tight together. We may be slower, but it's safer. A few of the rabble have turned out to try to get a sight of the prisoner.'

Dilks woke, blinking peevishly. 'They should think on their eternal souls and behave more decently.'

'They know he is innocent,' protested Jennet.

'Now is not the time, Jennet,' scolded Joshua through the window.

'Here, take some barley water,' said Tabitha. 'Keep up your strength, girl, or I shall have to give you a dose of the doctor's black remedy.'

Jennet gave a derisive laugh. 'That vile stuff? It made me feel half-dead, so I threw it in a ditch.'

Rising to adjust the window, Tabitha saw that a press of carts and barrows had gathered around them. An old man standing at the roadside called out to the prisoner's coach, 'God have mercy on your wicked soul!'

Now a couple of beggarly lads jeered at it, throwing clods of earth. Joshua trotted his horse towards them, waving his constable's staff. Then Tabitha saw his shoulders slump – what had he seen in their path?

A minute later, they were stuck tight in the middle of the market crowd, inching down the slope of Handbridge towards the river. The ancient Dee bridge, barely a wagon's width in extent, was filled with a great crowd, jostling among packed carts and carriages. At the further end, a herd of cattle was being sluggishly counted off the bridge through the tollgate. As the clamour grew riotous, a few opportunist hawkers began crying their wares.

Tantalizingly close, at the far side of the broad river, Chester Castle stood on a steep green hill, a mass of square castellated towers, mighty walls and semi-circular bastions. Tabitha had never ventured inside its walls before; her curiosity stirred, along with the natural apprehension of any free spirit on entering a prison. Nat circled back and doffed his hat to her as he passed. Squeezing open the glass, she called after him, asking how long their progress might take. She watched him caress Jupiter's neck with long soothing strokes and heartily wished it was her own throat he touched.

'Perhaps ten minutes, or it could be half an hour. Saxton is trying to hurry the toll-men.'

His gaze met hers and held it in a long look that said more than a hundred cumbersome words. Then, to her annoyance, a boy with an overloaded barrow pushed up behind them, and Nat was forced to pull away again.

Ten minutes later, they rattled on to the bridge, surrounded by marketgoers. At her first sight of the castle Jennet had again begun bewailing Darius's fate, prompting Mr Dilks to start up a lecture on the Devil, until Tabitha heartily wished that Old Nick himself might make a visit and carry off the parson. In spite of the stink from the riverside tanneries, she stood again at the window, admiring the straight line of Nat's back in the saddle. He was certainly one of the most engaging men she had ever met.

Would Nat know where she might best sell the skull timepiece? she wondered. That morning, pulling it out of its hiding place under her mother's eaves, she had been impressed anew by its elaborate gold chasing and its hefty weight of solid silver. Swinging it back and forth on its chain, she had at first intended to bring it to Chester to pawn, for she was much in need of funds. But it was too notable an object for the pawnbrokers of Chester, and she wished in no way to risk a spell in the cells herself. Instead, she decided to wait until she could lay it out with a trusted second-hand man off Covent Garden.

A sudden high-pitched scream cut through the hubbub, and she leaned out to peer through the crowd. The sound had been made by a horse, ahead of them on the bridge. Cries of protest erupted, along with the clash of metal horseshoes on stone cobbles. A melee of carts, carriages and frightened people pressed dangerously close on the bridge. Momentarily, she glimpsed the cause of the chaos.

'Jennet,' she said, reaching for the girl's hand. 'Mr Dilks, Sir John's carriage has hit the parapet.'

The grand armorial carriage had twisted sideways, blocking the only exit to the Chester gate. Then Tabitha saw why: the lead horse

of Sir John's carriage was rearing in its traces, screaming and terrifying the rest of the team. Mr Dilks pushed her aside, hogging the
window glass.

'Should we get out?' Jennet asked, clutching at Tabitha's skirts
like a child.

'I think not. It's too great a crowd.' At that moment, they felt
their own carriage rock as the barrow-boy attempted to force his
way past them. Tabitha went to the opposite window, where people
were crying out in alarm, fearful of being crushed against the
parapet.

Jennet sat down, trembling and very pale. Looking out again,
Tabitha saw that the boy had climbed on to his own handcart to
avoid being crushed by the surging mass. Then, all in a fleeting
moment, she saw a swarthy woman in a chequered shawl mount
the parapet and dive down into the river below, showing curiously
large bare feet.

'Mother Mary,' she whispered to herself, wondering if they must
soon follow suit and leap into the fast-flowing river. Would it be
worse to tumble into the water inside the coach or trust to their own
limbs and dive unencumbered? Then a loud 'Huzzah!' rose from
the crowd and a man cried out, 'They've cut the traces. The beast
has galloped all the way to the Market Cross.'

A flash of red signified a band of soldiers arriving from the castle.
To a chorus of commands, they were soon at work shifting Sir
John's carriage.

The company from Netherlea made a sorry procession up to the
castle, leading the skittering horses while the militia hauled the
carriage up the drawbridge. At last they came into the first of the
castle courtyards. Tabitha looked about at the half-ruined dreariness
of it: the square Roman towers, curtain walls, ancient chapel and
the prison. Even the once magnificent Shire Hall, seat of the ancient
Earls of Chester, was in need of repair.

'It is very quiet here,' Mr Dilks said testily. A moment later a
stout man in a dressing wrapper and bed cap emerged from a
doorway.

'Faithful Thomas,' Mr Dilks remarked. 'He is behind-times to
be slouching about half-dressed at this hour.'

As she dismounted from the carriage, Tabitha overheard Mr
Thomas beg Sir John's pardon.

'Nay, it is not the assizes today, your lordship. They are still to be held at Old Michaelmas Day on the tenth of October. The Justices don't come here till the tenth – there was a declaration that the assizes should remain as they always was, in the Old Style. We have been made all topsy-turvy, even before you came along. Parliament forgot we elect our Lord Mayor at St Denis's Day, and now there must be another Act of Parliament to put it right.'

Across the way, Nat caught her eye; Tabitha gave a tiny shake of her head, signifying disbelief. De Angelo had printed the wrong date of the assizes in hundreds of almanacks, and apparently brought them all to confusion.

'Do you jest, sir?' Sir John was growling like an old lion, telling the gaoler he'd be damned if he would take any further responsibility for the prisoner.

'Throw him in the Black Hole, for all I care. And throw that almanack writer in there with him, for wasting our time.'

All turned to survey the battered mourning coach, its blinds still drawn and quiet within. At Mr Thomas's signal, the turnkey and three guards marched over in readiness to accompany the prisoner to his cell. Tabitha held Jennet tight, wary of the girl's making some lamentable spectacle.

But when the turnkey opened the carriage door, musket in hand, no one emerged. Stepping inside, he gave a cry for assistance, and half-carried the tottering form of Godfrey, the mild-mannered Netherlea gaoler, out on to the cobbles. The poor fellow was dazed and bound about the eyes and wrists. The doctor hurried forward to loosen his bonds and sit him up to get some air.

Amid cries of 'What Devil's work is this?' a series of articles were carried from the carriage, each telling their own tale: here was Darius's coat, and here a chisel and file, of the type he handled daily in his work. Finally, the iron chains were lifted out and cast upon the ground.

'Fetch ale for this man,' Sir John cried, and Godfrey drank noisily, struggling for breath.

'When did the attack occur, my man?' Sir John was struggling to contain his fury.

'It were by Ord Farm, before we come to Handbridge, my lord. That ruffian hit me on the head, bound me and tied a blindfold upon me. From the sound of him, he used his tools to set himself free and pulled on fresh clothes. I fear some wicked accomplice hid those articles in the well of the coach.'

'A curious coincidence,' Nat said quietly, 'that we were shortly after delayed on the bridge.'

'Yes, Nathaniel,' Sir John agreed wearily. 'The timing is remarkable.'

Tabitha did not have time to think before she spoke.

'Begging your leave, Sir John. And sirs,' she added. 'When we were on the bridge I saw a swarthy woman in a chequered head cloth. It is possible – no, I am sure of it.'

'Tabitha.' Sir John eyed her reprovingly. 'Explain yourself.'

'Her feet were bare. I saw them as she, or it might have been he, leapt off the bridge into the Dee. Bare-naked they were, and very large and dirty.'

When Joshua and a band of soldiers had been dispatched to search the river and its environs, Sir John announced they might all take their leisure until four o'clock, when at least some of the party must return to Netherlea.

Tabitha looked into the coach and picked up one of Darius's boots. As she had guessed, a hobnail was missing, of just the size of that stud of metal she had found by her mother's fireplace.

A low whistle drew Tabitha towards a doorway outside the Gaoler's quarters. It was Nat, beckoning to her to join him.

'Tabitha, I'm taking the London coach now. If there's no trial, I must be on my way at once.' She gazed at him, feeling witless – and wondering again why he needed to leave in such haste. 'Well done. You had the sharpest eyes of all. Will you write to me?'

She nodded. 'And will you make enquiries about who printed the almanack?'

'Nothing will prevent me.'

Without quite knowing how it happened, she was suddenly locked in his arms and their lips met in a sudden, plunging kiss; then he pulled away as fast again, looking down into her face with a breathless smile.

'What was that?' she asked.

'The seal on my contract to return, lady. I shall be back for more.'

TWENTY-THREE

A Riddle

Lo! Here I stand with double face,
My name exalted in high place;
A creature, symbol or a crown,
Identifies me round the town.
I see below me all mankind:
In search of comfort of a liquid kind,
While some give out that I entice
To lust, and luxury, and dice,
And diverse oaths on me inflict,
Because they find their pockets picked.
Though I'm a comforter to many lives
'Tis said I steal health, wealth and wives.

The 29th day of September 1752

Michaelmas (New Calendar)

Luminary: Sun sets at 6 apparently,
allowing for refraction.
Observation: Saturn sets at 9 at night.
Prognostication: Men of viperous and sordid
principles will be active.

Happy to be at liberty, Tabitha and the rejoicing Jennet set off up Bridge Street, picking their way through milling shoppers, wooden barrows and straw baskets strewn with every sort of commodity. The barking dogs and ceaseless din of hawkers crying their wares gave Tabitha a chance to collect her wits before she spoke to the girl.

Where had Darius run to? She found herself eyeing dark corners of the galleried rows that stretched above the shops and bundled shapes behind lines of laundry and heaps of goods. No, once Darius had reached the river's shore, he must have struck out into the countryside. Or would he linger here, in the faceless crowds, where a stranger would not be remarked upon? Having witnessed his escape unnerved her; she recalled his vicious black eyes raking her countenance and was surprised to realize how much peace of mind the prospect of his imprisonment had brought her.

They halted at a linen stall but nothing pleased Tabitha in the prim array of shirt pieces and handkerchief squares.

'I want a drink,' she said, glancing down one of the town's gloomy passageways. 'The White Lion should be lively.'

She failed to mention that The White Lion was the inn where Nat would wait for the London coach. She could still feel a lingering but pleasing soreness upon her lips, and even more powerfully, a hastening within her body, like the release of a wheel that might spin away, who knew where.

The inn was as she remembered it: smoky, comfortable, and crowded with men. She looked about for Nat but saw no sign of

him. It was difficult to believe that a mere six – or was it seven?
– weeks had passed since she had walked through those doors in
all her flash rig-out, straight off the London coach. Again, heads
turned to inspect both her and Jennet: idle, lingering, drunken
appraisals. It made Tabitha want to spit in those wretches' eyes to
see how they leered at the girl. Jennet was no more than a child;
and as for herself, dressed in her mother's homespun, she was
scarcely looking for business.

Settling her charge down on a stool, she went to confirm that the
London coach had left on time, and to order a brandy for herself
and a barley water for Jennet. On her return, two ill-favoured carters
were attempting to coax Jennet to drink from their ale jug. The
younger one, a snub-nosed baboon, said, 'You two turned plenty of
heads when you come in here.'

'Aye, and no doubt you two turned plenty of stomachs,' Tabitha
snapped back. 'Be off with you.' With surly expressions, they
disappeared.

'I didn't fetch you any brandy,' she said tartly, 'for I can see you
are tipsy enough with joy.'

Jennet nodded, beaming. 'It's like a miracle. Like Darius said, it
was foretold in the stars that he would never go to trial.'

Tabitha rapidly downed the rough spirits, enjoying the pleasant
burn in her gullet.

'And what do you suppose he meant by that?'

'That he is innocent, of course.' She suddenly brimmed with
laughter. 'The way you spoke to those two men.' She giggled.

'That's what most of them deserve. You need to know that before
you throw yourself at a young devil like Darius.'

Jennet sipped her barley water, eyeing her friend. 'You told me
you were ill-treated in London. Is that why you don't like men?'

Tabitha laid her head back against the panelled wall and closed
her eyes. Why in Hell's name had she told the girl that?

'And how did you get away from that dreadful place?' Jennet
insisted.

Sighing, Tabitha explained. 'There was a girl in the next chamber
to me. Poll, she was called, as shining bright as a new penny. She
cultivated one of her beaux – a grizzled soldier, ugly but tender-
hearted, and begged him to help her get away, and made a thousand
promises to keep him sweet. For months she hid away his money
without the bawdy-house keeper's knowledge. And she took me

with her when she fled.' She smiled into the distance, remembering. '"Toujours pret, Madame!" was Poll's motto. "Always ready!" And so we were. Vauxhall Gardens had never seen the like of us.'

'You still have a gentleman friend in London?'

'Is that what my mother called him? I did have. Robert, yes.'

'Do you love him?'

Tabitha stifled a yawn. Truly, the girl was obsessed with that emotion. 'I should have met him here last week but I did not attend our rendezvous. So it would appear not.'

'Have you always been so—'

She never did learn what Jennet was about to say. Hard-hearted? Callous? Or worse – bitter, a second-rate beauty, a bold-shammer? Before she could conclude, Tabitha pinched her leg privately beneath the table. 'Do not look up,' she whispered, looking hard into Jennet's wide eyes. 'There is a man by the bar in a green braided coat. I stole something of great value from him. He may have me arrested if he claps eyes on me again.'

Jennet gave a tiny nod of comprehension.

'When I squeeze your hand, I want you to go to the door without looking backwards; I will follow behind.'

Jennet did as she was told. Then Tabitha followed, poker-stiff with fear. Skirting the Irishman's table, she saw that a set of coaching timetables was laid out before him, and that he was tracing across a line of departure times with his fingertip.

At any moment, she expected that hairy-backed hand to grip her shoulder, that husky brogue to whisper, 'Got you now, you prigging whore. So where's my damned timepiece?' But, unharmed, she reached the door, and breathed free air as she hustled Jennet out into the street.

'It's best we get back to the castle,' she said, setting a swift pace. 'Your father may have news.'

Joshua had no news; but before he sent them home to Netherlea, he pulled Tabitha aside. 'Where has that fellow Starling gone?'

She told him what she knew: that he must by now be a good hour down the road to London. His expression reminded her of a bear she had once seen baited at the Market Cross; the poor, baffled creature, striking out at its tormentors too slowly and too late.

'He has fled?'

'Fled?' she scoffed. 'He has gone to London on business.'

'He was directly next to that lead horse when it bolted. And now he has absconded.'

'Joshua, that is not true. He'll be back in a fortnight at the latest.'

'And his address in London?'

She frowned, having no notion. 'He said he would write to me.'

The worst of it was that, like that poor chained bear, Joshua's anger and pain was clear behind his eyes. 'I'll keep a lookout for his letters. I'd lay odds they'll make most interesting reading.'

When they got back to Netherlea, Nell Dainty and Bess were not at the cottage, nor were they at the doctor's house. Cutting through the grounds of Bold Hall to enquire at the stillroom, Tabitha stopped dead to listen. Was that the little chit's babbling voice, reaching her from the gloom of Lady Daphne's dairy? Inside were tables of marble, Delft tiles and churns, all of the most modern style. And there she found Nell Dainty watching her daughter, Zusanna, feed Bess from a bowl of curds and sugar.

'Here you are! I have looked everywhere,' Tabitha reproached the child, wishing she was not quite so hot and flustered.

'You said you was staying out for the night,' Nell complained, scowling. 'We was just talking about you. Where shall this little maid go when you traipse back to London, and start carrying on your old business?'

Zusanna chimed in. 'We heard you was looking to leave her with anyone as would have her.'

'I'll take her now,' Tabitha said, trying to hide the fury in her voice – but, as if deaf, Zusanna loaded another spoon, and nudged Bess's rosebud mouth.

'Me and my ma wouldn't want to see her sent down to the poorhouse. Only that's where most of the ill-gotten babes end up.'

Bess's huge eyes blinked in innocent pleasure as she swallowed another mouthful.

'No!' Tabitha swept the spoon from Zusanna's hand and pulled Bess into her arms. 'I don't care if you are as barren as the desert – you are not having her!'

All the way back to the cottage, Bess bawled so noisily that Tabitha wondered why in Hell's name she had bothered. Let them have the tiresome child. Her true life was in London, and that was no life for a child – especially a cherubic girl child. It was true that, once back in London, she hoped to continue her friendship with

Nat Starling; and, like her, he had no settled income or position to support a child, however charming. Charming? Bess cried on and on, at a tooth-wincingly high pitch.

'Oh, shut up!' She set Bess down on the ground. The child pulled herself upright, stamped her tiny feet and glared at her through teary eyes.

'Oh, mademoiselle is annoyed, is she?' Tabitha taunted. 'I can also stamp my feet.' She proceeded to do so, knowing herself to be quite ridiculous. Then she sank to her knees on the grass beside the little girl and placed a great smacking kiss on her mouth. 'Help me, Bess. What am I to do with you?'

To her surprise, Bess pushed her little lips against her mouth and kissed her in return.

TWENTY-FOUR

A Riddle

I am jet-black, as you may see,
The son of pitch, and gloomy night;
Yet all that know me will agree,
I'm dead except I live in light.

My blood this day is very sweet,
Tomorrow of a bitter juice,
Like milk 'tis cried about the street,
And so applied to different use.

Most wondrous is my magic power;
For with one colour I can paint;
I'll make the devil a saint this hour,
Next make a devil of a saint.

The 1st to the 6th day of October 1752

Luminary: Last Quarter of the Moon.
Observation: Opposition of Saturn and Mars.
Prognostication: Dissension between
notions of Differing Principles.

A day later Nat arrived in the city, hailing the pall of coal
smoke and the jangle of the crowds with joy. It had been a
troubled journey; the drama of Darius's escape blazed in
his head so fiercely that he was bursting to transform it into fresh-
inked news. Yet whenever he dozed, frissons of fear unnerved him:
he had the disturbing notion that the coach was in actuality travelling
backwards away from London, in ominous alignment with the new
calendar.

He had been relieved to wake from such nightmares, recalling,
instead, the kiss he had given to Tabitha. Oh, Tabitha! When he
reached his old haunts he would drink deep to her, the sharp-eyed
possessor of his heart.

At the printing house in Chandos Lane, he shook the plump
hand of Quare himself. The printer, a blubbery fellow with
ginger-lashed, piggish eyes, honoured him by rising from his
desk. An advance of payment was presented, and Nat agreed to
every term, signing a contract to write a pamphlet elaborating
every detail of the case, and all to be completed within the week.
An hour later, he had tracked down his fellow pen-smith Toby
in a private club on the piazza. Soon the witchery of French
brandy was upon Nat; as they raised toasts to women, to fortune
and fame, his every sinew sang with the pleasure of strong wine.
A future as a man of letters glowed before him like an answered
prayer.

He took Toby into his confidence about the arrangement with
Quare and saw with exultation the shadow of envy that crossed his
face. His friend laid his arm lazily across the back of the gilded
sofa. 'But what will your rustic friends in the north make of your
pamphlet?'

It was the first time Nat had considered his opus might be read by the villagers. Truly, it was not a pleasing prospect.

'Whatever Quare has given you, he will squeeze out ten times its value,' Toby added spitefully. 'He always pleads poverty; but remember, he has a house in the West End and keeps a coach and six.'

By midnight he wasn't too disappointed when Toby said he had a girl waiting for him down Nag's Head Court. 'The theatre trade will have finished now. She's a clean girl, not long from the country. She'll suffice – until she gets wise to London tricks.'

Once he was alone, Nat ordered a fresh bumper; then, tired of summoning the waiter, threw down a gold coin and seized the bottle itself.

Some unknowable amount of time had passed when he recovered his senses. He was sodden with drink, and stilettoes of pain skewered his skull. Out in the street he heard a watchman calling eleven of the morning. Only his parched desire to drink from the jug he glimpsed on the washstand forced him to stagger upright. At some time after his boozing spree, he had been carried by a set of rough hands; then he must have been transported to this fusty chamber, though he had no recollection of the journey. He pulled the window shutter back a half-inch, wincing, and saw that he was back at the printers on Chandos Lane, up near the roof in some kind of garret. And there, laid out upon the writing desk, were ink pot, quills, paper and sand.

Beside them stood a note in Quare's hand: *Drunken nights have always tomorrows. And one week today, good fellow, the press awaits your words.*

Nat generally excused himself from any labours when in such a painful state, but by the time Quare later paid him a visit, he had filled a page or two.

'Are you pursuing developments?' Quare wheezed. 'You do have a correspondent back in the north to keep you appraised?'

'Yes,' he mumbled, though the notion that Tabitha stood as such to him would have appalled her. She was pursuing De Angelo for motives far nobler than his.

'Scratch a line to him, then, and I'll drop it at the post office.'

'I shall take it myself,' Nat said.

'Nay, I fear you have shown your true colours. You must remain here until you have fulfilled your contract.'

Nat did not have the stamina to argue. Instead, he scribbled a few terse lines to Tabitha, asking for news of Darius, and only at the last moment remembering to enquire after her own health.

'And the – what is their name? The De Vallorys? My man Blunkett is searching out a likeness of the father for your pamphlet. But any further dirt you can expose . . .'

'Is that necessary?' Nat was feeling sick now, for more reasons than the surfeit of brandy.

Quare sidled his fat carcass towards him.

'It is a fair story, but it is for you to make it irresistible. It could be up there, lad, with Captain Maclean the Gentleman Highwayman, Jonathan Wild Gaol-Breaker, or Captain Morgan, Pirate. What shall we name it? *"The Bloody Harvest of a Northern Lord"*? Or *"A Noble House Cursed by a Curious Almanack"*?'

'These people are of my acquaintance. I believe a sensitive portrayal—'

'Poppycock! This searcher is female – a handsome piece, is she? Worth getting her portrait made? You hinted she has an interesting past.'

Hot bile was rising in Nat's throat. 'Pardon me,' he muttered, and ran to the closet where he vomited into the chamber pot, sweating and shaking. What, in his stupid pursuit of vainglory, had he unleashed?

As Nat's fuddlement eased, he gradually let more light in at the shutters. The garret was a decrepit repository of Quare's lurid business, the sloping walls hung with broadsheets that paraded anatomized corpses and scenes from Tyburn. Quare prided himself on his low beginnings, as a boy hawker of Last Dying Confessions at Newgate. It was rumoured he had then worked for a print-shop with a line in flagellation literature, just by the pit door at Drury Lane. After making a fortune stealing prints from gentlemen's houses, he bought out his master and struck out on his own.

Above Nat's desk hung a picture of Jack Sheppard the boy gaol-breaker, a puny youth with legs held in gigantic chains. Quare intended to use that very same copper-plate for Nat's own pamphlet, scratching out Sheppard's face and inserting a crude approximation of Darius's visage.

Slowly Nat grasped that it was he, Nat, who was prisoner here – sentenced to use his talents to slake the appetites of apprentices and hobbledehoys, and to titillate the seekers of penny sensations. His *Dramatis Personae* had shrunk to stock characters from *Commedia del Arte*: the foppish heir, the bombastic father, the plucky, beautiful village girl.

Yet, nonetheless, the more he wrote, the more he found the maw of Quare's printing press irresistible. It was refreshing to construct a publication of at least twelve pages; he gave an account of the murder, devised a map of the village, and rendered conversations as close to verbatim as he could recall. He described the finding of Francis's butchered body, the opinions of those at the Inn, he outlined the funeral oration, described Chester Castle and the daring escape. To his surprise, he found the exercise made his veins run with thrilling ichor.

'The trouble with you, Nat,' Quare announced, not unkindly, 'is that you were never whipped sufficiently hard.'

Nat bridled at first at the print-seller's words, but soon came to understand the truth of them. He had never worked so hard as now, when schoolroom discipline was imposed on his wayward habits. And, when his hands were too cramped from writing, he was free to clamber down through the roofspace to look through Quare's archives. There he found old copies of *The Newgate Calendar*, registries of past London, pamphlets recording Old Bailey trials. He felt like a hound on the scent, for Nat could not resist digging deeper into the story. He discovered that Parson Dilks had been dismissed from his post as chaplain to a Cambridge college; puzzling over how he might have overcome this impediment, he recalled that he was related to Lady Daphne. He now began to keep separate, secret notes from those he showed to Quare, and determined to visit his mother in Cambridgeshire, too, before he returned to Netherlea.

As the days passed, he began to feel towards Quare a loathing that stirred fantasies of violence. The uneducated, ill-bred Hackney print-seller had the temerity to alter Nat's work, adding florid descriptions of place, scandalous characters and inelegant hyperbole; he was a mercenary street peddler, squeezing every drop of blood from the drama. And somehow, where a thousand airy muses would have failed, Quare had succeeded – gutter trash though it was, Nat's pamphlet was rather good.

Nat showed Quare his copy of De Angelo's almanack and the print-seller regaled him with the story of the almanack's origins: the ancient desire to follow the movements of the sun and moon, first etched in notches on sticks and stones. His brain was as full of facts as a rat of fleas; he recalled the political prophecies of the Civil War, and the prediction of Cromwell's fall. Now, he told Nat, it was the Worshipful Company of Stationers who held the monopoly – though that was but the official view. Almanacks were the largest and most valuable commodity in the print world, for as many as one in a half-dozen Britons laid out their pennies every year. Grudgingly, Nat recognized that Quare was indeed a man of that encyclopaedic age; the Diderot of the vulgar.

As he dipped his pen he thought of Tabitha, venerating her like a private saint. She was no longer merely the alluring fast piece he had fallen for at the Haymarket; she was rather a vision of movement in the summer sunshine, miraculously living at just the same time as he had been granted life. Though he often recalled the softness of her hand, it was her vivacity he remembered best, the brightness she wore like a taffeta cloak. Half-mad with overwork, he kissed her letters and slid their coolness against the sweat that dampened his breast.

Only two letters had arrived from her. The first confirmed Darius's continued evasion and gave a warning, too: *The constable is (rather stupidly, in my opinion) claiming that your departure is a sign of guilt.*

His eyes scrabbled hastily over the paper; Saxton, the buffoon, believed that he had aided Darius and then absconded with him, having no notion yet of the fugitive's whereabouts.

Her second letter urged him again to investigate Dilks, and confirmed that Jennet had not, so far as she could tell, resumed communications with Darius. He was heartened to read that she was counting the days till his return.

The day the press was set to print, Nat knew not if he was playing a part in a triumph or a tragedy. There was an unstoppable appetite for the story, Quare had told him, and the pamphlet had been expanded to a whole sixteen pages, complete with illustrations. He had insisted that Quare must not use his own name, and the Latin term for scribe, *Demogrammateus,* had instead been substituted. But, like the ink stains on his shirt, he was unable to scrub away his unease.

He watched two printers working like automatons, inking and sliding and loading up paper, and producing an uncanny two hundred sheets per hour. Hawkers thronged at the door, snatching up corded stacks of pamphlets – sixpence for black and white, a shilling for coloured.

'We'll keep the press working through the night,' he heard Quare say, 'and get a third or fourth edition out by tomorrow.'

Next morning, the door to his garret was left unlocked. Nat stumbled down the stairs, his hands tarry black, his suit filthy and his hair tangled to his shoulders, feeling like a madman escaped from a peculiarly industrious asylum.

'Be off then, lad,' Quare called; then, seeing the parlous state of him, added, 'There's a *bagnio* across the road where you can tidy yourself.'

Taking his travelling box under his arm, he followed the print-seller's advice, and was shaved, bathed and dressed in a clean suit of clothes by noon. For Tabitha's sake, he declined the bouncing girl in a shift who offered him yet more attentive favours for a shilling. Then, with his fee from Quare and a barely dry copy of the pamphlet safe inside his coat, he headed out, still dazed, to find the Cambridge coach.

TWENTY-FIVE

A Riddle

My *first*, Adam's bone, is e'er by your side;
My *next* signals 'good' from those of French pride;
My *whole* is an ornament you love to wear
Tied round your waist, your neck, or your hair.

The 1st to the 6th day of October 1752

Luminary: Last quarter of the Moon.
Observation: Mercury, the Starry Messenger,
is with the Moon.
Prognostication: Beware mistaken zeal
in giving counsel to others.

T ime's leap forward had left everyone in Netherlea off balance.
The Feast of Saint Michael had always been the foremost
day in the country calendar, when land rents were due and
the fields were first ploughed for winter crops. Some villagers
attempted to pull Michaelmas forward to the twenty-ninth of
September, but most carried on as before, merely writing 'Old Style'
beside the Michaelmas they had grown up with, on the tenth of
October. It was easier to measure the seasons as they always had,
by the new nip in the air, the whirling departure of the swallows,
and the arrival of sloes and elderberries. Fruit and flesh were all
ripening in their eternal manner, the drinkers at the tavern agreed,
according to the steady pace of Old Mother Nature herself.

Each morning after Nat had left, Tabitha rose early, pulled on her
mother's red cloak and set off to gather wild stuffs at the edge of
the highway. Two solitary daybreaks passed with no reward from
the post boy – for she did not trust that Joshua would not open Nat's
letters. She reaped the magic of those pearly mornings; a world for
her alone, where golden beams pierced the vapours until the sun
burned through from a balmy blue sky. The summer was fading and,
after more than a year of seeing the world mostly through panes of
sooty London glass, the season filled her eyes with a melancholy
radiance. If only Nat had been there, they could have walked arm-
in-arm under leaves where cobwebs hung like lacework beaded with
glass. As she filled her basket she imagined Nat's lips pressing warm
against hers. To think about him produced a pleasant, elevating pain.

On the third morning, the post boy finally handed her a letter from
his sack. She tore it open at once, but after reading it, she felt like

flinging it into the ditch. Instead of protesting how violently he missed her, or penning glorious descriptions of town and all the coffeehouse news, he had included only a few half-intelligible lines. Was Darius yet found, and if so how and where? And had she any further information to give him? That was the whole of it, save for a cursory enquiry as to her health. She inspected it, front and back, for any news of his return, but found none. Devil take the wretch, she would show him what she was worth; she would find De Angelo herself.

As the moon grew to its full extent, waking her at two or three of the morning with its eerie mimicry of daylight, Tabitha turned the events of the last weeks over in her mind. Could Nat be the culprit? He had a store of astronomical and literary knowledge, true. Why, by his own account, he even wrote cryptic riddles of his own. And there was something slippery about him – she had to admit that.

She recalled those overheard remarks he had made to Sir John at the kennels. There were many questions for him to answer; not least, why he had fled so hurriedly to London – there were other women involved, she was convinced of it. At the heart of it all, her vanity was hurt. The rogue had deserted her, just as she felt a genuine liking for him.

In this mood, she itched to be alone. So one day, when Jennet and Bess had disappeared into the woods, Tabitha set off for the church, taking care all the while to be sure she was not watched. The church's back door led into a narrow passage, where she halted and listened to voices and the banging of tools that issued from the chancel. Damnation. The stonemason's men were at work on the De Vallory memorial. Slipping unseen past the chancel entrance, she found the vestry door locked, just as Mr Dilks had threatened. Quiet as a mouse, she applied a bent skewer she had brought for that purpose, holding her breath as she turned it in the keyhole. Feeling the catch release, she pushed it more strongly until it gave a satisfying click; then, once inside, she pulled the door closed and got down to work. Nat had been searching for records about his mother – now, while he was so far away, she would find out what he had been looking for.

She reckoned his mother, Hannah Dove, to be of a similar age to her own mother, and quickly found a record of her birth. She had been christened in April 1710, born to the Doves of Red End,

Netherlea. That address was surprising; a hamlet of parish tenements given to the needy, known to locals as 'Dead End'. Not so proud a family then, she crowed inwardly. She searched next for records of an older Hannah – first in the Marriage Register, then, not finding an entry, for something less respectable in the list of Baptisms. She found nothing – only the death of Hannah's father when she was no more than five years old, and ten years later the death of her mother, too. So many dead, she mused, glancing through mortalities from countless causes, from decline and mortification to fits and afflictions. But what had happened to Hannah?

A volley of echoing footsteps passed the vestry door, followed by a thud of dragged weights and tools. It would be circumspect to remain quiet while the stonemasons departed. At length she found a certificate in a wooden box set apart for Apprenticeship Indentures. On a parchment, beneath the crest of the De Vallorys, was written:

Parish Copy
These are to desire you, and every one of you, to permit and
suffer the Bearer hereof:
Hannah Dove, Spinster aged fifteen years
Peaceably and quietly to pass from Netherlea, Cheshire
into:
Whitewell, in the County of Cambridgeshire,
to be indentured to:
Sir James Robbins
As an Apprentice to the Art and Mystery of:
Housewifery
for a term of
Five years.

Tabitha looked at the list of signatures and seals. Sir John De Vallory was at its head, along with Mr Dilks, the doctor and other familiar names from the parish council. If this was what Nat had been searching for, it confirmed what he had told her on the way to Chester, that his mother had moved from Netherlea to work for Lord Robbins. She remembered Nat's words, that Hannah had been made housekeeper and married the estate's steward. For an orphan from Red End she had been fortunate.

Hearing the great front door of the church slam shut, she raised her head as the echoes died away. After neatly replacing all the documents, she had a fancy to inspect the new De Vallory memorial in private.

The vaulted chancel admitted only a trickle of light through its narrow windows, and Tabitha's footsteps sounded hesitant on the stone flags. Only as she approached the church tower did the sound of the new clock's mechanism reach her, a ceaseless thunk and tick. A new innovation, installed since her departure from Netherlea, the clock and bells were operated by gigantic chains and weights; and a copper pendulum the size of a frying pan swung back and forth along the whitewashed wall. She stood a while, watching it, with that peculiar sense of observing time. With each movement her life was passing and she was growing minutely older – further from birth and closer to death.

Unlike Nat, she thought of time as like a ribbon unspooling; the present moment was the only inch of the stuff you could grasp as it cascaded past you, framed by the diamond buckle of *now*. Life, in the moment of happening, was radiant with every colour at once, like a rainbow woven of thread, but once the moment had passed, it was nothing but grubby silk abandoned on the ground. All its freshness and lustre was spoiled and used up; her own folly, her poor choices, had ruined so many bright possibilities. And now her past lay in a sordid tangle at her feet.

As for the future, she had no ready picture of that at all. It was unknown, even frightening. That was why people sought out predictions of love, health, and good fortune; Nat thought there were choices to be made, but she was not so sure. She had once heard a sermon on the subject of God the Watchmaker, and how the world and its inhabitants were nothing but tiny cogs in a vast sphere of clockwork. Even as a child, that had sounded to her like a cold metal trap. Or was it the stars, perhaps, that wrote her fate? Well, even Nat knew no more of their futures than her, for all his philosophizing. No, the future was a dark place and her ribbon a fragile thread in a labyrinth by which she groped forwards.

Lord, was it her mother's dying that gave her such melancholy apprehensions? With a sigh of frustration, she turned from the pendulum. If only she could see the future; if only her shining ribbon could lead her to a better life than this.

The De Vallory memorial was being erected in the right-hand aisle, the most honoured of places, right up against the altar. At its foot gaped a deep and murky pit, some dozen feet across and as many deep. Lifting her apron to cover her nose, she silently reflected that even the great and noble rotted with the same stink as the poor. Peering down, she fancied she saw the gleam of ancient coffin boards and flecks of white bone. Next, her eye was caught by an array of sculptured stones propped against the chancel wall. She tried to read the inscription, but it was impossible; not only was the light failing, but the words were in a foreign tongue. The picture, however, she could make out, though barely. There was an air of deliberate mystery to it – a standing figure, seemingly without a face.

'And what does our searcher make of that?'

The voice spoke so close to the back of her neck that her heart leapt hard against her stays. She spun around and found Mr Dilks had joined her, on the softest of footfalls. Tabitha curtsied, but refused to be intimidated.

'Forgive me, sir. It is curious. What does it signify?'

'I doubt you would understand.'

Damn his eyes, she had seen plenty of remarkable sculptures with Robert. She had natural good taste and an eye for beauty, he had told her, and lent her books and improved her manner of speech. She cocked her head to one side. The figure was holding something in its right hand. A . . . scythe, perhaps?

'I should say it was Time.'

Mr Dilks nodded, reluctantly confirming that she was correct.

'Sir, is that a Latin motto?'

Dilks ignored her question. 'I should like to know your business here when no one else is about.'

'I was drawn, Mr Dilks, to wait upon God alone. I take it you do not object.'

'I do. The times of services are posted upon the door. That is when I expect to see you next, dressed modest and shamefaced, along with the rest of the congregation. Saxton may not charge you a fine for missing holy service, but I see all. Remember the pit awaits you, too. And it holds greater torment for those who are bloated with sin.'

As he spoke he took several small steps towards her. The parson needed only to push her hard in the chest and she would topple backwards into the cold earth. She moved from the edge towards him, meaning to pass him by. But he did not stand aside; his wide bulk stood as firm as a post to prevent her escape. Her eyes met his and he stood his ground like a pugilist; angry, assessing, belligerent.

'Your pardon, sir. Constable Saxton awaits my return.' She uttered the lie in a strong firm voice and he let her pass.

As she hurried outside she saw a veiled figure waiting by the churchyard wall beneath the shelter of the yew trees. Tabitha paused, though loath to draw attention to herself. It was Lady Daphne, standing motionless; waiting, perhaps, for the parson. She could not read the expression on her face behind the black lace.

By the time she reached home, she was sufficiently unsettled to write to Nat. She told him that Darius was still at large and believed to have fled by sea to Ireland or France. Also that Sir John was mortified at his son's murderer going free. And she told him again of her conviction that Dilks and Lady Daphne might in some way be conspiring together. It made no sense, but then neither did any other possibilities. Dilks was a hypocrite, a whited sepulchre; there was undoubtedly a viciousness about the parson that made her sensitive street-walker's hackles rise.

TWENTY-SIX

An Enigma

He who lacks it
Seeks it.
He who has it
Mistreats it.

The 4th to 6th day of October 1752

Luminary: Sun rises 18 minutes after 6.
Observation: Seven Stars rise 44 minutes
after 6 at night.
Prognostication: Princes and grandees will be
afflicted by disease and infirmities.

On the day she had agreed to begin work at the doctor's house, Tabitha followed his manservant Florian to a chamber where wealthy patients occasionally attended; a high-ceilinged room with walls lined with tiny shelves and drawers of medicaments. There she found the doctor sorting through his papers, beside an open window through which the scents of the garden drifted. He greeted her kindly and showed her a store of dusty boxes in a small wooden closet off the consultation room. In there, she must unpack the contents, and sort the papers into separate heaps of inventories, receipts, herbals, bills of charge and so on. It was duller work than she expected, for she had to pay full attention to his instructions and learn to use a reckoner to translate Roman numerals into their Arabic equivalent.

It was indeed a relief to be at liberty when the doctor was called away mid-morning. She waited until she heard his carriage depart – then leafed through the many papers he had left lying about. The contents were disappointing: there were no descriptions of feuds against the De Vallorys, or of poisons or means to murder. Most were crabbed abbreviations, cryptic symbols and strings of numbers. Gradually she came to understand these were formulae for medicines, or occasionally patients' case notes.

Her second day passed almost as dully. If she was to surprise Nat with a discovery, this was not moving her any further forward. Whenever she could, she observed the doctor as he worked; his tall figure had acquired a stoop, and the florid pink of his boyish face had a yellow cast. Then, when he was called to dinner, she saw him stumble against his desk and sit for a long while, noisily catching his breath. This, she reckoned, was a chance to draw him out.

'Sir,' she said, after fetching him some cordial from the cook. 'Your illness has come on very fast. Forgive me, but do you think it a natural ailment?'

His eyes were sharp, though increasingly sunk in a web of lines. 'Whatever do you mean, girl?'

'Again, forgive me, but there are rumours of poison. A dog belonging to Sir John died some months ago. This may sound presumptuous, sir, but your family – could you all be subject to attack?'

The doctor leaned against the cushion at his back, his face drawn. 'I did not know about this dog,' he said faintly. 'Tell me.'

Guiltily aware that she had distressed him, Tabitha told him of the dogman's suspicions.

'But why would anyone kill a dog?' The doctor pressed his fingers to his brow.

Tabitha leaned forward eagerly. 'Is it not the habit of anatomizers and other such butchers to test their poisons?'

He shook his head. 'On a rat or cat, perhaps. Though I see your argument, that a dog is closer in volume of blood to a person. Yet why kill Towler, the prize of my brother's pack?'

'We have a notion that the poisoner hates your brother.'

The doctor gave one of his rare peals of laughter. 'This is a lunatic story. And when you say "we" – do you mean you and that puddlehead Saxton?'

Tabitha nodded, not wanting to drag in Nat's name.

'So what have you discovered?'

She shrugged and laughed as prettily as she could. 'No more than that.'

'You must be very fond of my brother, to look out for him so assiduously.'

She hesitated a moment too long, aware of his pale eyes inspecting her closely.

'Ah – not so fond, then. John tells me you won't speak to him.'

'Sir, I do not want to appear ungrateful, but . . .' It was impossible to explain. She gave a little shake of her head.

'You want the past to be forgotten.'

'Yes.' That was it, exactly.

'I think my brother will not give up so easily. He may call here, you know.'

Tabitha could not stop herself. 'Sir, I will not be . . . used by Sir John.'

The doctor looked up, intent and alert. 'He is much in need of consolation.'

She stood and reached for her cloak. 'Then let him find consolation in the stews of Chester,' she said, her voice too loud, 'but not about my person.'

'Bravo,' the doctor murmured, clapping his dry hands together. 'Calm yourself. It will afford my brother a lesson, not to have all he desires.'

'He will find me here, though, soon enough.'

'Be easy. He has asked me your whereabouts; I will not let him find you.'

The doctor was true to his word, for when Florian announced Sir John the next day, he signalled that she might remain out of sight in the closeted room. She waited, standing by the wooden wainscoting and listening hard; she could just hear Sir John's blustering voice.

'Great God! She's giving me the devil of a run-around.'

His younger brother replied, too softly for Tabitha to distinguish.

'And I have such pains in my head!' cried Sir John peevishly. 'I never felt more fatigued in my life. How the devil did you gain a licence to practise as a physician?'

The doctor's reply was a conciliatory murmur.

'Are you deaf?' Sir John bawled so violently that Tabitha started back from the wall. 'No! Bleed me again. I need more vigour.'

Tabitha started when the doctor swung the door open, almost into her face; he passed serenely by, returning in a few moments with his box of cupping glasses and blades. She returned to the wainscot as the doctor prepared his patient.

'Have you heard? The common people are saying this assassin will harm me next.'

'They are only superstitious peasants.'

'Get on with it, if you're going to cut me.' Next came a yelp. 'Damn it, do you ever sharpen those blades? And have you seen this almanack? The manner in which it seems to predict events is extraordinary. It chills my bones.'

'What does it say?'

'Most of it is ignorant tattle – but it spoke of "blood on the corn" the very day Francis died. And as for the future, God forbid it is accurate. "Princes and grandees will be afflicted by disease and infirmities," is foretold this month. And in December, "A violent and bloody end." Think of it, man. Father always said my birth was foretold – so why not my death? Is it possible? Are there truly scrying crystals and magic mirrors?'

'Be sensible, brother. It will all be mere coincidence and suggestion.'

'I am not convinced. Who is this De Angelo? Could he be anyone you know of, in Chester?'

'The only writer I know hereabouts is that Starling fellow.'

'Not him. What about Dilks? He is an odd fish. What might Dilks have learned of us as he hangs about my wife's petticoats? I am troubled, and I don't mind confessing it.'

'You believe a minister of the church killed Francis?'

Tabitha could catch nothing of Sir John's reply, until he murmured, so quietly that she could barely catch it, '. . . the bishop to remove him.'

'How long will that take? Here. That's nearly ten ounces.'

Sir John yawned loudly. 'Well, your cure had better work this time. Call my man to bring up my horse. And get hold of that almanack and let me have your opinion of it.'

'You cannot expect an educated man to read such vulgar rubbish.'

After a long pause Sir John's voice replied, low and fierce, 'I don't ask you – I order. Which part of your grand education does not allow you to understand plain English?'

TWENTY-SEVEN

An Enigma

In looks I seem of human kind,
But yet I lack a human mind.
I bear a sad or frightful face
And linger long where wrongs take place.
I come and go, I shine and dim
Where'er the heavenly veil grows thin,
But chiefly when the sun is down
I'm often glimpsed on hallowed ground;
And yet despite my awful fame,
I'm but a creature of your brain.

The 5th day of October 1752

St Faith's Day Eve

Luminary: Sun rises 26 minutes after 6.
Observation: The Moon, Mars and Saturn
in malefic aspects.
Prognostication: Unthought-of alterations in events
bring troublesome consequences.

C ome the eve of Saint Faith's day, the virgin martyr, the
      weather changed. No beguiling glitter of dew spread across
      the meadow that morning when she set off for the doctor's
house and Tabitha knew at once that rain was on its way. By four
o'clock, when she fetched Jennet and Bess from Joshua's house,
there was still no smoke rising from the tall chimneys of Eglantine
Hall. So, Nat had disappointed her again. She hurried through the
woods, watching a fresh western wind ruffle the treetops.

'I've told Father I shall stay with you tonight,' Jennet said, ushering
Tabitha in at the door of the Grange. 'It's better than sleeping here
alone, what with him harrying back and forth to Chester.'

While Tabitha waited for Jennet she looked over Joshua's books.
There lay *The Pilgrim's Progress, Every Man His Own Lawyer* and
The Young Man's Guide. Alongside them were a number of journals:
The Universal Magazine and at least a dozen years' worth of De
Angelo's *Vox Stellarum.* Leafing through a copy of the latter, she
found notes written in Joshua's hand. Dates had been underlined
with names and addresses beside them.

Glancing up, she saw that Bess had toddled over to turn the
spinning wheel and watched in open-mouthed fascination as it slowly
spun.

'Stop that,' Tabitha scolded, feeling the baleful presence of Mary
Saxton lingering in the room as powerfully as ever. Bess moved
away from the spinning wheel and Tabitha returned to her reading.

Hetty to the Little Brown Bull at George Holt's, 13 July. It was
nothing but an account of his attempts to increase his stock. Further

on were dates of the assizes and parish councils. It was all as dull
as dust.

Bess had been silent for longer than was common. Sure enough,
the child looked up from a dark corner with wide guilty eyes. On
the floor in front of her was Joshua's document bag, its contents
spilled across the flagstones. Jennet was still busy in her chamber
so Tabitha dropped to the floor beside her.

'Shh,' she said softly and put her finger to her lips. Bess giggled
and inexpertly patted her own mouth. Handing her a ribbon to play
with, Tabitha pulled the bag on to her own lap. Inside were dull
orders from Sir John and the County Gaoler, old arrest warrants
and – God damn his spying eyes – a letter to herself from Nat. She
read it quickly.

> My dear Tabitha,
> Accept my heartfelt apologies for my recent scrawl. Forgive
> me, I have been out of sorts from an abominable surfeit of
> industry.
> I am now much recovered and rewarded with chinking
> guineas, and so with the assistance of your missive, I am again
> fired up to pursue the chase. I shall take this opportunity to
> call upon my mother in Cambridgeshire and dig a little deeper
> into the affairs of 'D'.
> I live in hope of returning by the fifth of October, should
> my mother's prattling tongue allow it. I count the minutes until
> the felicitous state of being once again,
> Your desiring and devoted servant,
> Nat Starling

The pleasure of reading the letter and learning of his eagerness
to see her was soured by the knowledge that Joshua had read it
first. Damnation – he had proof indeed that she corresponded fondly
with Nat, and also that they shared an investigation. Yet she slipped
it back into the bag, thinking it too cruel to confront Joshua yet,
for his theft of her letter was such a pitiful act. He had lost her
affections entirely and must know it.

When Jennet came in with an apron full of oak apples, Tabitha
got up to inspect her bounty.

'Such a crop foretells a hard winter coming and much snow at
Christmas,' Jennet announced.

Tabitha smiled, anticipating nights by the fireplace at Eglantine Hall.

'Winter in the country can be delightful. Soon we'll have All Hallows' Eve and Gunpowder Night – and Christmas.'

'If you want a comfortable Christmas, you must start collecting firewood now,' warned Jennet. 'It was so cold last winter that your mother was forever tramping out in the snow to tend to dying folk.'

Tabitha remained silent. Long dark nights and snow-blocked lanes would be far easier to bear with Nat paying her court and buying her pretty treats with his bag of guineas

By the time they reached the cottage an unnatural gloom had fallen and the wind was rising. Tabitha swept the dried petals of her mother's white rose out over the threshold. There were few stars, and the thinnest crescent of the moon was barely visible, just one day from the pitchy black of October's new moon. Jennet roused the fire and greased the iron griddle, laying out a bowl of water from the spring, a bowl of flour, salt and sugar.

'You forget, we need three girls to do the rite properly,' Tabitha reminded her.

'And so we do have three maids. Bess can take a turn.'

They both laughed and Bess comically joined in the good spirits by performing a clumsy little jig.

First Jennet, then Tabitha, kneaded the dough; then they both coaxed Bess to pat it in mimicry. Next, Jennet baked it on the griddle, and they each turned it thrice, counting up to the magical number nine. By the time they sliced it, night had fallen outside, and the wind was pummelling the garden fence, with rain rat-a-tatting against the thatch and plopping drips inside the windows that must be plugged with rags. They lit no lamp, only huddling closer around the red glow of the fire. Jennet's face was serious and intent, but Bess began yawning, losing interest in the long-winded game. The flat pancake had at first been cut into three, and then each portion was divided a further three times.

Tabitha pulled her mother's wedding ring out of her pocket, and they passed all their slivers of pancake through the circlet before Tabitha carried Bess into the back room to put her to bed.

'I wonder if Bess will dream of her future husband?' Jennet asked cheerfully.

'There is a new Prince of Wales who may do for her. Do you reckon she would have him?'

'Only if he has a good supply of sugarplums.'

'And what about you, Jennet? Have you forgotten Darius yet?'

Jennet had laid the slivers of dry cake on a plate, offering it to Tabitha.

'I shall never forget my first love.' Her voice was so thick with emotion that Tabitha restrained a mocking sigh. With reverence, they each ate a piece of the flat cake; then Tabitha and Jennet both touched the ring and beseeched the ancient saint:

'Oh good Saint Faith, be kind tonight
And bring to me my heart's delight.
Let me my future husband view
And be my vision chaste and true.'

Together they went to the bedroom and hung the charmed wedding ring from the headboard on a cord. Not yet sufficiently tired to sleep, they returned to the parlour and both sat, one on each side of the dim glow of the fire.

'Did you ever pray to Saint Faith when you were a girl, Tabitha?'

She looked up, startled from her reverie. She had been wondering if she would dream of Nat Starling, but a worry had waylaid her that the saint might recommend Joshua, or even Robert, as her husband. She was seized with a sudden impulse to tease. 'I did; but I dreamed of a dreadful hairy fellow who used to work with the pigs at Croft Farm.'

'Oh, no.' Jennet's mouth dropped open, and Tabitha shook her head dolefully.

'Then he began to follow me, whenever I walked alone, as if the spell had truly worked. And the worst of it was, he'd lost his hand, scything wheat. He had a wooden hand now, attached to the stump of his arm.' She struggled to keep her face straight.

'Oh, how dreadful.' Jennet had covered her face, aghast. 'What happened to him?'

Tabitha made a vast effort to look grave. 'He did very well; he's just as good as anyone now. Indeed, he has a *second-hand* stall!' She collapsed on the hearth, yelping with laughter at the foolish jest.

Jennet looked down at her, so stiff with disapproval that Tabitha fell on her and, seizing the wooden spoon, tickled her all over, asking, 'How would you like a wooden hand inside your smock every night?' Soon the two of them were shrieking with laughter.

It was a while until they regained their breath and settled down again before the fire. At length, Jennet looked up mischievously. 'Have you heard the tale of the Devil's bridegrooms over at Tranmere?'

Tabitha pretended she had not, simply for the pleasure of hearing Jennet tell the story. As the logs crackled and the wind whistled down the chimney like a wailing ghoul, Jennet recalled how five serving girls had stayed up on All Hallows' Eve, determined to see the faces of their intended husbands. They laid table and chairs out for ten persons; then, blasphemously, they read The Lord's Prayer backwards – and prayed in the name of His Satanic Majesty that their intended bridegrooms would come and seat themselves at the table.

'Just then, it being the hour of twelve, the doors flew open and five ghastly gentlemen came and seated themselves around the table,' Jennet whispered. 'The girls could barely move themselves for fright and had to sit up with the ghouls for most of the night before they disappeared, the same way as they came. And so,' she ended, 'at least one of the girls, named Martha, died that night of fright.'

The two of them sat for a moment. Then Tabitha lit a rushlight in the fire; the darkness only seemed the greater as it closed round the unsteady point of light.

'Do you believe in the Devil?' Jennet asked.

Tabitha shook her head. 'No. And Mother always said that story had been passed about for years. It is always said to happen in a different village.'

Yet it was easy to believe in such phantoms tonight. The rain lashed against the window in a high-pitched rattle; Tabitha's fingers were growing so cold that she splayed them to absorb the last heat of the fire. It was too wild now to walk down to the river and see if a light was lit at Nat's window. Great God, she hoped he was not travelling in this gale, but had found a comfortable inn upon the road.

Jennet's question lingered in her mind. Was not De Angelo some kind of devil, hounding her mother and ordering Darius to butcher Francis? The notion set off a series of unpleasant echoes in her mind. In London she had seen the worst sides of men's characters; discovering that some sheepish customers hid monstrous wolves beneath their skins. She was shaken from her thoughts by a sound from the garden; very close and low, and almost hidden by the bluster of the weather.

'Do you hear footsteps?' she asked Jennet suddenly.

The question set off a quiver of apprehensive laughter. 'Stop it. Don't tease me!'

The wind roused again, sending a whistling note down the chimney like a broken organ pipe; then, all at once, it dropped, and both could hear the slap of wet footfalls on the garden path. They seized each other's hands.

'Your father?' Tabitha whispered.

Three house-shaking thumps on the door came, loud enough to make them both jump up in fright.

'Get in the back room,' Tabitha commanded. Once Jennet had darted away, she smoothed her skirt and walked boldly to the front door. She had longed for Nat to come home, but this bludgeoning summons did not sound like him; neither was it Joshua, who had a distinctive rapping knock. It was no doubt some desperate neighbour in need of her services as searcher – if so, it was foolish to be frightened.

'Who is it?' she shouted through the oak door.

There was no answer, only another thump that made the boards shake. She shook her head, trying to cast away all the past hour's nonsense. What a pair of ninnies they were, terrifying themselves with tales of nightmarish bridegrooms. There was nothing for it but to discover who it was. She drew back the latch.

The door swung open, and the man who stumbled inside was so rain-drenched that at first she did not know him at all. His dark hair was plastered to his skull and rags clung to his body like a second skin. She stood back and watched as the fellow's large hand steadied himself against the wall. Then two jet-black eyes met hers and a short, pointed knife gleamed in her direction.

'I need food. Fire. Fresh clothes. Fetch Jennet here.'

TWENTY-EIGHT

A Riddle

Though I've no brains I have a head,
And eagerly lap though I'm never fed;
I often murmur but never weep,
Lie in a bed but never sleep.
I have not legs yet swiftly run,
And the larger I grow the quicker I run.
Yet when I'm enraged, I swell and grow faster,
Then no man or beast can my strength master.

St Faith's Day

Luminary: Sun rise at 8 minutes after 5
of the morning.
Observation: New Moon at noon.
Prognostication: As the trees are stripped of leaves,
so hopes also flee in winter.

'We must do as Darius says,' Tabitha urged Jennet, who was now cringing, terrified, in the back room. 'He has barely escaped the gallows; he has nothing to lose.'

Returning to the parlour, they found the fugitive in her mother's chair, dripping water on to the rug and attempting to set a fresh log alight. Grimly, they collected together what little food they could find: the end of a loaf, cheese, brambles and some cold hasty pudding intended for their breakfasts. He stuffed it untasted into his mouth, his black-bristling jaw working as he watched them collect what few clothes of her father's were left. There was an old coat that her mother had used in bad weather, a slouch hat and woollen leggings. He grumbled when they told him they had no liquor but closed his eyes with satisfaction as he drank hot sugared tea.

Setting the cup down, he said, 'You was always telling me you wanted to leave here, Jennet.'

'Me?' she squeaked. 'I have to go home. My father is waiting for me.'

'Don't lie to me! I seen your own house was empty or why else would I be here? There's a packet ship sails for Ireland in the morning, and you and me are taking it. I wouldn't go without you, sweetheart. I'll be looking after you now. Pack a bundle and be ready at first light.'

'She's not going with you,' Tabitha said fiercely, stepping up to him. Darius lifted the knife into his lap and ran the blade across his filthy fingertips.

'You,' he said with loathing. Tabitha could feel his venomous gaze raking her. 'I'll give your sluttish face a little knife-work if you speak another word.'

She lowered her eyes, commanding herself to hold her tongue for Jennet's sake.

'I need a rowing boat to take upriver.'

Jennet looked to her for help, but Tabitha dared not speak again; she only nodded mutely. 'There's a fishing boat in the rushes up the river,' said the girl shakily. 'My father keeps it hidden there.'

Darius yawned ferociously. 'I need to sleep first. Wake me at four. And you be ready, sweetheart. We'll live like kings when we get across the water.'

Once they had both escaped to the back room, Jennet stood trembling.

'I don't want to go. He might hurt me. I don't like him anymore.'

'I know. When he leaves I want you to do exactly what I tell you. Do you understand?'

'What should I do?'

Tabitha began to dress in her warmest clothes, tying her mother's quilted petticoat up around her waist.

'I'm still thinking. You lie still and try to rest.'

Jennet lay down very still on the bed, her narrow back trembling. Tabitha peeped through to where Darius was snoring, his head lolling, the knife still tight in his fist. She considered running for help, to the village or to Joshua; but as soon as she opened the front door the blast of wind and noise were certain to alert him. She looked at the tiny windows; they were too narrow even for Jennet to wriggle through. God help them, though she was growing foggy with tiredness, she had to think clearly. Should she try to follow Darius and Jennet when they set off? No, too risky – as soon as Jennet got into the rowing boat, she would be lost.

Trying not to make a sound, she stepped into the parlour and started to wrap the last scraps of food in a kerchief. There was scarcely anything left, only Bess's Saint Faith cake, a few withered apples and a handful of nuts.

The church bell had just rung out midnight when she returned to the bedroom.

'I'm feared I won't hear the time in this storm,' Jennet whimpered.

'I'll listen out for the bells.'

Setting a newly lit rushlight in its holder, Tabitha found her
mother's almanack, and leafed through the pages until she found
what she needed:

1752 October Hath XXXI Days

6th Day Saturday. St Faith, Virgin and Martyr. *Sunrise 8 minutes
past 5.*

Finally, she laid down next to the girl and placed a comforting
arm around her bony shoulders.

'Try to rest,' she whispered.

The next four hours were a purgatory, filled with snatched spells
of dozing and horrified awakenings. Soon after the bells rang out
four faint chimes, Tabitha got up, wanting plenty of time to arrange
matters. The wind was still raging outside, buffeting roof-boards
and whistling through the thatch. Going back to the parlour she
revived the fire and threw some oats into the pot. Darius pretended
to sleep on, but she caught him watching her through his long black
lashes. When she set the porridge down before him he asked for
light.

'All our candles are gone,' she said. 'Not even a rushlight until
we make some more.'

Putting on her red cloak, she unlatched the front door and was
blown backwards as the rain buffeted her, sending spitting darts into
her face. It was still pitch dark, and she could sense, rather than
see, tree branches lifting around her. The air was biting cold.

Stepping back inside, she saw Darius pulling on his boots.

'She ready?'

'I'll go and see.'

Jennet was still curled up on the bed, though her eyes were wide
and stared at nothing.

'Listen,' Tabitha said, so quietly that it was scarcely a breath.
'Get dressed and go with him, as far as the gate. Then tell him you
have forgotten your bundle of food. I'll be waiting inside.'

'I cannot go,' she whimpered. 'What will Father say?'

'Just do as I tell you and all will be well.'

It was a struggle to dress Jennet in her gown and grey cloak –
she recoiled at every touch. By the time she was ready Darius was
pacing the room, bundled in dry clothes.

'You,' he barked at Tabitha, grasping Jennet's arm and directing the point of his knife at her breast. 'Not a word to the law, or I'll slice her. Got it?'

She nodded. 'I'll stay low, wait here. I'll do anything to keep her safe.'

Then turning to Jennet, she said, 'Good luck. Be brave, my girl.'

Jennet cast her a despairing glance. Then, held tightly in Darius's grip, she was half-dragged out of the front door into the gale. Tabitha waited at the door, her nerves stretched to their limits. First Darius, then Jennet reached the garden gate. Timing was all.

'Jennet! Your bundle, with the food and money,' she shouted. 'You forgot it. Come back.'

She heard Darius curse, but a moment later Jennet stumbled back towards the cottage door. Tabitha hastened her inside, dragging off her wet grey cloak, and cast it around herself, pulling the hood down low. Then, snatching up the bundle, she stepped out into the rain and slammed the door on the bewildered Jennet.

Darius was a pale blur, waiting for her on the track. He called to her, but his words were snatched away by the wind. As soon as they moved from the cottage door, he was nothing but a grey phantom ahead of her, and she hoped she was little more to him. She followed him, striving to stay a few paces behind him, her feet moving blindly onwards, her shoes sinking into wet mud and puddles. In a minute she was soaked to the skin, her heavy skirts dragging around her ankles. On a night like this, even the countryside she knew so well could bewilder her like a foreign land. She strove to read her surroundings, trying to wipe her eyes free of stinging rain. Every few moments there came a lull in the wind when she could hear Darius's steady breathing and the wet slap of his footsteps. As her eyes grew stronger she could see his silhouette more clearly before her, as light on his feet as a muscled tomcat, well used to padding through woodland at night.

The mud beneath her feet stopped squelching and began to crunch as they reached the gravel path. The river was running high, and sounded like a hissing giant, waiting in ambush. Somewhere in the sky above her was a tiny sliver of moon, but it was obscured by rainclouds. The stars, too, gave off no glimmer of starlight. Could not this murk be turned to her advantage? For a few moments, she considered trying to lure Darius off the path, but that felt too perilous.

Then the mournful bleating of sheep told her they were passing to the right of the farmer's pasture. Darius was slowly descending ahead of her, and she felt herself, too, moving downhill. The river had to be her best chance, but what she could do with it was as yet unclear. Too quickly they came upon its roaring presence; a rush of pale movement hurtling past them, throwing freezing pinpricks into her face. She tried to sight the stepping stones but could see nothing breaking the surface's foam. If Darius wished to escape, he had been a fool, truly, to wait at the cottage while the waters rose so high.

His face was a smudge of pallor in the dark.

'Which way to the boat?'

Her hand was numb from holding her hood down over her face. Not daring to speak, she tugged his sodden sleeve, and motioned for him to follow her. Joshua kept his boat upriver towards Chester, by the bank where her mother's body had been found. Now that she led the way, she felt Darius watching her back, convinced he would notice from her figure and gait that she was an imposter.

Soon she had greater worries to occupy her. The last half-mile was like a maze built on a marsh; the usual riverside path had disappeared beneath the rising waters, and she had to move to higher land, feeling her way along the spongy banks. Little rills of panic assailed her. Once, when Darius startled her by coming too close, she lost her footing and slithered down a mud bank, arms flailing, only saving herself by clutching at a sapling. Beside her, the river roared, barely a hands' breadth away.

Painfully, she hauled herself back up to higher ground. She was frightened of falling, but more frightened still by visions of Darius's victims. Her mother's last moments had been spent near this very spot, in terror of this man. Poor, foolish Francis had also been butchered by him. She moved forward, calf-deep in the sinking marsh, as terrified exhaustion threatened to overwhelm her.

At last, she felt spikes of furry bulrush meet her outstretched hands. Just then, like an omen of good fortune, she heard the faint notes of Netherlea's church bell announcing five o'clock. She stopped in her tracks, trying to understand the lie of the land. A sickly glow in the east was illuminating the sky. Where was the boat? It was years since she had been here with Joshua, and now she could only sense hundreds of dark furry spikes, moving like waves in the wind. And if she found the boat, what then? Her usefulness would be over.

Darius's heavy hand fell like a dead weight on her shoulder.

'Where is it?'

Still holding her hood up with her frozen hand, she turned away from him and looked up-river. There it was, a dozen paces away; the stump of a mooring and the bobbing shape of a boat, covered in a dark oil-skin. Not daring to speak, she lifted her other arm and pointed, waiting for him to move towards it. If he would only be distracted by the boat, she could try to run away . . . But instead, he grasped her arm, and dragged her through knee-high water towards the boat. Too late, she remembered the strength and whiplash swiftness he had shown in Netherlea gaol. Clumsily, they both stumbled onwards in a flurry of splashes, and he whipped off the oilskin. Finally, he yanked Tabitha towards him, snatched down her hood, and pulled her face so close to his that she could smell his dog-like breath.

'Did you think I wouldn't know you?' he taunted. 'You'll wish you'd never tried your poxy tricks before I finish with you.'

The next moment, she felt herself thrown into the air; then, with a shriek of pain, she struck the solid bottom of the boat. For a long moment, she was winded, and her head spun. With a great effort she raised it and saw that Darius had turned his back on her as he untied the boat from its mooring. Testing her body, she found that the base of her spine hurt, but she could still move. This is your chance, her mind screamed.

She raised herself up on her elbows, reached for the gunwales, then hefted herself up and over the side of the boat and plunged into the water. Gasping, she spluttered as mud-thick water blocked her eyes and nose. Then, finding her feet in the slutch, she took a deep breath, kicked out, and launched herself towards a patch of rushes.

There was a sudden sound of rushing air behind her, culminating in a violent whack and splash. The end of the oar had barely missed her shoulder. She launched herself deeper and further away, through the hard but springy rushes. Burrowing into their centre, she crouched, trying to make herself as small as possible as Darius hit out again with the oar, cursing and raging.

'You stupid bitch! I'll make you beg for your last breath, just like I did your mother. The old baggage woke from the blow I gave to her head, but she didn't struggle long under water. But I'll draw it out sweet and slow for you.'

Tabitha listened in growing dread and rage, wishing to God she had a knife to drive deep into his black heart.

When he grew quieter she inched her way forward, observing him through a gap in the stalks. It was getting lighter every minute, and at last he sat down in the boat, attempting to paddle it through the reeds towards the main flow of the river. She was shivering from head to foot, and her teeth were chattering so violently that she feared the sound would betray her.

Just as he edged the boat forward he turned; his rage had not yet burned away. He yelled out at her, and she tried to shrink away beneath the water.

'I curse you, festering whore! You think this is ended, but you've still got my master to reckon with. I've seen you swallowing his every crafty word. You reckon him such a great good fellow, while all the time he plays you for a fool. May you rot in Hell!'

With dreadful slowness, he manoeuvred the boat through the rushes, until it hung at the very edge of the river's tidal flow. The main torrent was a dirty, foaming mass that swept along branches and debris in its flow. Gripping a handful of rushes with one hand and the oar with another, Darius steadied the boat, trying to judge the best moment to steer out into the current. Suddenly he let go, and the boat shot out into the race, spun around like a leaf in a whirlpool, tilted to vertical and capsized.

In an instant, Darius disappeared beneath the surface. Tabitha strained to look for him in the half-light; but, while the up-ended boat floated upstream, its oarsman never broke the surface again.

She stared at the spot for a long time, blinking sleepily, unable to rouse herself. She knew she had to act but was having difficulty remembering what it was she must do. Finally, she noticed the shoreline and tried to drag herself towards it. It was no use: her clothes dragged her backwards into the river, clinging and trapping her weakened limbs.

She shook her head and blinked. The sun was getting brighter with every moment; a marsh bird whooped and fluttered nervously in the sky. She drew heart from the slow transformation of the world around her, the retreat of the darkness and the fresh pinkish light of dawn. Pulling drenched hair from her eyes she noticed smoke rising from Eglantine Hall's tall chimneys behind the trees. With anguished cries of effort, she slithered up to the shore, until at last, with much panting and heaving, she hauled herself up and on to the grassy bank.

TWENTY-NINE

A Riddle

I grace the cottage, court and town,
My feathers are as soft as cygnets' down:
Four feet I have and yet my head is bare,
My curtains wrap and yet no window's there;
One half the year as if with leaden wand,
Death's elder brother does o'er me command,
But sometimes he to active love gives place,
And makes me fruitful with her warm embrace.

The 6th to the 30th day of October 1752

Luminary: The day shortened to 10 hours long,
decreased 6 hours 26 minutes.
Observation: Opposition of Saturn and Mars
from Virgo and Pisces.
Prognostication: It is not safe to be too secure.

When Nat first heard the sound of knocking, he thought it must be a shutter banging in the infernal wind. He pulled his coat more tightly around his shoulders and hunched over the fire, too exhausted to investigate. The Cambridge coach had rolled into Chester well after midnight, and all his fellow passengers had trailed into the golden-lit entrance of the Cross Keys Tavern. He alone had held back; his business in Cambridgeshire had already delayed him damnably, and he was rattled, as if the uneasy wind had infected him with its fretfulness. So he ordered a glass of negus to be sent to the stables, and after a delighted reunion with Jupiter, was soon up in the saddle. There had been no letter from Tabitha for three days, and anticipation of her surprise the next morning glowed like a hot coal inside him, through all the dark and drenching ride back home.

The banging continued to penetrate his reverie until he noticed that the knocks were being struck in weak beats of three. He stood and yawned, leaving his night robe warming before the fire. Taking only a candle, he went downstairs in a flurry of chasing shadows. In the hallway, he could hear nothing at all. Curious, he opened the front door and found daylight seeping into the sky, and a heap of wet clothing discarded on his steps. Investigating with the toe of his boot, he was horrified to find that a person lay within it; and, even worse, that it was Tabitha who lay there, senseless on the ground.

For sweet pity's sake, he cursed. Why had he not investigated sooner? Swiftly he carried her upstairs, her limbs hanging stone cold in their dripping garments. Then he laid her in a high-backed chair beside the fire, fetching a blanket and bottle of spirits. She was insensible and her face had a bluish cast; across her cheek, a swollen ridge was sliced, a wound the length of his finger. God spare him – but at least she breathed, faintly but regularly. In a panic, he pulled at her wet clothes, peeling off her sodden grey cloak, heavy skirts and petticoat. What price modesty when his sweet love might die?

Her garments were gritty and stained muddy brown and smelled of the river. He had got as far as her stays when he found the knots seized – he sliced through them with his knife. Trying not to look too hard at the curves and crannies of her nakedness, he dragged her clinging shift up over her head and began to dry her with the blanket. She shivered, her eyelids flickering, but remaining closed. Once his own green Chinese robe was wrapped around her, he reached for the cauldron of water warming by the fire. Gently, he washed her face, and then the skeins of her long hair, lathering it with almond soap and cradling her head as mud and broken leaves were rinsed away. Tenderly he dried the snake-like tangles that dripped down to her waist. He was thankful to see her colour improve, and a pulse beat at her neck. He carried her over to his bed and laid her down. Then he set a warm cup of brandy to her lips.

The spirits made her gasp, and her eyelids fluttered. Finally, she blinked, and looked at him for the first time.

'Dammit, Tabitha. Are you trying to scare me to death with such a greeting?'

She stared up at him, seeming not to see him. Fetching a hot stone from the fire and wrapping it in flannel, he pushed it inside the bed.

'I need warmth,' she whispered hoarsely. He obliged, and she clung to him, knotting trembling fingers into his shirt.

'What happened to you, my poor love?'

'Darius. Came to the cottage.' In fits and starts she recalled her ordeal. 'I think he's dead,' she ended. 'Save me, Nat. I thought I would die.'

Damn the rogue to hell! He had almost lost her. He kissed the wound on her face, tasting the iron-saltiness of her blood. As he did so, her mouth slid to his throat, exciting a pang of pleasure. He was holding her gently in his arms, but she pulled him tighter against her, bone to bone, locking them together. He tried to free himself. This could not be honourable, he told himself; to take advantage of a half-drowned woman.

'I am so cold,' she begged.

'Tabitha, stop.'

His blood was heating and hardening, nevertheless. He kissed the top of her head, as though she were a child. Still she clung to him, trying to absorb every ounce of his heat. Her eyes were open and glassy, her lips parted, her hair a Medusa's nest. She looked like a wild woodland creature, a tangled dryad of the forest.

'Warm me, Nat.'

Her breath tickled his neck, and a pang shot directly to his groin. She was a pitiable creature plucked from the hands of Death himself, but she was also an extraordinary being: *Agape*, the muse he had searched for all his life. She moved beneath him, and his bones grew incandescent. I am on the edge of the precipice, he marvelled; if I leap, everything will change. Then all argument ended – he could no longer think of anything but her.

Kissing her, he felt a deep tremor in her jaw; her mouth was warm and yielding, yet still her skin was cold as a shroud. He chafed her arms and found himself pulled closer still. Involuntarily, he groaned. Damn his blood, she was trembling in his arms, shuddering, her eyes half-closed. Her icy hand snaked down and lifted her robe, uncovering the length of her naked leg. Now she was tugging at his shirt.

'I thought I would die,' she whispered. 'Bring me to life again.'

Her wide eyes were no longer unfocussed but piercing him, shining with tears. For an instant he puzzled over the meaning of her words; then he lost himself, plunging into the crimson darkness.

He only returned to himself after the exquisite spasm of his own little death, when, as the ancients wrote, a man's soul leaps for an instant outside the bounds of Time itself. In their mutual pleasure, they had whispered together. Words, he understood for the first time, were rungs in a golden ladder that carried him to a place entirely new and glorious. She loved him, she had known it from her very first sight of him, and he had whispered in reply of his adoration, calling her his treasure, his true love, his wanton queen. Now she lay still and dreamy, her heart still thrumming fast. A frond of fern-like weed lay exquisitely pressed against her pink-tipped breasts. He rose to his elbow and surveyed her, every inch of her, like a bounty.

Her eyes opened. She did not smile but gazed at him with her unearthly eyes.

'I am a little warmer now,' she said.

She found his hand and pulled it to her secret cleft, drawing him closer in a greedy trance. He licked the cut on her cheek like a lascivious cat. He told her he would never ever leave her, that they were one now, and were bound together for all time.

Tabitha was content to stay on at Eglantine Hall. Nat had no wish ever to see another soul again; but when she asked, he dutifully sent for the constable to inform him of Darius's fate. Saxton barged in ill-temperedly, looking for a quarrel.

'Where were you when the prisoner was trying to abduct my daughter?'

'On the road from Chester,' Nat replied courteously.

'So you merely happened to arrive back upon the same night as that blackguard, Darius?'

If he had not been floating on a paradisiacal cloud, Nat might have shot the buffoon down with a well-aimed insult. Instead, he laughed.

'Yes, you have it, Saxton. I have been hiding the rogue in my portmanteau, all this time.'

Just then the constable caught sight of Tabitha lying in Nat's bed, and coloured like a virgin boy. Poor fellow, Nat thought; for now, he pitied any man who did not possess her. She sat up against a bolster, still wearing his own green robe, looking flushed and dishevelled and wonderfully provoking, as the constable questioned her. Impatiently, he listened as Saxton prepared a statement about her encounter with Darius. When she recounted Darius's confession that he was her mother's murderer, her voice shook. Nat was not certain, but it looked to him as if Saxton was holding her hand across his counterpane. At that moment, he could have knocked the constable's head clean from his hulking shoulders.

A few hours later, Saxton returned to announce that Darius's body had been found, bloodied and battered, trapped in the mill's weir.

'Sir John is jubilant at the news; and is overjoyed that your mother's murderer is found, Tabitha. As for me,' mumbled Joshua, 'I should never have believed you would risk your own life like that. I will never forget that you saved Jennet's life. There's no need to fret about Bess; Jennet will keep her with us till you are up and about.'

Nat paced like a panther, waiting for the constable to leave. If there was any rescuing to be done, he thought, Joshua had wished to do it himself. It must rankle him to be obliged to a woman, especially a woman he so violently wanted, and whom he had lost to Nat himself.

Nat had never before noticed that October was the most abundant month of the year. The summer was not dying; rather the earth was ripening in a short but vigorous explosion of life. Through autumn's copper-tinted days, he and Tabitha wandered slowly in the grounds of Eglantine Hall; within the crumbling walls grew brambles and yellow crab apples, soon succeeded by purple-bloomed sloes, rose hips and black elders. They unburdened themselves of their child-hoods and younger lives, of their secret whims and most profound beliefs. On warm afternoons they reclined in a leafy arbour, and Nat felt himself to be some bold knight from a long-lost tale, courting a beautiful sorceress. Tabitha was surprising, funny, spir-ited; and also, he marvelled, a most lascivious lover. Each night, in the universe of his bed, they were transformed into twin pulses chasing each other in the darkness. Time, if it existed, was a mere word – their lives were measured in spasms of pleasure before they tumbled into sleep as dawn approached, echoing each other's deep-ening breaths.

One such night, Nat told her his speculations on travel through time itself.

'I once read a collection of letters titled *Memoirs of the Twenty-first Century*. In it, a fellow possessed a guardian angel that carried letters back and forth into some future date, the year 2019, if I recollect.'

'I cannot even comprehend such a vast time into the future.'

'Why, it is only two hundred and sixty-seven years hence. Think of how it might be. I have heard engineers describe machines with near magical capacities quite unknown to us. We might have animated statues to be our servants.'

'I hope they can dress hair in the latest style and tie those difficult back laces.'

'Certainly, and pray let the female type be comely and pliant. I can think of many uses—'

She dug him with her elbow but he was in full flow now.

'And I have also heard of mighty cities run by clockwork. Picture it, coaches driving across the land without horses, their motion arising from the turning of a key. Mechanical looms, ovens and even ships. And flying carriages with powerful springs that send us careering up into the sky like fireworks. I would take my telescope on such a voyage.'

'I hope you would invite me.'

He pulled his arm even tighter around her and his tortoiseshell eyes shone.

'I may even give you your own telescope. And if these machines perform all our dreariest labours, there would be more time for love and poetry and bed.'

'Ah, your ideal world.'

'A better world. And I would be well paid for my scribblings. Or, listen to this. I would employ an angel of time to fly to a century distant in the future, where he finds my greatest poem. My time-leaping angel would return here with a fair copy. So I would possess my poem before I have written it!'

Tabitha laughed, saying only Nat would contrive such a world, in which poets had all the praise and none of the labour.

He began to laugh, his shoulders heaving with mirth so he could barely speak.

'So then I copy this poem and sell it to great esteem. The printers keep selling it, I grow rich, and my name becomes immortal. You agree? Yes! But who wrote it? Not me. I merely copied it!'

Their idyll was disturbed only when the doctor called on Tabitha. The man who hobbled in was a sadly diminished figure, bent over a walking stick and looking about himself with disapproval, as if he detected an air of lovers' deshabille about the place. Before Nat could stop him, he shambled to the wall displaying their speculations upon the murders.

'What is this?' he said, pointing belittlingly with his cane.

Nat blushed. On the wall, as clear as crystal, was a paper with the title *The Doctor*, and a list of reasons why he might have wished to kill his own nephew. He tried to remember if Saxton had also stopped to read their conjectures. Dammit, he was too short of sleep to remember.

'I am a writer,' he mumbled. 'Such matters intrigue me.'

'A scribbler, eh? We all, sir, believed you to be a gentleman. I pray you do not think to publish any scribblings about these persons to whom you are so greatly obliged.'

Nat felt a stab of shame that might have been his conscience at work. Why, this was the merest sampling of his sins. To his knowledge, his pamphlet on the Bloody Almanack had not yet been seen in Netherlea; each day such ignorance continued, he was filled with gratitude, and prayed it might remain so. Yes, he had enjoyed writing it, and had welcomed the money it earned – but now that it was finished, to be identified as its author struck him as a nightmare beyond endurance. Nat made a stiff little bow to the doctor, who dismissed him with a wave of his fingers.

When the doctor had departed, Tabitha relayed his diagnosis.

'The knocks to my head and back are pretty severe, and he has given me a salve for the cut to my cheek. He did not remark on the bruises to my thighs . . .' she teased. 'I must stay abed a whole month, though that will be no suffering if you will join me.'

'He does not like me,' said Nat.

Tabitha pulled an amused face. 'He is jealous. For an ailing man, he is rather a gallant; he has always cast a greybeard's twinkle in my direction.'

'He saw our speculations on the wall. If only I had covered them with a cloth. I don't care to think of him telling his brother about it.'

'I thought you were Sir John's friend?'

Nat felt trapped again. '"Friend" is not quite the correct term.' Even as he spoke, he hated his pedantic tone.

'Well, what is the correct term, then? They are all suffering heavy misfortune, Nat. The doctor is dying. Sir John is unwell, too. There is talk that neither may survive the winter.'

'Good God.' Nat turned aside to mask his consternation.

'I know. There is something sinister at the heart of this.'

He shook his head, unable to find any words.

'I am sorry you don't like the doctor,' Tabitha went on. 'I have told him I'll help him with his papers again as soon as I'm up and about.'

'Why?' He was irritated by the news, recalling the hostility in the man's jaundiced eye. 'We have money. There is no need for you to work.'

'It is a pleasure for me. Truly. He is sick; I enjoy helping him.'

'But do you trust him?'

'Yes, I do. He has helped me at every step, has he not? He has given me a cottage, respectable work, kindly regard; and even,' she hesitated, 'kept me out of the way of his brother when he calls.'

Nat nodded, placated. Then he glanced at the tattered pages on the wall and raked his fingers through his hair.

'Back to our inquiry, then. I have news of Mr Dilks.'

He saw he had her immediate attention. 'Firstly, I am afraid, I made inquiries and found that he was indeed at the Bishop's Palace the night your mother died. On the other hand, I made enquiries of a man I still know at Trinity and discovered that Dilks was dismissed from his position as chaplain there. The matter was kept quiet, for it involved a young pupil of his. The boy was punished much too brutally.'

'No! Poor boy.'

'It seems he was beaten – viciously beaten. His parents threatened to go to the law. And there was a question of – I would say this only to you, Tabitha – of unnatural practices.'

'Did you know that Dilks was also Francis's tutor? There was a falling out there, too; Dilks thrashed him so severely that he complained to his father. Perhaps Francis was killed to keep the parson's unnatural behaviour quiet? What else did your friend say?'

'That Dilks has powerful allies. Lady Daphne takes his side and will barely speak a word without his instruction. She and the De Vallory family made certain he took refuge in Netherlea after his dismissal.'

'Do you think he hopes, through her ladyship, to gain control of the estate?'

'Quite possibly. I heard, too, that her ladyship is prone to nervous attacks, and mystical – some might say lunatic – visions. God forbid Sir John were not fit and well. Dilks need only appoint himself her guardian to take the reins of all.'

'I am sure it is he,' Tabitha said. 'While you were away, I saw Lady Daphne waiting for Dilks outside the church. They both regarded me with the utmost malice, as if I had witnessed them conspiring in secret. As for her ladyship, I know she is disturbed in her mind; but remember how she threw that threat from De Angelo into the fire? I fear them both, Nat. I am only tolerated here because the doctor insists I stay on as searcher.'

Nat stroked her hair. 'I don't care to think of you in danger like this. Promise me that you will not pursue De Angelo alone.'

'I promise. But neither must you endanger yourself, Nat. Promise me that in return.'

'Very well.' He rapidly kissed her fingers. 'To other matters: I made enquiries in London about the almanack's printer. The address on the frontispiece is a sham. Number thirteen St Paul's Courtyard does not exist. Apparently, it is something of a joke; an ancient thoroughfare that did once exist but was destroyed in the Great Fire. It is commonly used as an address by printers hoping to evade their creditors.'

'So what do you construe from that?'

'That De Angelo is both clever and ruthless.'

'And do you believe he is Dilks?'

Nat pressed his lips together tightly and shook his head. 'He is a likely suspect. Without evidence, though, that is all I can say.'

THIRTY

A Riddle

I'm seen on high in yonder sky;
I'm seen below where waters flow;
I'm seen on breasts where honour rests.
My several meanings now determine:
Reverse me, and I stand for vermin.

The 30th day of October 1752

Luminary: Hunter's Moon in the Last Quarter.
Observation: Trine of Jupiter and Mars.
Prognostication: A beneficent aspect seems to
predominate over other malignant rays.

F or many days Tabitha stayed indoors by the fire, warm in the
crook, of Nat's body, as a deluge of rain rattled against the
high oriel windows. When the rain finally stopped, he told her
to wrap up warmly, as he wished to show her a great marvel of
nature. He dressed her in his swaggering shagreen coat, fastened
with shining buttons, and gold braid edging the deep cuffs. Laughing,
she set his second-best cocked hat on her head at a rakish tilt. Once
outside, she inhaled a lungful of frosty air, and it revived her like
an elixir.

'You must not see where we're going.'

He tied a kerchief over her eyes and led her by the arm like a
blind woman all the way down the lane. She squealed at her help-
lessness; from the way her shoes slipped on frozen mud, he seemed
to be taking her out towards open country.

'Are you hoping to drown me?' She laughed.

He made no answer, but slowly guided her through a gate, and
along a narrow path whose edges fell away into water. Finally he
turned her about and stood behind her.

'Open your eyes.'

He removed the kerchief and she looked. The water that
surrounded them was a vast black satin mirror, perfectly reflecting
the night sky, joining the heavens and watery earth in a giddy
diorama of infinity. She rocked on her heels, feeling that if she
stepped forward she might plummet down and down into the fath-
omless stars.

Nat threw a pebble into the water, and the universe at their feet
rippled as a million stars blurred and collided; gradually, the water
stilled and the whole glittering panoply returned. There were two
quarter moons, one above them like a silver feather, while its contrary

twin basked in the blackness below. Both moons appeared magically suspended, like an act of levitation performed on the grand stage of the sky.

Nat clasped her, and the length of his body pressed against her back as he breathed in her ear.

'For thousands of years men and women have watched that mysterious moon as it voyages through dark oceans, and have wished upon it, wished for their hearts' desires.'

She looked from one to the other of the twin moons, seemingly in two distant regions of the universe, yet each exerting the force of tides, directing blood and dreams and poets' fancies.

'Man, even with all his ingenious tinkering and invention, has made nothing to compare to this.'

It was true, she thought. What had paltry humans created to compare to God's great revolving universe? They had only their own little universe, the magnetic forces between hearts and minds.

'Do you see that shining light? It is Venus, the planet I worship.'

He pointed, and her eye followed his forefinger, landing on a twinkle of quicksilver-blue.

'Here.' He made a movement, as if plucking the planet from the heavens; then drew his cupped hand down to show her what he had caught. 'For you.'

He uncurled her fingers and dropped something into her palm – not a tiny planet, but something circular and metallic. He slipped the ring on to her finger and raised it high, so she could just glimpse a glittering speck of light. 'A star for you to wear forever.'

She flexed her hand, and felt emotion swell joyfully within her.

'Will you have me, then? To have and to hold?'

'To be buxom in bed and in board?' Her voice was breathless as she repeated the old country vow.

'Yes, please, lady.'

She turned about carefully on the narrow spit of land, and he was a silhouette of darkness, starless and gigantic, like the first ever shadow cast of a man. She fingered the jewel that jutted from the crown of the ring. She was happier than she could ever remember.

'I will love you till the stars fall, Nathaniel Starling. And I will wear my star forever, in remembrance of this night.'

Towards the end of another delicious evening, Nat reclined beside her on the bed, caressing the undulations of her body.

'I would never have known you had borne a child.'

It was innocently spoken, but Tabitha's every sinew tightened at his words. He didn't notice, but leaned over her, eager for love.

'My love,' he said, trailing his fingertips across her shoulder, 'I will be glad to take Bess as my own, if you wish it, and if her father does not object. Does he live here in the village?'

'I swore an oath,' she said dully.

'To this man? Surely any promise is null and void, now we are so content together.'

'No. The oath is binding.'

She turned away and covered herself. Sweet Cupid, the urge to confess was so strong she could barely resist it. Yet always it rang out in her head – that she had made a blood oath and must never break it. 'Maybe one day I will tell you. Only give me a little more time.'

Without protesting further, he kissed her on her brow. Grateful, but surprised, she wondered why he did not press her. Then, at some subterranean level, she recalled his own hedgings and evasions. But such troublesome thoughts, she decided, were best forgotten, for the time being at least.

THIRTY-ONE

A Riddle

What each one has received
Quite soon in their life;
What brave ones have achieved
By labour and strife;
What each man bestows
On her whom he espouses;
What some people choose
To put upon their houses.
What no groat has cost,
Yet may not be disdained;
For if once it is lost
It cannot be regained.

The 31st day of October 1752

All Hallows' Eve

Luminary: Daybreak at 15 minutes after 5.
Observation: The square of Jupiter and Mars will
initiate immoral actions.
Prognostication: A spirit of fanatic hypocrisy
animates mankind.

'Nat, get up!' Tabitha stood at the oriel window, looking down the drive of Eglantine Hall in dismay. Joshua and a band of men were marching between the ruined gate-posts; at their rear trundled the black prison coach. Ever since Joshua's visit, she had wondered if he would be able to stop himself from persecuting Nat. True, it had saddened her to see her old friend suffer, but she thought it for the best if Joshua finally knew he could not have her. At last, he might find someone new.

And now Joshua was striding up the driveway, his constable's staff like a cudgel in his hand. What a dunderhead she had been! He must have been plotting to ruin Nat during all these weeks she had been idling in bed. She ran to where Nat lay sleeping and pulled the tangle of bedsheets off him.

'Nat! Joshua is here. Get dressed and prepare to face whatever accusations he has invented.'

Nat's eyes opened in alarm.

'Here. Put on your best coat.' She handed him his articles, fussing over him like a fond mother. Too soon, loud knocking rang out from below. Tabitha pulled her mother's blue linsey gown over her night-shift and tried to smooth her hair as she clattered downstairs. She cursed her trusting nature as she reached the door. She and Nat should have left for London weeks ago. What a stupid pair of lummocks they were, so drunk on passion they could no longer think rationally.

She opened the door with a volley of protests, but Joshua signalled coolly for her to return upstairs. There Nat awaited them in his gold-laced coat, hat in hand, casting a mildly amused expression upon the proceedings. He made a bow to Joshua and waited, entirely unflustered. In that moment she loved him with a painful rush of pride.

'Mr Starling. Tabitha. I am commanded here by Sir John De Vallory . . .' Joshua faltered in his speech.

'Spit it out, Joshua,' she goaded. 'I see you cannot wait to arrest him.'

He shook his head, saying quietly, 'Forgive me. I do this upon compulsion.'

Then, in his official voice, he cried, 'Tabitha Hart. I command you to accompany me into the presence of Sir John De Vallory to a hearing of the Manor Court this day, All Hallows' Eve, in the name of the King.'

She was carried in that same mournful carriage in which Darius had been transported to Chester Castle. The notion that even that scoundrel at least had the wits to plan his escape did nothing to cheer her. All the way to Bold Hall she racked her brain as to why, in the Devil's name, she had been summoned; but even as the sour-smelling carriage rattled between the gates of Bold Hall, she could not revive her wits.

Dismounting, Joshua took her arm and led her down a labyrinth of passages until they reached the Great Hall where the Manor Court was in progress. A pair of magnificent double doors opened upon a row of men seated behind a long table. At their centre Sir John sat gowned in black, looking for all the world like a great shaggy lion at the head of his pride. She felt a small measure of relief to see the doctor sitting on his right-hand side, greeting her with a kindly nod. On the other side sat Mr Dilks, stone-faced in his parson's white bands and wig. The rest of the court was made up of Bold Hall's stewards, churchwardens and local dignitaries. She knew little of its process, save that as their baron, Sir John could order them to meet and deal with offences of back-rents, poaching and parish matters. Too late, she berated herself for dressing Nat in all his finery while she was thrust forward, sleepy-eyed and rumpled in her mother's threadbare gown. After weeks spent in bed, she felt fusty, and her hastily pinned hair threatened to tumble past her shoulders. Joshua guided her to a central spot some few yards from where Sir John sat enthroned beneath the gilded De Vallory crest.

Tabitha took a shaky breath as she felt the eyes of the assembled men bear down upon her.

'Tabitha,' Sir John said in his rumbling bass. 'It pains me to bring you here today, but you have avoided my messengers and ignored my own written summonses. You have forced my hand in calling you to this court.'

She felt her mouth fall open. If not for an assignation, for what reason had he wanted to meet her? Somehow, she had entirely misread his attentions. Then, remembering herself, she stood up straight and looked at each of the men before her in turn. Whatever the accusation, she must bear it with dignity.

'Mr Dilks has come to me with an accusation that I would not ordinarily have considered. However, as it relates to some concerns of my own, I have agreed to question you here.'

At the sound of Mr Dilks' name she looked over to the parson; the false benevolence upon his face made her want to spit.

'The parson tells me that you have refused to name the father of your child, contrary to the strict rules of this parish. This is further aggravated by your being appointed a parish officer yourself, namely the searcher of this village. And secondly, Mr Dilks tells me that you intend at some near date to depart this place and return to London, thereby leaving your child as a burden upon the parish of Netherlea. You force me to strike at the heart of this matter. The parish register holds only a blank against the name of your child's father, and that will not do. So I demand that you name that man.'

As she listened to Sir John's speech Tabitha felt ugly panic quickening in her veins. A dozen pairs of eyes watched her struggle to find an answer.

'I cannot say.'

Sir John grimaced as if in pain. 'Fetch the Bible, Constable.'

The Bible was fetched, and it fell to Joshua to assist her in swearing the oath, before God, to tell the truth. To her distress, she found that the black book shook in her hand.

Sir John leaned forward intently, his arms folded upon the oak table; the shadows of his grief scored his face.

'It is a simple question. Who is the father of that child?' To Tabitha's consternation, he pointed towards a wooden settle, where Bess slumbered on Jennet's knee.

'The truth is, Sir John. I do not know.'

'Do not trifle with me, Tabitha. It pains me to speak of it, but did we not meet together some years past? And did I not give you a guinea for a certain service?'

At that, an indignant intake of breath rose from a number of the crowd. Sir John looked about himself and raised a grin, an old stag enjoying rattling his antlers.

'Though I must add that this service was not, naturally, for my own satisfaction. I gave you a guinea, did I not, to lay out for a private room – to celebrate the coming of age of my late son, Francis.'

A creak from the minstrels' gallery above warned Tabitha that someone else was listening. Glancing up, she could see as the court could not, that Lady Daphne stood at the rail, dressed in her habitual mourning.

'You did, sir.'

'And did you follow my instructions? Did you make a man of the boy?' No sooner had he said it than his joviality leached away, remembering his only son's tragic death. 'Remember, you speak on oath.'

'I did lay out the money for a room, sir. And Francis did come to me, and I did invite him as you asked.'

An indiscreet snigger rose from an unseen man behind her.

'But . . . he was not willing.'

She remembered with great clarity how they had drunk a bottle together, while Francis courteously explained that though he liked her well enough, a woman's flesh was not at all to his taste. She had liked the lad; he had grown up as a funny, waspish young fellow, who mimicked his father's crude instructions with such pompous precision that she wept from laughing. After an hour or so of conversation they had ruffled up the bed, making saucy jokes together all the while. Then they left together, arm in arm, only separating once they were out of sight of onlookers. That was the last time she had ever spoken to Francis De Vallory, and she had wished him well, congratulating herself on earning a heavy gold guinea.

'So you are saying,' Sir John asked, his voice flat with disappointment, 'that you did not have congress with my son?'

'I am, sir. And I must add that the occasion of my meeting Mr Francis was upon his eighteenth birthday, and I believe that was in the autumn of 1750. Bess was born at Christmas of that year. If my calculations are correct, I should say she was conceived in March or thereabouts.'

Sir John collapsed back in his throne-like chair, and she understood with a pang that all this rigmarole was nothing but a sad
attempt to find a remnant of his lost son, in whatever manner he
could. He waved at Mr Dilks to continue the questioning, and Tabitha
braced herself.

'So, remembering you speak on oath – who is that child's father?'
The parson's interrogation was shrill with venom.

'I do not know. It is a mystery to me.'

Scandalized glances passed between those assembled.

'Do you mean to say that you were so free of your favours that
it is impossible to know who your child's father is? That, at that
time, you were whoring yourself with any number of men at once?'

Tabitha narrowed her eyes in disgust. Well, as they had driven
her to it, she must speak the truth. A flicker of movement attracted
her attention; she caught the glint of gold braid in the shadows.
Sweet Jesus, now even Nat had come to witness this mortification.
Her fingertips traced the outline of the ring on her finger, and it
gave her strength. A burst of perverse pleasure gripped her. Home
truths were as uncomfortable as jagged barbs – and that was what
this audience deserved.

'No. I mean nothing of the sort; and you insult me gravely, Parson
Dilks, in saying so. In March of that year, I was still a maid. I had
never even known a man.'

A murmur rose from the court, but Mr Dilks pressed on.

'Do not speak in riddles, girl. So how was this child of yours
created?'

She gathered her courage. A Bible oath, she assured herself, must
certainly trump a blood oath. So let them hear it.

'I do not know who Bess's father is – because I am not her
mother.'

THIRTY-TWO

A Riddle

My *first* is the half-point, not end nor beginning,
My *second* that woman we kiss without sinning;
My *whole* is a known introducer of strangers,
A life-saver too, and assistant in dangers.

The 31st day of October 1752

All Hallows' Eve

Luminary: Sun sets 46 minutes after 4
of the afternoon.
Observation: Saturn an evening star and Mars
under the Sun's beams and invisible.
Prognostication: Persons overcharged with honour
are malcontented.

T abitha's denial caused a ripple of mixed astonishment and
hilarity to spread throughout the hall. Sir John roused himself
enough to shake his head in bemusement.

'So tell us, Tabitha, for our parson has clearly leapt to some hasty
conclusions. Who is the child's mother?'

It was Tabitha's turn to grow sombre. 'I promised never to tell
another soul – and now you force me to break my word.'

'I take full responsibility for that,' insisted Sir John.

Tabitha hesitated until the silence rang in her ears.

'Bess was born to my own mother.'

'Widow Hart?' barked Dilks. 'A woman who paraded herself as
an example of virtue? And a parish officer, besides. This is an outrage!'

'Silence, Parson,' interrupted the doctor. 'Tabitha, how did this
come about?'

Reluctantly, Tabitha recalled the bitter events of 1750.

'My mother and I had a series of misfortunes. Firstly, our cow
died of some malady, and without her milk we had little to take to
market. We both fell sick, too. Then, at Easter I had the chance to
go to Chester fair, and earn a few shillings. I was away for only
two nights, but it was a hard price I paid for those coins. On my
return my mother seemed altered, forever in low spirits. But I had
more to consider than my mother's temperament that year; our stock
of goods had grown pitiful, and we scratched our way through the
summer upon only gleanings and wildstuffs. By Michaelmas, though,
even I could see that something serious ailed her. When I asked her,

she fell to weeping, and told me she had seen certain signs she would bear a child. I confess I was disgusted.

"'How could you?" I demanded. "At your great age?" For she was then aged three-and-forty. She then told me the strangest part of it, and this I tell you truly, on this Bible oath. She told me she had no recollection whatsoever of how it had occurred. At first, I did not believe her – I thought she was concealing some awful secret. But on one thing we were agreed: that it would be better to die than be a respectable widow who gave birth in a village of such cutting tongues as those of Netherlea.'

'Do you not think it more likely that your mother was confused in her mind?'

The doctor, she dimly felt, was trying to be kind. 'As to dates – it continually astonishes me how frequently women cannot recollect events. Then nine months later a child appears: *quod erat demonstrandum.*'

This raised a chorus of laughter.

'I am afraid I must disagree, Doctor. My mother had a certain method of understanding dates, known to many country women. She kept an almanack, and beside five or six days each month, she made a set of pinpricks as a guide. Indeed, it always amused her that menfolk fail to grasp why their wives are so fond of their almanacks; especially those who are weary of childbearing.'

The doctor nodded, interested, but she could see that many others were affronted at the notion of women exerting such private power. Her mother, in her brisk and country fashion, had gone on to explain how every woman should learn which quarter of the moon in which to have no man near her.

'Bearing too many children weakens the woman and risks her life. Once you have the method learned, the changes in your womb are clearly written in the sky for those who know moonlore.'

It was a lesson Tabitha had never forgotten; and in London, she and Poll had nailed a broadsheet almanack on their wall and arranged their adventures accordingly.

'We were both agreed on her staying here. There was nowhere else to go but Netherlea, and besides my mother was an excellent searcher, and many villagers put their trust in her. I was young and thoughtless. I complained that it was more usual that the daughter brought the babe home, than the mother. It was that remark which laid our plan. I told my mother she might pass the child off as mine.

What did I care? I longed to go to London and promised I would send her money for the child's upkeep. In that way, my mother could continue as the virtuous dame she deserved to be.'

Tabitha paused, remembering how simple their arrangement had seemed. The expression of joy and gratitude on her mother's face had sealed the agreement for her.

'You sacrificed your own reputation,' Sir John murmured.

'It did not seem so at the time. No one in London would know me. As for Netherlea, I cared not a whit. The ruse was easily achieved. That winter we both ventured outside only when bundled up in cloaks. The only difficulty was her work as searcher; as she grew less nimble, my mother no longer dared to visit the dead and dying. It was then that Mr Dilks threatened to take my mother's cottage from her, saying she must either work or be turned out. So I took on her duties, for I had seen her lay out the dead often enough; though I was careful to bolster my figure when I met our neighbours. Thankfully, Mother was too thin to show she was breeding, and no one was any the wiser.

'And then, on St Stephen's Day, the day after Christmas, her travail began. Our grain box was empty, but I dared not leave my mother to collect our longed-for Christmas dole from the hall. We neither of us ate for two light-headed days. But thankfully, my mother was safely delivered and, it not being her first child, she did well enough with only myself as midwife.'

Tabitha looked at the assembled men who sat in judgement upon her. She could not describe the horror of attending her own mother's birthing, as the distraught widow wept and prayed and convulsed in her torment. Without the familiar clutch of women to offer good cheer and encouragement, Tabitha had been forced to deal alone with the surprising fluids and profusion of blood, and to sever the navel-string herself. She remembered lifting the slippery red-faced creature, and bathing it, under her mother's panting instructions. Then she had wrapped it in torn cloths and, lacking any Christian blessing, her mother had whispered an ancient prayer and sprinkled the child with salt before placing her father's old seal, in lieu of a coin, inside Bess's tiny hand. Tabitha had looked on in stunned disgust, considering the child nothing but a memorial to her mother's folly.

It was then, on her bed of travail, that her mother had made Tabitha swear an oath on her own birthing blood.

'You must never tell a soul that she is mine, Tabitha. I wish to die here in Netherlea without rebuke. Do you promise, daughter? Do you promise never to break this vow?'

She had held out a bloodied hand and Tabitha had clasped its claggy warmth with scarcely a thought. All she wanted was to escape.

She looked up to find her audience waiting for her to continue. This time, she began to warm to her explanation.

'Once my mother could stand again, we changed places and I lay in her bed. My mother walked, frail and unfed, to visit the parish officers, and to borrow the birthing box of baby linen. When Mr Frith understood I was unwed, he told her it had been loaned to a respectable family. Mother wept, and made a petition for food and warm garments, but that too was refused by the parish overseer.' Tabitha turned to the same Mr Frith. 'We were starving in your midst, and you refused us charity,' she said, glad to see the man drop his eyes shamefacedly to the table.

Mr Dilks sprang to his defence. 'Your mother falsely represented that child as being yours, her errant daughter's!'

'Yes. And when my mother could not tell you a name, you threatened her with a whipping. You told me I deserved a spell in the house of correction.'

It was some gratification to see Sir John shake his head dolefully.

'Your mother lied in the parish books. And you,' Dilks said spitefully, 'summoned my curate to perform a baptism that was entirely deceitful.'

'Yes. And you continued to harry us for the shilling to pay for it. You may recall what a biting January it was that year. At the end of my wits, I set off one day to beg for food. And yes, I got your precious shilling by another method, but at least my mother and half-sister survived to see the spring.'

'You mean that you took up as a common prostitute?' said Mr Dilks, shining with triumph.

She nodded. 'Yes. Those rumours are true. I had to sell my body, so that we could live.' Her face grew hot, remembering that Nat was listening. God forgive her, he had admired her as an elegant lady of the town, passing almost as genteel beneath the tolerant gaze of the beau monde. The pitiful truth was that a gentleman had halted his carriage where she stood with an outstretched hand at the roadside. Her fingers were swollen with chilblains and she had been grateful to shelter from the sleet in his warm carriage. He had offered her a drink of spirits, and with uneasy apprehension, she had understood that he would pay her if he could make free with her body.

As a girl of nineteen, she had sold her maidenhead for ten shillings, and an uncomfortable quarter-hour later, she had trudged down the lane to buy food. It was not a decision she had struggled with. To escape, she needed not only to pay her fare, but also to leave her mother a good sum to tide her over. And so she had begun the flesh-trade, and steeled herself to visit the tavern and linger, shivering, in the cobbled yard that stank of ale lees and worse.

Money had been her only passion; if a man offered her a glass of ale she refused it and twisted the penny from his fingers instead. Greasy and warm, those coins jangled in her pockets like the golden keys to the gates of London. Then at last, one day in springtime, she handed her mother five whole pounds and told her she would leave the next day and send more money by the summer's end. Since then Tabitha had dutifully carried out every term of their agreement.

'It is a scandal that we harbour such a harlot,' the parson complained. 'I want the cottage back at once, and this filthy baggage set on her way.'

'Enough!' Sir John struck the table with his fist. 'I will not have Tabitha and the child ousted like that. Do you hear me? The terms of the tenancy must at least be honoured – to New Year's Eve, I believe.' He turned back to Tabitha, eyeing her sternly under his bushy brows. 'And you still have no idea of the child's father?'

She shook her head. 'No. But I am certain my mother would never have risked scandal.'

Turning to face the parson, she said, loudly and steadily, 'If I was forced to sell myself, it was only because no one here – not one of you – would help us. It was the same when my mother was attacked and drowned. Not one of you believed me. Only by facing death at Darius's hand did I find proof that you were all wrong; that he was an accomplice to a man hereabouts, hiding the terrible sin of her murder.'

She looked at everyone in the room, as steadily as her ragged breathing would allow; and no one answered, save for Sir John.

'That is not a matter for this court, Tabitha. But your accusation is noted.'

It was a hushed gathering that finally broke up that afternoon. Afterwards, Sir John came to her, his shoulders bowed and weary, as if the court had been as much of an ordeal for him as for her. In front of all the company, he called her a dutiful daughter who put many another to shame. But she excused herself and set off in search of solitude. The men sitting in that court had hounded her mother. And now she had been forced to murder her mother's reputation, too.

She halted, alone, in an empty corridor, and banged her bunched fists against the wall, grazing her knuckles so that Nat's ring dug painfully into her fingers. For the past month she had been slumbering, drunk on the draught of love, but she was wide awake now. Her mother's tragic history must have been resurrected for a greater purpose. For almost two years Tabitha had sheltered her mother from the cutting tongues of Netherlea; now she had only two months left before she herself would be turned out of the cottage. And in those final dark months of the year, she was damned if she wasn't going to restore her mother's name and unmask De Angelo. She would make him suffer for his crimes.

She rode back to Eglantine Hall on Jupiter, behind an attentive, gentle Nat. How did he feel towards her now? As they passed the darkening fields, a procession of men and boys marked the ancient boundaries of common land, gouging marks into the trunks of trees. As they caught up with them she did not at once recognize them; they were guisers, with blackened faces and ribbon-strewn garb.

She threw them a few coppers. She had forgot it was All Hallows' Eve, a night to perform old customs and appease the spirits. Well, tonight her mother's spirit felt palpably real, summoned like a chilly wraith from her grave. She could feel it alive in the bitterness of woodsmoke drifting on the wind, in the nip of cold on her nose and fingers, and the sun's descent into the winter darkness that soon would face them all.

When they returned to the apartment, she felt unnerved, as if the earth had jolted on its axis and was forever out of kilter. She watched Nat build up the fire.

'Well, Nat, now you know why I left Netherlea. And still you haven't said a word to me.'

At once he stood and pulled her into his arms, and the entire world righted again.

When he spoke, his voice was warm and gentle. 'You told the

harsh truth and they deserved it. Sweetheart, do you want to go to London? We can leave tomorrow. I will go wherever you go.'

She shook her head. 'They have given us two months longer. I shall brave it out.'

He brought her a glass of heated brandy, and she made a toast to the empty air. 'To you, Mother. Forgive my oath-breaking.'

She took a long draught and then sat, bewitched by the lively flames. Very quietly, she said, 'We must keep the fire burning all the night of Hallows' Eve, so no evil may enter this house.'

THIRTY-THREE

A Riddle

Why is ink like a scandal?

The 1st day of November 1752

All Hallows' Day

Luminary: Sunrise 15 minutes after 7.
Observation: Venus sets 18 minutes after 5
in the afternoon.
Prognostication: Those who boast of high degree will
likewise die in effigy.

L
ike a good omen for the future, the fire in the great carved
inglenook of Eglantine Hall still glowed in its embers the next
morning. Gazing at the wall that displayed their speculations,
Tabitha announced they must begin at once to tax their wits – for
no time could be lost.

'It is a shame that Darius, the surest witness, died before he could
be properly questioned,' Nat remarked, chewing on bread and cold
bacon.

At the mention of Darius, Tabitha picked up a pen and wrote in
a child-like, round hand: *You still have my master to reckon with.
I've seen you swallowing his crafty words. You reckon him such a
great good fellow while all the time he plays you for fools.*

'That is what he said to me – his very words.'

'There is an ambiguity about the word "great",' Nat said, musing.
'It could mean extremely good, as in virtuous; or that the man
himself is considered great – that is, of high rank. The reference to
craft certainly confirms the hypocrisy we have both detected in the
parson's character.'

Tabitha agreed and went on, slowly. 'I've been thinking, Nat,
about Joshua . . . He discovered my mother's body and was also
close by when Francis was discovered. And this escape Darius made
from the bridge – he certainly had a confederate among our party;
someone who had access to the prisoner's carriage.' Taking a slow
breath, she confided further. 'At Michaelmas, Bess opened Joshua's
document bag. He has been observing all your movements, over
many weeks. Don't look like that.'

He had sprung up from his chair, but slowly sat back down, saying caustically, 'That two-faced . . . Well, he is your fond friend. You know him best.'

She ignored the childishness of his tone. 'Be sensible. It is more likely that someone has asked him to watch over you than that he does so on his own account. He is not a likely creator of the almanack, even if he is not quite the dotard you imagine. More likely, he is under the influence of this unknown man. For Joshua does venerate power and rank.'

Nat strode over to the wall and inspected his own handiwork.

'Have you looked at all of the almanack's predictions?' she asked him.

'Blood, burning, and bones this month, if I recollect. Very cheering.'

'"*Those who boast of high degree will likewise die in effigy.*" Who do you suppose that is? We have underestimated these prognostications before.'

Nat found it hard not to show his contempt.

'It is styled exactly in the manner of most false predictions, from Nostradamus to Mother Shipton – vague, general, applicable to many cases.'

Tabitha frowned at the crude verse.

'Remember the "mighty confusion" he caused by giving out the wrong assizes date in September?'

'And so?'

'It could be that Sir John, or the doctor, or some other high-born person will die. Though why in effigy, I cannot say.'

'I pray it won't be so.'

'False or not, De Angelo, or someone styling himself as such, sent my mother and Francis those threatening verses. If there is a message it is the fall of a great family: the De Vallorys.'

'Well, what of your virtuous doctor?' he asked. 'You say he dislikes his brother.'

'They have always been at odds. It is common knowledge the doctor would have made a better overseer of the estate. But remember, if De Angelo was present at Francis's murder, it cannot be the doctor; a dozen people saw him at breakfast that morning.'

'Nevertheless, he is bookish, a classicist, of high rank and has a profession both great and good. You have been closest to him. Does he have any strange notions, any cruelty in his nature?'

'None at all. He is an unusually kind man. Don't pull that face;
I am an excellent judge of men.' Seeing him unconvinced, she
stepped over and sat on his knee, saying, 'Or else why would I be
here with you?'

They kissed but she pulled back before they could sink into
languorous lovemaking.

'Though, of course, there is still you to consider, Nat.'

She spoke sweetly, observing his face, glorying in the curves of
his mouth and his fine-boned features. 'For all I know, every word
of accusation you have made against others could be balderdash.'

He laughed, his shrewd eyes watching her under half-closed lids.

Leaving Nat to study the almanack further, Tabitha at length set off
for Netherlea. Stepping outside, no sun shone from the blankness
of the sky, while from above came only the sound of crows, fretfully cawing. The dark season in the countryside meant icy iron-hard
earth, and the labour of constantly collecting firewood. But by
January, London would welcome both her and Nat with gaiety and
the familiar luxuries of the playhouse, warm taverns and brightly
lit shops. As for Bess, she had formed a notion of where she might
foster her; she would return for her soon, when she and Nat were
settled in some decent lodging place.

Seeing a huddle of women near the church door selling leftover
Soul Cakes, she hailed them to buy a cake for Nanny. As she
waited for her farthing change, her eye was caught by the bonfire
rising on the Church Green. Piles of faggots and tree branches
were being heaped in preparation for the commemoration of
Parliament's delivery from the Gunpowder Plot. A group of young-
sters had made a remarkably ugly effigy from cast-off habiliments
stuffed with straw. Now they dragged it feet-first along the ground,
like a corpse across a battlefield. Turning back to the village
women, she caught them all staring intently at her. So, she thought
grimly, news of her appearance at the Manor Court the day before
had spread fast.

Going into the church she found the All Hallows' service had
just ended, leaving a welcome warmth from the newly departed
congregation. The De Vallory monument now dominated the nave;
the relief image of the standing figure had been sealed upright into
the wall. She could see now that it was a figure of a man, with a
remarkably well-carved cloth veiling his features. She approached

it and studied the Latin inscription, for only the oval lozenge bore words in English, stating Francis's name and rank.

Tabitha sat in an empty pew and pulled a piece of blank paper out of her pocket. It took a long, painstaking while to write down the words, letter by letter.

'You were my son's coming-of-age gift,' sneered a voice from a nearby pew. 'I am surprised such vermin is allowed on sacred ground.' She had been waylaid again by Lady Daphne, only this time the mistress of Bold Hall was alone. There was no polite answer Tabitha could make. She attempted a curtsy and began to back away.

'But we are all dust now,' said the haughty voice, behind the heavy mourning veil. Tabitha nodded, but just as she reached the church's aisle the woman lamented, 'He gives life and he takes it away.'

Tabitha stopped stock-still, looking back at the woman, a bowed figure shrunken within yards of black satin, frilled over outmoded wide skirts. Finally, when the silence grew too long, Tabitha quietly asked, 'Who takes life away, your ladyship?'

With great ill-timing, a ratcheting click from the clockwork above their heads started up, and the brass bell in the tower rang out nine ear-deafening times. Hastily, her ladyship rose with a sway of ancient hoops. Without another word, she dragged herself slowly up the aisle and out of the church.

It had been a laborious task to transcribe the inscription; but it was the work of moments to unpick the vestry door once more. She was pleased that Parson Dilks was not to be seen; though she figured that Sir John would defend her action to Hell and back. Opening up the Book of Mortalities she carefully removed the false page attached by dabs of wax. Beside her mother's original entry, she wrote clear across the margin: *Murdered by the hand of Darius Goff, who escaped trial by drowning on the 7th day of October 1752.*

Satisfied, she placed it back on its shelf and picked up the parish accounts that listed all the pennies and halfpennies handed out to itinerant beggars as an incentive to leave Netherlea. She leafed through the pages for all of spring 1750 but found no likely candidate who might have discovered her mother alone; only old folk, a nursing mother and wandering children, all of them harried back on to the highway. Impatiently, she drummed her fingers against the wooden table. Damn his blood, her mother's violator must be a Netherlea man, but he had left no trace of himself, save for the conception of little Bess.

The fog still hung in wispy skeins as she arrived on the High Street and let herself into Nanny's child-sized almshouse. The old lady lay motionless in a curtained box bed in the back room. The vitality she had possessed when Tabitha had last talked with her had vanished. Mottled skin hung now about her beaky nose and hollowed eyes. Tabitha pulled up a stool and took her claw-like hand into her own. Here was a foretaste of all of their fates, she mused. How heartily she wished she had been able to comfort her own mother at her end. Instead, she said a simple prayer, chastened to reflect on mankind's being forever close to death.

Tabitha was too late to learn any more from Nanny. She set the Soul Cake out on a communion tray, alongside untouched wine and wafers. She poured a measure of wine into the glass, and the scent of it rose, more palatable than any that she could recall sipping from the church goblet. With great gentleness she cradled Nanny's shoulders, and attempted to help her take a sip, but it was no use; the old lady's drooping lips remained shut tight. After straightening her bed linen and combing her hair, Tabitha could think of no other way to help her. Quietly, she let herself out, and began to retrace her steps down the High Street.

'Good day, Tabitha.' At the side of the highway the doctor was slowly dismounting from his carriage, leaning crookedly on his cane. Truly, she thought, Netherlea was peopled by a great many ailing folk.

'Are you back home at your cottage yet?' They fell into step together, though Tabitha had to slow to match his palsied gait.

'No. Though I am feeling stronger, now, with many thanks to you.' She told him she had just come from Nanny Seagoes: 'I am afraid her end is very close.'

'Indeed. It is a blessing that her neighbours care for her. I call as often as my other duties allow. But, Tabitha, we are well met.' He halted, leaning on his stick, panting with exertion. 'I need to sit.' He gasped and pointed to the tavern. 'Would you oblige me by sharing some refreshment?'

Even at ten of the morning, a group of village ne'er-do-wells hung about the inn. The sight of the door assailed her with a memory of standing in the reeking inn yard, as goosebumps of cold and distress rose beneath a too-thin gown. No, she would not torment herself by returning there.

'I'll not go inside, Doctor.'

Yet who could reprove her for resting outside a moment? Together they sat on a bench, where Tabitha accepted only small beer from the barmaid. The drinkers had hushed at their approach, and she was struck with the troubling notion that the whole village watched the pair of them in fascination. Was it her imagination, or did one of the local topers jeer under his breath, 'She don't look much like her picture, does she, then?' At the eruption of scornful laughter, she looked quickly in their direction, but they had turned aside.

'That was a fine performance yesterday,' the doctor said, with great warmth in his jaundiced eyes. 'What an extraordinary story you told. And my brother was so eager to claim that little maid as Francis's child. A lesser woman might have tried to deceive him and claim a birthright for Bess.'

'I am not a fraudster, Doctor.'

He courteously inclined his grey head. 'And you have helped me greatly in my work. I will not forget that. It is this Starling fellow I need to discuss with you – I have heard alarming news of him. I speak only as someone with a great regard for you, Tabitha, as I hope you will believe. I cannot repeat a confidence, but I believe he exploits you.'

Tabitha's chin jerked up. 'How is that, Doctor?'

'It is hard to speak and at the same time keep my promise. I do not simply mean he exploits you only as a – a very handsome woman.'

She felt unnerved. 'Then how?'

'Has he told you why he is here in Netherlea?'

His words could not have hit a more sensitive target. Crestfallen, she shook her head.

'Ask him. And whatever he tells you,' the doctor said, 'consider this. What can his true reason be for all those impertinent speculations about who killed poor Francis?'

She answered stiffly, 'I am sure there is a very good reason.'

Soon after, she made her excuses and left the doctor with a promise to return to her duties the following week. Resentment propelled her swiftly along the High Street. She had broken her vow to her mother, had been forced to confess that she had lived as a common whore in front of Sir John and his boorish cronies.

But as for Nat – why, he still kept his cards mighty close. Must she forever be the last to know of his schemes? If he did love her – and for the first time she pondered the distinction between love and feverish lust – he owed her his trust, and, above all, the truth.

One final incident rattled her entirely. As she hurried past the blacksmith's yard, she passed by the same bonfire-building young-sters she had first seen near the church, now begging for pennies around their guy. In all the bonfire celebrations that Tabitha could remember, only a narrow compass of characters had been repre-sented; the most usual was a feather-hatted Guy Fawkes, or an effigy of the pope in crimson and gold. But this year the effigy's face was daubed with round demonic eyes, its body hidden beneath a black coat tricked out with rags of gold. A tuneless but enthusiastic song reached her ears:

> *Guy Fawkes, Guy,*
> *Poke him in the eye,*
> *Shove him in the chimney pot*
> *And there let him die.*

Her eye was caught by a printed pamphlet pinned to the effigy's coat, and she snatched it up, despite the lads' protests – but she had read only the title, *A Noble House Cursed by a Curious Bloody Almanack*, before a thuggish youth whipped it away.

'Where did you get this?' she demanded.

'The tavern. Landlord had heaps of 'em, but they all sold out. He says they're the work of that writer fellow, Starling.' Then, smirking at her, he said, 'Ain't you 'er what's in it?' He opened it up beyond her arm's length, tantalizing her with a crude woodcut of a woman. Her own name, *Tabitha Hart*, was inked below it as clear as day.

She picked up her skirts and ran breathlessly home, trying to close her ears to any hints of laughter.

With a strong apprehension that her whole existence was about to change forever, she approached Eglantine Hall. Skin him alive, what had Nat done? She would give him such a tongue-lashing when she found him, true love or not. As she stumped up the stairs she rehearsed a stream of insults beneath her breath. He had behaved like a hired hackney, a poxy pen, a money-grubbing louse!

But the bitter words did not leave her lips, for Nat sat hunched over his desk, and when he raised his face it was gaunt with hopelessness. She could see at once that fate had struck him some great blow and, forgetting her anger, she rushed to comfort him.

'What is it, my love?'

'Tabitha,' he said, like a lost boy. 'I have betrayed everyone. And you, especially.'

'The pamphlet? I saw it. But I've not yet read it.'

He pushed a copy towards her across the desk, gingerly, as if it were dipped in poison, and her gaze flitted swiftly over the text. It was extraordinarily strange to read of Netherlea as if it were a town in a chapbook; as if she, Sir John and Francis and all the rest of them, were wooden puppets gallivanting on a painted stage. Then she turned the page and saw again the idiotic woodcut of a long-haired siren, with two spherical breasts protruding from a gown not fashionable since the days of Queen Anne. Beneath it was printed a caption: *The fair village searcher, Miss Tabitha Hart.*

'Dammit, Nat, I look like a ship's figurehead carved from oak, and twice as old besides,' she quipped, as lightly as she could. Next she saw an engraving of Sir John and Lady Daphne, done many years earlier, when they must first have been married.

Nat's voice was husky with sorrow when he spoke. 'Sir John has read it. He knows I wrote it. And, God forgive me, he fell to the ground in horrified surprise. An apoplexy, they say. He may die. The doors of Bold Hall are closed to me. I have brought everything to ruin.'

Tabitha took note of the bottle of brandy on the floor beside him, and of the sing-song lilt of his voice. Her anger, which had cooled a little, hardened now like metal ore – she was ready for a fight.

'So I see. You have done the murderer's work for him.'

'I need to find De Angelo. We need to unmask him.'

She raised her brows. 'Why, so you can earn a fee for writing about that, too?'

He shook his head wildly, as if a wasp had landed in his unkempt hair.

'No. I want to help you. And to catch this monster. But most of all – I need your good opinion.'

The greater consequences of what Nat had done were beginning to play out in her mind. 'La, it's my good opinion you seek, is it? Well you have already abused that with the absolute disdain you have shown me.' This time she was unable to disguise her hurt. 'Did you think I would be flattered at being paraded in public like this?' She threw the pamphlet down on the table, the sight of her own printed name burning in her mind.

The dismay in his face momentarily checked her. Then she remembered the doctor's remarks, and her words surged hotly from her mouth before she could restrain them.

'Have you used me, Nat? Did you befriend me only to write this scurrilous pamphlet?'

Her sorrow seemed to wake him from his fug. He stood, unsteadily, and threw his arms around her. For a moment she hoped that time could revert to a happier day; to yesterday, perhaps.

'No, never. I love you. I merely . . . I had a sudden hankering to write of these extraordinary matters and was possessed like a lunatic. I am heartily sorry. But I know the fate of these newspaper pieces – it will soon be forgotten.'

That was too much.

'You think so? Here, in Netherlea? Where any slight is remembered from a century back, and more? You have paraded me and all these others as an entertainment for the whole nation!'

'Damn me, then.' He sank his face against her shoulder. 'Let's go to bed,' he whispered.

'No.' She pulled back from him, keen to observe the effect of her words. 'Listen. No one here will ever freely speak to you again; and maybe not to me, either. Our pursuit of this villain is ended, for good and all. And the worst of it is that many folk out there believe now that *you* committed these murders, having written in such neat and nice detail of them. I felt it out there in the village – and I saw it, too. That damned pamphlet was pinned to the guy they will burn. The effigy in the almanack verse is meant to be you.'

'I wanted to keep this from you, Tabitha – but there's something else.' He staggered up and rifled through his mess of papers, handing her a neat page of verse. 'This was pinned on the door after you left.'

I observe how you meddle
My schemes to ensnare,
My wit has unmasked you,
Sir John's son and heir;
But you'll never unmask me

And fool, if you do
'Tis not me who will swing
By the neck – it is you.

De Angelo

Nat's hands shook as he set the paper down.

'Dear God.' Tabitha snatched it up and read it again. Sir John's son and heir.

Of course. Hannah Dove, a defenceless orphan, must have been given such generous parish assistance because she was carrying a child. Her move to Cambridgeshire was simply a means to rid Sir John of the nuisance of his merry-begotten child – who had grown up to be Nat.

'And what this says is true?' She searched his face, finding only a faint trace of the full De Vallory lips and high brow. 'You are Sir John's son?'

Nat groaned.

'His natural son. He got my mother with child when she was a fifteen-year-old in the care of the parish. I only learned the truth of it last year, after my stepfather died. Before you ask, I am here with my mother's blessing.'

Consequences, like a perilous pile of stones, seemed to be rising carelessly above her head. Tabitha looked at Nat with dawning horror. He had come to Netherlea, and met Sir John, in utmost secrecy; perhaps, having received no assurances from his father, he had sought to take his birthright by force. That was what any lawyer in the land would argue. The villagers and Joshua were all convinced of his guilt, even before they knew aught of this final damning fact.

'And when,' she said coldly, 'did you think to tell me this?'

He looked at her and shook his head, as if in pain.

Tabitha found she had risen from her chair. Now there were two Nat Starlings – her darling sweetheart and this other man, so secretive and sly. While she had confessed her every flaw and frailty, he had kept this dangerous secret hidden till it was forced from him.

'I must go,' she said weakly, and turned on her heel, feeling little spurs of fear speeding her away into the night.

THIRTY-FOUR

A Riddle

In young and old I do excite,
Painful sensations and delight.
All men me as their servant prize;
But when I'm wild, I tyrannize:
I can be seen, and heard, and smelt,
Yea, more, I'm at a distance felt,
There's but one death in nature found
For me, and that is to be drowned.

The 5th day of November 1752

Gunpowder Treason Day

Luminary: Night 14 hours and 42 minutes long.
Observation: Saturn in conjunction with
Venus and Mercury.
Prognostication: Secret plotters exert their malice.

Tabitha moved back to her mother's cottage. She wrote to Nat and begged him to leave at once – to go to London, or Cambridgeshire, or anywhere else in the world. Yet each day, when she walked to the river, she saw smoke still rising from the ornate chimneys of Eglantine Hall. Jennet had proved a loyal friend; she had solemnly taken both Tabitha's hands and, with the simplicity of youth, pronounced that from what she had heard at the Manor Court, she and her mother were two of the bravest women in the land.

Joshua was less generous when he called, though he had, at least, seemed unaware of Nat's secret relation to Sir John. Instead, he grumbled at how he had been hoodwinked by Tabitha and her mother. Like Mr Dilks, he took the view that any falsehood in the parish records should be punished, and the culprit made a public spectacle.

'Go to it, Joshua,' she taunted, lifting her arms up high. 'Hang, draw and quarter me, won't you? Is not that pamphlet sufficient entertainment?'

He scowled. 'Has Starling gone yet? Jennet told me you have given him his marching orders.'

She banged down the wooden spoon she was using to mix a hasty pudding that was too much water and too little oatmeal.

'As constable here, Joshua, you should know that a verse from De Angelo was pinned to Nat's door. Nat will be his next victim.'

'You ain't fallen for that old trick?' Joshua adopted his most annoying country drawl. 'He's wrote that himself. To garner sympathy from you, I should say.'

Had Nat indeed tried to deceive her? How simple it would be for him to compose a threat against himself . . .

'And what of November's prediction in the almanack – that "*traitors will burn*"? Don't you care about catching this villain in our midst?'

Joshua calmly spat into the fire. 'Oh, I do, Tabitha. You will soon see how much I do.'

By the time the evening bell rang out five times on Bonfire Night, the smell of wood smoke had drifted over to where Tabitha stood, captivated by the coral glow the fire cast into the darkening sky. Bess was sleepless, her small hand fidgeting in Tabitha's whenever she heard occasional shouts or snatches of song.

'Come on then,' Tabitha said at last, bundling the child inside a knitted shawl. 'If Nat truly is to be burned in effigy, we shall see it done.'

They halted in the shelter of the trees, well back from the crowd. Even from a stone's throw away, the blaze warmed her, the air taut and primed as a musket. Now the man-sized guy was being carried in triumph to the fire, then with the aid of hooks and poles, it was hoisted on to a stake at its apex. She eyed it carefully, needing to be sure it was only a straw-stuffed sack, not a pliable slender body. No, it was a crude likeness only, its ghoulish eyes round and staring. Hanging from its belt was what looked like a silver harvester's sickle.

A roar rose from the tankard-swilling revellers as the guy's body caught on fire and blossomed into flames, then the crowd watched in rapture as the effigy was transformed into a burning man-shaped brand. It was a sickening, yet exhilarating sight. First, the pamphlet pinned to its costume blazed; then the demonic face ignited and drifted away in tinsel sparks. Finally, the sickle combusted, revealing nothing but a piece of lath painted silver. Even Bess stood rapt, her round eyes filled with crimson reflections, and her arms raised in mute worship of the fire.

Soon it was over. The guy was only a man of straw, and rapidly consumed. The villagers began to move back from the fire; some to leave, while others poked the ashes for embers in which to bake food. One of those was Jennet, larking about happily with a boy who showed off to her, leaping across a burning log. Suddenly Jennet caught sight of Tabitha, and, without hailing her, walked over.

'That was a bonfire no one will forget,' Tabitha said as she approached. Jennet stayed silent, twisting her hair as she always did when uncertain how to speak her mind.

'I shouldn't tell you, but Father is out to get Mister Starling tonight.'

'No,' Tabitha groaned. 'Has that dunderhead still not left the hall?'

'He's been at the tavern all afternoon. That's where Father's gone to fetch him from.'

Jennet's reward for turning informant was to have sleepy Bess thrust in her arms while Tabitha trotted down the road to the tavern. She could have gladly slapped Nat's stupid, handsome face. What was his game? Courting the gallows for sport? Damn him!

As she hurried, she wondered why she still felt an ounce of loyalty to him.

Reaching the tavern, she shrunk back from its windows that cast lurid shapes into the darkness. From inside the walls, she could hear men singing like yawling cats. Now she would have to pass through that door of shameful memories – all to save a blockhead poet from himself. God in heaven, would she never learn?

'Damn you, Nat,' she whispered into the black air. Then, lowering her head, she strode quickly in through the door, and looked around. The front parlour was exactly as she remembered it as a timid nineteen-year-old: scratched blackened tables and rickety stools, gloomy from tallow candles that spread soot across the walls. Only the dregs of Netherlea's inhabitants slumped over their pots on Gunpowder Night. A half-dozen of them looked up with fuddled faces, until one red-faced toper cried, 'Look who it is, lads!'

'Where is Nat Starling?' she asked the landlord – but the insolent fellow only smirked as he wiped his pewter.

'What you want wi' him, Tabitha?' a voice bellowed from across the room. 'There be plenty of lusty lads hereabouts. Fancy a drink, do ye?' A chorus of drunken approval rose around her.

'Aye, and more 'n' a drink over here, my lovely!'

'She allus' liked 'em saucy, I hear.'

'No, she likes 'em rich.'

The landlord was laughing into his double chins, enjoying her discomposure. Where in Hell's name was Nat? Devil roast him, she would make him suffer for dragging her here.

A barmaid trudging past, foot-weary and well used to such straw-heads, whispered as she passed. 'He be outside, dearie.'

With as much dignity as she could muster, Tabitha headed for the inn-yard that had blighted her younger days. It was only a few steps, but they cost her dearly. At once she breathed in the stink of mildew, of ale lees, and the pails used to collect the beery piss that was sold as washing lye. If any smell evoked the dismal death of hope, it was this one.

Nat was slumped outside on a bench, his chin drooping to his chest, seemingly unaware of both the needling cold and his imminent danger. Tabitha halted out of sight, standing very still in the shadow of the wall. How could she get him to safety in such a state? Put gunpowder beneath him, perhaps? If she had not known him so well, she would have felt naught but contempt for such a drunken sot. His fine clothes were dishevelled; his hair untied, he wore no hat. She sighed, releasing a cloud of white vapour.

Another figure appeared from a side door, and walked uncertainly towards Nat, carrying two tankards with exaggerated care. The woman reached Nat's side and nudged him, giggling.

'Sup up now, Nat,' she said in a voice that Tabitha knew only too well. 'Budge up and tell me all about them stars and notions of your'n.' She set the tankards down and, swaying, teetered down upon his knee, throwing her arm around his shoulders.

Tabitha felt something far colder than the frost creep over her. She stood as still as a winter statue.

Zusanna giggled, and the sound stung Tabitha like broken glass thrown in her face. A burning sprang up in her eyes; she wished she could slink away like a rat into a hole. Still she could not move.

In a thunder of boots, Joshua emerged from the back door, striding business-like, holding his constable's staff aloft. Behind him were a band of the village watch, carrying torches.

'Well, Starling, how do you account for this?' He held a copy of the pamphlet aloft.

Nat remained motionless, dead drunk.

Joshua jerked his head in disdain. 'Nathaniel Starling, I arrest you in the name of the King for the wilful murder of Francis De Vallory.'

As if waking from a stupor, Tabitha ran from her place; she seized Joshua's coat sleeves and shook him.

'You cannot take him. Please, Joshua!'

Belligerent and unmoved, the constable gave an order, and strong hands hauled her backwards; she stumbled towards the icy wall and hit her shoulder hard.

'Keep her back,' Joshua commanded, and a thicket of men's bodies formed around her.

Nat did not even have the wit to protest when the constable's men dragged him upright and jostled him out towards the street. Zusanna shrieked incoherent curses, but no one paid her any mind.

In an instant, Tabitha was alone in the ice-bound yard. Alarm, confusion and a sickening sense of betrayal kept her hunched and still; she stayed in the shadows, listening, until all sounds of Joshua and his men had vanished into the night.

THIRTY-FIVE

A Riddle

My face resembles all mankind;
I'm ever blind when with the blind;
When I'm approached by ladies fair,
I'm just as handsome I declare;
And when an ugly cur I view;
By Jove, I'm just as ugly too:
If a beggar does draw near,
Then quick a beggar I appear;
And if a goddess I should see,
I'm raised as god-like just as she.

The 6th day of November 1752

Saint Leonard the Confessor

Luminary: New Moon at 2 in the morning.
Observation: Eclipse of the Sun at 1 in the morning.
Prognostication: Diverse and unexpected
changes at hand.

Tabitha stewed miserably in her bed. So now she knew it: Nat was not only a deceiver, he was just as worthless as every other man she had ever known. When she had first arrived in London she had been hopeful of meeting a fine man to be hers alone. But soon each face grew mazy, merging one into the next. And every one of them abandoned her, or ran out of money, or used her ill. Damn it, how had she been duped by a handsome face again?

As it darkened to afternoon, Jennet brought a sweet posset to warm her.

'I am sorry you did not reach the tavern in time.'

Tabitha gave a sad little shake of her head in reply.

Jennet watched her. 'He is in Chester Castle now. No one has visited him.'

'Do you think I care? It is what he deserves.' Tabitha squirmed away towards the wall.

Jennet sat down on the bed beside her. 'You loved him, Tabitha. I never saw a man and woman happier together. You can still go to him now.'

'Stop it.' She held the girl's wrist, not wanting to hear any more. 'Perhaps I loved him, Jennet, but I never even knew him.'

'Oh.' Jennet looked at her with her clear, guileless expression. 'Can we never truly know a man, Tabitha?'

'Only when it is too late. I could tell you some stories; my best friend, Poll Shepherd, for a start. She came home one day, bursting with news. A proposal of marriage. Mr Hartford Betts, the figure of a respectable bachelor, and well-connected, too. The wedding cost twenty pounds in gowns, white ribbons and bride cake. Then off she went to live in Mr Betts' new villa across town.

'It was all over in a twinkling. Hoping to improve his situation, that blockhead Betts lost his money on a speculation. His true character was then revealed: he was a despondent, miserable drunk. There was nothing for Poll to do but go back on the town. I did my best, I lent her five pounds – but Betts took it off her for drink. "Keep your pride and your purse to yourself," Poll told me. "Marriage is a rattrap – poxed easy to enter, but impossible to escape."

'And what is she now? A year later, I was leaving the Playhouse when I heard my name whispered. There was my dear, sweet Poll clutching the wall, half-cut on gin, half her teeth broken and her lovely yellow hair turned to grey. That jewel of London had been ground underfoot by that lazy dog, her husband. These days, he is no more than her drunken pimp – and there is a child now, a thin ragged creature lucky to get a bowl of milk. So you see, Jennet, we can never know a man.'

'But that is not always true. My mother was well content with Joshua as a husband. She, at least, died well loved. Poor man, I think he'll never find again what they once had.'

Tabitha rolled over and watched her narrowly. 'Truly?'

All these years, she had fancied it was herself whom Joshua wanted, and that he had merely married Mary as second-best. Now, she discovered, Mary had been his great love, and those long looks and kisses were nothing but a widower's loneliness.

Once Jennet had left Tabitha turned matters over and over, churning like butter that wouldn't come. For the first time in her life, she had let her bold husk be split, lain weak and exposed within cradling arms. She had believed she had found a true love; her own miraculous echoing heart, foretold in the stars to be hers alone.

The next day, while dressing, she paid attention to her costume and hair. At Eglantine Hall she found the door unlocked. She wandered the empty apartment, feeling the rawness of his absence, and picking up objects he had touched: a glass that bore the impress of his lips, a single chestnut hair, a linen stock. She buried her face in the linen's rumpled softness and smelled the traces of his body. Just a week earlier she had untied it from his throat and discarded it on the floor; then he had lifted his shirt from his naked shoulders. Venus save her, the memory made her body ache.

Nat's papers were cast over the desk, in heaps of ink-spattered scrawl. She picked up the pamphlet; the crude story that had so infuriated her and made sport of them all for any kitchen maid or street boy.

It was vulgar and crude – but now, viewing it from a little distance, she could comprehend its cleverness. If she did not know Netherlea, if she were reading about some other town – why, she would have sat down with a cup of sugared tea and devoured it with all the relish of a currant bun. And if the bag of guineas he had been paid was any guide, so would hundreds of other ordinary folk. In the city, no one cared now for the folktales of their grandsires; only for new legends of glamorous highwaymen, barbaric gangs and bloody outrages. They were tales of this new invention called a metropolis, where thousands of people lived crowded against their neighbours, all of them strangers, and many of them strange.

His bed was still unmade; he had left a paper under his pillow. She read it with slowly growing comprehension:

> *O future reader, in my glass I see,*
> *Two shining eyes and eager beating heart;*
> *And from an eerie distance back in Time,*
> *Shoot you a message with this poet's dart:*
> *Within our reach lies great transforming power,*
> *A partner soul to whom our soul is bound,*
> *Pray don't be cowardly, but grasp this hour –*
> *And know the bliss that I with T have found.*

Her heart thumped suddenly against her ribs. She forgave him all; his secret, the pamphlet, his drunkenness, and dallying with Zusanna. This verse was not written by a deceiver. No, here in his private moments was Nat's true and lovable self. She missed him so much, the damned rogue. Swiftly, she raised the stone where she knew he hid his money, counting what remained. There were still two pounds and sixteen shillings left. Whatever comforts she could buy for him in Chester gaol, he should have.

THIRTY-SIX

A Riddle

I'm all enigma, never was understood;
Some call me cruel, some the greatest good.
The world's my playground, and mankind my toys:
Kings, queens, lords, ladies, men and boys.
The lovely bride, though rich in worldly store,
Bereft of me, for all her wealth is poor.

The 8th day of November 1752

Luminary: Day shortened to 7 hours and 10 minutes.
Observation: Head of Andromeda south at 9 at night.
Prognostication: The vulgar are malcontented and
take great pains to excite discontent.

As she descended the dungeon stairs, Tabitha covered her
nose with her apron. Felons were kept in the Lower Court
of Chester Castle, a wretched vault reached by a set of slippery green steps. Here she found Nat alone, slumped on a stone
bench in the gloom. She could at first see only a crumpled silhouette,
for there was nothing but a grate to communicate with the daylight.
When he tried to rise and greet her, he stumbled, and she saw that
an iron chain fixed his leg to the floor.

She had tried to prepare herself for the ordeal, but still felt a
series of alarming pangs as her eyes adjusted and she saw him more
clearly. There was a new hollowness to his cheek, and his hair hung
in rat-tails.

'Nat. How is it here?'

'Tolerable. They treat me well enough.'

She shook her head in mystification. 'You speak as if you deserve
this.'

He raised his face, where shadows like old bruises surrounded
his eyes. 'Perhaps I do.'

'So – you are the murderer De Angelo, then?'

'No. But I know when I am bested.'

He lifted his face and met her gaze with overlarge eyes.

'Nat Starling, this is the first and last time I shall ask you. Did
you play any part in my mother's death, or in Francis's?'

'No. I did not. I swear it.'

'Thank Christ for that.'

She laid her hand upon his; it felt rough with grime. The atmos-
phere eased between them.

'Tell me. Does Sir John acknowledge you?' asked Tabitha gently.

Nat drew his long fingers over his brow. 'In private, yes. He was about to draw up a new will and make me his heir. Then he discovered I wrote that damnable pamphlet. He called me unworthy, a disgrace, a leech. Tabitha, he fell forward on to the table, his eyes seeing all, yet his body was powerless to move. And now he may die. I bring ruin to everything I do.'

'And so you deserve to hang in De Angelo's place?'

He hesitated, shook his head. 'If I hadn't come here, or written that pamphlet, my father would still be in health.'

'I don't believe that. I think it more likely he's being poisoned.'

Nat groaned. 'How fares he now?'

'No better, but no worse. The question is, how did De Angelo know you are Sir John's son?'

He sighed. 'I have no notion. Sir John and I swore an oath not to speak of it to anyone. At the time, there was Francis to consider, and his mother. But now he's on my trail. I had a letter from Quare, the London printer. He told me a fellow named Angelo or some such name, had a fat commission for me. Unwittingly, Quare gave out my name and particulars here in Netherlea. And now all of Netherlea knows I wrote the piece.'

As he shifted his position the chain clanked against the wet flagstones. 'I see now, he holds me like a fox at bay. He intends to finish me.'

'That's enough.' Surprised by her sharpness, his head jerked up. 'Do you not see that he works by fear? He enjoys his victim's sufferings. Nat Starling, after all that has passed, I will not abandon you. But henceforth there must be naught but honest dealing between us. Will you promise me that?'

He leaned towards her, bright and feverish. 'Yes. I swear it on you, our love, my life – on all that is good.'

'Then we can still defeat him.'

Tabitha offered him a pie from her basket, and he devoured it as if he had not eaten for days. After a long draught of cider, he looked a little restored.

'Thank you,' he said, 'both for your charity and for your faith in me. I couldn't tell you about Sir John; I could not break my oath to the man I'd just found was my father. Forgive me. I was going to tell you as soon as he acknowledged me. And I'm so devilish happy you had no close attachment to him after all.'

'Your father? Lord, I see your predicament now. No, none at all, thank heaven.' She laughed to think of his unnecessary suspicions. 'So what was your business with my mother?'

'Merely information. I needed to glean what I could of my own mother's circumstances before I confronted Sir John. God forgive me if I drew attention to your mother by searching the records.'

'I think not. It looks as if she did that herself.'

She reached in her pocket. 'Here is what is left of your money. I see from the notice it costs five shillings a week for a gentleman's parlour on the Master's side of the prison.'

'No need for that. It is Jupiter I fear for. I'd be obliged if you would take back five shillings and pay the ostler's boy to see him tended. As for me, not yet wanting to expire of gaol fever I will at least lay out some money to rent a private cell. As for food—'

'I shall come when I can, Nat. Every Saturday I'll bring food and whatever news I can.'

'You are too good.'

The gaol bell began to ring, announcing that it was time for any visitors to leave.

'You will see Jupiter is well cared for? And come again. Please.'

Tabitha got up. Suddenly, she could no more leave him than cut her own heart out. He had learned his lesson mighty hard. 'Have you any new scribblings in your head?'

'Too many to remember by heart,' he said.

'I shall fetch pen and paper, too.'

'Oh, Tabitha. Only you truly know me.'

'Next week, then.' She reached to him and kissed him quickly on the mouth.

Climbing up the dank stairs towards the light she felt the pain of parting seize her. Now she had seen him, she wished she had spent more precious time deep in his arms. Passing through the tunnelled gateway of the castle she had no clear notion of where to go next, only that she longed for the rocking emptiness of the cart on which she had arranged to ride back to Netherlea. For dreamy hours she would be able to conjure Nat's face – still dignified despite everything – and recollect the rough abrasion of his cheek as their lips briefly met. She had also to begin drawing up a scheme to set him free.

At the other side of the drawbridge, the Chester thoroughfare stood empty in the low afternoon light; a couple of prisoners, newly freed, shambled past her, led out by guards. Her eyes were searching for a clock to check the hour when the breath was suddenly knocked from her lungs. Before she could scream, a hand clapped over her mouth. Her attacker edged her backwards until, after a few painful steps, she was no longer in the public yard but pulled inside a murky sentry arch.

'Well met, you thieving brimstone,' a thick Irish brogue whispered in her ear. 'Where's my timepiece, you she-dog?'

His arm squeezed her throat. She shoved her elbow violently into his chest, so that his grip loosened sufficiently for her to suck in a breath.

'And all my goods and rig-out, you damned thief?' she gasped. A knee rammed into her back, and she groaned.

'My timepiece,' he hissed. 'Where is it? I have a customer that wants it bad. A man of learning with a heavy purse.'

'I sold it.'

The thick arm, wet with dungeon slime, pressed hard against her mouth.

'Bitch! Do you know what it's worth? It belonged to that cursed Scotch Queen who had her head sliced off. If you *have* sold it, you must get it back.'

He loosened his grip a half-inch, and she croaked, 'I might – if it were worth my while.'

With a shove, he sent her flying against the wall. Despite the blow, she was grateful to be free of his hold. Now he blocked her exit with his thick arms, braced against the narrow doorway. 'You think I'd give a strumpet like you a share?'

She smoothed her dress and smiled, with what she hoped was an appealing simper. 'Why ever not? I've been looking for a clever pal to work with. I could draw the cullies in while you strip their purses.'

He looked her over, from cap to buckles. In the November light his pewter-cold eyes made her want to shrink away and disappear.

'I only tumbled you because I knew the price of your gown. Maybe other dupes might bed you willingly enough.'

'So we renew our acquaintance?' she said heartily, extending her hand. When he took her fingers her skin recoiled from his hairy-handed touch. How had she ever let this lizard possess her?

'I'll tell you how it will be. Fetch me my timepiece, and I'll give you a try-out. You got any coin with you?'

'No.'

He poked her roughly in the back. 'You'd best get to work then.

I have a fancy for a fine feather bed in Chester town tonight. You can go work the Back Lanes.' Still wary of her, he led her by the arm out of the sentry box; she commanded herself to press close and friendly beside him and relax into his brutal grip. As they fell in step together, he held her a mite less tightly.

Passing down the drawbridge, they came upon a couple of soldiers wearing threadbare red coats. Tabitha began to chat to the Irishman of the city's different inns and pointed up towards the Exchange; as he turned in the direction she indicated, she reached across him and snatched the closest soldier's musket. Turning the muzzle towards her attacker, she announced, 'Gentlemen, this scoundrel attacked me before he had even left the prison grounds.'

The soldiers turned hard-bitten faces towards the Irishman.

'What a tale!' he protested, appealing to his fellow men. 'This whore tapped me for money and threatened to cry attack if I refused her.'

Keeping the musket trained on him, Tabitha spoke again: 'Sirs, I am the village searcher from Netherlea. I came here with food from the parish to give to a gentleman prisoner, Nat Starling. Pray check the gaoler's book. I was on my way out when this creature attacked me. Now ask him what his business is.'

The soldier whose musket she held grinned through broken teeth. 'No need to wave that piece about, sweetheart. We know this glib chancer well enough, don't we, Donoghue? Couldn't wait to be clear of the castle before you got up to your old game?'

When she'd handed him back his musket, he turned to his fellow. 'Put Donoghue back in the lock-up until he's repented his ways.' The Irishman was led away, spitting a string of curses in her direction, and she thanked the soldier warmly; he seemed a decent fellow, though he ribbed her for taking his gun. His name was Jansen, and though she declined a glass of spirits in his guardhouse, she stored away a morsel of his bragging talk; he was weary of the soldier's life and was saving his every penny to join an uncle in Virginia.

Ten useful minutes later she made her rendezvous with the Netherlea carter. Now, at last, she could think of Nat again and of how he might be freed from gaol. Two facts of bright significance jangled in her mind: that a learned man was willing to lay out a very large sum for the skull timepiece that she kept safely hidden back at the cottage; and secondly, that a soldier with access to a set of keys was in great want of coin to buy a fare to America.

THIRTY-SEVEN

A Riddle

I thrill when excited,
I boil when ignited,
By some I am said to be blue;
I am hot, I am cold,
Your heart I enfold,
Without me life bids you adieu.

The 11th day of November 1752

Martinmas (New Calendar)

Luminary: Sun sets 26 minutes after 4.
Observation: Venus sets a quarter hour after
5 in the evening.
Prognostication: Treacherous dealings of insinuating
and pretended friends.

Martinmas had always been the herald of winter at Netherlea; and it was therefore only with the greatest reluctance that the feast was celebrated eleven days early, on the eleventh of November. There was much grumbling from folk who felt it was too damned soon to kill their fattening creatures. Nevertheless, on strict orders from the Bold Hall estate, knives were sharpened on grinding wheels and the earth drank greedily of the blood of slaughtered cattle, sheep and pigs on Saint Martin's day. Neighbour worked with neighbour, gutting and skinning and singeing bristles, jointing and salting the carcasses.

Joshua brought a bowl of offal to the cottage, along with a pig's haunch to smoke in the chimney. He set the goods down with satisfaction: he was proud of his skill in slaying his own stock. 'Hog's pudding, do you say?'

Tabitha agreed, though she felt privately frustrated that the dish would turn bad before her next visit to Nat. Soon they had settled to their work; Jennet mixing herbs and oats, while Tabitha greased and floured the pudding cloths.

'Is Sir John any better?' Tabitha asked, enjoying an inward thrill to know she spoke of Nat's natural father.

'Much the same.' Joshua was peculiarly unmoved by Sir John's plight, she thought. 'He was able to sit up in bed and take communion with Parson Dilks yesterday, though he still cannot utter a word.'

'And if he does not recover?'

Joshua sat easily in her mother's chair, carving spills with his penknife. 'Not for me to say. No doubt the lawyers will profit from it.'

'I hear he's standing down in the election. Does it never trouble you, all these misfortunes heaped on your master's family?'

Joshua sighed impatiently. 'I've seen those comical speculations on Starling's wall. Has he infected you with his over-heated fancy?' He leaned forward, pointing his stubby finger towards her, and she saw his nails had crusted brown rims. 'Starling is the man behind the murders. I have half a dozen witnesses to his bad character, and his accomplice, Darius, is dead. Starling will be tried in January and, mark my words, that'll be the end of him.'

The squelching of spongy entrails beneath her fingers suddenly disgusted her.

'I heard you visited him.' He was watching her from the corner of his eye, making long strokes with his penknife.

'And why should I not?'

'That rogue has confounded you. We were all astonished you fell for his tricks. And he misled the whole village, too, turning Sir John's tragedy to his own profit.'

'Have some sense, Joshua. If he carried out these barbarities, why would he publicly parade them in writing?'

'You know little of these felons,' he replied with irritating certainty. 'They are forever boasting to the newspapers, taunting the public with their escapades.'

It was true that from Jack Shepherd to Jonathan Wild, it had become a low-bred fashion for villains to post vainglorious notices in the newspapers; but Tabitha knew that Nat would never have done the same.

'So what are you doing, Tabitha, come the year end? There's always room for you with me and Jennet.'

'I'll be back off to London,' she replied firmly.

'And Bess? She needs a family, not some bawdy house to be raised in.'

'I'll see she is cared for. In any case, what will happen to you, if Sir John dies?'

'I'm promised a new position in Chester. Money, a house.' He stood and came close to her, so close that she could almost taste the intensity of his feelings.

'Goodness. You have generous friends.'

The odour of blood on his hands filled her nostrils, making the bile rise in her throat. He slid his hands around hers and pressed them a little too hard.

'Is it a fine house?' she asked.

His slow grin told her he believed her nature to be entirely grasping.

'In the castle. Grand enough for you?'

'Somebody must like you, then. Someone powerful.'

He cocked his head. 'You could say so.'

He ran his hands up her sleeves and gripped her forearms. She assessed his build; he was as brawny as a young bull. She made a resolution not to be alone with him again. Jennet must be her chaperone at all times.

'Is it the same man who ordered Starling's arrest?'

Joshua stepped back, irritated. 'What are you after? I told you – there was open debate about Starling. The whole of the Manor Court agree he is guilty. You've behaved badly, Tabitha, falsifying the parish records and lying about Bess. But I can still forgive you, if you don't provoke me. And remember, you won't find a better home for Bess.'

'So would you take Bess on her own? At least until I decide?'

'No, I will not. Why should I take Bess so you can rattle off back to London without even a by-your-leave? No. And I will not allow Jennet to be your nursemaid.'

'I am glad that is settled then! But mark me, Joshua; you will not stop me visiting Nat.'

He stalked away and picked up his hat. 'Go. Visit him,' he said sharply. 'After all, he will be out of my way in eight short weeks.'

THIRTY-EIGHT

A Riddle

In vain you struggle to regain me,
When lost, you never can obtain me;
And yet, what's odd, you sigh and fret,
Deplore my loss and have me yet.

And often using me quite ill,
And seeking ways your slave to kill –
Then promise that in future you
Will give to me the homage due.

Thus we go on from year to year –
My name, dear reader, let me hear.

The 3rd day of December 1752

First Sunday of Advent (New Calendar)

Luminary: Day decreases 8 hours and 32 minutes.
Observation: Eclipse of the Sun at 1 in the morning.
Prognostication: Diverse and unexpected
changes at hand.

T he cold, mathematical region of Nat's brain would not refrain
from calculating his remaining life span. A gaoler had told
him that the Chester assizes were to meet when the Christmas
recess ended on the eighth of January. It was unlikely that his trial
would exceed one day, and he would probably hang the next morning.
That being so, he had a mere thirty-seven days left upon this earth;
a round figure of 888 hours. As the numbers steadily diminished, he
found his propensity for mathematics became a self-inflicted torture.

Every moment time was slipping through his mind like water
through splayed hands. He pictured little drops of *now* falling floor-
wards in that ceaseless flood we call the past. Only the future was
open and pliable, carving new channels into history. And so he
returned in a circle back to the damnable truth. By thinking such
thoughts he had wasted another hour, for he now had only 887 hours
of existence left. Manacled and shivering, he was becoming a shadow
of his former self. His only beacon of hope was Tabitha. Whenever
she could, she visited him, bringing candles, paper, ink, food and,
best of all, bottles of strong drink.

During one of her visits, Tabitha told him of the skull watch she
had stolen. Though she dared not carry it upon her person, she had
described the object minutely, and he had a dim memory of a legend
in which the Scottish Queen handed one of her maids of honour
just such a grim *vanitas*, upon the scaffold. On her next visit, she
gave him her crudely drawn versions of its designs, and the classical
axioms that graced it.

They had been sitting hand in hand in the midst of wet stones
and stinking straw. Tabitha was paler than he ever remembered. She

had lost her red cheeks; her vivacity seemed to have blown away with the autumn winds.

'Though the workmanship is extraordinary, it is a true horror. And, as the Irishman warned me, it has a vicious bite.' She described how the watch was opened, by lifting the underjaw on the hinge. 'The teeth are so devilish sharp that nine times out of ten it springs open and bites my fingers.'

'Is the mechanism working?'

'No, not at present. Yet it does work, for Donoghue had it running. Its weight in silver alone must make it worth a small fortune. If I sell it, what do you think I could ask for it?'

He blew out a long breath. 'My own watch cost forty shillings, but a fine gold watch commands as much as five guineas. You won't get a fair price for it, selling it on the sly, yet it is a great curiosity. I'll think on it.'

She had told him briskly of the Irishman's assault, just fifty paces from where they now sat.

'I will kill him if I see him here,' he muttered.

'Spare yourself; the law will see to that. He is to be hanged before Christmas.' Her face paled as the import of her words sank in.

He squeezed her hand. 'Be easy, my love. It won't come to that extremity for me. You will unmask De Angelo.'

Her lovely face emptied of hope as she attempted a smile.

'I only pray so. But I feel I'm on the wrong road, love. However much I try, I am forever chasing my tail.'

He grasped her hand, that felt so clean and soft. 'Every enquiry you make is a boon to me, sweetheart. What of the constable? Could he have brought these charges against me?'

She looked up at him and sighed. 'It was the manor court who charged you. But Joshua did tell me he'll soon have a new position, here in Chester – money, and a new house, too. That sounds suspiciously like a reward to me, though from whom, I cannot say.'

The precious visiting hour was passing. He braced himself to tell her his bad news. 'I have my trial date – the eighth of January.' He balled his fists angrily, unable to say more.

'When I saw Joshua, he said he was gathering statements against you. Can we not counter that? Nanny Seagoes would sign a deposition in your favour . . .' She was clutching his hand as if it were a rope that might haul her to safety.

'I am sorry, Tabitha, but that will not save me.' Seeing her crest-fallen, he added, 'But, if you would see to it, perhaps it would help. God help me, I am a man who has foolishly mislaid his friends. Lord Robbins has died, and now Sir John is mortally ill.'

The bell rang out for her to leave. He could not help himself; he clung to her warmth, knotting the fabric of her dress in his fingers like a child. The truth was, he could speak little sense to her. All he craved was her embrace, the sureness of her presence; the warmth of another human soul.

That evening, he found blessed distraction in the schoolboy task of translating the Latin dictums she had left, a fresh candle shining bright in the wall sconce. The first picture she had copied from the skull watch was the Holy Family in the stable, gathered about the infant Jesus. It took no great skill to construe: *Glory to God in the highest, and on earth peace to all men of goodwill.*

Only three Sundays remained until Christmas. It pierced him to be reminded of happier days with his parents, and Lord Robbins, who had been a generous host every Christmas season. The next phrase he chose from Tabitha's drawing also jolted a distant memory: the master at his grammar school had been especially fond of the poet Ovid. He recalled the famous lines from the *Metamorphoses* and undertook to make the finest translation: *Oh Time, great devourer, and thou, envious Age, together you destroy all things; and, slowly gnawing with your teeth, you finally consume all things in lingering death.*

Good God. These were hardly cheering words for a condemned man. It sobered him to think that the Scottish Queen must have read these same words in her own extremity. Secretly, he had always been more inclined to admire the Papist Temptress than the Virgin Queen. He pictured her as a pale French beauty in black velvet, a crucifix hanging on her lily-white breast.

He was too young to die, having found his beloved Tabitha – they had shared only the tiniest fraction of their lives so far. There was so much he still longed to do. He needed to gain his father's forgive-ness, to climb his tree of favour, to pick his ambition's harvest and live free.

He pictured the glories of his unlived life: waking each morning with Tabitha at his side; sharing Christmas revels; the books on which his name stood gold-tooled on the cover; his mother's kindly smile; and Sir John's blessing, too. There were smaller pleasures, too: a long-anticipated view of the sun's eclipse, two years hence; a hard gallop with Jupiter over the Cheshire plain; reading the *Gentleman's Magazine* with a fine brandy at his side; and each night holding Tabitha, in time-defying bliss.

Eight chimes rang out from the castle tower, and he emerged from his reverie in such pain that the bell's clapper might have swung physically against his own frail skull. The dark night had unpeeled to reveal a rotten, watery day, as the computational region of his brain restarted its calculations. Thirty-six days remained, 876 hours; a mere 52,560 seconds. And, in the instant of his thinking it, the total had inexorably shrunk. Time, his great absolute, was unstoppably moving ever closer with his razor-edged scythe.

THIRTY-NINE

A Riddle

I oft through lane, and street, and alley,
Officious in my duty, sally:
Yet was I born for nobler ends;
O'er prostrate crowds my voice descends.
The bridal joy and gay parade
Were cold and dim, without my aid.
Oh, would these cares were all the Fates
Had destined mine! – But yet awaits
Another and more sad employ;
I mourn the wreck of human joy,
When empty graves await us all,
And bid the tear-drops faster fall.

The 13th day of December 1752

St Lucy's Day (New Calendar)

Luminary: Sun rises 9 minutes after 8
in the morning.
Observation: Mercury sets half an hour after
4 in the afternoon.
Prognostication: Light will be shed on
unexpected places.

Tabitha woke before sunrise, bedevilled by forebodings about Nat. She felt fingers probing her closed eyelids, and then poke her nose and mouth. For a moment she was back in the featherbed at Eglantine Hall, waking sleepily to her lover's caresses. Then a high-pitched chuckle told her she was back at the cottage with Bess. It was still dark, but some inner mechanism told Tabitha it was time to rise and go to the doctor's house.

Bess giggled again, feeling the flutter of her sister's eyelashes.

Tabitha pulled her into the bed and hugged her, stroking her hair. While apprehensions about Nat plagued her every waking minute, Bess was at least an occasional distraction. Tabitha untangled her fair hair with her fingers, soft as the strands of a dandelion clock. Bess was growing into a remarkably pretty maid, her cheeks as plump as peaches and her eyes a pair of lively dark-ringed sapphires. Not that she was an angel; she could be huffy and petulant when the mischief took her, though the next moment she would caper into Tabitha's arms.

It was a pity she would have to leave Bess soon. Whatever happened at Nat's trial, she could not stay here past the first day of the new year, for Mister Dilks had taken great pleasure in announcing Nell Dainty would then move into the cottage as the new searcher. And Joshua was right, for once; London was no place for a child. Recently, she had caught herself wondering if London was the best place even for herself. 'A great city, a great solitude,' she told herself. If only she could get a glimpse of what the future would bring.

She pulled on her warmest clothes. Jack Frost, as children say, had called in the night, and left the window a swathe of icy ferns. Bess had fallen asleep again, wound into a snail-like curl. She pulled the blanket gently up to her chin. It was time to leave – Jennet must make the child's breakfast.

The almanack reminded her that it was Saint Lucy's day, a favourite saint of her mother's, famed to bring light to aged eyes. She pulled her mother's threadbare red cloak tight around her arms as she hurried up the drive to the doctor's house. Soon would come the darkest point of the year, for the sun was growing paler and weaker, each successive day. Around her, the doctor's garden was as unkempt as she had ever known it. Starved of the sun's rays, fruits and leaves had shrivelled and dropped, and now were turning into slime. Only the glossy green leaves of the holly tree, the laurel hedge, and the climbing ivy had survived. Most of nature had burrowed under-ground, bracing itself against a season of hoar frosts and northern blasts.

She felt a guilty pleasure at entering the doctor's comfortable home, unhappily recalling Nat's icy cell. There was a warm fire in the grate where she settled to her work, and a good supply of oil to light the lamps as soon as daylight failed. It grieved her that the doctor did not always rise from his bed. He was sick almost to death; it needed no physician to diagnose that.

To her surprise, Judith the cook knocked at the door with a slice of seed cake, and two more pieces wrapped in paper for Bess and Jennet.

'Master don't eat nearly nothing nowadays,' she grumbled. 'Best it goes to you young'uns.' The doctor, she said, was out visiting in Chester with his manservant, Florian. At once, Tabitha's heart leapt, for Judith would also be out marketing that morning. That would give her free rein to search the house.

Certain she would be uninterrupted, she began her study of those of the doctor's books that were written in the English tongue. The *Pharmacopeia Extemporanea* contained vast lists of ailments and remedies in English. She read avidly – of lack of speech, weak limbs and falling fits, nervous diseases and palsies. But, blinking her strained eyes an hour later, she had to admit that none of it gave her a clearer understanding of the De Vallory brothers' maladies.

She heard Judith close the door behind her and watched her stump off down the drive; then, at once, she began to explore the hall, parlour, dining room, library and servants' chambers. Sir John had stripped Bold Hall of what he called its morbid ancient follies; but not so the doctor. Most doors were open, and she moved along the creaking oak boards on stockinged feet, admiring fragments of pillars, patterned tiles and stones with peculiar lettering. By the light of windows set with jewel-like glass she admired large paintings, rich fabrics and Turkish carpets. To the rear was Judith's domain, an old-fashioned kitchen and scullery. Only two rooms were fastened tight: the wine cellar housing the prize casks of Florentine wine rumoured to be the doctor's great indulgence, and the strongroom that held his money. She remembered glimpsing the inside of the strongroom once, when passing on her way to the kitchen; a window-less room, in which padlocked chests were lined up along shelves. She made a rapid search for the keys but could find none.

Upstairs, there were ranged a series of bedchambers and closets. The doctor's small chamber she found a lonely room, furnished lavishly, but lacking the blessing of love or companionship. Now that she had observed him more closely, she understood he was not entirely a saint; wryly, she had noted a vaunting pride in his own great learning, and scorn for other country physicians. And why ever not? He had clearly won the brains in the battle with his brother. No one doubted that the doctor could have run the estate more profitably and astutely, either. If he had a fault, it was his stubborn-ness. He could be so clever, and yet so blind. She had urged him to look more carefully to his own safety but had met only with scorn.

By his bedside was a table of the sort that she, as searcher, often found beside a sickbed, stacked with tonics and elixirs, measuring spoons and an apothecary's weighing scale. Most interesting of all was a distillation of gold, labelled *aurum potabile*, that he had said was a wondrous cure-all. Poor fellow; for all his knowledge, this physician could not cure himself. As her fingers idly lifted and inspected what was spread upon the table – a jar of ointment, two large needles, a razor-sharp scarifying instrument to pierce the skin – Tabitha comprehended that she would never find a poison to match both Sir John's and the doctor's symptoms, for their ailments were entirely different.

The doctor, she mused, had gradually become breathless, fatigued, and was losing the strength in his limbs. Doubtless some disease was attacking his animal spirits. Sir John, on the other hand, had been suddenly struck down; all reports said that he could neither speak nor rise from his bed.

The ticking of a distant clock goaded her to use her time well. With the neat, precise movements of a housebreaker, she searched the rest of the doctor's chamber. Running her fingertips into the dusty bowl of a classical urn, she felt a familiar object; carefully, she shook it out on to the bed, and a ring of ancient keys rattled on to the blue velvet coverlet.

As she inspected them, a new sound reached her from the front of the house, distant, low and rhythmically steady. It was the passing bell at Netherlea church, tolling the news of a death. Dropping the keys back where she had found them, she satisfied herself that everything was just as it had been; then, silently returning downstairs, she pulled on her cloak and hurried away to the church. She must now collect her searcher's bag and learn the name of whichever of Netherlea's inhabitants had just passed away from this life.

According to her daughter Alice, Nanny Seagoes had left this world just an hour ago. Alice was a sensible woman, who kept a small herd of cows and sold butter at the market. Stocky and broad-faced, she greeted Tabitha with grave cordiality. 'The pity is she had a nasty sort of fit at her end time. We was all hoping for an easy passing – but the Lord din't choose to give it her.'

'You were with her, then? Was anyone else here?'

'No. Just meself. Though I'm right thankful Mister Dilks come this morning and spoke the proper words over her.'

Tabitha caught her breath. 'She could drink the wine, then?'

'Now, that I cannot say. I were out milking, and then I passed him on the lane; he said she were in God's good hands and whatever was needful was done.'

Oh, was it, indeed? Tabitha halted abruptly at her first sight of the old lady, lying on her box bed; her eyes were still open, colourless and rheumy, in a face of livid pink.

'She has a most high colour, Alice.'

'Aye, she does. That were the fit brought all the blood to her face.'

Sir John's face had also, by all reports, been scarlet from the apoplexy. Tabitha approached the dead woman and began unbinding the white plait of hair that hung over her shoulder. Pink patches also blotched Nanny's throat and chest. Tabitha held her tongue; she had never seen such livid marks upon a corpse.

Alice brought her a bowl of fresh water, and Tabitha began gently to wash the old lady's hands. Her fingers were as tight as knotted twigs of oak; she could not unbend them.

'Could your mother speak at the end?'

'No, she weren't up to talking, poor thing. She were proper badly. I come here and she's vomited all down her shift.'

'So you cleaned her up?'

'Aye, I used the best of her rosewater to make her nice and spruce again. I want people to see her as she always were, neat as a pin.'

Tabitha touched the woman's arm. 'I'll get started, if you like. You put some tea on, and rest your feet.'

Once alone, she went straight to the communion tray. The wafers remained on a little dish of pewter, but the wine bottle was unstoppered and empty. She sniffed it – the heady scent she had smelled last time was barely a ghost in the newly cleaned glass. Damn the parson. She had been hoping for a sample to steal away, for the doctor to make trial of.

'That's an odd thing,' she said in an even voice to Alice, when she joined her. 'The church wine bottle is cleaned out. It looks as if it's all been drunk. Or did you wash it out yourself?'

Alice had been staring into the fireplace and raised a pair of eyes that were tired and dull.

'I wouldn't know about that. It's all just as it were when I first come here.'

'I'll drop the parson's things off later,' Tabitha said.

'Save your feet; he'll be back later, he told me. 'Tis too bad, eh? Both of us losing our mothers this year.'

'It is a trial we never expect to face. Would you like me to tell anyone, Alice? Has anyone else come around to call yet?'

Alice took a long draught of hot tea. 'Well, Mrs Hay next door come round for a gawp once the bell started up. But no one else. Only the constable come round earlier on.'

'Whatever for? I thought Joshua had plenty on his plate, what with Sir John ailing and this trial coming up in January.'

'He brought a letter, all the way from Chester Castle. Seems some lawyer were going to ask Ma to be a witness to the character of that murderer fellow. Starling, is it? Well, he shall have to go to the gallows without my mother's word.'

A knock on the door interrupted them, and Tabitha rose to let in a gaggle of neighbours. Then she sidled back into the room where Nanny lay, her soul snuffed out before her time was due, and stroked the old woman's carnation-pink cheek. Coldly and secretly, someone had administered poison to this defenceless woman, she was sure of it.

'I am sorry I failed you,' Tabitha murmured.

FORTY

A Riddle

Come gentlemen you, I address myself to,
For the name of this flattering rogue;
You love it no doubt, so you'll soon find it out:
For amongst you it's greatly in vogue.
It smiles in your face, when the slave you embrace,
My words you will find to be true;
But it leaves a damned curse, like for better or worse,
Which your cunning can never undo.
But he that denies it, and with ease can despise it,
And makes it his servant, not master;
Will find it his friend, and on him it will tend,
And comfort him when in disaster.

The 21st day of December 1752

St Thomas's Day (New Calendar)

Luminary: The shortest day – 7 hours and
34 minutes long.
Observation: The Sun enters Capricorn 56
minutes after 11.
Prognostication: A loose stitch unravels
the greatest works.

N at had now been moved to a new cell on a higher floor of
the gaol. He was dismayed to find himself sharing it with
another inmate, an apothecary named Reuben Pearce, a
cadaverous fellow with watchful eyes that followed him about the
room. He wore a balding wig and a patched black gown, like the
wreck of a once-fine fellow. It was not cheering to Nat, either, that
Pearce had already been condemned to the gallows. He looked
around the small stone-hewn room, at the iron rings in the wall and
the large, though securely barred, window and wondered if he was
now in the notorious Dead Men's Cell.

When Tabitha visited on St Thomas's Day, Pearce watched her
keenly, not even shifting himself to the far end of the cell. Her
news was not good. Nanny Seagoes had been hastened to an early
death and so Nat's trial was going to prove a vastly speedy
performance with not even a single friend to stand up and
commend his character. She pulled some handwritten papers from
her pocket.

'For what it's worth, Nat, I've written out the words on the De
Vallory memorial.'

He pushed the papers inside the front of his coat that looked
none too clean now. Then, leaning towards Tabitha, he said, 'We
must speak softly. Our companion is listening.'

Tabitha raised her mouth close to his ear. 'I am full of apprehensions, Nat. You must consider escape.'

He started back. 'I would rather choose justice.'

'I would rather choose a living bridegroom.' She raised a hopeful smile.

'But how?' He spoke as quietly as he could.

'Jansen the guard is in need of a large sum to reach Virginia. He has an uncle there who needs his help to run a profitable farm. I think it better odds than discovering the identity of De Angelo.'

He nodded, cautioning her to speak even more softly.

'On the journey over here I talked with Joshua. Sir John's business brings him back and forth in his cart to Chester often. On Christmas Eve he'll carry me here again when there's to be a Goldsmith's Fair. There will be many strangers about, and I'll pass myself off as a genteel widow. It is my best chance to sell the timepiece and raise the money.'

'It is too dangerous. Consider, Tabitha, the object is known to be stolen – you could also risk the gallows. Sell the ring I gave you, instead.'

She pulled out the ring from where it hung on a ribbon inside her bodice. The gem sparkled like a tiny star, even in the gloom of the cell. 'I cannot. I have never possessed anything so precious,' she whispered, and he felt a lump grow in his throat.

'Very well. Then you must sell Jupiter, and any possessions of mine you can find of worth at Eglantine Hall.'

He reached out and pulled her to him. Her face was cold, but her mouth was warm and yielding; when they drew apart, she was half-smiling at him, a little hope restored.

When Tabitha had left him, Nat slumped back against the slippery stonework and unstoppered the bottle of brandy. Later that evening he would settle down to Latin translation, and then consign himself to blessed oblivion.

'You like to drink, Mr Starling.' The apothecary had an insinuating, wheezing voice that Nat found excessively provoking.

'What is it to you?' he answered sharply. 'I see you are lusting after my brandy, sir. Do you intend to spoil my enjoyment entirely?'

'Pray be kind, sir. If I might taste only a drop – at two o'clock this afternoon I will dance on the air, as they say. It would be my very last comfort on this earth.'

With ill grace, Nat carried it over to the apothecary, who snatched it from him and applied it speedily to his lips.

'That was a very fine woman,' Pearce said. 'Worth living for.'

The castle bell rang out the hour of one o'clock, and Nat shuddered to hear it; this man had less than an hour remaining until he was strung up at the Gallows Hill.

'I heard you talking of De Angelo as if he still lived,' Pearce said, taking a further slug of brandy. 'He's dead and gone, sir.'

Nat took a sharp breath. 'Dead? You knew him? The same fellow who wrote the almanack?'

'Indeed, sir. I was apprenticed to him years back. Plaguey old quack, God bless his bones.'

'Where was that?'

'Lamb Row here in Chester, it was. He had his so-called consulting rooms upon the top landing. Called himself an astrologer, blood-letter, magus, star-gazer, and any other esoteric art that he could get his aged tongue to pronounce. A prize charlatan, I'd call him. But he did have one great art, and that was his almanack. It is still printed, they say.'

Nat seized the man's arm. 'Who prints it now?'

Pearce shook his head. 'I wish I knew, sir. All the printing blocks were lost; I went to fetch them myself when I heard he'd snuffed it, but they had been stolen by then. The almanacks are a canny business – no need to change much, excepting the dates and a few novel predictions. Every year he had orders for two thousand copies. Sixpence a head; that made more money than even cakes and ale.'

Nat grasped both of Pearce's shoulders, shaking his bony frame. 'Think, man. Who could have taken them?'

Now a new sound drifted in through the barred grate; it was the rhythmic tramp of soldiers marching into the courtyard.

'Tell me. Who took them?'

Pearce's eyes were circular with fear as a hammering knock sounded on the door below them. When he spoke, Nat could scarcely hear what he said through his chattering teeth.

'If I knew . . . I'd have chased that poxed thief. And stolen them back.' He cowered away from Nat and drank deep from the bottle. Nat could not find the cruelty necessary to wrestle the brandy away.

'Did you ever know a ruffian of the name Darius?'

'No.' Pearce was shaking now like a hound in a rainstorm.

'How did this De Angelo die?'

'That's not his real name,' wheezed the apothecary. 'He was old Don Eagle – Don always loved an anagram.'

'And? How did he die?'

'It was a dropsy; he swelled up like a fish bladder.'

Now they both hearkened to the sound of voices in the yard, and
Nat's own stomach clutched with sympathetic fear as heavy footsteps
approached from the stairway. Pearce hugged the bottle to his heart.
'Thank you, my friend. Bless you and good luck.' He lifted off his
balding wig and, after poking around inside it, pulled a large black
tablet from out of the horsehair. 'Dutch courage,' he explained. 'The
best of my physic I've saved till last.'

He threw it into his mouth and swigged it back with the last few
gulps of brandy.

'My wits will be jigging with the fairies by the time they carry
me up to the scaffold. I always was a coward . . .'

'Have you a spare one for me, friend?'

Pearce shook out his wig by its pigtail and made a bleak face.
'All gone. A plucky fellow like you will have no need for it.'

Hell's teeth! 'Listen, Pearce – did De Angelo ever talk of
Netherlea?'

The door opened. At the first sight of the guards, Pearce tried to
flatten himself against the wall, his eyes as round as pebbles.

'Tell me! You owe me for the brandy,' Nat said fiercely, as the
soldiers seized Pearce by the arms and dragged him across the floor.

'Netherlea?' he said stupidly, as he crossed the threshold to the
stairs. 'Aye. That's where De Vallory lived.'

Nat stood at the barred window, drawn to witness Pearce's final
journey as a wasp is drawn to the honey trap he will drown in. The
apothecary tottered across the frosty yard to where the city boundary
was marked by the ancient white Gloverstone. There the sheriff's
men waited with a cart, ready to draw him to the crowd at Gallows
Hill. Pearce could no longer stand up straight, and was leaning
unsteadily against a guard. At least he would have a painless end
when the time came.

Nat squinted. As though to ape the dimming of the limelights at
the Playhouse, the sky had muted to the colour of dark lead. Was
a storm approaching? As he watched, a few large and feathery
snowflakes danced gracefully down to the earth and, in the distance,
he heard the orders for the cart to set off towards the gallows.

The sky was growing darker every moment, a low, charcoal
smudge. Would Tabitha be able to find out more about the real De
Angelo? He had a little money still to spare, but had quill, pen and
paper to hand. Quickly, he wrote her a few lines, giving Pearce's

story in brief and the address at Lamb Row. De Vallory, he recalled bitterly. Which De Vallory would have dealings with a charlatan astrologer? Calling out to the guard, he gave him sixpence and hoped that, with luck, the post boy might overtake Tabitha on the road.

FORTY-ONE

A Riddle

From Heaven I fall, though from Earth I begin,
No lady alive can show such a skin.
I'm bright as an angel, and light as a feather,
But heavy and hard, when you squeeze me together.
Though pure and unsullied my aspect I bear,
Yet many poor creatures I help to ensnare.

The 21st to the 23rd day of December 1752

Midwinter

Luminary: Day decreases 7 hours 34 minutes long.
Observation. Sun in Capricorn 56 minutes after 11.
Prognostication: All public actions at a standstill

The oilskin in the cart beneath which Tabitha sheltered soon resembled a little tent of snow. By the time they reached Moss Hill, the cart horses whinnied in distress, slithering in the ruts. Tabitha clambered down and walked behind the cart, her boot soles sliding on treacherous ice-glazed mud. With grim resolve, the carter coaxed the horses to the crown of the hill, where they stood, steaming and snorting clouds of vapour from their nostrils.

Tabitha looked back towards Chester, wiping away the flakes that stuck to her eyelashes. The distant curl of the river, the dozen church towers and wide roofs of the city were disappearing in a covering of muted grey and white. She wondered if Joshua and Jennet were also on the road, or more sensibly, had found lodgings that night. The carter motioned her to climb aboard again. Beneath her oilskin tent, she watched the snow tumble earthwards, smothering the familiar route like a shroud masking a well-loved face. Soon she and Nat would be fugitives, hiding from the world, scraping by in lodgings shared with those who also lived outside the law. And Nat was no longer the strong and vigorous man she had first met; more than six weeks in prison had left him thin and weakened, his ankle raw from the iron ring. She needed to nurse him, and to rebuild his strength. She felt unequal to such labours, for as well as anxious, she was vastly tired. Her eyes drooped as she watched the scene trundle past her: leafless trees laced with snow, the low sky turning bloodshot violet as the sun set.

Saint Thomas Grey, Saint Thomas Grey,
The longest night and the shortest day.

It was impossible to believe that from tomorrow the world would gradually spin back towards the brighter days of springtime.

She woke, rigid with cold, to find herself on the benighted high street of Netherlea. Hauling herself down from the cart, she was guided back to the cottage by the radiant silver disc of the Yuletide moon. The stepping stones glittered in the colourless light and felt treacherous as she teetered across them. Pale frills of ice were growing around each shimmering stone.

It was six o'clock by the church bell when she gratefully opened the cottage door and Nell Dainty rose from her place at the fireside. Bess ran towards her with plump arms extended, squealing with pleasure.

'I thought you was never coming back.'

Tabitha eyed the steaming teapot sitting within easy reach of Nell and bit her tongue. 'Have you any news of Joshua and Jennet?' she asked, instead. 'I've not seen them on the road – it seems they may have stayed in Chester.'

'Not a word.' Nell pulled on her cloak and black bonnet. 'She has been very quiet, the little maid. There's some milk in the pail for her in case the river ices up.'

Tabitha was still pulling off a great deal of wet woollen clothing. 'That's very generous of you.' In as friendly a fashion as she could muster, she asked, 'So, are you all set to move in here on the first day of January?'

'Aye. My old place is leaking like a rusty bucket. I reckon the constable kept this place in good order for your mother. It's a bit lonely, mind you, with not a neighbour about to call upon. But I'll send my goods over in a barrow then.'

Holding Bess against her hip, Tabitha twirled the girl's golden ringlets around her forefinger.

'When I leave, Nell, would you take care of Bess until I can fetch her? She's content here at the cottage, and now she knows you well enough. I'll pay her keep, naturally.'

Nell's face lit up like a lamp.

'I don't see why I can't take her off your hands, altogether.'

'Oh, I shall want her back.'

Nell's eyes narrowed, and the familiar twist to her mouth reappeared.

'So when will that be, then?'

'I shall write,' Tabitha said more airily than she had intended. 'And tell you when I'm settled.'

'You'll not stay for the trial, then?' She thought she glimpsed malice in Nell's face.

'No.'

Oh God, all of this weighs upon my shoulders, she thought. She wondered again how all these complicated matters could be arranged when she felt more despondent and weary than she ever had done in her life.

The next morning, she and Bess traipsed soggily into the village; Joshua and Jennet had still not returned. Though the baker had sold all his penny loaves, Tabitha bought a few stale rolls and a bag of flour.

'No one came up that road since last night,' the baker's boy told her. 'It were you and the carter last of all.'

'So the road is blocked with snow?'

'I reckon so. Some of the farmer's lads are setting off to take a look.'

By the time she and Bess turned for home, lamps were being lit in windows along the High Street and chimneys puffed woodsmoke into the air. She had firewood, plain food and drink. Trying to beat down her growing sense of alarm, she consoled herself that there was still time aplenty before Christmas Eve.

On the twenty-third of December Tabitha carried Bess above knee-high snow drifts to Eglantine Hall. She lit a fire in Nat's fireplace, for the apartment was damp and musty, and found a box of tea and some dry biscuits. While Bess scampered joyfully back and forth across the long chamber, Tabitha gathered up Nat's belongings. First she packed his fine clothes in his portmanteau; all save for the fine woollen coat with gold braid and brass buttons, which he had loved to see her wear. She pulled it on and felt as warm as if his arms encircled her. Standing in front of the mirror she placed his second-best tricorne hat on her hair. It was almost like seeing Nat swaggering before her in his lordly London costume. Damn – the mirror showed she was as pale as snow herself, save for the shadows around her eyes.

Next, she found his pocket watch draped over the headboard and tucked that into her pocket. There was a good engraved inkwell too, and some fine leather-bound books that she might sell. Yet, even as she calculated their value, her spirits sank. She had already decided it would be unforgiveable to sell Jupiter. She picked up Nat's telescope, but felt, again, that she could never deny Nat his passion for gazing at the stars.

While Bess played on the floor, Tabitha sank into a chair beneath the tall oriel windows. The early dusk revealed clear and glittering constellations, presaging another cold night. She raised the telescope to her eye and set the lens upon a few of those celestial bodies that Nat had taught her to locate: the blue diamond of Venus, yellow-ringed Saturn, the shining sword and girdle of Orion. The moon was still almost full tonight, as pock-marked as a sphere of shell.

If only the answer were in the pattern of the stars. She picked up Nat's copy of the almanack and noted with a heavy heart that after the morrow a mere fourteen days remained until his trial. Exiled from the sun's warming rays, the earth now hung upon the cusp of time, and so did they. Nat's box was packed and ready; her mind was set upon a new course of life, she was eager to forge ahead. Yet a disturbing premonition tainted her thoughts: that time had solidified. The future she desired was no longer certain: unseen and unstoppable forces were blocking her path.

FORTY-TWO

A Riddle

More numerous subjects has my *first,*
Than any mortal king can boast,
And yet for more he's still athirst
Till all the world compose his host.
My *second,* made with wondrous skill
Measures every live long day,
He bears a face and two thin hands,
That chase but never catch its prey.
When fear with superstition's joined
My fancied *whole* my first foretells,
And thus the enfeebled sick man's mind
To dread it constantly impels.

The 24th day of December 1752

Christmas Eve

Luminary: Sun rises 13 minutes after 8.
Observation: Conjunction of the Sun and Saturn.
Prognostication: Sly intrigues at hand.

On Christmas Eve, Tabitha awoke beside Bess, beneath a great weight of rugs and old clothes. The silence and unusual gloom filled her with alarm. She got up and rubbed her icy fingers, remembering with longing the London fashion for large swansdown muffs. Curse it, the casement window was half-blocked with snow, transforming her mother's chamber into a cave-like burrow. She wound more clothes around herself – eventually, by dint of some mighty shoves, she succeeded in opening the front door.

At least another foot of snow had fallen, lying in a spotless blanket over the garden and the brittle skeletons of trees. Rows of icicles hung in witchy fingers along the edges of the roof. Tabitha stamped her feet on the doorstep and cursed; she would never reach Chester that day. The realization left her feeling stupid and hopeless. Today was her last chance to sell the watch before all business ceased for Christmas, to meet Jansen and give him his ten pounds. All her hopeful plans – to be reunited with Nat and to board the coach to London – all of the intricate workings of transaction and timing were abruptly closed off to them.

She had failed and, with no other scheme to free Nat, his trial must be faced. A deposition had been made, but all the evidence stood against him. Vindictive character statements spoke of his midnight studies, star-gazing and night-wanderings. The pamphlet proved he had the rare skills necessary to compile an almanack. And, worst of all, it was possible that De Angelo would spread the knowledge that Nat was the natural-born heir to the De Vallorys, standing to gain a great fortune from Francis's death. The Devil roast him, she thought, De Angelo was an invisible, malevolent presence, working constantly to destroy them both.

After breakfast a messenger boy called, his hat and livery white from the morning's new fall of snow.

'It is me, Tom Seagoes, Nanny's nephew,' he explained, and Tabitha recognized the clear-faced lad, both as Jennet's friend and as the boy who had called with messages from Sir John.

'Any news from Chester?' She beckoned him inside.

'I was hoping for news from you, Miss Hart. What of the constable – and Jennet? Some fellow told us the road is blocked by fallen trees, over at Moss Hill.'

'So when will it be cleared?' She heard the anxiety clear in her own voice.

'No one knows. If the snow stops they might try to dig a bridle track through it. I cannot say, what with it being Christmas Eve.'

Despondent, she gave Tom the only warm drink she had, some tansy tea, with an apology for her lack of stronger spirit.

'I nearly forgot my proper business,' he said, holding his chapped hands over the fire. 'I'm to tell everyone that the doctor is making all the tenants welcome this Christmas Eve, for a wassail cup and some solid food. The Yule log is to be lit, so you can save your dry firewood.'

Weary of carrying Bess, Tabitha pulled on Nat's warm coat and braved the snow to see whether her mother had kept the sled she had used as a girl. She found it at the back of the woodshed, a crude wooden platform set upon two curved runners and pulled by a rope. Her father had made it during one of the Great Frosts, and now Bess shrieked with delight when Tabitha wrapped her in a rug and pulled her queen-like over undulating drifts. When they reached the river, they found it had frozen in waves and plaits of greenish ice. So they ignored the stepping stones, and the sled slithered straight across the ice to the far bank. It was a hard journey, and soon Tabitha's arms ached and her skirt was drenched to the knees. Yet perhaps the celebration might afford her some news, some hope.

On Church Green the oak tree stood laced with hoar-frost, like a duke in a coat made of diamonds. Nat had told her the sap of *now* was constantly rising up the trunk of time towards the many branches of their possible futures. Now she felt that their current troubles were a disease: De Angelo had lopped away her mother, Frances, and Nanny, and still he was creeping upwards, malevolent and invisible.

At Bold Hall a few dozen tenants had gathered in the Great Hall, where the doctor and Parson Dilks joined them to raise a toast to the forthcoming holiday. Tabitha stood apart with the serving women and watched as the door was flung open and a team of men came inside, dragging a gigantic log across the flagstones in a whirlwind of red cheeks and oaths.

'Must we suffer these heathen abominations every year, Doctor?' demanded Parson Dilks.

Tabitha looked to where the doctor was sitting. His face was flushed and cheerful, in spite of his sickness. 'I have a fondness for the old ways, Parson. Christmas, after all, has many echoes of the Saturnalia – which you, as a classicist, will of course know well. Pray take note, sir, of the similarity of customs: the hanging of evergreens, the lighting of lamps, the feasting and the frolics.'

Parson Dilks grimaced. 'Balderdash, Doctor. True believers deplore these heathenish routs. The feast days of the Church owe nothing whatsoever to paganism.'

Now the farmer appeared, with a flaming brand made from a little piece of last year's log.

'Stand well back; we must have no trouble with the lighting.'

As soon as the flame touched the dry tangle of roots, the kindling flared and caught, encouraging a loud shout and a cheer.

''Tis a lucky one, master,' said a greybeard. 'It be sure to burn the full twelve hour, an' give us a year's good luck, an' bring back the sun.'

Soon the Yule log was crackling and sparking, throwing off bright heat and barely a wisp of smoke. On Tabitha's knee, Bess clapped her hands and babbled happily in the delicious warmth.

Tabitha joined in a great cheer as the wassail cup was produced, a deep silver-chased bowl that shone in the firelight like a Viking treasure.

'A Merry Christmas to all,' announced the doctor, clumsily lifting the bowl to his lips. There were some sad expressions and head-shakes at the sight of the well-liked doctor, struggling to enjoy what would no doubt be his last Christmas. As he took a long draught, the gathering wished him the same, and the men doffed their caps. One by one, the brimming vessel was passed from mouth to mouth. At Tabitha's turn she allowed herself a good long drink, for she was still damp, and her toes wretchedly numb from the snow. Parson Dilks, on the other hand, gave a little shake of refusal when the bowl was offered to him. Tabitha wondered if he noticed the disapproving glances among the company.

When the supper was brought in, they fell on it like a flock of gannets; there was Yule cake, sliced and buttered, and minced pies, brawn and Zusanna's best cheeses. As soon as the hungry stomachs were filled, the wassail cup was again passed from hand to hand, while choruses were raised from old country carols, and young and old clapped along to the tune. Even the frail doctor supped deeply in the midst of the red-faced revellers.

But it was impossible for Tabitha to surrender to such pleasures while Nat was suffering such a desperate Christmas. She moved about the gathering, asking for news of any likely journeymen venturing to Chester in the next few days. All she got for her trouble were a few invitations to dance, and the same crude jests that labouring men unearthed, each and every Christmas.

Leaving Bess with Nell, Tabitha eventually found her way to the stillroom, where the air was sweet with the sugary fragrance of Christmas baking. Jane was working pell-mell, preparing macaroon biscuits and decorated marzipans.

Jane looked up. 'Tabitha. Thank goodness. What news of Joshua?'

'No news at all. And I've just learned there are other folk stranded. Judith, the doctor's cook, and the farmer's wife, who took her poultry to Chester market.'

'It's a sorry Christmas when folk are scattered so far from kin. And not a happy thought to have no constable in the village.'

Tabitha nodded, looking about herself for some distraction. 'Can I help you, Jane? I cannot bear to sit and rejoice when I cannot bring even a crumb of Christmas cheer to Nat.'

Jane's freckled face looked over to the groaning table.

'Well, I must take Sir John's tray up to him. If you could press these almonds in the centre of these dainties . . .'

'Please, Jane. Let me go up to Sir John. I would be forever beholden to you.'

'You?'

'Yes. I am leaving Netherlea as soon as this snow clears, and I should like to thank him for the kind words he spoke of me at the Manor Court. It is not likely I'll ever see him again.'

Jane gave her a long and doubtful look. Just then a footman burst through the door, demanding roasted apples for the cider.

'Yes, when they are ready!' she shouted back at him.

Then, turning back to Tabitha, she capitulated. 'Very well. His tray is over there. Only don't, for heaven's sake, upset him.'

As soon as Jane had turned her back, Tabitha pulled down a lace cap and apron from the row of hooks and, looking passably like a servant, picked up the tray and ascended the narrow back stairs. She found her way by trial and error, discovering Sir John's room at the end of the same passageway as his son's.

Tapping at the door and hearing no reply, she entered the grand apartment. Sir John made a slight figure in the centre of a vast tester bed, festooned with gilt and armorials and swathes of tasselled brocade. The chamber was in deep gloom; scarcely any light penetrated from the window, and only a few isolated candles burned in sconces. But Sir John was awake, propped up high on bolsters, and watched her approach through startled bloodshot eyes.

'Sir John,' she said softly, curtsying low. 'It is Tabitha. I am leaving soon and wanted to see you.'

She set the tray down and approached him. It was a blow to see the old man laid low like this.

'I want to thank you for speaking in my favour to Parson Dilks. I am sorry – I should have answered your messages.'

His gaze was fixed upon her and his lips worked anxiously, the spittle collecting at the corners.

'You cannot speak?' she whispered.

Sir John's purplish eyelids slowly closed, then opened, in a slow and deliberate blink.

Of a sudden, she unburdened herself of all her worries, convinced that Nat's father must have at least a fraction of the affection that she felt for his son.

'I have seen Nat in Chester gaol. Pray forgive him, but I forced him to tell me his secret. I know he is your son. I am doing all I can to free him, for I swear to you that he is innocent. But God help me, this snow has confounded my plans and I am at my wits' end.'

Suddenly all her heartfelt feelings burst out of her. 'I love him, Sir John. He's a fool at times, too clever for his own good; but Lord help me, I love him with all my soul. He must not be hanged. He is innocent.'

To her dismay, Sir John's eyes filled with tears, and two glistening tracks rolled down from the creased corners of his eyes.

'I am sorry,' she said again. 'You care for him too.'

She produced a handkerchief to gently wipe the tears away. 'Well, I swear to you that I will do my utmost to save him,' she said, sniffing hard.

Fearing that Lady Daphne might interrupt them, she offered him a spoonful of plum pottage, which he took as meekly as an infant. When he had taken all he could, she held the glass of ratafia to his lips, but Sir John was growing sleepy, and would take none of it, compressing his mouth in a stubborn line.

The cherry-scented liquor smelled sweet and appetizing and she was tempted to take a restorative sip. On hearing a movement on the stairs, she put the glass down and squeezed Sir John's great red fist and wished him a Christmas blessing.

She was distracted with sorrow as she emerged on to the passageway. From all she knew of the sick and dying, Sir John had the look of a man who would never recover his health. She finally comprehended the full force of guilt that Nat carried; that having so recently met his true father, he had caused this apoplexy, and perhaps brought about his imminent death.

'Tabitha?' She looked up to see the doctor leaning on his cane. 'You visited my brother?'

She curtsied. 'Yes, sir, I wanted to see him before I leave Netherlea. To say farewell.'

'Ah, I am sorry you are leaving. Well, my pharmacopoeia is in better order than it was before – and you and Bess have cheered an ailing man. Let me know if I can assist you, in any way at all. When is it you leave?'

'I leave as soon as the road to Chester is open. And – sir, perhaps you might help me.'

She set the tray down and surrendered to her sudden impulse. There was nothing for it; trapped here in Netherlea, she must try any possibility to save Nat.

'I have a curiosity I need to sell. A pocket watch of solid silver. It is a *memento mori*, engraved all over with mottos and Bible scenes. I'm told it once belonged to Mary, the Scottish Queen.'

The doctor lifted his grey brows and pursed his lips, nodding sagely. He was still flushed from the wassail cup; it had given his eyes a new, intoxicated glitter. 'Do you, indeed? I have heard tell of such a curious relic; engraved with mottoes from Horace and Ovid. I have a fascination for these *vanitas* objects. And you wish to part with it?'

'I must.'

'Do you have it here?'

'No. I would need to fetch it.'

He remained thoughtful, tapping his finger against his cheek. Finally, he looked up at her with a wan smile. 'I should like to give you a fair price, for friendship's sake – but to do that, I must discover more of the object's history. What say you to calling on me tomorrow? I will give you something for it, even if it is not of the provenance you hope.'

Tabitha hesitated; if the road were clear in the morning, she might be wasting precious hours with the doctor.

'I need at least fifteen pounds,' she said, not troubling herself about being so forthright.

The doctor narrowed his eyes as if deliberating hard. 'If the object is as you describe it, that price is certainly achievable. Tomorrow, being Christmas, I dine here at Bold Hall again. But if you will call upon me at my own house, I shall return at two o'clock.'

FORTY-THREE

A Riddle

Sometimes upright I am found,
As often laid along,
I'm also found on sacred ground
Amid a numerous throng.
Those whom I serve are cold as I:
No wages I receive,
But stand beneath the open sky,
To make their memory live.
In church I'm often placed more high,
With mournful trophies dressed:
Then speak in Latin frequently,
And wear a marble vest.

The 24th Day of December 1752

Christmas Eve

Luminary: Moon rises 4 minutes after 9.
Observation: Venus is an occidental evening star.
Prognostication: The minds of the people are filled
with ambiguous forebodings.

On Christmas Eve morning, Nat had taken such steps as he could to prepare himself for a rapid departure; he had paid for his face to be shaved and his hair to be dressed. Then there was nothing for it but to wait. He found himself repeatedly dragging the noisy leg iron back and forth to the window, hoping to gain his first glimpse of Tabitha. The snow in the castle yard had been mostly swept away by breakfast time, and he could see nothing beyond the high turreted walls. When a carriage rolled in through the gateway, however, its roof was white with snow. To his dismay, he saw the sheriff dismount from it, and beside him walked Constable Saxton, bearing his staff of office. They disappeared into the sheriff's lodgings while Nat continued to fret at the window.

The constable was in Chester devilish early; he envied him travelling with Tabitha from Netherlea. He told himself that Tabitha must even now be making her way to the Goldsmith's Fair. He had no doubt that she was as sharp as a razor, but still he wished that he could have accompanied her. Those merchants would try to swindle her – he silently urged her to hold out for as much as twenty guineas.

When might she come to the gaol – as early as noon? The castle bell rang out midday, then one, then two, and then three. An unpleasantly hollow feeling grew inside his ribcage; he feared that she had tried to sell the watch to someone who suspected it had been stolen. He sank his head into his hands and wondered how his conscience could bear it if he had delivered her up to the law, too.

Night had fallen by four o'clock. Torches were lit against the walls in the courtyard and he could just see moving silhouettes and hear drunken shouts. Heavy steps rang out on the stone stairs leading up to his cell; then the door opened, and the soldier he knew as Jansen pushed a drunken youth inside.

Nat sprang up. 'Have you seen Tabitha?'

Jansen busied himself attaching the drunken youth to a chain upon the wall.

'Looks like our lady has brought no Christmas gift, for me nor for you,' he said in a gruff undertone.

'Something must have gone wrong,' Nat hissed. 'She promised to be here. Some trouble must have delayed her.'

Jansen looked quizzically up at him, through his tangled hair. 'More's the shame if she don't come. The apprentice boys are out holidaying; there are fights on every street corner. I could have smuggled you out in all the hubbub.'

'Give her time,' Nat begged.

'Aye, but hark you, my watch ends at six – and I won't be back here till your trial day. I'm right sorry. I did my best.'

'If she comes before six?'

'If she has the money I stand by my word.'

For the next hour Nat stood upon the stool at the darkened window, conjuring a vision of Tabitha running up to his door, laughing about some foolish delay and spiriting him off to a coach that would speed them down the dark highway. He glanced over at his new cellmate, who was lying upon his stomach, groaning miserably from a surfeit of drink. The lad would not even bear witness to his escape.

The bells rang out six o'clock, and Nat collapsed back upon the stone ledge. His ignorance of Tabitha's whereabouts was the most appalling thing of all. For a long time he closed his eyes, confronting a series of horrific possibilities. The worst – and, it seemed to him, the most likely – eventuality was that De Angelo had seized her. He remembered her bold good sense, her loyal heart. He longed for brandy, or even a large black tablet such as Reuben Pearce had possessed, to consign himself to oblivion.

Striving to control his fears, he lit a candle, and for the first time grew concerned that the apprentice boy was gasping in a loud and painful fashion. Nat dragged himself across the chamber and prodded him then, reluctantly, heaved him over on to his back, and gave an involuntary cry. The freckle-faced lad was not drunk, but insensible from a wound to his chest that had stained his woollen coat dark with blood.

Nat shouted at his door, but no one answered. He hollered again before remembering Jansen's warning that most of the soldiery would be taking a holiday tonight. He felt quite empty of ideas; no one would call on him until at least seven the next morning. He made an attempt to staunch the lad's wound but had no doubt he was too badly injured for anyone but a surgeon to save. He raked his fingers through his hair and despaired. All his plans were confounded.

Forcing himself to grow calmer, he picked up the paper Tabitha had brought him, which bore the transcription of the De Vallory monument. He smiled indulgently over Tabitha's sketch, for, in truth, she was not the most skilled of artists. He could just identify what appeared to be a figure of a man with a sheet cast over his head, something like an All Hallows' ghost; certainly, the features of the effigy were entirely obscured. He could not at once think which god or character from the classical world this was meant to represent. Beneath the figure's raised foot lay a skeleton attempting to rise upon its elbows, twisting its skull to stare upwards at its conqueror. Nat read the inscription:

Francis John De Vallory,
Only Son of Sir John Lawrence De Vallory by Lady Daphne,
the daughter of Clement Fifield,
departed this life August fourth 1752, in the twentieth year
of His Age.

Only son, was he? Nat sighed, resigned to his own claim being never substantiated. He was truly sorry, however, that Sir John's only legitimate heir had died in such a violent manner. He had seen the despair in Sir John's face and would wish such pain upon no parent.

Below were inscribed a dozen lines of Latin. Nat's eyes speedily picked out a number of conventional and platitudinous words: sleep, truth, gentle. Well, he had the whole oppressive evening before him, so he supposed he might as well translate it from start to finish.

Behold the Veiled One,
Bringer of Truth

He was about halfway through the verse when it struck him, with a tiny thrill of interest, that he was reading a riddle. The effigy had to be a classical figure, for the Golden Age described by Ovid and Hesiod was clearly referred to; he racked his brain but could not find a solution. He caught his breath in excitement as the eighth line was revealed to him:

> *The sickle-bearer,*
> *Reaper of men.*

He dismissed his suspicion; surely this was a conventional description of Death, or Time, who traditionally carried a sickle. There were a number of jarring lines, however:

> *The serpent-twined staff*
> *Of victorious sleep . . .*

As quickly as he could, he completed the last few couplets.

> *My wandering twin,*
> *Be-ringed with light,*
> *Devourer of kin*
> *Reaper of years.*

Nat leaned back against the chilled wall of his cell and tapped his pen rhythmically against the rickety table. What the devil was this? It was a mighty odd funerary inscription, for it spoke nothing of Francis's qualities. Instead, it appeared to be a laudatory verse about the veiled figure standing above the inscription, and whoever had composed it had been extraordinarily free in his theme. Surely this was more than a personification of Time or Death? The figure also carried a serpent upon a staff and bore a ring of light. It had to be Saturn, he decided, remembering Ovid's lines about the god who had ruled a mystical Golden Age before the foundation of the world. And Saturn was another name for Chronos, or Time, and the twin was the planetary wanderer, Saturn, which also sported a ring of light.

Nat squeezed his eyes tight shut and tried to remember all he knew about Saturn. He had once seen a ghastly painting of Saturn destroying his own kin by eating them, thereby forbidding them dominion over himself. He was a cruel god, a forerunner of the grotesque figures of skeletal Death himself.

Nat shook his head in astonishment. Was he correct, to think this described Francis's murder by means of a reaping scythe, and the bringing of eternal night to Netherlea by use of poison? And a serpent carried upon a staff – why, the solution to the riddle was really rather easy.

Easy, but also terrifying. Where in Heaven's name was Tabitha? Both his mind and his body were suddenly so agitated that he felt he might scream if he could not at once go and search for her. If he had been cold before, he now found himself shivering like a plague victim.

For now, he had uncovered the identity of De Angelo. And the certainty grew like ice upon his limbs that the longer he was kept apart from Tabitha, the sooner De Angelo would strike.

FORTY-FOUR

A Riddle

I will always pursue you, although I am blind,
The more of me you take, the more follow behind,
There is only one means to escape me I've found,
And that's to evade me by taking hard ground.

The 24th day of December 1752

Christmas Eve

Luminary: The Yule Moon three days old.
Observation: Aldebaran south 30 minutes
after midnight.
Prognostication: Many subtle and unlawful actions
contrived among men.

I t was dark again when Tabitha and Bess set off home from Bold
Hall. All around them, the snow shone in the moonlight, like a
frozen fairytale world. It was a lonely journey dragging the sled,
once they had crossed the icy highway of the river. Bess was wakeful,
alert to the sounds of creatures stirring in the woods. Through the
clear night air they heard a vixen barking and, closer at hand, unseen
birds rustled in the trees sending falls of snow cascading to the
ground. To keep both their spirits up, she kept up a litany of stories
that her mother had told her: of how the dormouse was sleeping in
a furry knot in the hollows of the bank, and the spiked ball of the
hedgehog slumbered on through the winter in his dell. She related
how below the ice, on the river's floor, frogs crouched yellow-eyed
and motionless. And deep in the soil, buried seeds stirred and
dreamed of quickening in the springtime.

Afterwards, she remembered that both she and Bess had been
uneasy, even before she noticed footsteps leading towards the
cottage. The moon did not reveal them with the clarity of daylight,
and Tabitha could distinguish no details. She paused and set her
own booted foot beside the shape in the snow. These newer prints
were larger and heavier than hers. She could see the marks that she
had left earlier that afternoon very clearly, between the twin lines
of the sled's runners.

For a moment she hesitated, unsure whether to turn back to the
hall. The doctor had announced that any tenant who chose not to
venture out into the freezing night might sleep by the Yule fire. It
was tempting; yet she could already see the two squares of the

cottage windows gleaming golden-red from the remains of the fire. No, she was almost home – and besides, she felt curiously reluctant to turn back.

The prints continued up the path to the cottage door. She stopped halfway and inspected them, shushing Bess, who was making excited noises of pleasure to be home. To Tabitha's relief, she discovered that the footprints first led to the door and then turned back and away down the path. Now that she guessed there was no intruder waiting in the cottage, she considered other possibilities. With a jolt of excitement, she wondered if Nat had somehow broken free. Perhaps he had persuaded Jansen that she would pay him after Nat's release? Or maybe it was Joshua, returned from Chester up the newly opened road. Whoever it was, they had ventured out to call on her, and had then gone on their way.

Tabitha was therefore off her guard when she reached the wooden door and saw something square and pale had been fixed upon it. She pulled the paper down and, after beating away the excess snow from her clothes, she pushed the door open and carried Bess inside. It must be from Nat. Perhaps he was waiting for her at Eglantine Hall? Nevertheless, before reading the message, she made a rapid search of the cottage; so far as she could tell, no one had ventured inside since she had left. Bending low over the fireplace, she stoked the embers with the poker and peered at the message, making out the letters in the dim reddish glow.

To Tabitha

We have played the game to its merry end.
You long have amused me, my clever friend,
As a vain and dogged adversary;
'Tis a shame you are my enemy.
Only one of us can conqueror be,
So your death must crown my victory.

De Angelo

In a spasm of fright, she ran to the front door and, with fumbling fingers, succeeded in bolting it tight. Yet had not her mother relied on that frail barrier of wood and still been attacked in this very same cottage? She stood very still, listening for any movement from outside; then she dragged her mother's chair towards the door and jammed it hard against the latch. Next, she placed the heavy oak table behind the chair. It would not prevent a strong man with a hammer from entering the cottage, but she would have fair warning of an attacker's arrival.

Slowly she calmed herself, and a crazed desire to run out harum-scarum into the woods subsided. Tomorrow she would leave Netherlea, even if it took her a month of walking, through snowdrifts as deep as houses, to reach Chester. Her bundle of goods lay ready in the corner; after her visit to the doctor, she would have money enough to free Nat and escape. She need spend only one more night here. De Angelo had been here once tonight. Was he likely to return? In this weather, she wagered he would not.

Before she went to bed, Tabitha set metal pots and tins into the casements, so she would hear at once if an intruder tried to enter by the windows. Then, taking the poker in her hand, she led Bess into the bedroom, and prepared for her very last night in the cottage she had always known as home.

Too overwrought to sleep, she lit a candle and picked up her mother's almanack; she had searched it countless times, but still she re-read it, for she dimly remembered seeing mention of Christmas somewhere among her mother's cramped notes.

She caressed the softly worn pages, remembering her mother's ghostly appearance on the night of the calendar change, and grew steadily more certain that her mother must have left her a message inside the almanack. Though it was a waste of candlelight, she began wading through her mother's entries again, for what seemed the hundredth time. She read once more of her mother's fear of 'D', of the small calls on her mother's time to attend to the dying and dead, and of her impatience with Tabitha's tardiness in writing. There was nothing she had not read before. She turned back to the beginning, to January, February, March. She had reached April when she finally came across the elusive mention of Christmas:

2 April. St Urban's Day. *After calling at the hall, I rode in the cart, wherein the hedgers had gathered many laurel leaves. Such a remarkable scent of Christmas made me giddy, and I laid long in bed with a sore head.*

The scent of Christmas. She flicked through the pages of the almanack. The Prognostications for December spoke of Christmas, too. Perhaps it was the flickering of the candle flame, but her eye was caught by the appearance of a new word, spelled out by the first letter of each line. The verse hid an acrostic:

Lay evergreens above your fire,
And raise your glass with joy entire,
Unrest is over and an end to strife,
Rejoice in winter's death in life,
Ends now this year of fear and dread,
Lay victory's wreath high on his head.

Of course, the victor's wreath was made from laurel leaves! She was sure that the veiled figure on the De Vallory memorial was also crowned with a wreath. The threatening verse that had been pinned to the cottage door again repeated the same boast: '*So your death must crown my victory.*'

She was again standing in the stillroom at Bold Hall, breathing in the bittersweet fragrance of Christmas almond cakes. It was a subtle scent, one that had accompanied Tabitha often in these last months in Netherlea. It had been there in Nanny's communion wine, and she had also inhaled its fragrance when she had tried to tempt Sir John to drink his ratafia. What was the cordial Jane had added to Sir John's drink? Cherry laurel. Finally she knew De Angelo's identity, and with that knowledge came a shiver of pure and potent fear.

Too disturbed to sleep, Tabitha started violently at the sudden tolling of the doom bell that reached her across the night. For a moment she believed herself summoned to attend another death in the village; then she remembered it was Christmas Eve, and slumped back against the bolster. The tolling was only the traditional ringing for the Devil's funeral, in the final minutes before Christ's birth.

'Deliver us all from evil tonight,' she murmured. On and on the bell tolled, in mournful regular beats. If the universe were just, she thought, De Angelo, like the Devil, would not survive this night.

Then, as midnight heralded Christmas Day, a melodious peal of five bells rang out across the frosty air to summon the faithful to Midnight Mass. It was a long time since Tabitha had attended the ceremony, but she recalled the church radiant with candles, representing the Light of the World. She had always been drawn to the large candle that represented the Star of Bethlehem. The church had been dressed with evergreens, too – bay, mistletoe, holly, ivy – and also, she remembered, swagged bunches of glossy green laurel leaves.

Beside her, Bess stirred in her sleep, murmuring in a childish dream. Tabitha wondered if the cattle were even now falling upon their knees to worship, just as the beasts in the stable had worshipped the Child of Bethlehem. Or had the shift of the calendar confounded even the beasts and their ancient memories? No, Nat had told her that this year England's clocks were correct for the first time in centuries. This was the first true celebration of Christmas day's arrival, as calculated by the revolution of the sun.

She wondered if Nat was still awake at Chester gaol. She missed him – but she would never cease to fight for him. Instead of fretting and despairing, she put her arm around Bess and allowed her mind to fill with the mystery and magic of Christmas, and a scintillating star, sent to free the world of evil.

FORTY-FIVE

A Riddle

An instrument small, which has caused, on my word,
More mischief than ever was done by the sword;
Add a vowel – and a shelter from sun and from rain,
That can soon be raised up and then put down again;
United, will give what I hope you will be,
When your former transgressions you ruefully see.

The 25th day of December 1752

Christmas Day

Luminary: Sun rises 13 minutes after 8.
Observation: Mars is a morning star and rises at 6.
Prognostication: A lucky day to travel.

The apprentice boy was dead. Nat had barely slept, tormented not only by the thought of De Angelo pursuing Tabitha, but also by the suffering of the expiring youth, just a half-dozen feet from where he lay. At dawn, he had offered a cup of water to his cellmate; but when Nat touched his skin it was as cold as the stones beneath his feet. What a pitiful end to a young life, he cursed. No one came in answer to Nat's shouts for help, so he did his best to lay the body in a more dignified fashion – yet he failed even in that, for the limbs would not unbend.

When the guard finally came at eight o'clock, the surly drone was unrepentant, and merely cursed at the extra work of removing a man's corpse from a cell. So much for Christmas spirit. When Nat insisted on speaking to the high sheriff, the guard laughed in his face. 'You might want to see him, pal. But he don't want to see you.'

'Listen, fellow. I know who the Netherlea murderer is. I am innocent.'

'Aye. That's you and all the other innocent men here, wanting a parlay with the sheriff. On Christmas morning? Is your skull cracked?'

Nat tried again when a pair of soldiers arrived to remove the boy's corpse. 'I swear on my life, I am an innocent man. If a few soldiers can be spared, the villain will be arrested by this evening.'

This time his only replies were smirks, and scornful silence.

Nat's black mood was not improved when he looked outside and saw Saxton crossing the yard again, this time in a greatcoat and felt hat. The constable did not appear festive either; he kept his head down, and strode across the snow like an ill-tempered bear. Nat shook the iron bars and cursed him, along with all the gaolers and the sheriff, who were employed to uphold the law but didn't give a fig for justice.

He frowned to see Saxton walk past the guardhouse and make for the door that led to his own cell. When the constable burst in, his broad pink face was as stern as Nat had ever seen it. Rummaging in his pocket, the constable pulled out a letter, and waved it before his face.

'Who told you of this? Don Eagle and his almanack?' Nat was in a mood to be affronted.

'Where did you get my private letter, you scurrilous dog?'

'That is my business. Answer me in the name of the law.'

'I will not. What have you done with Tabitha?'

Saxton's blue eyes were as cold as beads of ice. 'You've got this all arsey-versey, Starling. I question you first, and then, only if my humour takes me, do I allow you to speak.'

'And Tabitha?'

'Tell me about Eagle.'

The constable's grim tone and bearing were beginning to unnerve Nat so he let the facts tumble out of his mouth as speedily as he could.

'I had a cellmate with the name of Reuben Pearce; he went to the gallows a few days past. Listen, Saxton, I beg you go and make enquiries at Lamb Row. This Don Eagle was an astrologer, the original De Angelo. Pearce said the printing blocks of his almanack were stolen, and that the name De Vallory was known to him. And there is more. I have translated the De Vallory inscription in Netherlea church and can tell you that De Angelo is taunting us. I know who that murdering devil is.'

Saxton's mouth set in a hard line. 'As do I. I've been to this Don Eagle's lodgings and questioned his servants. All his almanack paraphernalia was taken by the man who attended him at his death.'

So Saxton knew too. Nat felt he might burst. 'So I am right. And what of Tabitha?'

'The road to Netherlea has been blocked by snow and fallen trees since Saint Thomas's day. So far as I can reckon it, Tabitha travelled the road just before the worst of the weather. I tried to get back home, late that night, but had to return here. And now I've been given this letter of yours that was never passed on to her. And she is stranded in Netherlea.'

'And is that devil in Netherlea, too?'

Saxton nodded with clenched teeth, and Nat saw that what he had taken to be fury was fierce desperation.

'How is the road today?'

'Still blocked. And damn this cowardly town, there is not a man who will make a trial of it.'

Nat stood up smartly, the chain at his ankle clanking at his side. 'I will.'

'It will be on foot, man – no horse can climb over the trees that have fallen across that steep road. The only way is for us to haul our way up with hatchets and ropes.'

'We can do it, Saxton. Every minute that passes puts her in greater danger.'

Saxton folded his arms and looked intently at Nat.

'You know I will do whatever is needful to help Tabitha,' Nat urged him. 'Come on, man. Let's go.'

The constable brooded a moment longer – then, suddenly, he roared over his shoulder.

'Amos!'

When the guard hurried in, Saxton pointed at the chain holding Nat's ankle.

'Unlock it. I must question this rascal at greater length.'

At the rapid turn of a key, the chain tumbled to the floor, and the constable clapped Amos on the back. 'Here's your Christmas box, good fellow. Go and fetch some hot ale for the lads in the guardhouse. Don't gawp, man, but go to it! Only leave me your keys – I had a roaring night on the ale last night and am in much want of the privy.'

Once the guard had left, Saxton pulled off his own coat to reveal a second set of garments beneath. 'Put these on, and stuff your old rags with straw.'

Nat did as he was told, leaving a crude mannequin of himself upon the floor of his cell. At a signal, he limped after the constable, and out through the door, dressed in a black watchman's hat that he wore low over his eyes, with the collar of his greatcoat pulled up around his chin. Without the least attempt at secrecy, the constable led the way downstairs.

'Wait here,' Saxton ordered.

Nat leaned against the guardhouse wall. He felt lightheaded, and his newly freed leg was a devil to manage. But the chill air of liberty entered his lungs, firing his blood like the strongest brandy.

A few feet away Saxton was bawling good-humouredly into the guardhouse door.

'No, no more ale till dinnertime. I'll be on my way now. I'll get a confession out of that prig by New Year, see if I don't!' He rubbed his knuckles, as if they were sore. 'Here be your keys, Amos. Starling is knocked senseless – be a good fellow and leave him dinnerless until I call again tomorrow. Merry Christmas, lads!'

Nat heard a chorus of good wishes from the smoky fug of the guardhouse. Then Saxton took Nat's arm and steered him briskly through the gateway and down the drawbridge, where not even a single guard was inclined to endure Christmas Day in the snow.

As Saxton drove a hired cart along the empty snow-smooth road out of Chester, Nat's eyes watered in the blinding outdoor light. He felt overcome by the sea-blue sky and the disc of silver sun that shed warming rays upon his cheek. Wisps of freezing vapour moved across the fields, with the silent stealth of drifting smoke. After six weeks in a dark cell there was something paradisiacal about the light and distance and beauty of the open world.

Nat was compelled to speak, at last, of De Angelo.

'He used his profession as the craftiest of disguises. Do you remember, when Francis died, he told everyone with absolute assurance that the murder had taken place that morning?'

Saxton nodded as he adjusted the reins, guiding the horse up the lower slope of the hill. 'Aye, I was there, being duped with the rest.'

'He insisted that Francis had died that morning and, naturally, there were witnesses aplenty to his being present at breakfast. He even quarrelled with Sir John, so all the company would remember it. Yet Tabitha said Francis was so rigidly fixed in a kneeling posture that she couldn't straighten his limbs. Idiot that I am, I questioned her judgement, instead of doubting his word. Then, last night, a wretched boy died in my cell. Right after he died, only his head and face were in a state of rigor; but this morning, his limbs were entirely inflexible, just as Francis's had been. Francis died the night before.'

Saxton looked at him sideways and nodded. 'Even the law can be misled, when our medical man is a liar.'

It was ten thirty in the morning by the constable's pocketwatch when the wheels refused to budge further. They left the cart at the last cottage on the edge of town and walked on with a few tools.

Soon they reached the first fallen tree, a good-sized beech that had crashed down at an angle across the road, its leafless branches and tangle of roots thickly covered in ice-hard snow.

'Ready for a scramble, Starling?'

'Assuredly.'

Saxton climbed up first, using his hatchet to steady himself against the icebound tree. At the top, he crawled over the slippery trunk, and Nat soon followed after him. Then, with great care, they descended over a powdery snowdrift as tall as a man.

It was desperate work after that, dragging broken branches and shrubs out of their path. Nat was feverish and unsteady on his feet by the time they reached a tree that entirely blocked their way, an oak of colossal size that had crashed down awkwardly across the road, exactly where it wound into a gully. Its trunk was suspended like a bridge above their heads, yet beneath it the way was blocked with debris and compacted snow.

'I should say it is twenty feet to its highest point,' Nat said.

'I shall go first,' the constable insisted.

Saxton tied a rope around his hatchet and, taking a few steps backwards, threw it with a strong aim into the air. It glittered and spun as it arced up, lodging between two strong-looking branches. Then, with all his burly strength, he seized the rope and began to shin up its length, using his hands and feet to haul himself up.

After much exertion, the constable straddled the tree trunk and secured the rope to a branch high above Nat's head.

Nat grasped the rope, strangely reluctant to leave the solid ground behind him.

'Come along, Starling,' the constable called down. 'It's well after noon by the height of the sun. Or are you not man enough?'

Damn, he was more of a books-and-brandy man than a circus tumbler. Still, he grasped the rope and hauled himself up a few feet, though his limbs were sapped of vigour. Death and fire, his muscles were stretched beyond their capacity. Raising his head, he saw the constable watching him, the bright sun casting his face entirely in shadow. With great effort, he scrambled up a few more feet of slippery rope.

'We haven't got all day, Starling.'

Nat caught the flash of the hatchet's ironwork in the sunshine. He steadied himself to look up again; the constable was a dark shape waiting above him.

'What the devil are you doing with that hatchet?' Nat gasped.

'Thinking on your future.'

'Well, think on Tabitha's future, won't you? Give me a hand up.'

He could not see the constable's face – but he did feel the rope slowly lift his weight, and scrabbled, in a most ungainly fashion, to drag himself up. With a gasp of relief Nat threw himself up beside the constable and clung there. He could do nothing but lie and pant, with a heaving chest, for a good few minutes.

'Well,' Nat said at last, pulling himself upright, 'now for De Angelo.'

Together they clambered down the other side and, with great joy, saw they had reached the long, flat road to Netherlea.

FORTY-SIX

A Riddle

No vast device beneath the sky,
Can keep a secret bound as I;
All things for safety are to me consigned,
Although I often leave them far behind;
I never act but by another's will,
And what is twisted from me, I must fulfil.

The 25th day of December 1752

Christmas Day

Luminary: Day 7 hours and 34 minutes long.
Observation: Jupiter is retrograde in the 10th
degree of Cancer.
Prognostication: Affliction of some eminent person.

Tabitha had woken to find herself not only still alive, but in possession of a new scheme she had devised in her sleep. She would open the doctor's strongroom while he was absent at Bold Hall, help herself to fifteen pounds, and leave the skull watch in its place. That was mighty close to honest dealing, she convinced herself. Then, good and early, with her money in hand, she need only leave Bess with Nell before setting off across the snow for the safe haven of Chester. With luck, the road would be open, and a cart or carriage would offer her a ride. And if it were not, she would just have to dig her way to Nat through the snow.

It was a glorious, glittering, blue-skied Christmas day. Approaching the doctor's house, she found only one set of wheel and hoof marks in the snow. All was well; the carriage had transported her former employer to his Christmas dinner at Bold Hall. She let herself and Bess in at a servants' door that was generally left on a latch. Shushing Bess, she waited for a moment in the gloom of the passage, hearkening for any sounds from the empty house. All was so still that she could almost hear the dust settling.

As quietly as she could, she crept upstairs and found the ring of old keys in the doctor's chamber. In a moment she was downstairs again, trying each key in the strongroom lock. But try as she might, not one of them fitted; the brass lock was of an ancient type, with a series of catchments quite impervious to any key but its own. A pick-lock would also be useless in so antiquated a device. Cursing under her breath, she tried each key again. Death and fire. None of them would turn.

A clock on the wall showed the time to be fifteen minutes past noon. To be sure of avoiding the doctor, she needed to be far away on the path to Nell's by the time he returned at two o'clock. What the devil were these keys for, if not the strongroom?

'Let's look downstairs,' she whispered to Bess, who had been toddling about the kitchen in search of sugarplums. Together, they went to the nail-studded door that led to the wine cellar; it was possible, she thought, that there might be a small store of money in there. The very first key she inserted turned in the lock with a satisfying creak. Taking Bess by the hand, she took a few steps down a set of stone stairs that plummeted away into the cold bowels of the cellar.

A sudden gust of cold air, and a loud bang, made Tabitha cry out in surprise; the door had slammed closed at their backs, leaving the two of them standing unsteadily in complete darkness. Tabitha groped around herself with outstretched hands. Bess began to wail, a high-pitched, frightened sound that could have woken the Devil in that enclosed space.

'Hush!' she hissed to Bess. At last she found the wooden flatness of the door and, after a long search, the raised metal of the lock; but she could find no inside handle. The key was still where she had left it, on the outside. After endless frantic minutes, she understood that they were trapped.

Looking down, she noticed for the first time that a faint glow of light emanated from the bottom of the stairs. Bess was already moving steadily away from her down the steps towards the light. Perhaps there was another way out? With new hope, Tabitha followed Bess down the stairs.

It grew colder as they moved deeper underground. Reaching the bottom stair, they entered a barrel-ceilinged room like a chapel from an antique age. The flames of oil lamps revealed walls painted with pastel figures of great delicacy, all of them dressed in classical garb; she wondered if they might be relics of the days of the Roman invaders, for they were mighty old. Truly, this was a jewel box of a room.

It also appeared to be inhabited. Shelves displayed bound volumes of books with incomprehensible titles, a brass telescope of breathtaking intricacy, and a clock like a golden castle, set with tiny winged figures. The time, she read with dismay, was forty-five minutes after noon. At the centre of the room stood a spherical contraption like a gilded cage, in which cogs and tiny globes were suspended. She guessed that it was a mechanical model of the sky, the golden globe at its centre representing the sun, and a small ball of lapis lazuli signifying the earth.

Bess clung to her hand as they entered a second chamber, in which she was just able to see the glint of many glass jars in the faint light of further oil lamps. Peculiar shapes, that were neither foods or fruits, were suspended in the jars; peering into them, she gave an involuntary gasp to see various parts of human bodies. Here was a human heart, the great veins waving like tentacles; there the grey, sponge-like matter of the brain. She had to swallow back bile at the sight of a glass case containing two tiny twins with blue cords encircling them, clasping each other in an endless sleep. She hurried on past lidless blood-veined eyes, and unborn babies scrawny as newborn kittens.

Tabitha was grateful that, in her ignorance, Bess looked about her with nothing more than wary interest. At the furthest corner of the room stood another door; passing through it, she felt another shock of unexpected strangeness. This final chamber was dominated by an image sculptured in relief upon the furthest wall, and she recognized it as the same veiled figure carved upon the De Vallory monument. Before it was a black marble altar, bearing an open book. It was the almanack, its pages open at that day's date.

Behind her, the bell of the golden clock rang out the hour: one o'clock. Tabitha looked back in the direction of the locked door. She had only one precious hour left before the doctor returned.

Trying to master her panic, she inspected every nook and cranny of all three chambers, rummaging for a trapdoor, a tunnel or even a cupboard. To her increasing dismay, she found nothing.

Catching her breath, she again paused by the almanack. It was the same book as her mother's common sixpenny edition; only this was printed as large as the Bible chained to the pulpit in the church. She flicked through the pages and found the entry for her mother's last day of life, the thirtieth of July. Below it, notated in Latin, was the word 'Hart' – and another familiar term from the parish records – 'mort', the ancient word for death.

The twelfth of August bore a similar account of Francis's death; and ever more frequently, on the subsequent pages, the word *Johanus* appeared, alongside frequent doses of *Aqua Laurocerasi,* or, by its English name, cherry laurel water. Damn her dullard wits, she had been blind to a dozen indications. The doctor's house was surrounded by laurel hedges, and there was an elaborate glass still on hand,

ready to distil abundant quantities of the cordial that was delicious
by the drop but deadly by the spoonful.

Bess tugged at her skirt, growing fretful. To quiet her, she felt
in her pocket and, finding nothing else, gave her the skull watch.
Gleefully, Bess grasped it and settled down on the stone floor, poking
its empty eye holes with her stubby fingers.

A wooden cabinet stood beneath the black marble altar. Opening
it, Tabitha found a lump of liquorice-like tar that she sniffed
cautiously – it smelled powerfully of dried flowers: sweet, yet with
a bitter tang. It was, she supposed, a lump of pure opium, for the
doctor prepared his own tinctures, combining the drug with wine
and spirituous waters. A flask of spirits of Ether stood beside it –
that, she knew, he employed to sedate those patients in great agita-
tion. Next, she lifted a dark blue bottle bearing the handwritten
inscription for the doctor's most favoured physic, Black Drop – and
here, too, was a bottle of *Aqua Laurocerasi*. Even its cork emanated
that sweet odour, of slightly over-toasted almonds. She wished she
could serve the doctor a dose of his own medicine – yet how might
she make him ingest it?

As the golden clock in the next room chimed the half hour, she
pressed her fingers to her brow, cudgelling her wits as she had never
done before. Snatching up an oil lamp, she ordered Bess to stay where
she was, and hurried back up the stairs to study every inch of the door;
intently, she guided the flickering lamp across its surface, in the hope
of finding a hidden latch or a release. Still she found nothing.

Then a shriek rang out from the chamber below, followed by
ear-piercing sobs. She hastened down again, and found Bess sitting,
red-faced and tearful, with the skull watch beside her. Tabitha
comforted her, seeing that the skull's mouth had opened up wide;
its jaw hung as if in grotesque mimicry of laughter.

Bess tearfully displayed her finger, smeared with crimson blood,
and Tabitha petted her and kissed the scratch, promising that the
pain would soon be gone. On the upper side of the skull's elongated
palate was the clock face, set with golden Roman numerals. When
she flicked an inner plate open, she found the clock's mechanism
was just where the brain would sit, a jumble of brass clockwork.
The lower jaw piece had sprung back violently on its silver hinge,
showing both upper and lower mandibles lined with rows of tiny,
rodent-sharp teeth; the lower jaw was smeared with Bess's blood.
She wiped it away on her apron.

'Damn,' she muttered; the razor-sharp teeth had also nipped her finger as effectively as if by the doctor's scarifying instruments. Gently, she tried to close the mechanism, but its snapping jaws were as stiff as a rusty nutcracker's. Finally, using her apron to protect her hands, she forced the jaws back together.

She felt, rather than heard, the change in the mechanism – inside the watch's entrails of cogs, catchments and springs, a quivering movement began. At the same time, she heard it: a faint but steady ticking. She held it to her ear and listened to a rushing metallic whirr.

On the instant, a loud high-pitched note rang directly into her head, so painful that she dropped the watch to the floor. Bess and Tabitha stared at it, astonished as if a rock had begun to play a tune. Somewhere in the skull's clockwork was a piercing silvery bell that had just woken, as if from long sleep, and was now shrilling like a death's head summoning its living subjects.

Once it had stopped chiming, Tabitha stared dully at the damnable object. Why had it sprung to life just now? Sweet God, was she not sufficiently terrified by the ceaseless pitter-pattering of time, faster and faster, towards two o'clock?

Giddily, she tried to think of a means to overcome the doctor – but there was not even enough space behind the door for her to hide and attempt to push him down the stairs. There had to be a means to overpower him.

If only they had not become trapped in here. Then she could have offered him the skull clock, and . . . Suddenly a ploy came to her; she grasped at it and made her preparations.

Muffled sounds reached her from the floor above; soon after came the sound of a door distantly slamming. Taking Bess by the hand, Tabitha went to the bottom of the stone steps, fixing her eyes upon the locked door. A tight pain gripped her chest. How soon would he notice the key standing in the lock? Scarcely able to breathe, Tabitha picked Bess up and held her close against her heart, stroking the little girl's hair.

Before she could gather her scattered thoughts, the door sprang open and the doctor's tall silhouette filled the rectangular frame of the doorway. She saw him turn around to lock the door from the inside before pocketing the key and descending slowly towards them.

FORTY-SEVEN

A Riddle

My *first* is valued more than gold,
Because 'tis seldom found;
Many there be, that name do hold,
With whom 'tis nought but sound.
My *second* sails the skimming flood,
And makes a sight full fair;
Its fabric is of carven wood,
And its motion springs from air.
My *whole*, mid life's distressing cares,
Is company, sweet and kind;
Happy who call this blessing theirs –
But few that solace find.

The 25th day of December 1752

Christmas Day

Luminary: Day decreased 8 hours and 52 minutes.
Observation: Moon in Gemini and lately
separated from opposition of Mars.
Prognostication: Differences may be reconciled
and a better understanding reached.

An hour later, as they trudged through knee-deep snow, Nat and the constable hitched a ride on a cart that overtook them in the muffled silence and threw themselves down among the sacks and barrels loaded behind the driver.

The constable had the means, and the good sense, to pay for some victuals from the man's cargo. Their Christmas dinner felt like the best Nat had ever eaten: cold capons, minced pies and white rolls. Soon afterwards, he fell fast asleep, warm in the winter's sun and rocked by the cart's slow progress down the undulating road.

It was after one o'clock by the time the carter set them down, half a mile from Netherlea. Nat felt extraordinarily refreshed, well-fed and eager to search every house in the village.

'The cottage first?' he asked Saxton.

'I reckon so.'

They struck off across white fields towards the distant spire of Netherlea church. Once they had set up a good pace, Nat forgot his soaking feet and raw hands.

'What are your intentions towards Tabitha?' the constable asked suddenly.

'The Devil knows what business that is of yours,' Nat flared.

'A rake like you will treat her ill,' said Saxton. 'Tabitha deserves better. You will abandon her and scuttle back to London.'

'Pox you, Saxton! If we do not hurry, we will both have abandoned her in her hour of greatest need. But – if she survives this Christmas day – it's agreed we will marry. I've given her a diamond ring.'

They walked on in silence across another field.

'Anyway, it is devilish impudent of you to say you cannot trust me,' Nat said jovially. 'What about your new position at the castle? Who was it made you that promise?'

Saxton shook his head dolefully.

'You catch me there. He made a fine dupe of me. He told me he would speak to the high sheriff, and obtain a position of power, and good lodgings in the castle. "Think of Jennet," he said. "And think of how such a position might be favourable in finding a fine new wife."

'Thank God my conscience pricked me,' he continued. 'And damn me, I'm glad you wrote that letter about De Angelo. I saw it then, the slavish way in which I had followed his orders – he cast snares in my path like Old Nick himself.'

'You know him, Joshua. What is he capable of?'

'Any cruelty, manipulation, murder,' said Joshua grimly. 'Only think of this almanack he printed, with these vicious predictions. Spreading fear is meat and drink to him, and all the while he laughs behind a mask of virtue.'

'True. I've had time to run over the events of the day Sir John collapsed. An apoplexy – like damnation it was! That monster saw to our refreshments, then retired and no doubt set his ear to the wall until I called for assistance. And these predictions for the year's end, "a violent bloody end". We have to stop him.'

'If it's in our powers, together we will.'

And though they both were as eager as the other to reach the end of their journey, Nat touched his arm and for an instant the two men stood face-to-face and shook ice-cold hands together.

Tabitha was not to be found at the cottage.

'The grate is still warm,' announced Joshua, kneeling at the fireplace. 'And look, a bundle of her belongings lies there, in the corner.'

Nat picked up a piece of paper written in a hand he knew all too well.

'He has her.' He passed the verse to Joshua, who crumpled it in his hand, banging his fist on the table.

'Hanging will be too good for that murdering charlatan. Where d'you think he is, Nat?'

'Let's look about. Perhaps we can follow her traces?'

Nat went outside and cast his eyes over the deep snow, that had lain so long it now had a top layer of crystallised ice. Joshua joined him. They saw prints from large, almost rectangular boots, and also more frequent, smaller prints that came and went, along twin lines that Nat guessed must have been made by a small sled.

Their deliberations were interrupted by a lad in the De Vallory livery, crunching through the snow towards them from the woods.

'Constable Saxton,' the youth called warmly. 'I am right glad to see you. Is Jennet Saxton here?'

'She's still in Chester, Tom. When did you last see Tabitha?'

'Why, yesterday. She came to the hall.'

'And today?'

'I came along earlier, but no one answered my knocking.'

Joshua gave a series of sharp orders, seeing Nat's impatience.

'Tom. Run back to Bold Hall and raise the watch, or gather together any other sturdy men you can find. Then meet us at the doctor's house. Get to it, lad. Run as fast as you can.'

FORTY-EIGHT

A Riddle

Long before Adam, I have lived,
And liveth still in certain souls,
A Prince by name, right royal I am,
As also Lord and gentleman;
Men frequently cry out my name,
And celebrate my ageless fame,
And yet they seem to take offence,
If called down to my residence,
If you cast back through all these lines,
My common name reversed you'll find.

The 25th day of December 1752

Christmas Day

Luminary: Sun sets at 48 minutes after 3.
Observation: Mercury in Capricorn opposing
Jupiter in Cancer.
Prognostication: The fall of a great one
by sickness or death.

'Ah, Tabitha. Whatever brings you here?'

The doctor sounded remarkably unconcerned at finding her and Bess behind a locked door in his cellar. He descended the stairs with some difficulty, leaning on his cane and wheezing at the effort. On reaching the bottom he straightened up and smiled; a benevolent old gentleman from his silver buckles to his thin and courtly face.

'I have brought you the timepiece,' she said, her voice shaking only a little. 'The door slammed behind us. Shall we do our business upstairs?'

She found herself squeezing Bess's hand as he came closer towards them, smiling at her in the same benign manner he always had.

'Oh, but now you are here, why don't I show you around?'

'We need to leave, sir.'

'Leave? And where are you thinking of going?'

Tabitha's smile felt entirely stiff and artificial. 'To London.' She was near to choking on her words.

'Ah yes. Nell did tell me. You are abandoning the child.'

Tabitha swallowed and did not reply.

'So, what do you make of my wine cellar?'

As he ushered her through to his hidden chambers, his face grew lively with pleasure. It was self-satisfaction, she decided; a chilling confirmation that she had truly stepped inside his trap.

'You see here the remnants of the greatest of civilizations. There had always been legends of lost Roman temples hereabouts, sunk into the ground and destroyed by time. And then, one day, as I was surveying to create my cellar, I discovered this. Or, as I like to believe, I was led here. Look around you.'

He pointed with the end of his cane to different characters rendered in chalky paint on the walls.

'Here is Hermes, and there Zeus and Minerva. You are fortunate; I have never shared this room with anyone, save for Darius, who appreciated such things, and my manservant Florian, who would no more question me than God himself. If my brother John knew of it, he would of course be entirely Philistine in his views. Have you noticed what a fool that man is?

'As Plato said, only the clever should rule – don't you agree? John has always resented my intellect. Every day, as I selflessly gave of my time for the healing of others, that buffoon persecuted and belittled me. If I could only have taken his place I would have run a model estate here, set up a seat of learning, endowed a university. Do you have a brother, Tabitha?'

She shook her head.

'All my life he has cast a shadow upon me; the heir, the eldest son, who must always be paramount. Yet he is a creature of naught; he frittered away his days in hunting, eating, and coupling, like any low brainless animal.

'And now Time has cheated me.' He shook his head in stiff disdain. 'Just as I had finally found the means to take John's place, this ailment struck me. It is a fatal disorder of the blood. I above all should know it, for my aim in training as a physician was always to outlive my brother . . . Come along, let me show you my greatest treasure.'

The doctor limped into the second chamber, and Tabitha hesitated before following. She had no key, even if she dashed up to the cellar door with Bess. No, she must play along, and pray that he would let them go.

'There is not such a perfect collection of medical curiosities in all of England,' he boasted, waving his graceful hand towards the macabre jars.

'Where did you find these . . .' Tabitha could think of no words to describe them.

'Oh, the commonest sorts of persons were privileged to play a part in my studies.' He peered into a jar of bloodshot eyes. 'Sacrifice is always needful in the pursuit of knowledge.' He raised his open hand towards another jar. 'Perhaps you recognize your father's heart?'

Tabitha reeled in horror; clutching at the wall to stop herself swooning. She would not look in the direction this fiend was pointing.

'And here he is,' announced the doctor as he moved into the final chamber. 'Behold: the only perfect image in relief of the great god Saturn. He is my true twin soul, my godhead, my divine shadow. Like me, he is the bringer of life and the servant of death. And here he was, waiting for me to discover him beneath my own floor.'

Tabitha looked up at the veiled figure, for the first time apprehending its victory crown of laurel leaves.

'You placed his image on the monument,' she murmured.

'Yes,' he said breezily. 'If I cannot be ennobled in life, I am resigned to be ennobled in death, at least. Sir John, as you observed yesterday, has very little time left on this earth; I am intending to complete his course of physic tonight. And I need only outlive him for a few minutes to be entombed as Baronet De Vallory. It appeals to me thus to have the final jest in this long game.'

Tabitha understood all too clearly now that this man had entirely lost his reason. Her every instinct screamed to her to scoop up Bess and run away from him; instead she prayed that he was crazed enough to be diverted by a little play-acting.

'Well, I have brought the skull watch for your inspection.'

She lifted it from her pocket and held it in her palm, a little out of his reach, and he smiled greedily.

'A powerful relic for a man in my circumstances. So, have you made your farewells yet? You are packed and ready to leave?'

'Yes.' As she spoke the word, she realized that she had tolled her own death knell; if she never left this cellar, no one would make even a brief inquiry.

The thought made her frantic. 'If you give me the money I shall go, and never come back. And never speak a word of this again.'

Serenely, the doctor turned to pick up a wooden box – when he opened it, she saw it was full of shining coins. His bright eyes creased as he observed her.

'I have made arrangements for the child.'

She was perplexed. 'I don't understand, sir.'

Bess, growing bored, had by now settled on the floor to play with the model of the planets, and had removed the golden sphere of the sun to roll upon the ground. She was in the act of loosening the lapis ball that represented the earth when she glanced up and, seeing them both intent upon her, chuckled and rolled it along the floor, to knock against the sun as if they were two balls upon a billiard table.

The doctor watched Bess with a peculiarly benevolent expression.

'She will live a life of great privilege. I have made a trust for the little orphan, to provide funds for her education and every advantage the De Vallory fortune can buy her.'

'But why?' Tabitha's voice rose in perplexity.

He watched Bess throw more parts of the astrolabe petulantly across the floor.

'Come here, Bess,' he crooned. 'Would you like a sugarplum, my little maid?'

Obediently, Bess rose and toddled towards him, her plump fingers outstretched and a greedy grin upon her lips. The doctor scooped her up and pulled a confection from his robe, and Bess sat chewing happily in his arms.

'You reminded me, Tabitha, at the Manor Court. I had almost forgotten how, when I called upon her once, I found your mother lying in confusion from an ague and administered physic to make her sleep. Even I, trained to channel my animal spirits into my intellect, suffer occasional troublesome urges, and allow myself certain small indulgences. My medications do confer a most delicious stupor in my subjects, as well as providing a surety against detection. Indeed, I have always had a preference for insensible flesh.

'And then you brought the child here – and she is delightful. I had no notion I could ever feel such pleasure at being confronted by my own flesh, a living descendant I can leave on this earth.'

Cramps of disgust assailed her as she understood his meaning – that her mother had been attacked by this madman while she lay insensible. She had a stupid desire to punch the doctor in his smooth, triumphant face. But now he held Bess before him like a shield; and he was watching her carefully, flushed with triumph.

Tabitha edged her way backwards, towards the door.

'And then you had Darius kill my mother.'

'That was her own fault entirely. Killing that hound was not only a test of my laurel distillation, but also a most amusing strike against my brother. Your mother was such a meddler in other people's affairs.

'I confess, Tabitha, you have been an entertaining opponent. Once that mongrel pretender to the De Vallory title, Starling, was arrested, I fancied you would retire from our contest. But, as I said, there can only be one victor.'

He watched her, his benign visage entirely erased; triumph and madness now combined in his countenance, so that he more resembled a cunning beast than a dignified old man. She felt her blood freeze, as if a poisonous snake reared before her. Yet if she were going to act, she must do so now, she commanded herself. She could not abandon her little sister to this murderous lunatic. Nevertheless, she could not bring herself to look at Bess as she spoke.

'You will pay me to be rid of Bess? That's good. I feared I should be out of pocket to be rid of her.' She forced herself to look with avarice at the box of coins. 'Fifteen pounds will purchase my silence.'

She looked up from the box and knew at once he would not be duped so easily. Yet there was another matter that drove her on and made her lay her hand protectively across her stomach. There was a natural reason for her recent weariness. A miscalculation of the calendar's lost days against the moon was now growing within her, into a fruitful future to be shared with Nat. She must overcome the monster for this new child's sake.

She pulled out the skull watch. 'Before I part from it, would you grant me one last favour? Would you show me the trick of how to open it? It defeats me.'

Impatiently, he compressed his lips, but she sensed his vanity had been aroused, for he was a man who loved above all things to display his prowess. In the lamplight, the silver skull gleamed with malice. Now she thought it the most ugly piece of craftsmanship she had ever seen, and held her breath as he reached out to take it. Please God, she prayed, let the teeth only break his skin, and the mixture enter his blood. Her heart seemed to stop as his graceful fingers attempted to prise apart the jaws.

With a chilling smile, he met her eyes. Using the thick cloth of his robe as protection, he slowly drew the skull's jaws apart.

'Tabitha,' he said, in a gentle voice, 'did you truly think I would let you poison me? I see your spirit is all a mere front for your stupidity. A self-flattering harlot is how Netherlea thinks of you, and that is all you are. I must confess, I was especially amused that you were vain enough to imagine yourself enticing to me.'

This was too much. Fury at her own failure made her boil over at last.

'Yes, we are all so stupid, are we not? Mere dolts who believed in the myth of your virtue! We are nothing but animated carcasses to you. God help me, but I hope you suffer on your own deathbed as my mother did.'

He grasped her wrist; his grip was surprisingly strong. It took only an instant before she felt the skull's needle-sharp teeth bite deep into her flesh.

Her last thought was of how mighty fast-working was the medicament she had chosen to anoint the skull's needling teeth. Then the room span around her and her skull banged hard against the stone-flagged floor.

FORTY-NINE

A Riddle

In Paradise first, 'twas agreed, I believe,
That I should attend upon Adam and Eve,
And shed my kind influence over the earth,
On birds, beasts, and fishes, and all who had birth;
On the healthy I rarely forget to attend:
And by the hard-working am styled their best friend;
I alleviate cares and enable them still,
To rise with the lark, and employ all their skill:
At balls and assemblies and routs I'm ne'er seen,
At church in a corner I sometimes have been;
In short, I'm so odd, I confess with a sigh,
Too much of me kills, and without me you die.

The 25th day of December 1752

Christmas Day

Luminary: Sun sets 48 minutes after 3.
Observation: Venus and Mercury are both
occidental evening stars.
Prognostication: Hope well and trust to providence.

L ike a pair of hounds chasing a scent, Joshua and Nat followed
the footprints. Soon the light failed, but by then they knew
the way, even without the tracks to guide them. When they
reached the drive of the doctor's house, however, all the windows
were blank and dark.

'She is still here,' Joshua murmured, following the runner tracks
into a stand of bushes and pulling out the sled. As they deliberated,
a band of farm lads and a few watchmen met them at the drive.
Then a rustling sound amongst the trees alerted Nat to a stealthy
movement; a man was furtively heading off across the garden.

'Catch him!'

Three or four men hurtled after the dark shape, yelling and
cursing. Soon they returned with the doctor's servant Florian, his
head hanging low and both arms locked tight in the lads' strong
grip.

Nat dipped a torch down to the ground, seeking the impression
of the servant's footwear in the snow. Instantly, he recognized its
pattern.

'You pinned that paper to Tabitha's door?'

The little man jerked away from the potent fury in Nat's voice.
'I never harmed her!'

'Where is she? Tell me now, or you'll swing from that tree before
you can catch your breath.' Joshua shook the man's collar with his
meaty hands.

'In the cellar,' Florian gasped. 'Through the kitchen; the low
door, stuck with iron nails.'

'Take him to the lock-up,' ordered the constable.

If Nat had been alone, the heavy door to the cellar would have defeated him; but a half-dozen villagers, using a heavy oak bench as a ram, broke it open with a few thundering blows. He was the first to spring through the splintered debris and race down the stairs.

The first chamber was empty, as was the second. As he entered the third, the sound of a child weeping reached him. Tabitha lay prone on the ground, her body crumpled where it had fallen. Weeping beside her was Bess, who raised round, tear-filled eyes as he approached, and shook Tabitha's inert hand in an attempt to wake her.

He was too late. Nat fell on his knees and caressed Tabitha's cheek. She was not yet cold to his touch. Bess tugged at her sister's hand again and attempted to speak to Nat in her infant prattle.

'What happened, little one?' His question set her weeping again.

Taking one of Tabitha's hands in his, he saw a curious horseshoe-shape of blood spots upon it, as if her skin had been punctured by a small creature's teeth.

He looked around the room and, for the first time, became aware of the doctor, who was held fast by the watchmen.

'I am a sick man,' he quavered. 'Have pity, Saxton.'

'What happened to her?' Nat demanded. 'What are these marks?'

The doctor answered him with a flash of his old arrogance. 'She came here to try to poison me. But I was too clever for her; she took a dose of her own medicine.'

Nat stood up, barging the doctor's captors aside. Then he did what he had ached to do since he had first read the vaunting hubris of the inscription; with the flat of his hand he slapped the old man's conceited face, sending him flying against the wall.

'How do I restore her?'

'How dare you strike me?' demanded the doctor, cringing away from him.

'The remedy? What is it?'

'I don't know what she used,' the doctor muttered.

'Damn you, I cannot listen to this,' said the constable bleakly. 'May you suffer what your victims suffered – a hundredfold.' Turning to his men, he ordered them to walk the old man through the snow, and chain him to the wall of the lock-up's coldest cell.

Nat carried Tabitha up the stairs. Here she was at last; he felt her pliable flesh pressed against his chest, her tumbling hair, her smooth but chilly skin. He laid her on the couch and wrapped her in blankets, then built a fire, praying that he might once more be allowed to revive her. Joshua took his leave, insisting he would run no risk of the doctor's escape.

Nat nodded stiffly; he had tried to pour brandy between Tabitha's lips, but she did not stir. Bess clambered on to her sister's prone form and anxiously patted her face. Getting no response, she lay down on Tabitha's lap, and soon quieted. Nat chafed Tabitha's feet, stroked her head, squeezed her hand. The fire crackled and slowly sunk away into ash.

The bright possibilities of a life with Tabitha hung before him in the firelight like a trembling vision that was every moment draining of its power. He knew that if she left him, he would face a great void, stretching before him like a pit of hell. If Tabitha ceased, he would rather his own time stopped altogether.

Bess yawned and clambered down to join him at the fireside, tear-swollen eyes staring dully at the flames. Recollecting himself, Nat coaxed her to follow him into the kitchen. One thing he did have a notion of was that children needed to be fed.

As he provided Bess with a piece of cake and a cup of milk, he heard something stir in the drawing room. Running back, to his joy he found Tabitha half raised upon the couch, feeling her head, and blinking wearily. He folded her in his arms and she sank against him.

'I thought I had lost you,' he whispered. 'Thank God the poison did not prove fatal.'

She flung her head back, pale but gaining in strength. 'I only intended to make him sleep; I have seen too much of death.'

He studied the greenish-bronze of her iris, the obsidian gateway of the pupil, as if he could journey into her soul itself.

'It is time to welcome life, Nat.'

She took his hand and laid it on to the rounded swelling of her stomach.

FIFTY

A Riddle

Deprived of root and branch, and rind,
Yet flowers I bear of every kind,
And such is my prolific power,
They bloom in less than half an hour;
My head with giddiness goes around,
And yet I firmly stand my ground.
No noble bishop in the land
E'er joined such numbers hand in hand;
I link them roundly in a ring,
And e'en our Parson joins the thing;
And though no marriage words are spoke,
They part not till the ring is broke.

The 1st day of May 1753

May Day

Luminary: Sun rises 19 minutes after 4:
no dark nights.
Observation: Venus an oriental evening star;
Mercury is in the sunbeams.
Prognostication: The stars are most propitious
bringing Amity and Friendship to all.

The pungent odour of May blossom releases its scent across the village; all of Netherlea has abandoned daily chores and drudgery to gather on the Church Green. Above the hum of chatter rises the rhythmic squawking of two fiddle players, their heads bent close together in pursuit of a melody. All the revellers wear their holiday best: white gowns and fancy stockings, treasured lace and pink-speckled blossom pinned at their breasts. The maypole stands at the centre, near twenty feet of tree trunk rising to the sky, bedecked with flowers and herbs and bound with a rainbow of ribbons from tip to tail. A circle of matrons and maidens are dancing, wheeling around the pole, reversing and advancing.

Nat's consciousness is spinning circles, too: a Wheel of Fortune, the *ouroboros* snake biting its tail, the revolutions of two hands upon a clock face. To sow and reap, to circle-dance by day, to make love by night – are these our puny efforts to imitate the orbits of moons and planets? For an instant he is overcome by his own paltriness; he is nothing but a speck on an insignificant planet amongst the multitudes of stars – then he banishes such pessimism. Here and now is this May time, and it stands green-garlanded and glorious in the calendar of all his days.

The May cart arrives, dressed in boughs and flowers and drawn by a beribboned team of horses. Tabitha, Queen of the May, stands at its helm, her hair crowned with a loosely woven garland of lady's smock, blue speedwell and red campion. Nat warms at the sight of her. Her white taffeta gown is rich with embroidered flowers, gathered across her swollen belly, where their unborn child grows like a miraculous harvest.

Nat greets his wife and leads her by the arm to the long table beneath the oak. Sir John sits at the table's head, still slow and palsied, and costumed in black mourning for his brother, who died just as the New Year came in. The spring frolics seem to have given the old master new strength, though it is not likely he will ever again be the bluff and bumptious fellow he once was. Nonetheless, he rises tremulously to make a toast. He wishes good health and prosperity to them all: the May maidens, garland gatherers, wood wardens, cooks and, last of all with shining eyes, his son and heir Nathaniel, and his daughter-in-law, Tabitha.

Then all fall upon the feast, each taking a portion of the great pie flourished with a pastry Eden; sun's rays, creatures and songbirds. It is the month of milk and increase, and all the villagers who can have contributed the cream of their cows so that Zusanna and her milkmaids may whip a gigantic syllabub. The wine has been donated by the new parson, a gesture that Mr Dilks, now exiled to a chaplaincy at a hospital for poor women's foundlings, would never have countenanced. Nat looks around the table with settled pleasure; at the old folk nodding their white heads in the sunshine, the children ferociously feeding, and a crafty cat that steals away with jaws full of scraps. Bess is chattering with her young playmates; his little cousin is growing fearsomely clever. Tabitha has told him she will soon engage a governess for her.

As the ale is passed around the singing begins; the men's voices tuneless and gruff and the women piping in an off-key.

For summer is a-come O!
And winter is a-gone O!

The earth has spun back to the healing warmth of spring, and all their blood is warming with reawakening urges. He watches as Jane brings Joshua a dish of sweetmeats and, soon afterwards, the pair eat from a shared plate, as Jane casts shy glances into his broad face. Tabitha has told him that though they know nothing of it themselves, it is as good as decided that they will be married by the summer's end.

And the village women predict, too, that Jennet and Tom Seagoes will soon afterwards visit the altar. He hopes it will be a good year for bridals and bride cakes; a perpetual season of lusty hearts, and the staining of gowns on the green grass.

By evening time, Nat has found himself a leafy, solitary arbour in the garden at Bold Hall. He casts his mind back across a thousand pinpoints of time, dancing like fireflies in his memory. He has decided to fuse those kaleidoscopic pictures into one beam of steady light: a half-naked woman glimpsed through a telescope's lens, the starry universe shining at the bottom of a water meadow, the sound of a silver skull's jaws snapping closed, and the sweet almond scent of distilled laurel.

He wants to make a bubble in the tide of time and inhabit it. Can he fix on paper something greater than a crude pamphlet or foolish riddle? He wants to attempt it; to try his hand at a new-fangled fiction, with a heroine both ever-changing and immortal. Silently, he dedicates it to those time-leaping angels that he and Tabitha once speculated upon. Will they carry his words into the future, where beings command animated statues and inhabit cities made of curious clockwork? Today, he has hope of immortality, if only by means of ink and paper. So, dipping his quill, he begins to write that curious assortment of words some call a novel:

An unlucky day for travel. The phrase tolled like a doom bell in Tabitha's skull when she woke to find all her possessions stolen . . .

A hand appears on his shoulder, and he looks up to see Tabitha reading his lines, her mouth twitching in amusement.

'And does it have a happy ending?' she asks.

He puts down his pen, slides his hand over her body's ripeness, and feels the child quicken. It seems to him that all he has to do is direct his pen, and he can halt time.

'In this present time of now,' he replies carefully, 'on this page, for this reader, I promise you it does.'

Solutions to the Riddles

The eighteenth century saw an explosion of 'riddlemania', as word puzzles were widely printed in almanacs, magazines and books. Creating and solving ingenious puzzles was a popular pastime and some of the greatest wits of the day contributed to the golden age of enigmatography. The majority of the riddles set out in this book are anonymous, although others are based on the work of notable contributors listed below. In almost all cases I have rendered the language and style more accessible to the modern reader.

Preface: A Riddle

1. A letter
2. A telescope *(Friedrich von Schiller, Dramatist and Poet)*
3. Death
4. Jealousy
5. A candle
6. A coffin
7. Darkness
8. Fashion
9. Heart
10. An eye
11. The letter D
12. Moon
13. Scythe
14. A quill pen *(Jonathan Swift, Satirist)*
15. The gallows *(Jonathan Swift, Satirist)*
16. Tell-tale
17. Cherries
18. A dog
19. (1) Rue, (2) Sage, (3) Bay, (4) Laurel, (5) Pennyroyal, (6) Rosemary, (7) Savory, (8) Monkshood, (9) Marigold, (10) Thyme, (11) Mint, (12) Balm

20. The Planets
21. A dream
22. Fare-well *(Charles James Fox, Statesman)*
23. Inn sign
24. Ink *(Jonathan Swift, Satirist)*
25. A ribbon
26. Health
27. Ghost
28. River *(Mrs A L Barbauld, poet and author)*
29. Bed
30. Star
31. A name
32. Midwife
33. Because it blackens all it touches
34. Fire
35. A looking glass
36. Love
37. Blood
38. Time
39. Church bells
40. Brandy
41. Snow *(Jonathan Swift, satirist)*
42. Death-watch
43. Tomb stone
44. Footsteps
45. Pen-i-tent
46. A key
47. Friendship
48. The Devil
49. Sleep
50. A maypole

Acknowledgements

It was something of a revelation when I first discovered eighteenth-century almanacs; pocket-sized booklets combining calendars, astronomical observations, general knowledge and predictions. Contemporary records show they were indispensable references: for planning parties on nights when a full moon would ease travel, as guides in sowing crops and to carry out trade at local fairs. They offer tantalizing insights into the daily life of our ancestors: care of livestock, herbal remedies, weather lore, reckoning of money, and even lucky and unlucky times to travel or cut one's hair.

There was an almanac for almost every taste and town; during the seventeenth century over two thousand different almanacs were published. The predictions on subjects from daily weather to world affairs attracted a vast number of readers. By the mid-eighteenth century, the leading almanac by far was the original 'Old Moore's', *Vox Stellarum* ('The Voice of the Stars'). In 1768 it sold 107,000 copies, reaching its peak in the nineteenth century, in spite of astrologer Francis Moore having died in 1714 – a drawback blithely ignored to this day.

Almanacs were generally bought from street hawkers, at a cost of twopence to sixpence depending on their quality, and it is said that at times their sales in England exceeded the Bible. Such was their profitability that unlicensed editions, such as De Angelo's fictional production in this novel, were produced in great numbers by hack writers and charlatan astrologers.

Predictions were typically cryptic and ambiguous. So, for example, *Wing's Almanack* predicted the death of a great man in August 1658 and later claimed this foretold the demise of Oliver Cromwell on 3 September. *Moore's Almanack* cited the 1755 Lisbon earthquake as the beginning of the fall of the Antichrist, and claimed to unveil Bonnie Prince Charlie as the horn of the beast of Daniel. Much like today's tabloid newspapers, the enemy was generally any foreigner, particularly from the Catholic mainland of Europe, with special vitriol reserved for the French.

At the same time almanacs were evolving to meet a largely middle-class desire for amusement and instruction. *The Ladies' Diary,* founded in 1704, successfully featured essays on famous women, a short story, recipes and ferociously difficult mathematical problems. At the heart of its success, however, were the rhyming riddles or 'enigmas'. Folk riddles had long featured in penny chapbooks but soon 'riddlemania' gripped British readers. Unlike cryptic crosswords or sudoku, riddling was often a communal activity, as we see in Jane Austen's *Emma*, where the Hartfield party is invited to contribute 'any really good enigmas, charades or conundrums' to form a written collection.

The better sort of almanacs ran contests to compose and solve erudite riddles. Readers were left puzzling for a year before learning the solutions or winning a prize comprising both the kudos of getting one's name in print, plus a free copy of the next Almanack. Such puzzles give an insight into the lofty intellectual levels in the Georgian era.

Certainly, in comparison to the present editions of *Old Moore's Almanack*, with its celebrity horoscopes and lucky bingo dates, we can only be impressed – if not shamed – by the mental dexterity of our ancestors.

A great many books, articles, and experiences helped me in writing this book but the following deserve a special mention:

Mark Bryant, *Dictionary of Riddles* (Routledge 1990)
Bernard Capp, *Astrology and the Popular Press: English Almanacs, 1500-1800* (Faber and Faber, 1979)
David Cressy, *Birth, Marriage, and Death: Ritual, Religion, and the Life-Cycle in Tudor and Stuart England* (Oxford University Press, 1997)
Paul Glennie and Nigel Thrift, *Shaping the Day: A History of Timekeeping in England and Wales 1300-1800* (Oxford University Press, 2009)
Tristan Gooley, *The Lost Art of Reading Nature's Signs (*Experiment, 2014*)*
Herbert Green, *Village Life in the Eighteenth Century* (Longman, 1976)
Charles Kightley, *The Perpetual Almanack of Folklore* (Thames and Hudson, 1994)
Robert Poole, *Time's Alteration: Calendar reform in early modern England* (UCL Press, 1998)

Laura J. Rosenthal (editor), *Nightwalkers: Prostitute Narratives from the Eighteenth Century* (Broadview Press, 2008)
Aaron Skirboll, *The Thief-Taker Hangings: How Daniel Defoe, Jonathan Wild, and Jack Sheppard Captivated London and Created the Celebrity Criminal* (Lyons Press, 2014)
David Vaisey (editor), *The Diary of Thomas Turner 1754-1765* (Oxford University Press, 1984)

In the early days of my research I anticipated long hours studying archives of almanacs in libraries, but instead found the best collections online. Google Play provided some of my favourites, including sight of the 1752 calendar change almanacs in 'A Collection of English Almanacs for the Years 1702-1835'.

A daily delight was following nature's changes through the seasons from my writing window. At night, I loved following the moon and stars using the app *Sky Map*.

As ever, while I have tried to capture some of the spirit of the Georgian age, I have played with certain facts to write this fiction. For example, the village of Netherlea is entirely fictional and its location is imaginary.

I would like to thank the many generous people who helped and inspired me:

My writer friends, Alison Layland and Elaine Walker, who continued to give invaluable feedback and guidance on my work in progress. Dr Derek Nuttall MBE, and his wife Ruth, also kindly read the early manuscript and offered valuable advice.

My friends in The Prime Writers, a group of hugely supportive writers who all had their fiction debuts commercially published at the age of forty or more.

The Society of Authors for part-funding an unforgettable spell as Artist-in-Residence at Hawkwood College, Stroud.

The staff at Acton Scott Historic Working Farm (the location of the BBC's *Victorian Farm*), where I loved spending 'A Day in the Life of a Farmer's Wife'.

Chester Archives for a place on their 'Horrible Handwriting' course where I learned to read old parish records.

For their encouragement and belief in the novel, many thanks to agents Charlotte Seymour and Sarah Nundy at Andrew Nurnberg Associates. Imogen Russell Williams again provided invaluable assistance.

A special thank you to Kate Lyall Grant and Sara Porter at Severn House Publishers, for their crucial enthusiasm and commitment to the book.

And finally, thanks to my son Chris and my husband Martin, both ever ready with their encouragement and suggestions.